ISLAND LANDFALLS

Beset by chronic ill health and in perennial search of sunshine and clean air, Robert Louis Stevenson (1850–94) spent the last seven years of his life travelling in North America and the South Seas. He craved news of his native land, and his advisors in Britain encouraged him to produce more books and stories on Scottish themes. Indeed, Stevenson's most famous later novels, *The Master of Ballantrae* (1888), *Catriona* (1893), and *Weir of Hermiston* (1896), were all produced during the Pacific years, or from what was to become his home when he settled at Vailima on the island of Upolu in Samoa.

Yet Stevenson had become increasingly aware of the white man's failings and the colonial exploitation of the island peoples, and some of his finest writing relates to this issue. At a time when exiled Scots around the world were enjoying the fashion for a more homely 'Kailyard' fiction, Stevenson produced *The Beach at Falesá* and *The Ebb Tide* in imaginative response to the South Pacific experience. Jenni Calder's selection from Stevenson's creative prose, essays and letters will help to remind readers that he had a penetrating artistic and human interest in cultures far from the shores of Forth and the Weaver's Stone.

Robert Louis Stevenson

ISLAND LANDFALLS:
REFLECTIONS FROM THE SOUTH SEAS

*Selected and introduced
by Jenni Calder*

**CANONGATE
CLASSICS
3**

First published as a Canongate Classic in 1987
by Canongate Publishing Limited
17 Jeffrey Street
Edinburgh EH1 1DR

Professor Barry Menikoff's edition of
The Beach of Falesá is reproduced
by permission of Stanford University Press
and Edinburgh University Press.

British Library Cataloguing in Publication Data
Stevenson, Robert Louis
Island landfalls: reflections from
the South Seas.—(Canongate classics).
I. Title   II. Calder, Jenni
823'.809   PR5482

ISBN 0-86241-144-0

The publishers gratefully acknowledge
general subsidy from the Scottish Arts Council
towards the Canongate Classics series
and a specific grant towards the
publication of this title.

Set in 10 pt Plantin
by Alan Sutton Publishing Ltd, Gloucester
Cover printed by Wood Westworth, St Helens
Printed and bound in Great Britain
by Cox and Wyman Ltd, Reading

Contents

INTRODUCTION   vii

LETTERS   1
  To Charles Baxter 6 ix 1888   2
  To Thomas Archer xi 1888   3
  To R.A.M. Stevenson ii 1889   5
  To Adelaide Boodle 6 iv 1889   8
  To Sidney Colvin vi 1889   12
  To Sidney Colvin viii 1889   14
  To Sidney Colvin x 1889   15
  To Sidney Colvin 2 xi 1890   18
  To Henry James 29 xii 1890   22
  To Sidney Colvin xii 1891   25

IN THE SOUTH SEAS   31
  Making Friends   32
  The Maroon   41
  Depopulation   47
  The Story of a Plantation   55
  A House to Let   64
  Butaritari   72
  Around Our House   78
  A Tale of a Tapu   87
  Husband and Wife   103

FICTION   111
  The Bottle Imp   112
  The Isle of Voices   142
  The Beach of Falesá   174

Introduction

It was ill health that drove Robert Louis Stevenson away from Scotland. It was an urge for new and adventurous places and experiences that drew him to the Pacific. In June 1888 he and members of his family sailed out of San Francisco Bay on the schooner yacht *Casco*. For the next six and a half years, until his death on 3 December 1894, Stevenson was never out of Pacific regions.

For the first two of those years he wandered from island to island, on the *Casco*, the *Equator* and the *Janet Nichol*, and spent some time in Australia. It was hopeful voyaging, relished for its own sake, and most of the time with the bonus of good health. Sometimes there were pauses of weeks or months, stays occasioned by personal inclination, or the exigencies of Pacific trade, Pacific weather or Pacific ships. Wherever he was, and for whatever reason, Stevenson was continually alert to sights, sounds and happenings that were new, fresh and vivid. Many of his letters catch the exoticism and excitement of it all.

> This climate; these voyagings; these landfalls at dawn; new islands peaking from the morning bank; new forested harbours; new passing alarms of squalls and surf; new interests of gentle natives,—the whole tale of my life is better to me than any poem.[1]

But Stevenson was not carried away by the romance and adventure of the Pacific, although some of his published work up until that time might have suggested such a response. Another letter, written within days of the one above, suggests his awareness of some of the contradictions and difficulties of the islands.

> The Pacific is a strange place; the 19th century only exists there in spots: all round, it is a no man's land of

the ages, a stir-about of epochs and races, barbarisms and civilisations, virtues and crimes.[2]

The Pacific was a challenge because it not only lived up to his most extravagant ideas of adventure, the ideas that had flowered in *Treasure Island*, but it also presented him with realities that were tantalising and instructive. His understanding of human nature and human history, which is so apparent in *Kidnapped*, in *Strange Case of Dr Jekyll and Mr Hyde*, in stories such as 'Thrawn Janet' and 'The Merry Men', was sharpened and extended.

By the end of 1890 Stevenson, his wife Fanny, and a fluctuating entourage were more or less settled in Vailima, the home he built near Apia on the Samoan island of Upolu. Throughout these years, whether at sea, or encamped in a palm-thatched hut, or living in squalor or in splendour—he sampled both extremes—at Vailima, he was writing. Both the world that he had left and the world in which he was now living were the subject of his pen.

The content of his writing was more diverse and wide-ranging than at any other time of his life. In the early months of his travels he was working on *The Master of Ballantrae*, which he had begun in a sub-arctic winter spent in the Adirondacks in New York State, and finished in a beach house at Waikiki. But although at this distance he could recreate Scotland and Scots, Scottish habits and Scottish speech, the Pacific environment equally commanded his attention. He kept a journal, and when he could he wrote letters. The opportunites to send them were irregular, so there were necessarily long silences. Stories began to suggest themselves, plots and people unfolded from the endless fascination of the Pacific. Yet all the time Scotland was never very far from his mind

Soon he found himself concerned with much more than simply recording impressions. His interest in the peoples and cultures he encountered became involvement, both personal and, after a while, political. This is reflected in his writing, and worried greatly those at home who would have been happier to see him as a spinner of the picturesque, making delightful capital out of exotic sensations, than as an investigator of colonialism and its impact. But Stevenson could not close his eyes to what he saw going on around him, especially as it provided him with such rich material for continuing an exploration of moral ambiguity that was already a primary current in his work.

He began to write fiction directly inspired by his South Sea experience: *The Wrecker*, in collaboration with his stepson Lloyd Osbourne, *The Ebb Tide*, begun as *The Pearl Fisher* with Lloyd, set aside and later worked over again by Stevenson alone, the short stories 'The Bottle Imp' and 'The Isle of Voices' aimed at a Polynesian audience, and the masterly novella *The Beach of Falesá*. At the same time his growing understanding of expansionist politics and of the native Polynesians led him to engage with the warring interests of the colonial powers in the Pacific. Inevitably, he wrote about that too.

Stevenson's interest in Samoa and the political situation there had been aroused during a six month stay in Hawaii. There he spent many enjoyable and interesting hours in the company of King Kalakaua, a convival, extravagant and plausible figure who consumed quantities of champagne and had serious if ambivalent convictions about traditional Polynesian values. Kalakaua had an interest in Samoa, for he felt that a possible solution to colonial squabbling could be that he should take the islands under his wing. At this time Samoa was uneasily supervised by a trio of powers— Germany, Britain and the United States—a situation created by the 1868 Treaty of Berlin, the great nineteenth-century colonial carve-up. Of the three, Germany dominated, both politically and economically, the political influence owing a great deal to Germany's long-established economic presence.

Stevenson was outraged by the political manoeuvrings and manipulations of all three powers, none of which showed much regard for the needs or traditions of the Samoans. His indignation was sharply expressed in a series of letters to *The Times* which rehearsed, with an ironic wit that surely owed something to his Edinburgh legal training, a tale of imperialist treachery and doublethink. Once in Samoa Stevenson openly allied himself with the chief Mataafa, a man for whom he had great personal regard and political respect. Mataafa was the main rival to the German-backed puppet chief Malietoa. The British, while recognizing privately Mataafa's claims, disliked him because he was a Catholic, and were anyway reluctant to disturb a situation that suited them quite well. Stevenson was regarded as an interfering innocent, causing trouble through his naive idealism—words often used to dismiss the awkwardly honest. The situation erupted into war in July 1883, much of the conflict enacted literally in the Stevensons' back yard. Not content with sending lengthy correspondence to *The Times* Stevenson produced his own account of the situation and the background to the conflict in a book which he called *A Footnote to History*.

We do not usually think of Stevenson as being either a 'straight' historian or a political commentator, but there is clear evidence of his attraction to historical fact. An interest in Scottish history was reflected in more than his fiction and essays: he had applied for the Chair of History and Constitutional Law at Edinburgh University, a post for which he was academically ill-qualified and didn't get. Nevertheless, the intellectual and psychological challenge of Scotland's past always appealed to him, and more significant, perhaps, was his project to write a history of Scotland.

In Samoa Stevenson's involvement in events and his determination to set the record straight was as much the result of his highly developed sense of justice as of the magnetism of historical fact. He was witness to words and actions that were hypocritical, deceitful, and manipulative. He could not stand back from such a state of affairs. He felt a moral obligation to commit to paper—his only effective weapon—his understanding of events. But amongst his friends and associates at home there was alarm. At an early stage in his career Stevenson had been identified as a torch-carrier for a revitalized fiction. In 1878 Leslie Stephen, a highly respected member of the literary establishment, had written to Stevenson saying that he was on the lookout for a new novelist, a Scott or a Dickens or a George Eliot, suggesting that perhaps Stevenson could be the answer. It was an extraordinary profession of faith in a young man who was in the early stages of his literary career, and that aura, the feeling that he was destined for great things, clung to him.

From the other side of the world it looked as if Stevenson was spending his time in wild and ill-conceived political adventures with a gang of savages. It did not conform with an image of him as not merely a serious novelist, but as the saviour of English literature at a time when it was judged to be in the doldrums.

What Stevenson realized was that such adventures were not only the stuff of history, they were the stuff of fiction. Although he had gained a reputation as a fine weaver of imaginative tales he was no ivory-tower fabulist. To write he had to live, and for the first time in his life he was well and strong enough to throw himself into the thick of things, whether it was the struggle against the jungle growth on his Vailima land, or riding secretly across the island to consort with the rebels, or tending the wounded in the aftermath of battle, or the emotional conflicts that were a part of daily life amongst the Vailima extended family.

Stevenson's refusal to withdraw was partly the result of his unending enthusiasm for life, partly of moral conviction. Both these aspects of his mind and personality are evident in his writing. They were if anything heightened by his South Seas experience, and certainly reflected in the material brought together in this volume. In it we can se⸚ three levels of response, in the letters, in the extracts from his book *In the South Seas*, and in the fiction. In the letters, with which the selection begins, there is all the lively immediacy of instant communication. From them we get a vivid picture of the activities that filled his days, the demanding physical work, the even more intense demands of writing, and the serendipity for which he had a particular talent. These were years in which, in some respects, Stevenson tasted a freedom from conventional restrictions which previously had been overshadowed by parental and social authority. One of those parents, his mother, had travelled with him and was as aware as anyone of the lack of restraint. 'It is a strange, irresponsible, half-savage life,' she wrote, '& I sometimes wonder if we shall ever be able to return to civilised habits again.'[3]

The absence of civilization suited Stevenson wonderfully. He would have loved this description, written after his death, and would have recognized himself immediately.

. . . I met a little group of three European strangers—
two men and a woman. The latter wore a print gown,
large gold crescent earrings, a Gilbert-Island hat of
plaited straw, encircled by a wreath of small shells, a
scarlet silk scarf round her neck, and a brilliant plaid
shawl across her shoulders; her bare feet were encased
in white canvas shoes, and across her back was slung a
guitar. . . . The younger of her two companions was
dressed in a striped pyjama suit—the undress costume
of most European traders in these seas—a slouch hat of
native make, dark blue sun-spectacles, and over his
shoulders a banjo. The other man was dressed in a
shabby suit of white flannels that had seen many better
days, a white drill yachting cap with a prominent peak,
a cigarette in his mouth, a photographic camera in his
hand. Both the men were bare-footed. They had, evidently, just landed from the little schooner now lying
placidly at anchor, and my first thought was that,
probably, they were wandering players en route to New
Zealand, compelled by their poverty to take the cheap
conveyance of a trading vessel.[4]

They were not, of course, wandering players, but Stevenson,
his wife, and Lloyd Osbourne. This was written by W.E.
Clarke, missionary on Upolu, subsequently a respected
friend of Stevenson who had no great sympathy for the
missionary breed on the whole, and mentioned in one of the
letters included here.

It was in may ways a delightful existence, but Stevenson
had to work, especially once the bills for Vailima started
coming in. There was a large and proliferating household to
maintain, which was not only a financial burden but often an
emotional and psychological one too. There were extreme
pressures and profound anxieties, money problems, illness
and unhappiness amongst the members of the household,
worries over work in hand that foundered. Indeed, all of this
almost certainly contributed to his death, brought by a sudden brain haemorrhage. These pressures hardly surface in his
letters, for he did not like to dwell on his difficulties and was
concerned that the folk at home should not worry. Nor do we
detect them in his more literary writing during this period.

In the South Seas represents another level of response to the Pacific, considered, ordered, and crafted. If the writing here is without the spontaneity of the letters, it still has sparkle and humour, and Stevenson's avid interest in all he encountered is apparent. The scenery was intoxicating; the expanses of ocean, the islands taking shape as they approached, the mountains, streams and forests, the stretches of sand and shore—all these he found irresistible. The people were equally a temptation. He became absorbed by island customs and behaviour, by beliefs and folklore, and comparisons with Scotland came readily. It wasn't just homesickness that kept Scotland in the forefront of his mind throughout his time in the Pacific, but the chords that were struck by anything from a mountainside to a myth. Sometimes it was the very unlikeliness of similarity that made the discovery such a delight. Most striking of all is Stevenson's sense of a common humanity. He recognized that the fears and vulnerabilities of the South Sea islanders were little different from those of men and women everywhere.

From time to time the modern reader may be brought up sharply by words or phrases that suggest a colonialist condescension. Stevenson, for example, refers to the adult Samoan workers on his Vailima land as 'boys'. 'Nigger' appears to describe blacks of African origin. And the paternalism of some of his attitudes at times reads uncomfortably. But it would be ungenerous and misleading to be overcritical. This was the language of the times, and he was in fact far ahead of his time in his respect for the islanders and his interest in them as individuals with a culture of their own. There is no doubt that he enjoyed being gaffer at Vailima, but he shared in their work and although he was of course in a position of power (even if he didn't have the political influence he would have liked) he was very aware that he was also in a position of responsibility. He was disgusted by white exploitation of the islanders, angry at the way many missionaries totally disregarded Samoan traditions, and saddened at the erosion of human spirit, in victims and perpetrators alike, that followed from the diminishment of a people.

Always uncompromisingly himself Stevenson was at the

same time genuinely internationalist and sought out common ground with whomever he encountered. During an enforced stay at Tautira on Tahiti while the *Casco*'s masts were being repaired, he established a flourishing relationship with the local chieftain, Ori a Ori. They feasted each other, and swapped songs and stories. When on Christmas Day 1888 the *Casco* pointed north for Hawaii the handsome Ori and another local dignitary, the aristocratic Princess Moë, wept; Louis and Fanny Stevenson wept also. They left behind them not only good friends, but a wonderful source of story and fable.

This and other meetings inspired the stories 'The Bottle Imp' and 'The Isle of Voices'. Stevenson readily adapted to the resonance and cadences of myth, for legendary tales had suffused his own upbringing. If he had absorbed such sources into his Scottish fiction, he was equally primed to make something of the Polynesian story-telling to which he was now exposed. Thus 'The Bottle Imp' is an ancient tale with a contemporary feel, and it provides an interesting glimpse of some of the incidentals of the Polynesian encounter with whites. The scene and the viewpoint are Polynesian, and the white presence is not conspicuous. If readers are inclined to question the success of Stevenson's attempt at getting under the skin of his Polynesian characters, it is worth noting that the fable itself has an impulsion that overrides this. 'The Isle of Voices' has a more specifically Polynesian reference, and Stevenson's grasp on the tale is less confident. But there is an ambience, a personalized environment, that still remains powerful.

Stevenson was acutely aware of the kinship between traditional story-telling in the Pacific and in Scotland. He continually drew parallels between Scottish and Polynesian customs, traditions and tribes. He recognized that this was a useful way of gaining the confidence of the islanders from whom he sought acceptance. As an amateur anthropologist he was unusual for that time, since he looked at alien cultures as much in terms of their similarities with his own as of their differences. At the same time he seems to have shared the belief held by even the most enlightened investigators that tribal societies represented a primitive stage in human evolution which would inevitably give way to 'civilization'. What was less usual was his regret at the loss this would entail, and his indignation at what he described as '. . . the unjust (yet I can see the inevitable) extinction of Polynesian Islanders by our shabby civilisation'.

There is no doubt that his sensitivity towards this loss was a direct result of his engagement with his own cultural origins. There was mutual nourishment. As his writing responded to the challenge of the Pacific he was also probing and examining the Scottish past and the Scottish character. The traditions of Border reiving and rivalry which play so important a part in *Weir of Hermiston,* his last substantial piece of fiction, have their parallels in Pacific life. The authoritarian attitudes of the novel's Lord Braxfield towards human frailty were not dissimilar to those of the imperialist powers towards the native populations. The harsh land-scapes and harsher actions of Scotland might have seemed very different from the sun-dazzled, easy-going South Seas, yet the roots of human behaviour were sustained by the same kind of needs and feelings.

In the South Seas is not a continuous record of Stevenson's travels. It is a series of worked up, almost self-contained pieces. His letters, some of them written over several days, convey a sense of day-to-day living, of a continuum, a pattern of progress and setbacks, of events not just following upon each other but entangled with each other. Life is tidier in the book version of these events. Hindsight and the literary imagination lend shape and meaning. I am not suggesting that reality is being tampered with, but literary skills are at work and an inevitable process of selection and reordering is going on. Stevenson was a conscious and delib-erate craftsman, and this process was part of his commit-ment, of his sense of responsibility as a writer. The directness of his style can be pleasantly informal, yet at the same time there is a literary, almost an ornate quality. Stevenson combines close observation, an awareness of lang-uage as well as of sensation, sympathetic humour, and a strong feeling for the potential absurdity that lies in the clash of mutual ignorance. Here is an example, taken from 'The Maroon', one of the pieces included here.

It chanced one day that I was ashore in the cove with Mrs Stevenson and the ship's cook. Except for the *Casco* lying outside, and a crane or two, and the ever-busy wind and sea, the face of the world was of a prehistoric emptiness; life appeared to stand stockstill, and the sense of isolation was profound and refreshing. On a sudden, the tradewind, coming in a gust over the isthmus, struck and scattered the fans of the palms above the den; and, behold! in two of the tops there sat a native, motionless as an idol and watching us, you would have said, without a wink. The next moment the tree closed, and the glimpse was gone. This discovery of human presences latent overhead in a place where we had supposed ourselves alone, the immobility of our tree-top spies, and the thought that perhaps at all hours we were similarly supervised, struck us with a chill. Talk languished on the beach. As for the cook (whose conscience was not clear), he never afterwards set foot on shore, and twice, when the *Casco* appeared to be driving on the rocks, it was amusing to observe that man's alacrity; death, he was persuaded, awaiting him upon the beach. It was more than a year later, in the Gilberts, that the explanation dawned upon myself. The natives were drawing palm-tree wine, a thing forbidden by law; and when the wind thus suddenly revealed them, they were doubtless more troubled than ourselves.

Here is an incident contained in a paragraph. Hindsight rounds the story off. The visual context, the island ambience, the culture clash are all there. And so is the author, taking a step back, looking at himself and his companions. The writer of first person documentary has to be observer, participant and artist. Stevenson highlights these roles by adopting a tone of mild irony, which also softens the nuts and bolts of his style, and maintains the distance between observer and actor. Twentieth-century writers would probably feel it was not so important to be scrupulous about distinguishing these roles, yet Stevenson's control of tone gives a true modernity to his prose.

It is now around one hundred years since Stevenson was in

the Pacific. From this distance we can see that he was engaged in one of the most important arenas of nineteenth-century history, both geographically and psychologically. We are now aware of the long-term effects of imperialism and are living with their consequences. What Stevenson witnessed, and what he recorded with considerable acuity, was colonialism in action in the Pacific one hundred years after the voyages of Captain Cook in the 1770s and 80s, a convenient date for locating the origins of imperialism in that part of the world.

Literary convention associates one great novelist in particular with the exploration and exposure of the tensions and conflicts inherent not just in the confrontation between imperialist powers and native populations, but in the sensations of the representatives of imperialism. This writer is Joseph Conrad, and his *Heart of Darkness* has become an emblem of the rotten core of exploitation. But a parallel and a companion to Conrad's great novella can be found in the earlier and equally impressive story by Stevenson, *The Beach of Falesá*.

Stevenson saw the Pacific as a huge melting-pot, or perhaps 'stew' is a more appropriate word, remembering that he wrote about the islands as 'a stir-about of epochs and races, barbarisms and civilisations, virtues and crimes'. He did not mean that these attributes belonged to one race or another. What his fiction tells us is that this 'stir-about' was a melange of peoples, none of which had any special claim to virtue or criminality. His particular interest, as it was Conrad's later, was in the moral and psychological effects of an environment of exoticism and exploitation on people with differing backgrounds and assumptions.

All Stevenson's fiction reveals a pre-eminent concern with the moral dimensions of man—of man in particular, rather than woman. Before coming to the Pacific he had examined moral ambivalence in the context mainly of Scotland's past, although his most famous venture into this territory, *Strange Case of Dr Jekyll and Mr Hyde*, was ostensibly set in London. Scottish history offered event after event, situation after situation, which seemed to demonstrate and confirm what Stevenson saw as fundamental divisions within humankind,

between emotional life and the instinct for survival—
sometimes an instinct for evil—and the need for controlled
social relations. Towards the end of his life he wrote to his
cousin Bob, who had been a close companion of his experi-
mental youth, 'The prim obliterated polite face of life, and
the broad, bawdy, and orgiastic—or maenadic—foundation,
form a spectacle to which no habit reconciles me.'[6] He did
not have to search far in Scotland's past to find extremes of
feeling and belief, extremes that led to violence of action and
language.

In spite of *Jekyll and Hyde*, where in fact the extremes of
behaviour are not entirely convincing, Stevenson has not had
the reputation of a writer engaged with violence. Yet we need
look no further than *Treasure Island* or *Kidnapped* to find
naked conflict starkly expressed. The adventure story genre
of course accommodates violence quite comfortably. In *The
Master of Ballantrae* it is rather more sinister. But physical
violence is only one aspect of confrontation. In the unfinished *Weir of Hermiston* there is an attempt to illuminate the
whole spectrum of division and extremity through one pow-
erfully knotted plot. The bold language of the elder Kirstie
warning the hero Archie about the dangers of his relationship with a young and vulnerable girl catches the essence
of at least part of Stevenson's concern. Kirstie's words echo
those of Stevenson's to Bob.

> Man, do ye no' comprehend that it's God's wull we
> should be blendit and glamoured, and have nae
> command over our ain members at a time like that? My
> bairn . . . think o' the puir lass! have pity upon her,
> Erchie! and O, be wise for twa! Think 'o the risk she
> rins! I have seen ye, and what's to prevent ithers? I saw
> ye once in the Hags, in my ain howf, and I was wae to
> see ye there—in pairt for the omen, for I think there's a
> weird on the place—and in pairt for puir nakit envy and
> bitterness o' hairt. It's strange ye should forgather there
> tae! God, but yon puir, thrawn, auld Covenanter's seen
> a heap o' human natur since he lookit his last on the
> musket-barrels, if he never saw nane afore . . .

Even without specific knowledge of the references here, to
the Covenanting conflicts and martyrdoms for example, the

vibrance of Kirstie's language alerts us to many of the aspects of human feelings and behaviour that were a preoccupation during Stevenson's years at Vailima. On the one hand there was human nature, willed by God, as the Calvinists believed, to lead to sin unless kept in check. On the other hand were the rules and rigid structures imposed to keep humanity under control, but which themselves were dangerous in their capacity to distort.

Weir of Hermiston is set in eighteenth-century Scotland. Stevenson was living in late nineteenth-century Samoa. The wayward Archie is fenced in with social, moral and judicial rules. What was the situation in the Pacific? There was certainly plenty of opportunity to witness human nature in the raw. Traditional tribal life was breaking down. It had once been firmly stratified and organized, contrary to how it seemed to white incomers who were only too ready to exploit economic innocence and an apparently easy-going sexuality. There was a system of morality that was as strong, however different, as anything devised in the Christian world. To the whites, tribal life looked like moral anarchy while they themselves were a long way from the accustomed boundaries of behaviour—indeed that was part of the place's attraction. The result was a breeding ground of moral ambivalence which fascinated Stevenson.

The novelist could no longer write about human nature in terms of a contest between Dr Jekyll and Mr Hyde, or a balance between prim, whiggish, sensible David Balfour and flamboyant, self-conceited, courageous Alan Breck. The edges of moral responsiblity and the margins of moral judgment were too blurred. All around him were people whose customary moral and social structures were destroyed or left behind. This is the territory he explores in the novel *The Ebb Tide* (1893) where he looks at the varieties of disintegration exhibited in three individuals who find themselves 'on the beach' in Tahiti, a form of destitution that was common in the islands. One of *The Ebb Tide*'s characters shows himself to be totally evil. Another is desperately weak and when a figure of authority appears, he submits thankfully to that dubious power. The third, the central character, struggles to maintain his self-respect by seeking resources within himself.

The Beach of Falesá is equally a moral tale. Wiltshire, the hero, is a small-time trader. By the end of the nineteenth century the focus of white trading in the Pacific was copra, dried coconut meat valuable for its oil. Coconuts were plentiful, native labour to collect them not difficult to harness. Stevenson himself had taken a close look at the copra trade as the *Equator* had made her way from island to island. 'The mystery of the copra trade tormented me,' he wrote in 'Around Our House' (*In the South Seas*), 'as I sat and watched the profits drip on the stair and sands.' Traders like Wiltshire, established on island stations, had come to expect an easy time. They offered cheap trade goods in exchange for the copra the islanders brought in, cheated the islanders whenever they could—everyone, it seemed, cheerfully watered the copra to bump up the weight, hence the dripping profits—and assumed there would be no lack of bodily comforts. Women were available, liquor was cheap, and sunshine inexhaustible.

Stevenson's Wiltshire is no different from any other trader, and in many respects this is still true at the end of the story. He does not change, and his identity as hero does not blot out his shortcomings. He retains the prejudices and limitations with which he started out. We are in no doubt that he is in the business of exploitation, and although there is a certain charm in his frankness the reader quickly recognizes him as an ordinary and unremarkable sort of man. The tone and rhythm of his thought and speech tell us this. But they also tell us that, plain man though he is, he is not unresponsive to his surroundings. He appreciates the setting moon, the scent of the mountains, the prospect of fresh experience.

Stevenson's portrayal through the first person of a character who gives away more about himself than he states is a fine achievement. As the oblique unfolding of personality is continued, deeper levels of moral ambivalence are revealed. Wiltshire has no scruples about cheating the natives, yet he is troubled, not so much by exploitation itself as by the hypocrisy that surrounds it. His feelings about the marriage to Uma, the island girl who is acquired for him, demonstrate this. He does not object to being provided with a woman.

That he sees as an unexceptionable part of the life of the white man in the islands. But he is unhappy about the phony marriage, although he rationalizes and in the course of rationalizing unwraps a whole nexus of ambivalence and double standards. 'A man might easily feel cheap for less,' is his comment on the worthless marriage certificate. 'But it was the practice in these parts, and (as I told myself) not the least the fault of us White Men but of the missionaries. If they had let the natives be, I had never needed this deception, but taken all the wives I wished, and left them when I pleased, with a clear conscience.'

By any standards Wiltshire's morality is dubious. He is ready to exploit the islanders both economically and sexually. When Uma first appears he and his supposed ally Case size her up like a marketable object, an impression confirmed by Case's 'That's pretty'—not 'she's pretty'. The image modulates from object to animal to child. Wiltshire describes her as having 'a sly, strange, blindish look between a cat's and a baby's' and then, 'she looked up at men quick and timid like a child dodging a blow'. It is only later and, significantly, away from Case, that he sees her differently. 'She showed the best bearing for a bride conceivable, serious and still; and I thought shame to stand up with her in that mean house and before that grinning negro' (the latter not an islander but an associate of the degenerate Randall). Wiltshire has not only become aware of Uma as an individual; that awareness has implications for his sense of himself.

The two strands of the story are closely interwoven, with Uma providing the binding force. One strand follows Wiltshire's discovery of his love and respect for Uma, and his wish to do the decent thing by her. The other is the story of how he destroys Case, more out of self-preservation than a sense of public duty. He has considerable courage, but he does not see himself as champion of the native.

The story that Wiltshire tells proceeds like the peeling of an onion. With each episode, in themselves inexplicable and incomplete, he reveals more of himself and adds to his own understanding. He makes it quite clear that he acts throughout largely through self-interest, although concern for another, Uma, has translated self-interest onto a more heroic level. Yet he emerges as a decent and relatively honourable man, if not honest with the islanders at least honest with himself, and not attempting to disguise his prejudices.

The most striking feature of *The Beach of Falesá*, and the feature that disturbed some cotemporary readers, is its frankness. Its frankness about sex distressed its first editor. Readers one hundred years later probably feel that the story's frankness about exploitation and deceit is more significant. In many ways it is more direct than anything Conrad was to write later, and this is largely because Stevenson's vehicle is a man of limited understanding and imagination. He is not preoccupied with his own soul or a struggle to come to terms with guilt or collusion. Wiltshire has no problems of that kind. He adjusts cheerfully. When his modest ambition of returning to England and running a pub fades, because of his commitment to his family, he accepts it. He lives comfortably with his own prejudices, assuming, probably rightly, that they are the norm. All this is clear in the final paragraph. But much more than that is clear. Stevenson, through his inadvertent hero, precisely exposes an ambivalence that is at the heart of imperialism.

> My public house? Not a bit of it, nor ever likely; I'm stuck here, I fancy: I don't like to leave the kids, you see; and there's no use talking—they're better here than what they would be in a white man's country. Though Ben took the eldest up to Auckland, where he's been schooled with the best. But what bothers me is the girls. They're only half castes of course; I know that as well as you do, and there's nobody thinks less of half castes than I do; but they're mine, and about all I've got; I can't reconcile my mind to their taking up with kanakas, and I'd like to know where I'm to find them whites?

Falesá was a kind of breakthrough for Stevenson. Most of his fiction had drawn back from the problems of the contemporary world by placing character and action in the past. But we know Stevenson was keen to take on the confusions and contradictions of late Victorian life. In Scotland all kinds of inhibitions stood in the way of his tackling these in fiction, not the least of which was the unacceptability of being honest about sex. In the South Seas those inhibitions dwindled. In a letter to Colvin he claimed that *Falesá* was the first ever realistic story set in the South Seas.

> Everybody else who has tried, that I have seen, got carried away by the romance, and ended in a kind of sugar candy sham epic, and the whole effect was lost— there was no etching, no human grin, consequently no conviction. Now I have got the smell and the look of the thing a good deal. You will know more about the South Seas after you have read my little tale than if you had read a library.

Stevenson's own judgment of his story remains valid.

None of Stevenson's writing about the South Seas is 'sugar candy'. Indeed, although the adulation of Stevenson in the years after his death was somewhat sickly, candy is rare in any of his writing. And of all that he experienced in the Pacific *The Beach of Falesá* is a distillation. We meet aspects of it in letters and scattered through *In the South Seas*. Although in *The Ebb Tide* he takes the theme of moral degeneration further, nowhere else does he examine with such clarity and consistency this crucial accompaniment to expansionism. In many ways—in its perception, in its language and in its lessons—it is an astonishingly radical book, and of all his work it most strongly suggests that had Stevenson lived longer he might now be remembered more as a novelist of Britain's nineteenth-century imperialist present than of Scotland's contentious past.

Jenni Calder

NOTES TO INTRODUCTION

1. Letter to James Payne, *The Letters of Robert Louis Stevenson*, ed. Sidney Colvin (London 1911), vol. iii, p.131

2. Letter to Sidney Colvin, *ibid.*, p.134

3. Margaret Stevenson, *From Saranac to the Marquesas and Beyond* (London 1903), p.63

4. W.E. Clarke, *Reminiscences of Robert Louis Stevenson*, n.d., no page numbers.

5. In Arthur Johnstone, *Recollections of Robert Louis Stevenson in the Pacific* (London 1905), p.103.

6. Letter to R.A.M. Stevenson, *Letters*, vol. iv, p.303.

7. Robert Louis Stevenson, *Weir of Hermiston*, Skerryvore Edition (London 1925), p.129.

8. Letter to Sidney Colvin, *Letters*, vol. iii, p.292.

Letters

Throughout his life Stevenson was a prolific letter writer. While in the South Seas he wrote to many of his friends in England and Scotland, most regularly to Sidney Colvin, who acted as his literary agent in London. From the following letters, written between the ages of thirty-nine and forty-one, we get a flavour of Stevenson's experiences and responses in the Pacific which has a spontaneous liveliness often muted in his more polished work. His delight in fresh encounters and his boyish enthusiasm are expressed in the letters without inhibition. But an attentiveness to detail and nuance is also apparent, and a disarming directness. When he wrote for publication, there were times that Stevenson felt he had to curb his frankness and subdue his criticism. This was less likely to be true of his letters.

The text of the letters in this selection is taken from the Swanston edition of Stevenson's work, 1925, which includes some letters not published in earlier editions.

TO CHARLES BAXTER[1]

Yacht 'Casco', at sea, near the Paumotus
7 A.M., *September 6th, 1888, with a dreadful pen.*

My Dear Charles,—Last night as I lay under my blanket in the cockpit, courting sleep, I had a comic seizure. There was nothing visible but the southern stars, and the steersman there out by the binnacle lamp; we were all looking forward to a most deplorable landfall on the morrow, praying God we should fetch a tuft of palms which are to indicate the Dangerous Archipelago; the night was as warm as milk, and all of a sudden I had a vision of—Drummond Street. It came on me like a flash of lightning: I simply returned thither, and into the past. And when I remember all I hoped and feared as I pickled about Rutherford's[2] in the rain and the east wind; how I feared I should make a mere shipwreck, and yet timidly hoped not; how I feared I should never have a friend, far less a wife, and yet passionately hoped I might; how I hoped (if I did not take to drink) I should possibly write one little book, etc. etc. And then now—what a change! I feel somehow as if I should like the incident set upon a brass plate at the corner of that dreary thoroughfare for all students to read, poor devils, when their hearts are down. And I felt I must write one word to you. Excuse me if I write little: when I am at sea, it gives me a headache; when I am in port, I have my diary crying 'Give, give.' I shall have a fine book of travels, I feel sure; and will tell you more of the South Seas after very few months than any other writer has done—except Herman Melville[3] perhaps, who is a howling cheese. Good luck to you, God bless you.—Your affectionate friend,   R.L.S.

1. Baxter was an old friend and fellow-student of Stevenson's. An Edinburgh lawyer, he handled Stevenson's financial affairs while he was abroad.
2. A public house in Drummond Street, a stone's throw from Edinburgh University's Old College, and still standing.
3. Stevenson had read Melville's *Typee* (1846), a record of a four month stay in the Marquesas, with great enthusiasm.

Tautira, Island of Tahiti [November 1888].

Dear Tomarcher,—This is a pretty state of things! seven o'clock and no word of breakfast! And I was awake a good deal last night, for it was full moon, and they had made a great fire of cocoa-nut husks down by the sea, and as we have no blinds or shutters, this kept my room very bright. And then the rats had a wedding or a school-feast under my bed. And then I woke early, and I have nothing to read except Virgil's *Æneid*, which is not good fun on an empty stomach, and a Latin dictionary, which is good for naught, and by some humorous accident, your dear papa's article on Sker-ryvore. And I read the whole of that, and very impudent it is, but you must not tell your dear papa I said so, or it might come to a battle in which you might lose either a dear papa or a valued correspondent, or both, which would be prodigal. And still no breakfast; so I said 'Let's write to Tomarcher.'

This is a much better place for children than any I have hitherto seen in these seas. The girls (and sometimes the boys) play a very elaborate kind of hopscotch. The boys play horses exactly as we do in Europe; and have very good fun on stilts, trying to knock each other down, in which they do not often succeed. The children of all ages go to church and are allowed to do what they please, running about the aisles, rolling balls, stealing mama's bonnet and publicly sitting on it, and at last going to sleep in the middle of the floor. I forgot to say that the whips to play horses, and the balls to roll about the church—at least I never saw them used elsewhere—grow ready made on trees; which is rough on toy-shops. The whips are so good that I wanted to play horses myself; but no such luck! my hair is grey, and I am a great big, ugly man. The balls are rather hard, but very light and quite round. When you grow up and become offensively rich, you can charter a ship in the port of London, and have it come back to you entirely loaded with these balls; when you could

1. 'Tomarcher' was the son of writer, critic and translator William Archer, who had visited Stevenson in his Bournemouth house, called Skerryvore after the famous Stevenson lighthouse in the Hebrides.

satisfy your mind as to their character, and give them away when done with to your uncles and aunts. But what I really wanted to tell you was this: besides the tree-top toys (Hush-a-by, toy-shop, on the tree-top!), I have seen some real *made* toys, the first hitherto observed in the South Seas.

This was how. You are to imagine a four-wheeled gig; one horse; in the front seat two Tahiti natives, in their Sunday clothes, blue coat, white shirt, kilt (a little longer than the Scotch) of a blue stuff with big white or yellow flowers, legs and feet bare; in the back seat me and my wife, who is a friend of yours; under our feet, plenty of lunch and things: among us a great deal of fun in broken Tahitian, one of the natives, the sub-chief of the village, being a great ally of mine. Indeed we have exchanged names; so that he is now Rui, the nearest they can come to Louis, for they have no *l* and no *s* in their language. Rui is six feet three in his stockings, and a magnificent man. We all have straw hats, for the sun is strong. We drive between the sea, which makes a great noise, and the mountains; the road is cut through a forest mostly of fruit trees, the very creepers, which take the place of our ivy, heavy with a great and delicious fruit, bigger than your head and far nicer, called Barbedine. Presently we came to a house in a pretty garden, quite by itself, very nicely kept, the doors and windows open, no one about, and no noise but that of the sea. It looked like a house in a fairy-tale, and just beyond we must ford a river, and there we saw the inhabitants. Just in the mouth of the river, where it met the sea waves, they were ducking and bathing and screaming together like a covey of birds: seven or eight little naked brown boys and girls as happy as the day was long; and on the banks of the stream beside them, real toys—toy ships, full rigged, and with their sails set, though they were lying in the dust on their beam ends. And then I knew for sure they were all children in a fairy-story, living alone together in that lonely house with the only toys in all the island; and that I had myself driven, in my four-wheeled gig, into a corner of the fairy-story, and the question was, should I get out again? But it was all right; I guess only one of the wheels of the gig had got into the fairy-story; and the next jolt the whole thing vanished, and we drove on in our sea-side forest as before,

and I have the honour to be Tomarcher's valued correspondent, TERIITERA, which he was previouly known as
ROBERT LOUIS STEVENSON

TO R.A.M. STEVENSON[1]
Honolulu, Hawaiian Islands, February 1889.

My Dear Rob,—My extremely foolhardy venture is practically over. How foolhardy it was I don't think I realised. We had a very small schooner, and, like most yachts, over-rigged and over-sparred, and like many American yachts on a very dangerous sail plan. The waters we sailed in are, of course, entirely unlighted, and very badly charted; in the Dangerous Archipelago, through which we were fools enough to go, we were perfectly in ignorance of where we were for a whole night and half the next day, and this in the midst of invisible islands and rapid and variable currents; and we were lucky when we found our whereabouts at last. We have twice had all we wanted in the way of squalls: once, as I came on deck, I found the green sea over the cockpit coamings and running down the companion like a brook to meet me; at that same moment the foresail sheet jammed and the captain had no knife; this was the only occasion on the cruise that ever I set a hand to a rope, but I worked like a Trojan, judging the possibility of haemorrhage better than the certainty of drowning. Another time I saw a rather singular thing: our whole ship's company as pale as paper from the the captain to the cook; we had a black squall astern on the port side and a white squall ahead to starboard; the complication passed off innocuous, the black squall only fetching us with its tail, and the white one slewing off somewhere else. Twice we were a long while (days) in the close vicinity of hurricane weather, but again luck prevailed, and we saw none of it. These are dangers incident to these seas and small craft. What was an amazement, and at the same time a powerful stroke of luck, both our masts were

1. Bob Stevenson was Stevenson's cousin, son of Alan Stevenson, the designer of the Skerryvore lighthouse. Three years older than Stevenson, he was a favourite playmate in childhood and a valued friend as a young man.

rotten, and we found it out—I was going to say in time, but it was stranger and luckier than that. The head of the main-mast hung over so that hands were afraid to go to the helm; and less than three weeks before—I am not sure it was more than a fortnight—we had been nearly twelve hours beating off the lee shore of Eimeo (or Moorea, next island to Tahiti) in half a gale of wind with a violent head sea: she would neither tack nor wear once, and had to be boxed off with the mainsail—you can imagine what an ungodly show of kites we carried—and yet the mast stood. The very day after that, in the southern bight of Tahiti, we had a near squeak, the wind suddenly coming calm; the reefs were close in with, my eye! what a surf! The pilot thought we were gone, and the captain had a boat cleared, when a lucky squall came to our rescue. My wife, hearing the order given about the boats, remarked to my mother, 'Isn't that nice? We shall soon be ashore!' Thus does the female mind unconsciously skirt along the verge of eternity. Our voyage up here was most disastrous— calms, squalls, head sea, waterspouts of rain, hurricane weather all about, and we in the midst of the hurricane season, when even the hopeful builder and owner of the yacht had pronounced these seas unfit for her. We ran out of food, and were quite given up for lost in Honolulu: people had ceased to speak to Belle[2] about the *Casco*, as a deadly subject.

But the perils of the deep were part of the programme; and though I am very glad to be done with them for a while and comfortably ashore, where a squall does not matter a snuff to any one, I feel pretty sure I shall want to get to sea again ere long. The dreadful risk I took was financial, and double-headed. First, I had to sink a lot of money in the cruise, and if I didn't get health, how was I to get it back? I have got health to a wonderful extent; and as I have the most inter-esting matter for my book, bar accidents, I ought to get all I have laid out and a profit. But, second (what I own I never considered till too late), there was the danger of collisions, of damages and heavy repairs, of disablement, towing, and

2. Mrs Isobel Strong, daughter of Stevenson's wife Fanny
   Osbourne. Belle was living in Honolulu with her artist
   husband Joe Strong.

salvage; indeed, the cruise might have turned round and cost me double. Nor will this danger be quite over till I hear the yacht is in San Francisco; for though I have shaken the dust of her deck from my feet, I fear (as a point of law) she is still mine till she gets there.

From my point of view, up to now the cruise has been a wonderful success. I never knew the world was so amusing. On the last voyage we had grown so used to sea-life that no one wearied, though it lasted a full month, except Fanny, who is always ill. All the time our visits to the islands have been more like dreams than realities: the people, the life, the beachcombers, the old stories and songs I have picked up, so interesting; the climate, the scenery, and (in some places) the women, so beautiful. The women are handsomest in Tahiti, the men in the Marquesas; both as fine types as can be imagined. Lloyd reminds me, I have not told you one characteristic incident of the cruise from a semi-naval point of view. One night we were going ashore in Anaho Bay;[3] the most awful noise on deck; the breakers distinctly audible in the cabin; and there I had to sit below, entertaining in my best style a negroid native chieftain, much the worse for rum! You can imagine the evening's pleasure.

This naval report on cruising in the South Seas would be incomplete without one other trait. On our voyage up here I came one day into the dining-room, the hatch in the floor was open, the ship's boy was below with a baler, and two of the hands were carrying buckets as for a fire; this meant that the pumps had ceased working.

One stirring day was that in which we sighted Hawaii. It blew fair, but very strong; we carried jib, foresail, and mainsail, all single-reefed, and she carried her lee rail under water and flew. The swell, the heaviest I have ever been out in—I tried in vain to estimate the height, *at least* fifteen feet—came tearing after us about a point and a half off the wind. We had the best hand—old Louis—at the wheel; and really, he did nobly, and had noble luck, for it never caught us once. At times it seemed we must have it; Louis would look over his shoulder with the queerest look and dive down

3. The Stevenson party had spent some time at Anaho
   Bay in the Gilbert Islands.

his neck into his shoulders; and then it missed us somehow, and only sprays came over our quarter, turning the little outside lane of deck into a mill race as deep as to the cockpit coamings. I never remember anything more delightful and exciting. Pretty soon after we were lying absolutely becalmed under the lee of Hawaii, of which we had been warned; and the captain never confessed he had done it on purpose, but when accused, he smiled. Really, I suppose he did quite right, for we stood committed to a dangerous race, and to bring her to the wind would have been rather a heart-sickening manoeuvre.   R.L.S.

TO MISS ADELAIDE BOODLE[1]
Honolulu, April 6th, 1889.
My Dear Miss Boodle,—Nobody writes a letter better than my Gamekeeper: so gay, so pleasant, so engagingly particular, answering (by some delicate instinct) all the questions she suggests. It is a shame you should get such a poor return as I can make, from a mind essentially and originally incapable of the art epistolary. I would let the paper-cutter take my place; but I am sorry to say the little wooden seaman did after the manner of seamen, and deserted in the Societies.[2] The place he seems to have stayed at—seems, for his absence was not observed till we were near the Equator—was Tautira,[3] and, I assure you, he displayed good taste, Tautira being as 'nigh hand heaven' as a paper-cutter or anybody has a right to expect.

I think all our friends will be very angry with us, and I give the grounds of their probable displeasure bluntly—we are not coming home for another year. My mother[4] returns next month. Fanny, Lloyd, and I push on again among the islands on a trading schooner, the *Equator*—first for the

1. A neighbour in Bournemouth who became very friendly with both Fanny and Louis Stevenson. Stevenson nicknamed her 'the Gamekeeper'.
2. The Society Islands, of which Tahiti is the largest.
3. On the opposite side of Tahiti from Papeete, the island's main town and capital of French Polynesia. The Stevensons had spent a very happy time there.

Gilbert group, which we shall have an opportunity to explore thoroughly; then, if occasion serve, to the Marshalls and Carolines; and if occasion (or money) fail, to Samoa, and back to Tahiti. I own we are deserters, but we have excuses. You cannot conceive how these climates agree with the wretched house-plant of Skerryvore: he wonders to find himself sea-bathing, and cutting about the world loose, like a grown-up person. They agree with Fanny too, who does not suffer from her rheumatism, and with Lloyd also. And the interest of the islands is endless; and the sea, though I own it is a fearsome place, is very delightful. We had applied for places in the American missionary ship, the *Morning Star*, but this trading schooner is a far preferable idea, giving us more time and a thousandfold more liberty; so we determined to cut off the missionaries with a shilling.

The Sandwich Islands[5] do not interest us very much; we live here, oppressed with civilisation, and look for good things in the future. But it would surprise you if you came out tonight from Honolulu (all shining with electric lights, and all in a bustle from the arrival of the mail, which is to carry you these lines) and crossed the long wooden causeway along the beach, and came out on the road through Kapiolani park, and seeing a gate in the palings, with a tub of gold-fish by the wayside, entered casually in. The buildings stand in three groups by the edge of the beach, where an angry little spitfire sea continually spirts and thrashes with impotent irascibility, the big seas breaking further out upon the reef. The first is a small house, with a very large summer parlour, or *lanai*, as they call it here, roofed, but practically open. There you will find the lamps burning and the family sitting about the table, dinner just done: my mother, my wife, Lloyd, Belle, my wife's daughter, Austin her child, and tonight (by way of rarity) a guest. All about the walls our South Sea curiosities, war clubs, idols, pearl shells, stone axes, etc.; and the walls are only a small part of a lanai, the rest being glazed or latticed windows, or mere open space.

4. Stevenson's mother, Margaret Isabella Balfour Stevenson, recently widowed, accompanied him for the first part of the South Seas trip.
5. Hawaiian Islands.

You will see there no sign of the Squire, however; and being a person of a humane disposition, you will only glance in over the balcony railing at the merry-makers in the summer parlour, and proceed further afield after the Exile. You look round, there is beautiful green turf, many trees of an outlandish sort that drop thorns—look out if your feet are bare; but I beg your pardon, you have not been long enough in the South Seas—and many oleanders in full flower. The next group of buildings is ramshackle, and quite dark; you make out a coach-house door, and look in—only some cocoanuts; you try round to the left and come to the sea front, where Venus and the moon are making luminous tracks on the water, and a great swell rolls and shines on the outer reef; and here is another door—all these places open from the outside—and you go in, and find photography, tubs of water, negatives steeping, a tap, and a chair and an inkbottle, where my wife is supposed to write; round a little further, a third door, entering which you find a picture upon the easel and a table sticky with paints; a fourth door admits you to a sort of court, where there is a hen sitting—I believe on a fallacious egg. No sign of the Squire in all this. But right opposite the studio door you have observed a third little house, from whose open door lamplight streams and makes hay of the strong moonlight shadows. You had supposed it made no part of the grounds, for a fence runs round it lined with oleander; but as the Squire is nowhere else, is it not just possible he may be here? It is a grim little wooden shanty; cobwebs bedeck it; friendly mice inhabit its recesses; the mailed cockroach walks upon the wall; so also, I regret to say, the scorpion. Herein are two pallet beds, two mosquito curtains, strung to the pitch-boards of the roof, two tables laden with books and manuscripts, three chairs, and, in one of the beds, the Squire busy writing to yourself, as it chances, and just at this moment somewhat bitten by mosquitoes. He has just set fire to the insect powder, and will be all right in no time; but just now he contemplates large white blisters, and would like to scratch them, but knows better. The house is not bare; it has been inhabited by Kanakas,[6] and—you know what children are!—the bare wood walls are pasted over with pages from the *Graphic, Harper's Weekly*, etc. The floor is matted, and I am bound to say the matting is filthy. There are two windows and two doors, one of which is condemned; on the panels of that last a sheet of paper is pinned up, and covered with writing. I cull a few plums:—

A duck-hammock for each person.

A patent organ like the commandant's at Taiohae.[7]

Cheap and bad cigars for presents.

Revolvers.

Permanganate of potass.

Liniment for the head and sulphur.

Fine tooth-comb.

What do you think this is? Simply life in the South Seas foreshortened. These are a few of our desiderata for the next trip, which we jot down as they occur.

There, I have really done my best and tried to send you something like a letter—one letter in return for all your dozens. Pray remember us all to yourself, Mrs. Boodle, and the rest of your house. I do hope your mother will be better when this comes. I shall write and give you a new address when I have made up my mind as to the most probable, and I do beg you will continue to write from time to time and give us airs from home. Tomorrow—think of it—I must be off by a quarter to eight to drive in to the palace and breakfast with his Hawaiian Majesty at 8.30: I shall be dead indeed. Please give my news to Scott, I trust he is better; give him my warm regards. To you we all send all kinds of things, and I am the absentee Squire,

ROBERT LOUIS STEVENSON.

6. In the Hawaiian language Kanaka is the word for man, but was widely used to refer to all native Pacific islanders.

7. A village in the Marquesas Islands.

TO SIDNEY COLVIN

Honolulu, June 1889.

My Dear Colvin,—I am just home after twelve days journey to Molokai,[1] seven of them at the leper settlement, where I can only say that the sight of so much courage, cheerfulness, and devotion strung me too high to mind the infinite pity and horror of the sights. I used to ride over from Kalawao to Kalaupapa (about three miles across the promontory, the cliff-wall, ivied with forest and yet inaccessible from steepness, on my left), go to the Sisters' home, which is a miracle of neatness, play a game of croquet with seven leper girls (90° in the shade), get a little old-maid meal served me by the Sisters, and ride home again, tired enough, but not too tired. The girls have all dolls, and loved dressing them. You who know so many ladies delicately clad, and they who know so many dressmakers, please make it known it would be an acceptable gift to send scraps for doll dressmaking to the Reverend Sister Maryanne, Bishop Home, Kalaupapa, Molokai, Hawaiian Islands.

I have seen sights that cannot be told, and heard stories that cannot be repeated: yet I never admired my poor race so much, nor (strange as it may seem) loved life more than in the settlement. A horror of moral beauty broods over the place: that's like bad Victor Hugo,[2] but it is the only way I can express the sense that lived with me all these days. And this even though it was in great part Catholic, and my sympathies flew never with so much difficulty as towards Catholic virtues. The passbook kept with heaven stirs me to anger and laughter. One of the sisters calls the place 'the ticket office to heaven'. Well, what is the odds? They do their darg, and do it with kindness and efficiency incredible; and we must take folk's virtues as we find them, and love the better part. Of old Damien,[3] whose weaknesses and worse perhaps I heard fully, I think only the more. It was a European peasant: dirty, bigoted, untruthful, unwise,

1. One of the Hawaiian Islands, on which there was a leper colony. Stevenson made a point of visiting Molokai during his stay in Honolulu.
2. Stevenson came to admire the French novelist, though with certain reservations.

tricky, but superb with generosity, residual candour and
fundamental good-humour: convince him he had done
wrong (it might take hours of insult) and he would undo
what he had done and like his corrector better. A man, with
all the grime and paltriness of mankind, but a saint and hero
all the more for that. The place as regards scenery is grand,
gloomy, and bleak. Mighty mountain walls descending sheer
along the whole face of the island into the sea unusually
deep; the front of the mountain ivied and furred with
clinging forest, one viridescent cliff: about half-way from
east to west, the low, bare, stony promontory edged in
between the cliff and the ocean; the two little towns (Kalawao and Kalaupapa) seated on either side of it, as bare
almost as bathing machines upon a beach; and the
population—gorgons and chimaeras dire. All this tear of the
nerves I bore admirably; and the day after I got away, rode
twenty miles along the opposite coast and up into the mountains: they call it twenty, I am doubtful of the figures: I
should guess it nearer twelve; but let me take credit for what
residents allege; and I was riding again the day after, so I
need say no more about health. Honolulu does not agree with
me at all: I am always out of sorts there, with slight headache, blood to the head, etc. I had a good deal of work to do
and did it with miserable difficulty; and yet all the time I
have been gaining strength, as you see, which is highly
encouraging. By the time I am done with this cruise I shall
have the material for a very singular book of travels: names
of strange stories and characters, cannibals, pirates, ancient
legends, old Polynesian poetry,—never was so generous a
farrago. I am going down now to get the story of a shipwreck-
ed family, who were fifteen months on an island with a
murderer: there is a specimen. The Pacific is a strange place;

3. Father Damien was the Belgian priest who presided
   over the leper colony. Although he never met
   Damien, who died before Stevenson's visit to
   Molokai, he admired him greatly. Damien was
   considered a reprobate by many. Stevenson defended
   him against what he considered sanctimonious Protestant attack in 'An Open Letter to the Rev. Dr Hyde
   of Honolulu' (1890).

the nineteenth century only exists there in spots: all round, it is a no man's land of the ages, a stir-about of epochs and races, barbarisms and civilisations, virtues and crimes.

It is good of you to let me stay longer, but if I had known how ill you were, I should be now on my way home. I had chartered my schooner and made all arrangements before (at last) we got definite news. I feel highly guilty; I should be back to insult and worry you a little. Our address till further notice is to be c/o R. Towns and Co., Sydney. That is final: I only got the arrangement made yesterday; but you may now publish it abroad.—Yours ever,   R.L.S.

TO SIDNEY COLVIN
Schooner 'Equator,' Apaiang Lagoon
22nd August, 1889.

My Dear Colvin,—The missionary ship is outside the reef trying (vainly) to get in; so I may have a chance to get a line off. I am glad to say I shall be home by June next for the summer, or we shall know the reason why. For God's sake be well and jolly for the meeting. I shall be, I believe, a different character from what you have seen this long while. This cruise is up to now a huge success, being interesting, pleasant, and profitable. The beachcomber is perhaps the most interesting character here; the natives are very different, on the whole, from Polynesians: they are moral, stand-offish (for good reasons), and protected by a dark tongue. It is delightful to meet the few Hawaiians (mostly missionaries) that are dotted about, with their Italian *brio* and their ready friendliness.. The whites are a strange lot, many of them good, kind, pleasant fellows; others quite the lowest I have ever seen even in the slums of cities. I wish I had time to narrate to you the doings and character of three white murderers (more or less proven) I have met. One, the only undoubted assassin of the lot, quite gained my affection in his big home out of a wreck, with his New Hebrides wife in her savage turban of hair and yet a perfect lady, and his three adorable little girls in Rob Roy Macgregor dresses, dancing to the hand organ, performing circus on the floor with startling effects of nudity, and curling up together on a mat to sleep, three sizes, three attitudes, three Rob Roy dresses, and six little clenched fists: the murderer meanwhile brooding and gloating over his chicks, till your whole heart went out to him; and yet his crime on the face of it was dark: disembowelling, in his own house, an old man of seventy, and him drunk.

It is lunch-time, I see, and I must close up with my warmest love to you. I wish you were here to sit upon me when required. Ah! if you were but a good sailor! I will never leave the sea, I think; it is only here that a Briton lives: my poor grandfather, it is from him I inherit the taste, I fancy, and he was round many islands in his day: but I, please God, shall beat him at that before the recall is sounded. Would you be surprised to learn that I contemplate becoming a shipowner? I do, but it is a secret. Life is far better fun than people dream who fall asleep among the chimney stacks and telegraph wires.

Love to Henry James and others near.—Ever yours, my dear fellow　　　　　　ROBERT LOUIS STEVENSON.

TO SIDNEY COLVIN
Equator Town,[1] *Apemama, October* 1889.

No *Morning Star* came, however; and so now I try to send this to you by the schooner *J. L. Tiernan.* We have been about a month ashore, camping out in a kind of town the king set up for us: on the idea that I was really a 'big chief' in England. He dines with us sometimes, and sends up a cook for a share of our meals when he does not come himself. This sounds like high living! alas, undeceive yourself. Salt junk is the mainstay; a low island, except for cocoanuts, is just the same as a ship at sea: brackish water, no supplies, and very little shelter. The king is a great character—a thorough tyrant, very much of a gentleman, a poet, a musician, a historian, or perhaps rather more a genealogist—it is strange

1. At Apemama in the Gilberts King Tembinoka constructed a compound of huts for the Stevenson party's stay. It was known as 'Equator Town', after the schooner *Equator* in which they were voyaging.

to see him lying in his house among a lot of wives (nominal
wives) writing the History of Apemama in an account-book;
his description of one of his own songs, which he sang to me
himself, as 'about sweethearts, and trees, and the sea—and
no true, all-the-same lie', seems about as compendious a
definition of lyric poetry as a man could ask. Tembinoka is
here the great attraction: all the rest is heat and tedium and
villainous dazzle, and yet more villainous mosquitoes. We
are like to be here, however, many a long week before we get
away, and then whither? A strange trade this voyaging: so
vague, so bound-down, so helpless. Fanny has been planting
some vegetables, and we have actually onions and radishes
coming up: ah, onion-despiser, were you but awhile in a low
island, how your heart would leap at sight of a coster's
barrow! I think I could shed tears over a dish of turnips. No
doubt we shall all be glad to say farewell to low islands—I had
near said for ever. They are very tame; and I begin to read up
the directory, and pine for an island with a profile, a running
brook, or were it only a well among the rocks. The thought of
a mango came to me early this morning and set my greed on
edge; but you do not know what a mango is, so—

I have been thinking a great deal of you and the Monu-
ment[2] of late, and even tried to get my thought into a poem,
hitherto without success. God knows how you are: I begin to
weary dreadfully to see you—well, in nine months, I hope;
but that seems a long time. I wonder what has befallen me
too, that flimsy part of me that lives (or dwindles) in the
public mind; and what has befallen *The Master*,[3] and what
kind of a Box[4] the Merry Box has been found. It is odd to
know nothing of all this. We had an old woman to do
devil-work for you about a month ago, in a Chinaman's
house on Apaiang[5] (August 23rd or 24th). You should have
seen the crone with a noble masculine face, like that of an old

2. Stevenson referred thus to the British Museum, where
   Colvin was Curator of Prints.

3. *The Master of Ballantrae*, recently published.

4. *The Wrong Box*, written in collaboration with Lloyd
   Osbourne before leaving the United States for the
   Pacific, and recently published.

5. One of the Gilbert Islands.

crone [*sic*], a body like a man's (naked all but the feathery
female girdle), knotting cocoanut leaves and muttering
spells: Fanny and I, and the good captain of the *Equator*, and
the Chinaman and his native wife and sister-in-law, all
squatting on the floor about the sibyl; and a crowd of dark
faces watching from behind her shoulder (she sat right in the
doorway) and tittering aloud with strange, appalled, em-
barrassed laughter at each fresh adjuration. She informed us
you were in England, not travelling and now no longer sick;
she promised us a fair wind the next day, and we had it, so I
cherish the hope she was as right about Sidney Colvin. The
shipownering has rather petered out since I last wrote, and a
good many other plans besides.

Health? Fanny very so-so; I pretty right upon the whole,
and getting through plenty work: I know not quite how, but
it seems to me not bad and in places funny.

South Sea Yarns:[6]

1. *The Wrecker*   R.L.S.
2. *The Pearl Fisher*   } *by*   *and*
3. *The Beachcombers.*   LLOYD O.

The Pearl Fisher, part done, lies in Sydney. It is *The
Wrecker* we are now engaged upon: strange ways of life, I
think, they set forth: things that I can scarce touch upon, or
even not at all, in my travel book; and the yarns are good, I
do believe. *The Pearl Fisher* is for the *New York Ledger*: the
yarn is a kind of Monte Cristo one. *The Wrecker* is the least
good as a story, I think; but the characters seem to me good.
The Beachcombers is more sentimental. These three scarce
touch the outskirts of the life we have been viewing; a
hot-bed of strange characters and incidents: Lord, how
different from Europe or the Pallid States! Farewell. Heaven
knows when this will get to you. I burn to be in Sydney and
have news.   R.L.S.

6. *The Wrecker* (1892) had been begun, in collaboration
with Lloyd Osbourne, a few months earlier. *The Pearl
Fisher* was begun by Lloyd Osbourne in Honolulu the
previous spring. The final version was written by
Stevenson and published as *The Ebb Tide* (1893). *The
Beachcombers* was never written.

TO SIDNEY COLVIN

In the Mountain, Apia, Samoa
Monday, November, 2 1890.

My Dear Colvin,—This is a hard and interesting and beautiful life that we lead now. Our place is in a deep cleft of Vaea Mountain, some six hundred feet above the sea, embowered in a forest, which is our strangling enemy, and which we combat with axes and dollars. I went crazy over outdoor work, and had at last to confine myself to the house, or literature must have gone by the board. *Nothing* is so interesting as weeding, clearing, and pathmaking; the oversight of labourers becomes a disease; it is quite an effort not to drop into the farmer; and it does make you feel so well. To come down covered with mud and drenched with sweat and rain after some hours in the bush, change, rub down, and take a chair in the verandah, is to taste a quiet conscience. And the strange thing that I mark is this: if I go out and make sixpence, bossing my labourers and plying the cutlass or the spade, idiot conscience applauds me: if I sit in the house and make twenty pounds, idiot conscience wails over my neglect and the day wasted. For near a fortnight I did not go beyond the verandah; then I found my rush of work run out, and went down for the night to Apia; put in Sunday afternoon with our consul, 'a nice young man', dined with my friend H. J. Moors[1] in the evening, went to church—no less—at the white and half-white church—I had never been before, and was much interested; the woman I sat next *looked* a full-blood native, and it was in the prettiest and readiest English that she sang the hymns; back to Moors', where we yarned of the islands, being both wide wanderers, till bedtime; bed, sleep, breakfast, horse saddled; round to the mission, to get Mr Clarke[2] to be my interpreter; over with

1. Henry Moors was a trader in Apia who acted as agent for the building of Vailima. He was a close associate of Stevenson and wrote about their relationship in *With Stevenson in Samoa* (1910).

2. W.E. Clarke was from the London Missionary Society and a man for whom Stevenson, often critical of missionaries, had considerable regard. See the passage quoted in the Introduction.

him to the King's whom I have not called on since my return; received by that mild old gentleman; have some interesting talk with him about Samoan superstitions and my land—the scene of a great battle in his (Malietoa Laupepa's[3]) youth—the place where we have cleared the platform of his fort—the gully of the stream full of dead bodies—the fight rolled off up Vaea mountain-side; back with Clarke to the mission; had a bit of lunch and consulted over a queer point of missionary policy just arisen, about our new Town Hall and the balls there—too long to go into, but a quaint example of the intricate questions which spring up daily in the missionary path.

Then off up the hill; Jack very fresh, the sun (close on noon) staring hot, the breeze strong and pleasant; the ineffable green country all around—gorgeous little birds (I think they are humming-birds, but they say not) skirmishing in the wayside flowers. About a quarter way up I met a native coming down with the trunk of a cocoa palm across his shoulder; his brown breast glistening with sweat and oil: 'Talofa'—'Talofa, alii—You see that white man? He speak for you.' 'White man he gone up here?'—'Ioe' (Yes)—'Tofa, alii'—'Tofa, soifua!' I put Jack up the steep path, till he is all as white as a shaving stick—Brown's euxesis, wish I had some—past Tanugamanomo, a bush village—see into the houses as I pass—they are open sheds scattered on a green—see the brown folk sitting there, suckling kids, sleeping on their stiff wooden pillows—then on through the wood-path—and here I find the mysterious white man (poor devil!) with his twenty years' certificate of good behaviour as a book-keeper, frozen out by the strikes in the colonies, come up here on a chance, no work to be found, big hotel bill, no ship to leave in—come up to beg twenty dollars because he heard I was a Scotchman, offering to leave his portmanteau in pledge. Settle this, and on again; and here my house comes in view, and a war whoop fetches my wife and Henry (or Simelé), our Samoan boy, on the front balcony; and I am home again, and only sorry that I shall

3. The puppet king of Samoa, supported by the Germans.

have to go down again to Apia this day week. I could, I would, dwell here unmoved, but there are things to be attended to.

Tuesday, 3rd.—I begin to see the whole scheme of letter-writing; you sit down every day and pour out an equable stream of twaddle.

This morning all my fears were fled, and all the trouble had fallen to the lot of Peni himself, who deserved it; my field was full of weeders and I am again able to justify the ways of God. All morning I worked at *The South Seas*, and finished the chapter I had stuck upon on Saturday. Fanny, awfully hove-to with rheumatics and injuries received upon the field of sport and glory, chasing pigs, was unable to go up and down stairs, so she sat upon the back verandah, and my work was chequered by her cries. 'Paul, you take a spade to do that—dig a hole first. If you do that, you'll cut your foot off! Here, you boy, what you do there? You no get work? You go find Simelé; he give you work. Peni, you tell this boy he go find Simelé: suppose Simelé no give him work, you tell him go 'way. I no want him here. That boy no good.'—*Peni* (from the distance in reassuring tones), 'All right, sir!'—*Fanny* (after a long pause), 'Peni, you tell that boy go find Simelé! I no want him stand here all day. He no do nothing.'—Luncheon, beef, soda-scones, fried bananas, pine-apple in claret, coffee. Try to write a poem; no go. Play the flageolet. Then sneakingly off to farmering and pioneering. Four gangs at work on our place; a lively scene; axes crashing and smoke blowing; all the knives are out. But I rob the garden party of one without a stock, and you should see my hand—cut to ribbons. Now I want to do my path up the Vaituliga single-handed, and I want it to burst on the public complete. Hence, with devilish ingenuity, I begin it at different places; so that if you stumble on one section, you may not even then suspect the fullness of my labours. Accordingly I started in a new place, below the wire, and hoping to work up to it. It was perhaps lucky I had so bad a cutlass, and my smarting hand bade me stay before I had got up to the wire, but just in season, so that I was only the better of my activity, not dead beat as yesterday.

A strange business it was, and infinitely solitary; away

above, the sun was in the high tree-tops; the lianas noosed
and sought to hang me; the saplings struggled, and came up
with that sob of death that one gets to know so well; great,
soft, sappy trees fell at a lick of the cutlass, little tough
switches laughed at and dared my best endeavour. Soon,
toiling down in that pit of verdure, I heard blows on the far
side, and then laughter. I confess a chill settled on my heart.
Being so dead alone, in a place where by rights none should
be beyond me, I was aware, upon interrogation, if those
blows had drawn nearer, I should (of course quite unaf-
fectedly) have executed a strategic movement to the rear;
and only the other day I was lamenting my insensibility to
superstition! Am I beginning to be sucked in? Shall I
become a midnight twitterer like my neighbours? At times I
thought the blows were echoes; at times I thought the
laughter was from birds. For our birds are strangely human
in their calls. Vaea Mountain about sundown sometimes
rings with shrill cries, like the hails of merry, scattered
children. As a matter of fact, I believe stealthy woodcutters
from Tanugamanono were above me in the wood and
answerable for the blows; as for the laughter, a woman and
two children asked Fanny's leave to go up shrimp-fishing in
the burn; beyond doubt, it was these I heard. Just at the
right time I returned; to wash down, change, and begin this
snatch of letter before dinner was ready, and to finish it
afterwards . . . .

Dinner: stewed beef and potatoes, baked bananas, new
loaf-bread hot from the oven, pine-apple in claret. These are
great days: we have been low in the past; but now we are as
belly-gods, enjoying all things.

TO HENRY JAMES[1]

Vailima, Apia,[2] Samoa, December 29th, 1890

My Dear Henry James,—It is terrible how little every-body writes, and how much of that little disappears in the capacious maw of the Post Office. Many letters, both from and to me, I now know to have been lost in transit: my eye is on the Sydney Post Office, a large ungainly structure with a tower, as being not a hundred miles from the scene of disappearance; but then I have no proof. The *Tragic Muse* you announced to me as coming; I had already ordered it from a Sydney bookseller: about two months ago he advised me that his copy was in the post; and I am still tragically museless.

News, news, news. What do we know of yours? What do you care for ours? We are in the midst of the rainy season, and dwell among alarms of hurricanes, in a very unsafe little two-storied wooden box 650 feet above and about three miles from the sea-beach. Behind us, till the other slope of the island, desert forest, peaks, and loud torrents; in front green slopes to the sea, some fifty miles of which we dominate. We see the ships as they go out and in to the dangerous roadstead of Apia; and if they lie far out, we can even see their topmasts while they are at anchor. Of sounds of men, beyond those of our own labourers, there reach us, at very long intervals, salutes from the warships in harbour, the bell of the cathedral church, and the low of the conch-shell calling the labour boys on the German plantations. Yesterday, which was Sunday—the *quantième* is most likely erroneous; you can now correct it—we had a visitor—Baker of Tonga. Heard you ever of him? He is a great man here: he is accused of theft, rape, judicial murder, private poisoning, abortion, misappropriation of public moneys—oddly enough, not for-gery, nor arson: you would be amused if you knew how thick the accusations fly in this South Sea world. I make no doubt

1. The novelist and critic Henry James was a close friend of Stevenson, and had visited him often in Bour-nemouth. *The Tragic Muse* (1889) was his most recent novel.
2. The main town on the island of Upolu, and Samoa's capital.

my own character is something illustrious; or if not yet, there is a good time coming.

But all our resources have not of late been Pacific. We have had enlightened society: La Farge[3] the painter, and your friend Henry Adams:[4] a great privilege—would it might endure. I would go oftener to see them, but the place is awkward to reach on horseback. I had to swim my horse the last time I went to dinner; and as I have not yet returned the clothes I had to borrow, I dare not return in the same plight; it seems inevitable—as soon as the wash comes in, I plump straight into the American consul's shirt or trousers! They, I believe, would come oftener to see me but for the horrid doubt that weights upon our commissariat department; we have *often* almost nothing to eat; a guest would simply break the bank; my wife and I have dined on one avocado pear; I have several times dined on hard bread and onions. What would you do with a guest at such narrow seasons?—eat him? or serve up a labour boy fricaseed?

Work? work is now arrested, but I have written, I should think, about thirty chapters of the South Sea book; they will all want rehandling, I dare say. Gracious, what a strain is a long book! The time it took me to design this volume, before I could dream of putting pen to paper, was excessive; and then think of writing a book of travels on the spot, when I am continually extending my information, revising my opinions, and seeing the most finely finished portions of my work come part by part in pieces. Very soon I shall have no opinions left. And without an opinion, how to string artistically vast accumulations of fact? Darwin[5] said no one could

3. John La Farge was an American artist, and friend of another American artist Will Low, a companion of Stevenson in France in the 1870s.
4. American historian and friend of Henry James. He and La Farge were rather appalled at the Stevenson household. Adams described Stevenson as 'a bundle of sticks in a bag, with dirty striped pyjamas' and Fanny Stevenson as 'an Apache squaw'.
5. Stevenson was intrigued by the theories of Charles Darwin, whose *Origin of Species* was published in 1859.

observe without a theory; I suppose he was right; 'tis a fine point of metaphysic; but I will take my oath, no man can write without one—at least the way he would like to, and my theories melt, melt, melt, and as they melt the thaw-waters wash down my writing and leave unideal tracts—wastes instead of cultivated farms.

Kipling[6] is by far the most promising young man who has appeared since—ahem—I appeared. He amazes me by his precocity and various endowment. But he alarms me by his copiousness and haste. He should shield his fire with both hands 'and draw up all his strength and sweetness in one ball'. ('Draw all his strength and all His sweetness up into one ball'? I cannot remember Marvell's[7] words.) So the critics have been saying to me; but I was never capable of—and surely never guilty of—such a debauch of production. At this rate his works will soon fill the habitable globe; and surely he was armed for better conflicts than these succint sketches and flying leaves of verse? I look on, I admire, I rejoice for myself; but in a kind of ambition we all have for our tongue and literature I am wounded. If I had this man's fertility and courage, it seems to me I could heave a pyramid.

Well, we begin to be the old fogies now; and it was high time *something* rose to take our places. Certainly Kipling has the gifts; the fairy godmothers were all tipsy at his christening: what will he do with them?

I am going to manage to send a long letter every month to Colvin, which, I dare say, if it is ever of the least interest, he will let you see. My wife is now better, and I hope will be reasonably right. We are a very crazy couple to lead so rough a life, but we manage excellently: she is handy and inventive, and I have one quality, I don't grumble. The nearest I came was the other day: when I had finished dinner, I thought

6. Rudyard Kipling's first stories were being published in the 1880s.

7. Stevenson is quoting, slightly inaccurately, from the seventeenth-century poet Andrew Marvell's poem 'To His Coy Mistress'. The lines should read 'Let us roll all our strength and all/Our Sweetness up into one ball.'

awhile, then had my horse saddled, rode down to Apia, and
dined again—I must say with unblunted appetite; that is my
best excuse. Goodbye, my dear James; find an hour to write
to us, and register your letter.—Yours affectionately,

R.L.S.

TO SIDNEY COLVIN

Tuesday, Dec., 1891.

Sir,—I have the honour to report further explorations of
the river Vaea, with accompanying sketch plan. The party
under my command consisted of one horse, and was
extremely insubordinate and mutinous, owing to not being
used to go into the bush, and being half-broken anyway—
and that the wrong half. The route indicated for my party
was up to the bed of the so-called river Vaea, which I
accordingly followed to a distance of perhaps two or three
furlongs eastward from the house of Vailima, where the
stream being quite dry, the bush thick, and the ground very
difficult, I decided to leave the main body of the force under
my command tied to a tree, and push on myself with the
point of the advance guard, consisting of one man. The
valley had become very narrow and airless; foliage close shut
above; dry bed of the stream much excavated, so that I
passed under fallen trees without stooping. Suddenly it
turned sharp to the north, at right angles to its former
direction; I heard living water, and came in view of a tall face
of rock and the stream spraying down it; it might have been
climbed, but it would have been dangerous, and I had to
make my way up the steep earth banks, where there is
nowhere any footing for man, only for trees, which made the
rounds of my ladder. I was near the top of this climb, which
was very hot and steep, and the pulses were buzzing all over
my body, when I made sure there was one external sound in
my ears, and paused to listen. No mistake; a sound of a
mill-wheel thundering, I thought, close by yet below me, a
huge mill-wheel, yet not going steadily, but with a *schott-
isch*[1] movement, and at each fresh impetus shaking the

1. An energetic dance, similar to a polka.

mountain. There, where I was, I just put down the sound of the mystery of the bush; where no sound now surprises me—and any sound alarms; I only though it would give Jack a fine fright, down where he stood tied to a tree by himself, and he was badly enough scared when I left him. The good folks at home identified it; it was a sharp earthquake.

At the top of the climb I made my way again to the watercourse; it is here running steady and pretty full; strange these intermittencies—and just a little below the main stream is quite dry, and all the original brook has gone down some lava gallery of the mountain—and just a little further below, it begins picking up from the left hand in little boggy tributaries, and in the inside of a hundred yards has grown a brook again. The general course of the brook was, I guess, S.E.; the valley still very deep and whelmed in wood. It seemed a swindle to have made so sheer a climb and still find yourself at the bottom of a well. But gradually the thing seemed to shallow, the trees to seem poorer and smaller; I could see more and more of the silver sprinkles of sky among the foliage instead of the sombre piling up of tree behind tree. And here I had two scares—first, away up on my right hand I heard a bull low; I think it was a bull from the quality of the low, which was singularly songful and beautiful; the bulls belong to me, but how did I know that the bull was aware of that? and my advance guard not being at all properly armed, we advanced with great precaution until I was satisfied that I was passing eastward of the enemy. It was during this period that a pool of the river suddenly boiled up in my face in a little fountain. It was in a very dreary, marshy part among dilapidated trees that you see through holes in the trunks of; and if any kind of beast or elf or devil had come out of that sudden silver ebullition I declare I do not think I should have been surprised. It was perhaps a thing as curious—a fish, with which these head waters of the stream are alive. They are some of them as long as my finger, should be easily caught in these shallows, and some day I'll have a dish of them.

Very soon after I came to where the stream collects in another banana swamp, with the bananas bearing well. Beyond, the course is again quite dry; it mounts with a sharp

turn a very steep face of the mountain, and then stops
abruptly at the lip of the plateau, I suppose the top of Vaea
mountain: plainly no more springs here—there was no smal-
lest furrow of a watercourse beyond—and my task might be
said to be accomplished. But such is the animated spirit in
the service that the whole advance guard expressed a sentiment of disappointment that an exploration, so far success-
fully conducted, should come to stop in the most promising
view of fresh successes. And though unprovided either with
compass or cutlass, it was determined to push some way
along the plateau, marking our direction by the laborious
process of bending down, sitting upon, and thus breaking
the wild cocoanut trees. This was the less regretted by all
from a delightful discovery made of a huge banyan tree
growing here in the bush, with flying-buttressed flying buttresses, and huge arcs of trunk hanging high overhead and
trailing down new complications of root. I climbed some way
up what seemed the original beginning; it was easier to climb
than a ship's rigging, even rattled; everywhere there was a
foot-hold and hand-hold. It was judged wise to return and
rally the main body, who had now been left alone for perhaps
forty minutes in the bush.

The return was effected in good order, but unhappily I
only arrived (like so many other explorers) to find my main
body or rear-guard in a condition of mutiny; the work, it is to
be supposed, of terror. It is right I should tell you the Vaea
has a bad name, an *aitu fatine*—female devil of the woods—
succubus—haunting it, and doubtless Jack had heard of her;
perhaps, during my absence, saw her; lucky Jack! Anyway,
he was neither to hold nor to bind, and finally, after nearly
smashing me by accident, and from mere scare and insubor-
dination several times, deliberately set in to kill me; but poor
Jack! the tree he selected for that purpose was a banana! I
jumped off and gave him the heavy end of my whip over the
buttocks! Then I took and talked in his ear in various voices;
you should have heard my alto—it was a dreadful, devilish
note—I *knew* Jack *knew* it was an *aitu*. Then I mounted him
again, and he carried me fairly steadily. He'll learn yet. He
has to learn to trust absolutely to his rider; till he does, the
risk is always great in thick bush, where a fellow must try

different passages, and put back and forward and pick his way by hair's-breadths.

The expedition returned to Vailima in time to receive the visit of the R.C. Bishop. He is a superior man, much above the average of priests.

Thursday.—Yesterday the same expedition set forth to the southward by what is known as Carruthers' Road. At a fallen tree which completely blocks the way, the main body was as before left behind, and the advance guard of one now proceeded with the exploration. At the great tree known as *Mepi Tree*, after Maben the surveyor, the expedition struck forty yards due west till it struck the top of a steep bank which it descended. The whole bottom of the ravine is filled with sharp lava blocks quite unrolled and very difficult and dangerous to walk among; no water in the course, scarce any sign of water. And yet surely water must have made this bold cutting in the plateau. And if so, why is the lava sharp? My science gave out; but I could not but think it ominous and volcanic. The course of the stream was tortuous, but with a resultant direction a little by west of north; the sides a whole way exceeding steep the expedition buried under fathoms of foliage. Presently water appeared in the bottom, a good quantity; perhaps thirty or forty cubic feet, with pools and waterfalls. A tree that stands all along the banks here must be very fond of water; its roots lie close-packed down the stream, like hanks of guts, so as to make often a corrugated walk, each root ending in a blunt tuft of filaments, plainly to drink water. Twice there came in small tributaries from the left or western side—the whole plateau having a smartish inclination to the east; one of the tributaries is a handsome little web of silver hanging in the forest. Twice I was startled by birds; one that barked like a dog; another that whistled loud ploughman's signals, so that I vow I was thrilled, and thought I had fallen among runaway blacks, and regretted my cutlass which I had lost and left behind while taking bearings. A good many fishes in the brook, and many cray-fish; one of the last with a queer glow-worm head. Like all our brooks, the water is pure as air, and runs over red stones like rubies. The foliage along the banks very thick and high, the place close, the walking exceedingly laborious. By the time the expedition reached the fork, it was felt exceedingly questionable whether the *morale* of the force were sufficiently good to undertake more extended operations. A halt was called, the men refreshed with water and a bath, and it was decided at a drumhead council of war to continue the descent of the Embassy Water straight for Vailima, whither the expedition returned, in rather poor condition, and wet to the waist, about 4 P.M.

Thus in two days the two main watercourses of this country have been pretty thoroughly explored, and I conceive my instructions fully carried out. The main body of the second expedition was brought back by another officer despatched for that purpose from Vailima. Casualties: one horse wounded; one man bruised; no deaths—as yet, but the bruised man feels today as if his case was mighty serious.

In the South Seas

The following excerpts are from the book *In the South Seas* which Stevenson based on the journals he kept during his voyaging on the *Casco* and the *Equator*, and while visiting the Marquesas, the Paumotus (or Dangerous Archipelago, now Tuamotu) and the Gilbert Islands (now Kiribati). The Marquesas and Tuamotu are part of Polynesia, a collection of widely scattered volcanic islands and coral atolls. Culturally and historically the Polynesian islands have much in common, but, as Stevenson recorded, there are many differences in detail of character, belief and lifestyle. Kiribati belongs to the Micronesian group, although just next door, Tuvali (the old Ellice Islands) is in Polynesia.

The *Casco*'s first landfall was at Nukahiva in the Marquesas on 28 July 1888, where the Americans had established a whaling station early in the century. It was whaling that first drew Americans and Europeans in significant numbers to the Pacific. From the Marquesas the *Casco* sailed westward through the Dangerous Archipelago, an experience that proved as alarming as the name suggests, to Fakarava atoll, the administrative centre of this group of islands. In early October they carried on to Tahiti, where repairs to the *Casco* kept them until December. They left on Christmas Day 1888 to sail north, for Honolulu.

The Stevensons were six months in Hawaii where, amongst other activities including socializing with King Kalakaua, Stevenson finished *The Master of Ballantrae*, and revised *The Wrong Box*. In June 1889 they left on a trading schooner, the *Equator*, which took them to Butaritari and Apemama in the Gilbert Islands. The following pieces describe aspects of Stevenson's experience in the Marquesas, at Fakarava, and in the Gilberts.

from The Marquesas

MAKING FRIENDS

The impediment of tongues was one that I particularly over-estimated. The languages of Polynesia are easy to smatter, though hard to speak with elegance. And they are extremely similar, so that a person who has a tincture of one or two may risk, not without hope, an attempt upon the others.

And again, not only is Polynesian easy to smatter, but interpreters abound. Missionaries, traders, and broken white folk living on the bounty of the natives, are to be found in almost every isle and hamlet; and even where these are unserviceable, the natives themselves have often scraped up a little English, and in the French zone (though far less commonly) a little French-English, or an efficient pidgin, what is called to the westward 'Beach-la-Mar', comes easy to the Polynesian; it is now taught, besides, in the schools of Hawaii; and from the multiplicity of British ships, and the nearness of the States on the one hand and the colonies on the other, it may be called, and will almost certainly become, the tongue of the Pacific. I will instance a few examples. I met in Majuro a Marshall Island boy who spoke excellent English; this he had learned in the German firm in Jaluit,[1] yet did not speak one word of German. I heard from a gendarme who had taught school in Rapa-iti[2] that while the children had the utmost difficulty or reluctance to learn French, they picked up English on the wayside, and as if by accident. On one of the most out-of-the-way atolls in the Carolines, my friend Mr

1. Majuro, Jaluit. Both in the Marshall Islands, Micronesia.
2. A small volcanic island 300 miles southeast of the Tubai Islands.

Benjamin Hird was amazed to find the lads playing cricket on the beach and talking English; and it was in English that the crew of the *Janet Nicoll*,[1] a set of black boys from different Melanesian islands, communicated with other natives throughout the cruise, transmitted orders, and sometimes jested together on the fore-hatch. But what struck me perhaps most of all was a word I heard on the verandah of the Tribunal at Noumea.[2] A case had just been heard—a trial for infanticide against an ape-like native woman; and the audience were smoking cigarettes as they awaited the verdict. An anxious, amiable French lady, not far from tears, was eager for acquittal, and declared she would engage the prisoner to be her children's nurse. The bystanders exclaimed at the proposal; the woman was a savage, said they, and spoke no language. '*Mais, vous savez,*' objected the fair sentimentalist; '*ils apprennent si vite l'anglais!*'

But to be able to speak to people is not all. And in the first stage of my relations with natives I was helped by two things. To begin with, I was the showman of the *Casco*. She, her fine lines, tall spars, and snowy decks, the crimson fittings of the saloon, and the white, the gilt, and the repeating mirrors of the tiny cabin, brought us a hundred visitors. The men fathomed out her dimensions with their arms, as their fathers fathomed out the ships of Cook;[3] the women declared the cabins more lovely than a church; bouncing Junos were never weary of sitting in the chairs and contemplating in the glass their own bland images; and I have seen one lady strip up her dress, and, with cries of wonder and delight, rub herself bare-breeched upon the velvet cushions. Biscuit, jam, and syrup was the entertainment; and, as in European

1. *SS Janet Nicholl*, the trading steamer in which the Stevensons left Sydney and visited the Gilberts, the Marshalls and New Caledonia. The spelling '*Nicholl*' is incorrect.

2. Capital of New Caledonia, part of the Melanesian group, in the West Pacific.

3. Captain James Cook, who made three expeditions to the Pacific in the 1770s and initiated British involvement in that part of the world.

parlours, the photograph album went the round. This sober gallery, their everyday costumes and physiognomies, had become transformed, in three weeks' sailing, into things wonderful and rich and foreign; alien faces, barbaric dresses, they were now beheld and fingered, in the swerving cabin, with innocent excitement and surprise. Her Majesty was often recognised, and I have seen French subjects kiss her photograph; Captain Speedy—in an Abyssinian war-dress, supposed to be the uniform of the British army—met with much acceptance; and the effigies of Mr Andrew Lang[6] were admired in the Marquesas. There is the place for him to go when he shall be weary of Middlesex and Homer.

It was perhaps yet more important that I had enjoyed in my youth some knowledge of our Scots folk of the Highlands and the Islands. Not much beyond a century has passed since these were in the same convulsive and transitory state as the Marquesans of today. In both cases an alien authority enforced, the clans disarmed, the chiefs deposed, new customs introduced, and chiefly that fashion of regarding money as the means and object of existence. The commercial age, in each, succeeding at a bound to an age of war abroad and patriarchal communism at home. In one the cherished practice of tattooing, in the other a cherished costume, proscribed. In each a main luxury cut off: beef, driven under cloud of night from Lowland pastures, denied to the meat-loving Highlander; long-pig, pirated from the next village, to the man-eating Kanaka. The grumbling, the secret ferment, the fears and resentments, the alarms and sudden councils of Marquesan chiefs, reminded me continually of the days of Lovat and Struan. Hospitality, tact, natural fine manners, and a touchy punctilio, are common to both races: common to both tongues the trick of dropping medial consonants. Here is a table of two widespread Polynesian words:—

	House.	*Love.*★
Tahitian	FARE	AROHA
New Zealand	WHARE	
Samoan	FALE	TALOFA

6. Scottish historian, poet and folklorist, and friend of Stevenson.

	House.	*Love.**
Manihiki	FALE	ALOHA
Hawaiian	HALE	ALOHA
Marquesan	HA'E	KAOHA

The elision of medial consonants, so marked in these Marquesan instances, is no less common both in Gaelic and the Lowland Scots. Stranger still, that prevalent Polynesian sound, the so-called catch, written with an apostrophe, and often or always the gravestone of a perished consonant, is to be heard in Scotland to this day. When a Scot pronounces water, better, or bottle—*wa'er, be'er,* or *bo'le*—the sound is precisely that of the catch; and I think we may go beyond, and say, that if such a population could be isolated, and this mispronunciation should become the rule, it might prove the first stage of transition from *t* to *k*, which is the disease of Polynesian languages. The tendency of the Marquesans, however, is to urge against consonants, or at least on the very common letter *l*, a war of mere extermination. A hiatus is agreeable to any Polynesian ear; the ear even of the stranger soon grows used to these barbaric voids; but only in the Marquesan will you find such names as *Haaii* and *Paaaeua*, when each individual vowel must be separately uttered.

These points of similarity between a South Sea people and some of my own folk at home ran much in my head in the islands; and not only inclined me to view my fresh acquaintances with favour, but continually modified my judgment. A polite Englishman comes today to the Marquesans and is amazed to find the men tattooed; polite Italians came not long ago to England and found our fathers stained with woad; and when I paid the return visit as a little boy, I was highly diverted with the backwardness of Italy: so insecure, so much a matter of the day and hour, is the pre-eminence of race. It was so that I hit upon a means of communication which I recommend to travellers. When I desired any detail of savage custom, or of superstitious belief, I cast back in the story of my fathers, and fished for what I wanted with some trait of equal barbarism: Michael

* Where that word is used as a salutation I give that form. [R.L.S.]

Scott,[1] Lord Derwentwater's head, the second-sight, the Water Kelpie,—each of these I have found to be a killing bait; the black bull's head of Stirling procured me the legend of *Rahero*;[2] and what I knew of the Cluny Macphersons, or of the Appin Stewarts, enabled me to learn, and helped me to understand, about the *Tevas*[3] of Tahiti. The native was no longer ashamed, his sense of kinship grew warmer, and his lips were opened. It is this sense of kinship that the traveller must rouse and share; or he had better content himself with travels from the blue bed to the brown. And the presence of one Cockney titterer will cause a whole party to walk in clouds of darkness.

The hamlet of Anaho stands on a margin of flat land between the west of the beach and the spring of the impending mountains. A grove of palms, perpetually ruffling its green fans, carpets it (as for a triumph) with fallen branches, and shades it like an arbour. A road runs from end to end of the covert among beds of flowers, the milliner's shop of the community; and here and there, in the grateful twilight, in an air filled with a diversity of scents, and still within hearing of the surf upon the reef, the native houses stand in scattered neighbourhood. The same word, as we have seen, represents in many tongues of Polynesia, with scarce a shade of difference, the abode of man. But although the word be the same, the structure itself continually varies; and the Marquesan, among the most backward and barbarous of islanders, is yet the most commodiously lodged. The grass huts of Hawaii, the birdcage houses of Tahiti, or the open shed, with the crazy Venetian blinds, of the polite Samoan—none of these can be compared with the Marquesan *paepae-hae*, or dwelling platform. The paepae is an oblong terrace built without cement of black volcanic stone,

1. Michael Scott etc. These all feature in Scottish legend. Stevenson was fascinated by the common cultural ground he discovered.
2. 'The Song of Rahero', a narrative poem in ballad form which Stevenson based on a story heard from Princess Moë at Tautira.
3. A Tahitian tribal name, which Stevenson compares with warlike figures and clans in Scottish history.

from twenty to fifty feet in length, raised from four to eight
feet from the earth, and accessible by a broad stair. Along the
back of this, and coming to about half its width, runs the
open front of the house, like a covered gallery: the interior
sometimes neat and almost elegant in its bareness, the
sleeping space divided off by an endlong coaming, some
bright raiment perhaps hanging from a nail, and a lamp and
one of White's sewing-machines the only marks of civilisation. On the outside, at one end of the terrace, burns the
cooking-fire under a shed; at the other there is perhaps a pen
for pigs; the remainder is the evening lounge and *al fresco*
banquet-hall of the inhabitants. To some houses water is
brought down the mountain in bamboo pipes, perforated for
the sake of sweetness. With the Highland comparison in my
mind, I was struck to remember the sluttish mounds of turf
and stone in which I have sat and been entertained in the
Hebrides and the North Islands. Two things, I suppose,
explain the contrast. In Scotland wood is rare, and with
materials so rude as turf and stone the very hope of neatness
is excluded. And in Scotland it is cold. Shelter and a hearth
are needs so pressing that a man looks not beyond; he is out
all day after a bare bellyful, and at night when he saith, 'Aha,
it is warm!' he has not appetite for more. Or if for something
else, then something higher; a fine school of poetry and song
arose in these rough shelters, and an air like '*Lochaber no
more*' is an evidence of refinement more convincing, as well
as more imperishable, than a palace.

To one such dwelling platform a considerable troop of
relatives and dependants resort. In the hour of the dusk,
when the fire blazes, and the scent of cooked breadfruit fills
the air, and perhaps the lamp glints already between the
pillars of the house, you shall behold them silently assemble
to this meal, men, women, and children; and the dogs and
pigs frisk together up the terrace stairway, switching rival
tails. The strangers from the ship were soon equally
welcome: welcome to dip their fingers in the wooden dish, to
drink cocoa-nuts, to share the circulating pipe, and to hear
and hold high debate about the misdeeds of the French, the
Panama Canal, or the geographical position of San Francisco
and New Yo'ko. In a Highland hamlet, quite out of reach of

any tourist, I have met the same plain and dignified hospitality.

I have mentioned two facts—the distasteful behaviour of our earliest visitors, and the case of the lady who rubbed herself upon the cushions—which would give a very false opinion of Marquesan manners. The great majority of Polynesians are excellently mannered; but the Marquesan stands apart, annoying and attractive, wild, shy, and refined. If you make him a present he affects to forget it, and it must be offered him again at his going: a pretty formality I have found nowhere else. A hint will get rid of any one or any number; they are so fiercely proud and modest; while many of the more lovable but blunter islanders crowd upon a stranger, and can be no more driven off than flies. A slight or an insult the Marquesan seems never to forget. I was one day talking by the wayside with my friend Hoka, when I perceived his eyes suddenly to flash and his stature to swell. A white horseman was coming down the mountain, and as he passed, and while he paused to exchange salutations with myself, Hoka was still staring and ruffling like a gamecock. It was a Corsican who had years before called him *cochon sauvage—coçon chauvage*, as Hoka mispronounced it. With people so nice and so touchy, it was scarce to be supposed that our company of greenhorns should not blunder into offences. Hoka, on one of his visits, fell suddenly in a brooding silence, and presently after left the ship with cold formality. When he took me back into favour, he adroitly and pointedly explained the nature of my offence: I had asked him to sell cocoa-nuts; and in Hoka's view articles of food were things that a gentleman should give, not sell; or at least that he should not sell to any friend. On another occasion I gave my boat's crew a luncheon of chocolate and biscuits. I had sinned, I could never learn how, against some point of observance; and though I was drily thanked, my offerings were left upon the beach. But our worst mistake was a slight we put on Toma, Hoka's adoptive father, and in his own eyes the rightful chief of Anaho. In the first place, we did not call upon him, as perhaps we should, in his fine new European house, the only one in the hamlet. In the second, when we came ashore upon a visit to his rival, Taipi-kikino, it was Toma whom we saw standing at the head of the beach, a magnificent figure of a man, magnificently tattooed; and it was of Toma that we asked our question: 'Where is the chief?' 'What chief?' cried Toma, and turned his back on the blasphemers. Nor did he forgive us. Hoka came and went with us daily; but, alone I believe of all the countryside, neither Toma nor his wife set foot on board the *Casco*. The temptation resisted it is hard for a European to compute. The flying city of Laputa[1] moored for a fortnight in St James's Park affords but a pale figure of the *Casco* anchored before Anaho; for the Londoner has still his change of pleasures, but the Marquesan passes to his grave through an unbroken uniformity of days.

On the afternoon before it was intended we should sail, a valedictory party came on board: nine of our particular friends equipped with gifts and dressed as for a festival. Hoka, the chief dancer and singer, the greatest dandy of Anaho, and one of the handsomest young fellows in the world—sullen, showy, dramatic, light as a feather and strong as an ox—it would have been hard, on that occasion, to recognise, as he sat there stooped and silent, his face heavy and grey. It was strange to see the lad so much affected; stranger still to recognise in his last gift one of the curios we had refused on the first day, and to know our friend, so gaily dressed, so plainly moved at our departure, for one of the half-naked crew that had besieged and insulted us on our arrival: strangest of all, perhaps, to find, in that carved handle of a fan, the last of those curiosities of the first day which had now all been given to us by their possessors—their chief merchandise, for which they had sought to ransom us as long as we were strangers, which they pressed on us for nothing as soon as we were friends. The last visit was not long protracted. One after another they shook hands and got down into their canoe; when Hoka turned his back immediately upon the ship, so that we saw his face no more. Taipi, on the other hand, remained standing and facing us with gracious valedictory gestures; and when Captain Otis

1. The flying island in the third part of Swift's *Gulliver's Travels* (1726).

dipped the ensign, the whole party saluted with their hats. This was the farewell; the episode of our visit to Anaho was held concluded; and though the *Casco* remained nearly forty hours at her moorings, not one returned on board, and I am inclined to think they avoided appearing on the beach. This reserve and dignity is the finest trait of the Marquesan.

THE MAROON

Of the beauties of Anaho books might be written. I remember waking about three, to find the air temperate and scented. The long swell brimmed into the bay, and seemed to fill it full and then subside. Gently, deeply, and silently the *Casco* rolled; only at times a block piped like a bird. Oceanward, the heaven was bright with stars and the sea with their reflections. If I looked to that side, I might have sung with the Hawaiian poet:

Ua maomao ka lani, ua kahaea luna,
Ua pipi ka maka o ka hoku.
(The heavens were fair, they stretched above,
Many were the eyes of the stars.)

And then I turned shoreward, and high squalls were overhead; the mountains loomed up black; and I could have fancied I had slipped ten thousand miles away and was anchored in a Highland loch; that when the day came, it would show pine, and heather, and green fern, and roofs of turf sending up the smoke of peats; and the alien speech that should next greet my ears must be Gaelic, not Kanaka.

And day, when it came, brought other sights and thoughts. I have watched the morning break in many quarters of the world; it has been certainly one of the chief joys of my existence, and the dawn that I saw with most emotion shone upon the bay of Anaho. The mountains abruptly overhang the port with every variety of surface and of inclination, lawn, and cliff, and forest. Not one of these but wore its proper tint of saffron, of sulphur, of the clove, and of the rose. The lustre was like that of satin; on the lighter hues there seemed to float an efflorescence; a solemn bloom appeared on the more dark. The light itself was the ordinary

light of morning, colourless and clean; and on this ground of
jewels, pencilled out the least detail of drawing. Meanwhile,
around the hamlet, under the palms, where the blue shadow
lingered, the red coals of cocoa husk and the light trails of
smoke betrayed the awakening business of the day; along the
beach men and women, lads and lasses, were returning from
the bath in bright raiment, red and blue and green, such as
we delighted to see in the coloured pictures of our
childhood; and presently the sun had cleared the eastern hill,
and the glow of the day was over all.

The glow continued and increased, the business, from the
main part, ceased before it had begun. Twice in the day there
was a certain stir of shepherding along the seaward hills. At
times a canoe went out to fish. At times a woman or two
languidly filled a basket in the cotton patch. At times a pipe
would sound out of the shadow of a house, ringing the
changes on its three notes, with an effect like *Que le jour me
dure* repeated endlessly. Or at times, across a corner of the
bay, two natives might communicate in the Marquesan
manner with conventional whistlings. All else was sleep and
silence. The surf broke and shone around the shores; a
species of black crane fished in the broken water; the black
pigs were continually galloping by on some affair; but the
people might never have awaked, or they might all be dead.

My favourite haunt was opposite the hamlet, where there
was a landing in a cove under a lianaed cliff. The beach was
lined with palms and a tree called the purao, something
between the fig and mulberry in growth, and bearing a flower
like a great yellow poppy with a maroon heart. In places
rocks encroached upon the sand; the beach would be all
submerged; and the surf would bubble warmly as high as to
my knees, and play with cocoa-nut husks as our more
homely ocean plays with wreck and wrack and bottles. As
the reflux drew down, marvels of colour and design streamed
between my feet; which I would grasp at, miss, or seize: now
to find them what they promised, shells to grace a cabinet or
be set in gold upon a lady's finger; now to catch only *maya* of
coloured sand, pounded fragments and pebbles, that, as
soon as they were dry, became as dull and homely as the
flints upon a garden path. I have toiled at this childish

pleasure for hours in the strong sun, conscious of my incurable ignorance; but too keenly pleased to be ashamed. Meanwhile, the blackbird (or his tropical understudy) would be fluting in the thickets overhead.

A little further, in the turn of the bay, a streamlet trickled in the bottom of a den, thence spilling down a stair of rock into the sea. The draught of air drew down under the foliage in the very bottom of the den, which was a perfect arbour for coolness. In front it stood open on the blue bay and the *Casco* lying there under her awning and her cheerful colours. Overhead was a thatch of puraos, and over these again palms brandished their bright fans, as I have seen a conjurer make himself a halo out of naked swords. For in this spot, over a neck of low land at the foot of the mountains, the trade-wind streams into Anaho Bay in a flood of almost constant volume and velocity, and of a heavenly coolness.

It chanced one day that I was ashore in the cove with Mrs Stevenson and the ship's cook. Except for the *Casco* lying outside, and a crane or two, and the ever-busy wind and sea, the face of the world was of a prehistoric emptiness; life appeared to stand stockstill, and the sense of isolation was profound and refreshing. On a sudden, the trade-wind, coming in a gust over the isthmus, struck and scattered the fans of the palms above the den; and behold! in two of the tops there sat a native, motionless as an idol and watching us, you would have said, without a wink. The next moment the tree closed, and the glimpse was gone. This discovery of human presences latent overhead in a place where we had supposed ourselves alone, the immobility of our tree-top spies, and the thought that perhaps at all hours we were similarly supervised, struck us with a chill. Talk languished on the beach. As for the cook (whose conscience was not clear), he never afterwards set foot on shore, and twice, when the *Casco* appeared to be driving on the rocks, it was amusing to observe that man's alacrity; death, he was persuaded, awaiting him upon the beach. It was more than a year later, in the Gilberts, that the explanation dawned upon myself. The natives were drawing palm-tree wine, a thing forbidden by law; and when the wind thus suddenly revealed them, they were doubtless more troubled than ourselves.

At the top of the den there dwelt an old, melancholy, grizzled man of the name of Tari (Charlie) Coffin. He was a native of Oahu, in the Sandwich Islands; and had gone to sea in his youth in the American whalers; a circumstance to which he owned his name, his English, his down-east twang, and the misfortune of his innocent life. For one captain, sailing out of New Bedford,[1] carried him to Nuka-hiva and marooned him there among the cannibals. The motive for this act was inconceivably small; poor Tari's wages, which were thus economised, would scarce have shook the credit of the New Bedford owners. And the act itself was simply murder. Tari's life must have hung in the beginning by a hair. In the grief and terror of that time, it is not unlikely he went mad, an infirmity to which he was still liable; or perhaps a child may have taken a fancy to him and ordained him to be spared. He escaped at least alive, married in the island, and when I knew him was a widower with a married son and a granddaughter. But the thought of Oahu haunted him; its praise was for ever on his lips; he beheld it, looking back, as a place of ceaseless feasting, song, and dance; and in his dreams I daresay he revisits it with joy. I wonder what he would think if he could be carried there indeed, and see the modern town of Honolulu brisk with traffic, and the palace with its guards, and the great hotel, and Mr Berger's band with their uniforms and outlandish instruments; or what he would think to see the brown faces grown so few and the white so many; and his father's land sold for planting sugar, and his father's house quite perished, or perhaps the last of them struck leprous and immured between the surf and the cliffs on Molokai. So simply, even in South Sea Islands, and so sadly, the changes come.

Tari was poor, and poorly lodged. His house was a wooden frame, run up by Europeans; it was indeed his official residence, for Tari was the shepherd of the promontory sheep. I can give a perfect inventory of its contents: three kegs, a tin biscuit-box, an iron saucepan, several cocoa-shell cups, a lantern, and three bottles, probably containing oil; while the clothes of the family and a few mats were thrown

1. Massachusetts whaling port.

across the open rafters. Upon my first meeting with this exile
he had conceived for me one of the baseless island friend-
ships, had given me nuts to drink, and carried me up the den
'to see my house'—the only entertainment that he had to
offer. He liked the 'Amelican', he said, and the 'Inglishman',
but the 'Flessman' was his abhorrence; and he was careful to
explain that if he had thought us 'Fless', we should have had
none of his nuts, and never a sight of his house. His distaste
for the French I can partly understand, but not at all his
toleration of the Anglo-Saxon. The next day he brought me a
pig, and some days later one of our party going ashore found
him in act to bring a second. We were still strange to the
islands; we were pained by the poor man's generosity, which
he could ill afford; and, by a natural enough but quite
unpardonable blunder, we refused the pig. Had Tari been a
Marquesan we should have seen him no more; being what he
was, the most mild, long-suffering, melancholy man, he
took a revenge a hundred times more painful. Scarce had the
canoe with the nine villagers put off from their farewell
before the *Casco* was boarded from the other side. It was
Tari; coming thus late because he had no canoe of his own,
and had found it hard to borrow one; coming thus solitary
(as indeed we always saw him), because he was a stranger in
the land, and the dreariest of company. The rest of my
family basely fled from the encounter. I must receive our
injured friend alone; and the interview must have lasted hard
upon an hour, for he was loath to tear himself away. 'You go'
way. I see you no more—no, sir!' he lamented; and then
looking about him with rueful admiration. 'This goodee
ship—no, sir!—goodee ship!' he would exclaim: the 'no, sir'
thrown out sharply through the nose upon a rising inflection,
an echo from New Bedford and the fallacious whaler. From
these expressions of grief and praise he would return
continually to the case of the rejected pig. 'I like give plesent
all 'e same you,' he complained: 'only got pig: you no take
him!' He was a poor man; he had no choice of gifts; he had
only a pig, he repeated; and I had refused it. I have rarely
been more wretched than to see him sitting there, so old, so
grey, so poor, so hardly fortuned, of so rueful a countenance,
and to appreciate, with growing keenness, the affront which

I had so innocently dealt him; but it was one of those cases in
which speech is vain.

Tari's son was smiling and inert; his daughter-in-law, a
girl of sixteen, pretty, gentle, and grave, more intelligent
than most Anaho women, and with a fair share of French;
his grandchild, a mite of a creature at the breast. I went up
the den one day when Tari was from home, and found the
son making a cotton sack, and madame suckling mad-
emoiselle. When I had sat down with them on the floor, the
girl began to question me about England; which I tried to
describe, piling the pan and the cocoa shells one upon
another to represent the houses, and explaining, as best I was
able, and by word and gesture, the over-population, the
hunger and the perpetual toil. '*Pas de cocotiers? pas de popoi?*'
she asked. I told her it was too cold, and went through an
elaborate performance, shutting out draughts, and crouch-
ing over an imaginary fire, to make sure she understood. But
she understood right well; remarked it must be bad for the
health, and sat a while gravely reflecting on that picture of
unwanted sorrows. I am sure it roused her pity, for it struck
in her another thought always uppermost in the Marquesan
bosom; and she began with a smiling sadness, and looking
on me out of melancholy eyes, to lament the decease of her
own people. '*Ici pas de Kanaques*,' said she; and taking the
baby from her breast, she held it out to me with both her
hands. '*Tenez*—a little baby like this; then dead. All the
Kanaques die. Then no more.' The smile, and this instan-
cing by the girl-mother of her own tiny flesh and blood,
affected me strangely; they spoke of so tranquil a despair.
Meanwhile the husband smilingly made his sack; and the
unconscious babe struggled to reach a pot of raspberry jam,
friendship's offering, which I had just brought up the den;
and in a perspective of centuries I saw their case as ours,
death coming in like a tide, and the day already numbered
when there should be no more Beretani, and no more of any
race whatever, and (what oddly touched me) no more
literary works and no more readers.

from The Marquesas

DEPOPULATION

Over the whole extent of the South Seas, from one tropic to
another, we find traces of a bygone state of over-population,
when the resources of even a tropical soil were taxed, and
even the improvident Polynesian trembled for the future.
We may accept some of the ideas of Mr Darwin's theory of
coral islands, and suppose a rise of the sea, or the subsidence
of some former continental area, to have driven into the tops
of the moutains multitudes of refugees. Or we may suppose,
more soberly, a people of sea-rovers, emigrants from a
crowded country, to strike upon and settle island after
island, and as time went on to multiply exceedingly in their
new seats. In either case the end must be the same; soon or
late it must grow apparent that the crew are too numerous,
and the famine is at hand. The Polynesians met this
emergent danger with various expedients of activity and
prevention. A way was found to preserve breadfruit by
packing it in artificial pits; pits forty feet in depth and of
proportionate bore are still to be seen, I am told, in the
Marquesas; and yet even these were insufficient for the
teeming people, and the annals of the past are gloomy with
famine and cannibalism. Among the Hawaiians—a hardier
people, in a more exacting climate—agriculture was carried
far; the land was irrigated with canals; and the fishponds of
Molokai prove the number and diligence of the old inhabitants. Meanwhile, over all the island world, abortion and
infanticide prevailed. On coral atolls, where the danger was
most plainly obvious, these were enforced by law and sanc-
tioned by punishment. On Vaitupu, in the Ellices, only two
children were allowed to a couple; on Nukufetau,[1] but one.

1. An atoll in the Ellice Islands, Southwest Pacific.

47

On the latter the punishment was by fine; and it is related that the fine was sometimes paid, and the child spared.

This is characteristic. For no people in the world are so fond or so long-suffering with children—children make the mirth and the adornment of their homes, serving them for playthings and for picture-galleries. 'Happy is the man that has his quiver full of them.' The stray bastard is contended for by rival families; and the natural and the adopted children play and grow up together undistinguished. The spoiling, and I may almost say the deification, of the child, is nowhere carried so far as in the eastern islands; and furthest, according to my opportunities of observation, in the Paumotu group, the so-called Low or Dangerous Archipelago. I have seen a Paumotuan native turn from me with embarrassment and disaffection because I suggested that a brat would be the better for beating. It is a daily matter in some eastern islands to see a child strike or even stone its mother, and the mother, so far from punishing, scarce ventures to resist. In some, when his child was born, a chief was superseded and resigned his name; as though, like a drone, he had then fulfilled the occasion of his being. And in some the lightest words of children had the weight of oracles. Only the other day, in the Marquesas, if a child conceived a distaste to any stranger, I am assured the stranger would be slain. And I shall have to tell in another place an instance of the opposite: how a child in Manihiki[1] having taken a fancy to myself, her adoptive parents at once accepted the situation and loaded me with gifts.

With such sentiments the necessity for child-destruction would not fail to clash, and I believe we find the trace of divided feeling in the Tahitian brotherhood of Oro. At a certain date a new god was added to the Society-Island Olympus, or an old one refurbished and made popular. Oro was his name, and he may be compared with the Bacchus of the ancients. His zealots sailed from bay to bay, and from island to island; they were everywhere received with feasting; wore fine clothes; sang, danced, acted; gave exhibitions of dexterity and strength; and were the artists, the

1. Polynesian island in the central South Pacific.

acrobats, the bards, and the harlots of the group. Their life was public and epicurean; their initiation a mystery; and the highest in the land aspired to join the brotherhood. If a couple stood next in line to a high-chieftaincy, they were suffered, on grounds of policy, to spare one child; all other children, who had a father or a mother in the company of Oro, stood condemned from the moment of conception. A freemasonry, an agnostic sect, a company of artists, its members all under oath to spread unchastity, and all forbidden to leave offspring—I do not know how it may appear to others, but to me the design seems obvious. Famine menacing the islands, and the needful remedy repulsive, it was recommended to the native mind by these trappings of mystery, pleasure, and parade. This is the more probable, and the secret, serious purpose of the institution appears the more plainly, if it be true, that after a certain period of life, the obligation of the votary was changed; at first, bound to be profligate: afterwards, expected to be chaste.

Here, then, we have one side of the case. Man-eating among kindly men, child-murder among child-lovers, industry in a race the most idle, invention in a race the least progressive, this grim, pagan salvation-army of the brotherhood of Oro, the report of early voyagers, the wide-spread vestiges of former habitation, and the universal tradition of the islands, all point to the same fact of former crowding and alarm. And today we are face to face with the reverse. Today in the Marquesas, in the Eight Islands of Hawaii, in Mangareva,[1] in Easter Island,[2] we find the same race perishing like flies. Why this change? Or, grant that the coming of the whites, the change of habits, and the introduction of new maladies and vices, fully explain the depopulation, why is that depopulation not universal? The population of Tahiti, after a period of alarming decrease, has again become stationary. I hear of a similar result among some Maori tribes; in many of the Paumotus a slight increase is to be observed; and the Samoans are today as healthy and at least as fruitful as before the change. Grant that the Tahitians, the Maoris,

1. Principal island of the Gambiers, French Polynesia.
2. Polynesian volcanic island now belonging to Chile.

and the Paumotuans have become inured to the new conditions; and what are we to make of the Samoans, who have
never suffered?

Those who are acquainted only with a single group are apt
to be ready with solutions. Thus I have heard the mortality
of the Maoris attributed to their change of residence—from
fortified hill-tops to the low, marshy vicinity of their plantations. How plausible! And yet the Marquesans are dying
out in the same houses where their fathers multiplied. Or
take opium. The Marquesas and Hawaii are the two groups
the most infected with this vice; the population of the one is
the most civilised, that of the other by far the most barbarous, of Polynesians; and they are two of those that perish the
most rapidly. Here is a strong case against opium. But let us
take unchastity, and we shall find the Marquesas and Hawaii
figuring again upon another count. Thus, Samoans are the
most chaste of Polynesians, and they are to this day entirely
fertile; Marquesans are the most debauched: we have seen
how they are perishing; Hawaiians are notoriously lax, and
they begin to be dotted among deserts. So here is a case
stronger still against unchastity; and here also we have a
correction to apply. Whatever the virtues of the Tahitian,
neither friend nor enemy dares call him chaste; and yet he
seems to have outlived the time of danger. One last example:
syphilis has been plausibly credited with much of the
sterility. But the Samoans are, by all accounts, as fruitful as
at first; by some accounts more so; and it is not seriously to
be argued that the Samoans have escaped syphilis.

These examples show how dangerous it is to reason from
any particular cause, or even from many in a single group. I
have in my eye an able and amiable pamphlet by the Rev.
S.E. Bishop:[1] 'Why are the Hawaiians Dying Out?' Any
one interested in the subject ought to read this tract, which
contains real information; and yet Mr Bishop's views would
have been changed by an acquaintance with other groups.
Samoa is, for the moment, the main and the most instructive
exception to the rule. The people are the most chaste and one
of the most temperate of island peoples. They have never

1. Sereno Bishop, Hawaiian-born American missionary.

been tried and depressed with any grave pestilence. Their clothing has scarce been tampered with; at the simple and becoming tabard of the girls, Tartuffe,[1] in many another island, would have cried out; for the cool, healthy, and modest lava-lava or kilt, Tartuffe has managed in many another island to substitute stifling and inconvenient trousers. Lastly, and perhaps chiefly, so far from their amusements having been curtailed, I think they have been, upon the whole, extended. The Polynesian falls easily into despondency: bereavement, disappointment, the fear of novel visitations, the decay or proscription of ancient pleasures, easily incline him to be sad; and sadness detaches him from life. The melancholy of the Hawaiian and the emptiness of his new life are striking; and the remark is yet more apposite to the Marquesas. In Samoa, on the other hand, perpetual song and dance, perpetual games, journeys, and pleasures, make an animated and a smiling picture of the island life. And the Samoans are today the gayest and the best entertained inhabitants of our planet. The importance of this can scarcely be exaggerated. In a climate and upon a soil where a livelihood can be had for the stooping, entertainment is a prime necessity. It is otherwise with us, where life presents us with a daily problem, and there is a serious interest, and some of the heat of conflict, in the mere continuing to be. So, in certain atolls, where there is no great gaiety, but man must bestir himself with some vigour for his daily bread, public health and the population are maintained; but in the lotos islands, with the decay of pleasures, life itself decays. It is from this point of view that we may instance, among other causes of depression, the decay of war. We have been so long used in Europe to that dreary business of war on the great scale, trailing epidemics and leaving pestilential corpses in its train, that we have almost forgotten its original, the most healthful, if not the most humane, of all field sports—hedge-warfare. From this, as well as from the rest of his amusements and interests, the islander, upon a hundred islands, has been recently cut off.

1. Character in Molière's play of the same name, a religious hypocrite.

And to this, as well as to so many others, the Samoan still makes good a special title.

Upon the whole, the problem seems to me to stand thus:—Where there have been fewest changes, important and unimportant, salutary or hurtful, there the race survives. Where there have been most, important and unimportant, salutary or hurtful, there it perishes. Each change, however small, augments the sum of new conditions to which the race has to become inured. There may seem, *a priori*, no comparison between the change from 'sour toddy' to bad gin, and that from the island kilt to a pair of European trousers. Yet I am far from persuaded that the one is any more hurtful than the other; and the unaccustomed race will sometimes die of pin-pricks. We are here face to face with one of the difficulties of the missionary. In Polynesian islands he easily obtains pre-eminent authority; the king becomes his *mairedupalais*; he can proscribe, he can command; and the temptation is ever towards too much. Thus (by all accounts) the Catholics in Mangareva, and thus (to my own knowledge) the Protestants in Hawaii, have rendered life in a more or less degree unliveable to their converts. And the mild, uncomplaining creatures (like children in a prison) yawn and await death. It is easy to blame the missionary. But it is his business to make changes. It is surely his business, for example, to prevent war; and yet I have instanced war itself as one of the elements of health. On the other hand, it were, perhaps, easy for the missionary to proceed more gently, and to regard every change as an affair of weight. I take the average missionary; I am sure I do him no more than justice when I suppose that he would hesitate to bombard a village, even in order to convert an archipelago. Experience begins to show us (at least in Polynesian islands) that change of habit is bloodier than a bombardment.

There is one point, ere I have done, where I may go to meet criticism. I have said nothing of faulty hygiene, bathing during fevers, mistaken treatment of children, native doctoring, or abortion—all causes frequently adduced. And I have said nothing of them because they are conditions common to both epochs, and even more efficient in the past than in the present. Was it not the same with unchastity, it may be asked? Was not the Polynesian always unchaste? Doubtless he was so always: doubtless he is more so since the coming of his remarkably chaste visitors from Europe. Take the Hawaiian account of Cook: I have no doubt it is entirely fair. Take Krusenstern's[1] candid, almost innocent, description of a Russian man-of-war at the Marquesas; consider the disgraceful history of missions in Hawaii itself, where (in the war of lust) the American missionaries were once shelled by an English adventurer, and once raided and mishandled by the crew of an American warship; add the practice of whaling fleets to call at the Marquesas, and carry off a complement of women for the cruise; consider, besides, how the whites were at first regarded in the light of demigods, as appears plainly in the reception of Cook upon Hawaii; and again, in the story of the discovery of Tutuila, when the really decent women of Samoa prostituted themselves in public to the French; and bear in mind how it was the custom of the adventurers, and we may almost say the business of the missionaries, to deride and infract even the most salutary tapus. Here we see every engine of dissolution directed at once against a virtue never and nowhere very strong or popular; and the result, even in the most degraded islands, has been further degradation. Mr Lawes, the missionary of Savage Island, told me the standard of female chastity had declined there since the coming of the whites. In heathen time, if a girl gave birth to a bastard, her father or brother would dash the infant down the cliffs; and today the scandal would be small. Or take the Marquesas. Stanislao Moanatini told me that in his own recollection the young were strictly guarded; they were not suffered so much as to look upon one another in the street, but passed (so my informant put it) like dogs; and the other day the whole school-children of Nuka-hiva and Ua-pu escaped in a body to the woods, and lived there for a fortnight in promiscuous liberty. Readers of travels may perhaps exclaim at my

1. Adam Ivan Krusenstern, a Russian explorer, navigator and hydrographer of the late eighteenth and early nineteenth centuries. He was the first Russian to circumnavigate the world.

authority, and declare themselves better informed. I should prefer the statement of an intelligent native like Stanislao (even if it stood alone, which it is far from doing) to the report of the most honest traveller. A ship of war comes to a haven, anchors, lands a party, receives and returns a visit, and the captain writes a chapter on the manners of the island. It is not considered what class is mostly seen. Yet we should not be pleased if a Lascar foremast hand were to judge England by the ladies who parade Ratcliffe Highway, and the gentlemen who share with them their hire. Stanislao's opinion of a decay of virtue even in these unvirtuous islands has been supported to me by others; his very example, the progress of dissolution amongst the young, is adduced by Mr Bishop in Hawaii. And so far as Marquesans are concerned, we might have hazarded a guess of some decline in manners. I do not think that any race could ever have prospered or multiplied with such as now obtain; I am sure they would have been never at the pains to count paternal kinship. It is not possible to give details; suffice it that their manners appear to be imitated from the dreams of ignorant and vicious children, and their debauches persevered in until energy, reason, and almost life itself are in abeyance.

from The Marquesas

THE STORY OF A PLANTATION

Taahauku, on the south-westerly coast of the island of
Hiva-oa—Tahuku, say the slovenly whites—may be called
the port of Atuona. It is a narrow and small anchorage, set
between low cliffy points, and opening above upon a woody
valley: a little French fort, now disused and deserted, over-
hangs the valley and the inlet. Atuona itself, at the head of
the next bay, is framed in a theatre of mountains, which
dominate the more immediate settling of Taahauku and give
the salient character of the scene. They are reckoned at no
higher than four thousand feet; but Tahiti with eight
thousand, and Hawaii with fifteen, can offer no such picture
of abrupt, melancholy alps. In the morning, when the sun
falls directly on their front, they stand like a vast wall: green
to the summit, if by any chance the summit should be
clear—watercourses here and there delineated on their face,
as narrow as cracks. Towards afternoon, the light falls more
obliquely, and the sculpture of the range comes in relief,
huge gorges sinking into shadow, huge, tortuous buttresses
standing edged with sun. At all hours of the day they strike
the eye with some new beauty, and the mind with the same
menacing gloom.

The mountains, dividing and deflecting the endless airy
deluge of the Trade, are doubtless answerable for the
climate. A strong draught of wind blew day and night over
the anchorage. Day and night the same fantastic and attenu-
ated clouds fled across the heavens, the same dusky cap of
rain and vapour fell and rose on the mountain. The land-
breezes came very strong and chill, and the sea, like the air,
was in perpetual bustle. The swell crowded into the narrow
anchorage like sheep into a fold; broke all along both sides,

high on the one, low on the other; kept a certain blowhole sounding and smoking like a cannon; and spent itself at last upon the beach.

On the side away from Atuona, the sheltering promontory was a nursery of coco-trees. Some were mere infants, none had attained to any size, none had yet begun to shoot skyward with that whip-like shaft of the mature palm. In the young trees the colour alters with the age and growth. Now all is of a grass-like hue, infinitely dainty; next the rib grows golden, the fronds remaining green as ferns; and then, as the trunk continues to mount and to assume its final hue of grey, the fans put on manlier and more decided depths of verdure, stand out dark upon the distance, glisten against the sun, and flash like silver fountains in the assault of the wind. In this young wood of Taahauku, all these hues and combinations were exampled and repeated by the score. The trees grew pleasantly spaced upon a hilly sward, here and there interspersed with a rack for drying copra, or a tumbledown hut for storing it. Every here and there the stroller had a glimpse of the *Casco* tossing in the narrow anchorage below; and beyond he had ever before him the dark amphitheatre of the Atuona mountains and the cliffy bluff that closes it to seaward. The trade-wind moving in the fans made a ceaseless noise of summer rain; and from time to time, with the sound of a sudden and distant drum-beat, the surf would burst in a sea cave.

At the upper end of the inlet, its low, cliffy lining sinks, at both sides, into a beach. A copra warehouse stands in the shadow of the shoreside trees, flitted about for ever by a clan of dwarfish swallows; and a line of rails on a high wooden staging bends back into the mouth of the valley. Walking on this, the new-landed traveller becomes aware of a broad fresh-water lagoon (one arm of which he crosses), and beyond, of a grove of noble palms, sheltering the house of the trader, Mr Keane. Overhead, the cocos join in a continuous and lofty roof; blackbirds are heard lustily singing; the island cock springs his jubilant rattle and airs his golden plumage; cow-bells sound far and near in the grove; and when you sit in the broad verandah, lulled by this symphony, you may say to yourself, if you are able: 'Better fifty

years of Europe . . .' Farther on, the floor of the valley is flat
and green, and dotted here and there with stripling coco
palms. Through the midst, with many changes of music, the
river trots and brawls; and along its course, where we should
look for willows, puraos grow in clusters, and make shadowy
pools after an angler's heart. A vale more rich and peaceful,
sweeter air, a sweeter voice of rural sounds, I have found
nowhere. One circumstance alone might strike the experienced: here is a convenient beach, deep soil, good water, and
yet nowhere any paepaes, nowhere any trace of island
inhabitation.

It is but a few years since this valley was a place choked
with jungle, the debatable land and battle-ground of cannibals. Two clans laid claim to it—neither could substantiate
the claim, and the roads lay desert, or were only visited by
men in arms. It is for this very reason that it wears now so
smiling an appearance: cleared, planted, built upon,
supplied with railways, boat-houses, and bath-houses. For,
being no man's land, it was the more readily ceded to a
stranger. The stranger was Captain John Hart: Ima Hati,
'Broken-arm', the natives call him, because when he first
visited the islands his arm was in a sling. Captain Hart, a man
of English birth but an American subject, had conceived the
idea of cotton culture in the Marquesas during the American
War, and was at first rewarded with success. His plantation
at Anaho was highly productive; island cotton fetched a high
price, and the natives used to debate which was the stronger
power, Ima Hati or the French: deciding in favour of the
captain, because, though the French had the most ships, he
had the more money.

He marked Taahauku for a suitable site, acquired it, and
offered the superintendence to Mr Robert Stewart, a
Fifeshire man, already some time in the islands, who had just
been ruined by a war on Tauata. Mr Stewart was somewhat
averse to the adventure, having some acquaintance with
Atuona and its notorious chieftain, Moipu. He had once
landed there, he told me, about dusk, and found the remains
of a man and woman partly eaten. On his starting and
sickening at the sight, one of Moipu's young men picked up
a human foot, and provocatively staring at the stranger,

grinned and nibbled at the heel. None need be surprised if
Mr Stewart fled incontinently to the bush, lay there all night
in a great horror of mind, and got off to sea again by daylight
on the morrow. 'It was always a bad place, Atuona', com-
mented Mr Stewart, in his homely Fifeshire voice. In spite of
this dire introduction, he accepted the captain's offer, was
landed at Taahauku with three Chinamen, and proceeded to
clear the jungle.

War was pursued at that time, almost without interval,
between the men of Atuona and the men of Haamau; and
one day, from the opposite sides of the valley, battle—or I
should rather say the noise of battle—raged all the afternoon: the shots and insults of the opposing clans passing
from hill to hill over the heads of Mr Stewart and his
Chinamen. There was no genuine fighting; it was like a
bicker of schoolboys, only some fool had given the children
guns. One man died of his exertions in running, the only
casualty. With night the shots and insults ceased; the men of
Haamau withdrew; and victory, on some occult principle,
was scored to Moipu. Perhaps, in consequence, there came a
day when Moipu made a feast, and a party from Haamau
came under safe-conduct to eat of it. These passed early by
Taahauku, and some of Moipu's young men were there to be
a guard of honour. They were not long gone before there
came down from Haamau, a man, his wife, and a girl of
twelve, their daughter, bringing fungus. Several Atuona lads
were hanging round the store; but the day being one of truce
none apprehended danger. The fungus was weighed and
paid for; the man of Haamau proposed he should have his
axe ground in the bargain; and Mr Stewart demurring at the
trouble, some of the Atuona lads offered to grind it for him,
and set it on the wheel. While the axe was grinding, a
friendly native whispered Mr Stewart to have a care of
himself, for there was trouble in hand; and, all at once, the
man of Haamau was seized, and his head and arm stricken
from his body, the head at one sweep of his own newly
sharpened axe. In the first alert, the girl escaped among the
cotton; and Mr Stewart, having thrust the wife into the
house and locked her in from the outside, supposed the affair
was over. But the business had not passed without noise, and

it reached the ears of an older girl who had loitered by the way, and who now came hastily down the valley, crying as she came for her father. Her, too, they seized and beheaded; I know not what they had done with the axe, it was a blunt knife that served their butcherly turn upon the girl; and the blood spurted in fountains and painted them from head to foot. Thus horrible from crime, the party returned to Atuona, carrying the heads to Moipu. It may be fancied how the feast broke up; but it is notable that the guests were honourably suffered to retire. These passed back through Taahauku in extreme disorder; a little after the valley began to be overrun with shouting and triumphing braves; and a letter of warning coming at the same time to Mr Stewart, he and his Chinamen took refuge with the Protestant missionary in Atuona. That night the store was gutted, and the bodies cast in a pit and covered with leaves. Three days later the schooner had come in; and things appearing quieter, Mr Stewart and the captain landed in Taahauku to compute the damage and to view the grave, which was already indicated by the stench. While they were so employed, a party of Moipu's young men, decked with red flannel to indicate martial sentiments, came over the hills from Atuona, dug up the bodies, washed them in the river, and carried them away on sticks. That night the feast began.

Those who knew Mr Stewart before this experience declare the man to be quite altered. He stuck, however, to his post; and somewhat later, when the plantation was already well established, and gave employment to sixty Chinamen and seventy natives, he found himself once more in dangerous times. The men of Haamau, it was reported, had sworn to plunder and erase the settlement; letters came continually from the Hawaiian missionary, who acted as intelligence department; and for six weeks Mr Stewart and three other whites slept in the cotton-house at night in a rampart of bales, and (what was their best defence) ostentatiously practised rifle-shooting by day upon the beach. Natives were often there to watch them; the practice was excellent; and the assault was never delivered—if it ever was intended, which I doubt, for the natives are more famous for false rumours than for deeds of energy. I was told the late French war was a case in point; the tribes on the beach accusing those in the mountains of designs which they had never the hardihood to entertain. And the same testimony to their backwardness in open battle reached me from all sides. Captain Hart once landed after an engagement in a certain bay; one man had his hand hurt, an old woman and two children had been slain; and the captain improved the occasion by poulticing the hand, and taunting both sides upon so wretched an affair. It is true these wars were often merely formal—comparable with duels to the first blood. Captain Hart visited a bay where such a war was being carried on between two brothers, one of whom had been thought wanting in civility to the guests of the other. About one-half of the population served day about upon alternate sides, so as to be well with each when the inevitable peace should follow. The forts of the belligerents were over against each other, and close by. Pigs were cooking. Well-oiled braves, with well-oiled muskets, strutted on the paepae or sat down to feast. No business, however needful, could be done, and all thoughts were supposed to be centred in this mockery of war. A few days later, by a regrettable accident, a man was killed; it was felt at once the thing had gone too far, and the quarrel was instantly patched up. But the more serious wars were prosecuted in a similar spirit; a gift of pigs and a feast made their inevitable end; the killing of a single man was a great victory, and the murder of defenceless solitaries counted a heroic deed.

The foot of the cliffs, about all these islands, is the place of fishing. Between Taahauku and Atuona we saw men, but chiefly women, some nearly naked, some in thin white or crimson dresses, perched in little surf-beat promontories— the brown precipice overhanging them, and the convolvulus overhanging that, as if to cut them off the more completely from assistance. There they would angle much of the morning; and as fast as they caught any fish, eat them, raw and living, where they stood. It was such helpless ones that the warriors from the opposite island of Tauata slew, and carried home and ate, and were thereupon accounted mighty men of valour. Of one such exploit I can give the account of an eye-witness. 'Portuguese Joe', Mr Keane's cook, was once pulling an oar in an Atuona boat, when they spied a stranger in a canoe with some fish and a piece of tapu. The Atuona men cried upon him to draw near and have a smoke. He complied, because, I suppose, he had no choice; but he knew, poor devil, what he was coming to, and (as Joe said) 'he didn't seem to care about the smoke'. A few questions followed, as to where he came from, and what was his business. These he must needs answer, as he must needs draw at the unwelcome pipe, his heart the while drying in his bosom. And then, of a sudden, a big fellow in Joe's boat leaned over, plucked the stranger from his canoe, struck him with a knife in the neck—inward and downward, as Joe showed in pantomime more expressive than his words—and held him under water, like a fowl, until his struggles ceased. Whereupon the long-pig was hauled on board, the boat's head turned about for Atuona, and these Marquesan braves pulled home rejoicing. Moipu was on the beach and rejoiced with them on their arrival. Poor Joe toiled at his oar that day with a white face, yet he had no fear for himself. 'They were very good to me—gave me plenty grub: never wished to eat white man,' said he.

If the most horrible experience was Mr Stewart's, it was Captain Hart himself who ran the nearest danger. He had bought a piece of land from Timau, chief of a neighbouring bay, and put some Chinese there to work. Visiting the station with one of the Godeffroys,[1] he found his Chinamen trooping to the beach in terror; Timau had driven them out, seized their effects, and was in war attire with his young men. A boat was despatched to Taahauku for reinforcement; as they awaited her return, they could see, from the deck of the schooner, Timau and his young men dancing the war-dance on a hill-top till past twelve at night; and so soon as the boat came (bringing three gendarmes, armed with chasse-pots, two white men from Taahauku station, and some native warriors) the party set out to seize the chief before he should awake. Day was not come, and it was a very bright moonlight morning, when they reached the hill-top where

1. The German firm J. C. Godeffroy and Son led the exploitation of copra in the Pacific.

(in a house of palm-leaves) Timau was sleeping off his debauch. The assailants were fully exposed, the interior of the hut quite dark; the position far from sound. The gendarmes knelt with their pieces ready, and Captain Hart advanced alone. As he drew near the door he heard the snap of a gun cocking from within, and in sheer self-defence—there being no other escape—sprang into the house and grappled Timau. 'Timau, come with me!' he cried. But Timau—a great fellow, his eyes blood-red with the abuse of kava, six foot three in stature—cast him on one side; and the captain, instantly expecting to be either shot or brained, discharged his pistol in the dark. When they carried Timau out at the door into the moonlight, he was already dead, and, upon his unlooked-for termination of their sally, the whites appeared to have lost all conduct, and retreated to the boats, fired upon by the natives as they went. Captain Hart, who almost rivals Bishop Dordillon in popularity, shared with him the policy of extreme indulgence to the natives, regarding them as children, making light of their defects, and constantly in favour of mild measures. The death of Timau has thus somewhat weighed upon his mind; the more so, as the chieftain's musket was found in the house unloaded. To a less delicate conscience the matter will seem light. If a drunken savage elects to cock a fire-arm, a gentleman advancing towards him in the open cannot wait to make sure if it be charged.

I have touched on the captain's popularity. It is one of the things that most strikes a stranger in the Marquesas. He comes instantly on two names, both new to him, both locally famous, both mentioned by all with affection and respect—the bishop's and the captain's. It gave me a strong desire to meet with the survivor, which was subsequently gratified—to the enrichment of these pages. Long after that again, in the Place Dolorous—Molokai—I came once more on the traces of that affectionate popularity. There was a blind white leper there, an old sailor—'an old tough' he called himself—who had long sailed among the eastern islands. Him I used to visit, and, being fresh from the scenes of his activity, gave him the news. This (in the true island style) was largely a chronicle of wrecks; and it chanced I mentioned the case of one not very successful captain, and how he had lost a vessel for Mr Hart; thereupon the blind leper broke forth in lamentation. 'Did he lose a ship of John Hart's?' he cried; 'poor John Hart! Well, I'm sorry it was Hart's,' with needless force of epithet, which I neglect to reproduce.

Perhaps, if Captain Hart's affairs had continued to prosper, his popularity might have been different. Success wins glory, but it kills affection, which misfortune fosters. And the misfortune which overtook the captain's enterprise was truly singular. He was at the top of his career. Ile Masse belonged to him, given by the French as an indemnity for the robberies at Taahauku. But the Ile Masse was only suitable for cattle; and his two chief stations were Anaho, in Nuka-hiva, facing the north-east, and Taahauku in Hiva-oa, some hundred miles to the southward, and facing the south-west. Both these were on the same day swept by a tidal wave, which was not felt in any other bay or island of the group. The south coast of Hiva-oa was bestrewn with building timber and camphor-wood chests, containing goods; which, on the promise of a reasonable salvage, the natives very honestly brought back, the chests apparently not opened, and some of the wood after it had been built into their houses. But the recovery of such jetsam could not affect the result. It was impossible the captain should withstand this partiality of fortune; and with his fall the prosperity of the Marquesas ended. Anaho is truly extinct, Taahauku but a shadow of itself; nor has any new plantation arisen in their stead.

from The Paumotus

A HOUSE TO LET IN A LOW ISLAND
Never populus, it was yet by a chapter of accidents that I
found the island[1] so deserted that no sound of human life
diversified the hours; that we walked in that trim public
garden of a town, among closed houses, without even a
lodging-bill in a window to prove some tenancy in the back
quarters; and, when we visited the Government bungalow,
that Mr Donat, acting Vice-President, greeted us alone, and
entertained us with cocoa-nut punches in the Sessions Hall
and seat of judgment of that widespread archipelago, our
glasses standing arrayed with summonses and census
returns. The unpopularity of a late Vice-President had
begun the movement of exodus, his native employés
resigning court appointments and retiring each to his own
cocoa-patch in the remoter districts of the isle. Upon the
back of that, the Governor in Papeete[2] issued a decree: All
land in the Paumotus must be defined and registered by a
certain date. Now, the folk of the archipelago are half
nomadic; a man can scarce be said to belong to a particular
atoll; he belongs to several, perhaps, holds a stake and
counts cousinship in half a score; and the inhabitants of
Rotoava in particular, man, woman, and child, and from the
gendarme to the Mormon prophet and the schoolmaster,
owned—I was going to say land—owned at least coral blocks
and growing coco-palms in some adjacent isle. Thither—
from the gendarme to the babe in arms, the pastor followed
by his flock, the schoolmaster carrying along with him his

1. Stevenson had arrived at the port of Rotoava on Fakarava atoll in the Paumotus group.
2. Main town of Tahiti and capital of French Polynesia.

64

scholars, and the scholars with their books and slates—they had taken ship some two days previous to our arrival, and were all now engaged disputing boundaries. Fancy overhears the shrillness of their disputation mingle with the surf and scatter sea-fowl. It was admirable to observe the completeness of their flight, like that of hibernating birds; nothing left but empty houses, like old nests to be reoccupied in spring; and even the harmless necessary dominie borne with them in their transmigration. Fifty odd set out, and only seven, I was informed, remained. But when I made a feast on board the *Casco*, more than seven, and nearer seven times seven, appeared to be my guests. Whence they appeared, how they were summoned, whither they vanished when the feast was eaten, I have no guess. In view of Low Island tales, and that awful frequentation which makes men avoid the seaward beaches of an atoll, some two score of those that ate with us may have returned, for the occasion, from the kingdom of the dead.

It was this solitude that put it in our minds to hire a house, and become, for the time being, in-dwellers of the isle—a practice I have ever since, when it was possible, adhered to. Mr Donat placed us, with that intent, under the convoy of one Taniera Mahinui, who combined the incongruous characters of catechist and convict. The reader may smile, but I affirm he was well qualified for either part. For that of convict, first of all, by a good substantial felony, such as in all lands casts the perpetrator in chains and dungeons. Taniera was a man of birth—the chief a while ago, as he loved to tell, of a district in Anaa of 800 souls. In an evil hour it occurred to the authorities in Papeete to charge the chiefs with the collection of the taxes. It is a question if much were collected; it is certain that nothing was handed on; and Taniera, who had distinguished himself by a visit to Papeete and some high living in restaurants, was chosen for the scapegoat. The reader must understand that not Taniera but the authorities in Papeete were first in fault. The charge imposed was disproportioned. I have not yet heard of any Polynesian capable of such a burden; honest and upright Hawaiians—one in particular, who was admired even by the whites as an inflexible magistrate—have stumbled in the narrow path of the trustee. And Taniera, when the pinch came, scorned to denounce accomplices; others had shared the spoil, he bore the penalty alone. He was condemned in five years. The period, when I had the pleasure of his friendship, was not yet expired; he still drew prison rations, the sole and not unwelcome reminder of his chains, and, I believe, looked forward to the date of his enfranchisement with mere alarm. For he had no sense of shame in the position; complained of nothing but the defective table of his place of exile; regretted nothing but the fowls and eggs and fish of his own more favoured island. And as for his parishioners, they did not think one hair the less of him. A schoolboy, mulcted in ten thousand lines of Greek and dwelling sequestered in the dormitories, enjoys unabated consideration from his fellows. So with Taniera: a marked man, not a dishonoured; having fallen under the lash of the unthinkable gods; a Job, perhaps, or say a Taniera in the den of lions. Songs are likely made and sung about this saintly Robin Hood. On the other hand, he was even highly qualified for his office in the Church; being by nature a grave, considerate, and kindly man; his face rugged and serious, his smile bright; the master of several trades, a builder both of boats and houses; endowed with a fine pulpit voice; endowed besides with such a gift of eloquence that at the grave of the late chief of Fakarava he set all the assistants weeping. I never met a man of a mind more ecclessiastical; he loved to dispute and to inform himself of doctrine and the history of sects; and when I showed him the cuts in a volume of Chambers's *Encyclopaedia*—except for the one of an ape—reserved his whole enthusiasm for cardinals' hats, censers, candlesticks, and cathedrals. Methought when he looked upon the cardinal's hat a voice said low in his ear: 'Your foot is on the ladder.'

Under the guidance of Taniera we were soon installed in what I believe to have been the best-appointed private house in Fakarava. It stood just beyond the church in an oblong patch of cultivation. More than three hundred sacks of soil were imported from Tahiti for the Residency garden; and this must shortly be renewed, for the earth blows away, sinks in crevices of the coral, and is sought for at last in vain. I know not how much earth had gone to the garden of my villa; some at least, for an alley of prosperous bananas ran to the gate, and over the rest of the enclosure, which was covered with the usual clinker-like fragments of smashed coral, not only coco-palms and mikis but also fig-trees flourished, all of a delicious greenness. Of course there was no blade of grass. In front a picket fence divided us from the white road, the palm-fringed margin of the lagoon, and the lagoon itself, reflecting clouds by day and stars by night. At the back, a bulwark of uncemented coral enclosed us from the narrow belt of bush and the nigh ocean beach where the seas thundered, the roar and wash of them still humming in the chambers of the house.

This itself was of one story, verandahed front and back. It contained three rooms, three sewing-machines, three sea-chests, chairs, tables, a pair of beds, a cradle, a double-barrelled gun, a pair of enlarged coloured photographs, a pair of coloured prints after Wilkie and Mulready,[1] and a French lithograph with the legend: '*Le brigade du Général Lepasset brûlant son drapeau devant Metz.*' Under the stilts of the house a stove was rusting, till we drew it forth and put it in commission. Not far off was the burrow in the coral whence we supplied ourselves with brackish water. There was live stock, besides, on the estate—cocks and hens and a brace of ill-regulated cats, whom Taniera came every morning with the sun to feed on grated cocoa-nut. His voice was our regular réveillé, ringing pleasantly about the garden: 'Pooty—pooty—poo—poo—poo!'

Far as we were from the public offices, the nearness of the chapel made our situation what is called eligible in advertisements, and gave us a side look on some native life. Every morning, as soon as he had fed the fowls, Taniera set the bell agoing in the small belfry; and the faithful, who were not very numerous, gathered to prayers. I was once present: it was the Lord's day, and seven females and eight males composed the congregation. A woman played precentor, starting with a longish note; the catechist joined in upon the

1. Sir David Wilkie, historical and genre painter, 1785–1841. William Mulready, genre painter in the Wilkie style, 1786–1863.

second bar; and then the faithful in a body. Some had
printed hymn-books which they followed; some of the rest
filled up with 'eh—eh—eh', the Paumotuan tol-de-rol. After
the hymn, we had an antiphonal prayer or two; and then
Taniera rose from the front bench, where he had been sitting
in his catechist's robes, passed within the altar-rails, opened
his Tahitian Bible, and began to preach from notes. I
understood one word—the name of God; but the preacher
managed his voice with taste, used rare and expressive
gestures, and made a strong impression of sincerity. The
plain service, the vernacular Bible, the hymn-tunes mostly
on an English pattern—'God save the Queen', I was
informed, a special favourite—all, save some paper flowers
upon the altar, seemed not merely but austerely Protestant.
It is thus the Catholics have met their low island proselytes
half-way.

Taniera had the keys of our house; it was with him I made
my bargain, if that could be called a bargain in which all was
remitted to my generosity; it was he who fed the cats and
poultry, he who came to call and pick a meal with us like an
acknowledged friend; and we long fondly supposed he was
our landlord. This belief was not to bear the test of experience; and, as my chapter has to relate, no certainty
succeeded it.

We passed some days of airless quiet and great heat;
shell-gatherers were warned from the ocean beach, where
sunstroke waited them from ten till four; the highest palm
hung motionless, there was no voice audible but that of the
sea on the far side. At last, about four of a certain afternoon,
long cats-paws flawed the face of the lagoon; and presently in
the tree-tops there awoke the grateful bustle of the trades,
and all the houses and alleys of the island were fanned out.
To more than one enchanted ship, that had lain long becalmed in view of the green shore, the wind brought
deliverance; and by daylight on the morrow a schooner and
two cutters lay moored in the port of Rotoava. Nor only in
the outer sea, but in the lagoon itself, a certain traffic woke
with the reviving breeze; and among the rest one François,
a half-blood, set sail with the first light in his own half-
decked cutter. He had held before a court appointment;

being, I believe, the Residency sweeper-out. Trouble arising with the unpopular Vice-Resident, he had thrown his honours down, and fled to the far parts of the atoll to plant cabbages—or at least coco-palms. Thence he was now driven by such need as even a Cincinnatus[1] must acknowledge, and fared for the capital city, the seat of his late functions, to exchange half a ton of copra for necessary flour. And here, for a while, the story leaves to tell of his voyaging.

It must tell, instead, of our house, where, toward seven at night, the catechist came suddenly in with his pleased air of being welcome; armed besides with a considerable bunch of keys. These he proceeded to try on the sea-chests, drawing each in turn from its place against the wall. Heads of strangers appeared in the doorway and volunteered suggestions. All in vain. Either they were the wrong keys or the wrong boxes, or the wrong man was trying them. For a little Taniera fumed and fretted; then had recourse to the more summary method of the hatchet; one of the chests was broken open, and an armful of clothing, male and female, baled out and handed to the strangers on the verandah.

These were François, his wife, and their child. About eight A.M., in the midst of the lagoon, their cutter had capsized in jibbing. They got her righted, and though she was still full of water put the child on board. The mainsail had been carried away, but the jib still drew her sluggishly along, and François and the woman swam astern and worked the rudder with their hands. The cold was cruel; the fatigue, as time went on, became excessive; and in that preserve of sharks, fear haunted them. Again and again, François, the half-breed, would have desisted and gone down; but the woman, whole blood of an amphibious race, still supported him with cheerful words. I am reminded of a woman of Hawaii who swam with her husband, I dare not say how many miles, in a high sea, and came ashore at last

1. Lucius Octavius Cincinnatus, 5th century B.C. Roman senator who put devotion to the republic before personal fame and power. Appointed Dictator in a crisis, he resigned and returned to his farm when the danger was past.

with his dead body in her arms. It was about five in the
evening, after nine hours' swimming, that François and his
wife reached land at Rotoava. The gallant fight was won, and
instantly the more childish side of native character appears.
They had supped, and told and retold their story, dripping
as they came; the flesh of the woman, Mrs Stevenson helped
to shift, was cold as stone; and François, having changed to
a dry cotton shirt and trousers, passed the remainder of the
evening on my floor and between open doorways, in a
thorough draught. Yet François, the son of a French father,
speaks excellent French himself and seems intelligent.

It was our first idea that the catechist, true to his evan-
gelical vocation, was clothing the naked from his superfluity.
Then it came out that François was but dealing with his
own. The clothes were his, so was the chest, so was the
house. François was in fact the landlord. Yet you observe he
had hung back on the verandah while Taniera tried his
'prentice hand upon the locks; and even now, when his true
character appeared, the only use he made of the estate was to
leave the clothes of his family drying on the fence. Taniera
was still the friend of the house, still fed the poultry, still
came about us on his daily visits, François, during the
remainder of his stay, holding bashfully aloof. And there was
stranger matter. Since François had lost the whole load of
his cutter, the half ton of copra, an axe, bowls, knives, and
clothes—since he had in a manner to begin the world again,
and his necessary flour was not yet bought or paid for—I
proposed to advance him what he needed on the rent. To my
enduring amazement he refused, and the reason he gave—if
that can be called a reason which but darkens counsel—was
that Taniera was his friend. His friend, you observe; not his
creditor. I inquired into that, and was assured that Taniera,
an exile in a strange isle, might possibly be in debt himself,
but certainly was no man's creditor.

Very early one morning we were awakened by a bustling
presence in the yard, and found our camp had been surprised
by a tall, lean, old native lady, dressed in what were obvi-
ously widow's weeds. You could see at a glance she was a
notable woman, a housewife, sternly practicable, alive with
energy, and with fine possibilities of temper. Indeed there

was nothing native about her but the skin; and the type abounds, and is everywhere respected, nearer home. It did us good to see her scour the grounds, examining the plants and chickens; watering, feeding, trimming them; taking angry, purpose-like possession. When she neared the house our sympathy abated; when she came to the broken chest I wished I were elsewhere. We had scarce a word in common; but her whole lean body spoke for her with indignant eloquence. 'My chest!' it cried, with a stress on the possessive. 'My chest—broken open! This is a fine state of things!' I hastened to lay the blame where it belonged—on François and his wife—and found I had made things worse instead of better. She repeated the names at first with incredulity, then with despair. A while she seemed stunned, next fell to disembowelling the box, piling the goods on the floor, and visibly computing the extent of François's ravages; and presently after she was observed in high speech with Taniera, who seemed to hang an ear like one reproved.

Here, then, by all known marks, should be my landlady at last; here was every character of the proprietor fully developed. Should I not approach her on the still depending question of my rent? I carried the point to an adviser. 'Nonsense!' he cried. 'That's the old woman, the mother. It doesn't belong to her. I believe that's the man the house belongs to,' and he pointed to one of the coloured photographs on the wall. On this I gave up all desire of understanding; and when the time came for me to leave, in the judgment-hall of the archipelago, and with the awful countenance of the acting Governor, I duly paid my rent to Taniera. He was satisfied, and so was I. But what had he to do with it? Mr Donat, acting magistrate and a man of kindred blood, could throw no light upon the mystery; a plain private person, with a taste for letters, cannot be expected to do more.

from The Gilberts

BUTARITARI

At Honolulu we had said farewell to the *Casco* and to Captain
Otis, and our next adventure was made in changed conditions. Passage was taken for myself, my wife, Mr Osbourne,
and my China boy, Ah Fu, on a pigmy trading schooner, the
Equator, Captain Dennis Reid; and on a certain bright June
day in 1889, adorned in the Hawaiian fashion with the
garlands of departure, we drew out of port and bore with a
fair wind for Micronesia.

The whole extent of the South Seas is desert of ships; more
especially that part where we were now to sail. No post runs
in these islands; communication is by accident; where you
may have designed to go is one thing, where you shall be able
to arrive is another. It was my hope, for instance, to have
reached the Carolines, and returned to the light of day by
way of Manila and the China ports; and it was in Samoa that
we were destined to re-appear and be once more refreshed
with the sight of mountains. Since the sunset faded from the
peaks of Oahu six months had intervened, and we had seen
no spot of earth so high as an ordinary cottage. Our path had
been still on the flat sea, our dwellings upon erected coral,
our diet from the pickle-tub or out of tins; I had learned to
welcome shark's flesh for a variety; and a mountain, an
onion, an Irish potato or a beef-steak, had been long lost to
sense and dear to aspiration.

The two chief places of our stay, Butaritari and Apemama,
lie near the line; the latter within thirty miles. Both enjoy a
superb ocean climate, days of blinding sun and bracing
winds, nights of a heavenly brightness. Both are somewhat
wider than Fakarava, measuring perhaps (at the widest) a
quarter of a mile from beach to beach. In both, a course kind

72

of *taro*[1] thrives; its culture is a chief business of the natives, and the consequent mounds and ditches make miniature scenery and amuse the eye. In all else they show the customary features of an atoll: the low horizon, the expanse of the lagoon, the sedge-like rim of palm-tops, the sameness and smallness of the land, the hugely superior size and interest of sea and sky. Life on such islands is in many points like life on shipboard. The atoll, like the ship, is soon taken for granted; and the islanders, like the ship's crew, become soon the centre of attention. The isles are populous, independent, seats of kinglets, recently civilised, little visited. In the last decade many changes have crept in; women no longer go unclothed till marriage; the widow no longer sleeps at night and goes abroad by day with the skull of her dead husband; and, fire-arms being introduced, the spear and the shark-tooth sword are sold for curiosities. Ten years ago all these things and practices were to be seen in use; yet ten years more, and the old society will have entirely vanished. We came in a happy moment to see its institutions still erect and (in Apemama) scarce decayed.

Populous and independent—warrens of men, ruled over with some rustic pomp—such was the first and still the recurring impression of these tiny lands. As we stood across the lagoon for the town of Butaritari, a stretch of the low shore was seen to be crowded with the brown roofs of houses; those of the palace and king's summer parlour (which are of corrugated iron) glittered near one end conspicuously bright; the royal colours flew hard by on a tall flagstaff; in front, on an artificial islet, the gaol played the part of a martello. Even upon this first and distant view, the place had scarce the air of what it truly was, a village; rather of that which it was also, a petty metropolis, a city rustic and yet royal.

The lagoon is shoal. The tide being out, we waded for some quarter of a mile in tepid shallows, and stepped ashore at last into a flagrant stagnancy of sun and heat. The lee side of a line island after noon is indeed a breathless place; on the ocean beach the trade will be still blowing, boisterous and

1. A food plant with starchy roots and succulent leaves.

cool; out in the lagoon it will be blowing also, speeding the canoes; but the screen of bush completely intercepts it from the shore, and sleep and silence and companies of mosquitoes brood upon the towns.

We may thus be said to have taken Butaritari by surprise. A few inhabitants were still abroad in the north end, at which we landed. As we advanced, we were soon done with encounter, and seemed to explore a city of the dead. Only, between the posts of open houses, we could see the townsfolk stretched in the siesta, sometimes a family together veiled in a mosquito net, sometimes a single sleeper on a platform like a corpse on a bier.

The houses were of all dimensions, from those of toys to those of churches. Some might hold a battalion, some were so minute they could scarce receive a pair of lovers; only in the playroom, when the toys are mingled, do we meet such incongruities of scale. Many were open sheds; some took the form of roofed stages; others were walled and the walls pierced with little windows. A few were perched on piles in the lagoon; the rest stood at random on a green, through which the roadway made a ribbon of sand, or along the embankments of a sheet of water like a shallow dock. One and all were the creatures of a single tree; palm-tree wood and palm-tree leaf their materials; no nail had been driven, no hammer sounded, in their building, and they were held together by lashings of palm-tree sinnet.

In the midst of the thoroughfare, the church stands like an island, a lofty and dim house with rows of windows; a rich tracery of framing sustains the roof; and through the door at either end the street shows in a vista. The proportions of the place, in such surroundings, and built of such materials, appeared august; and we threaded the nave with a sentiment befitting visitors in a cathedral. Benches run along either side. In the midst, on a crazy dais, two chairs stand ready for the king and queen when they shall choose to worship; over their heads a hoop, apparently from a hogshead, depends by a strip of red cotton; and the hoop (which hangs askew) is dressed with streamers of the same material, red and white.

This was our first advertisement of the royal dignity, and presently we stood before its seat and centre. The palace is

built of imported wood upon a European plan; the roof of
corrugated iron, the yard enclosed with walls, the gate
surmounted by a sort of lychhouse. It cannot be called
spacious; a labourer in the States is sometimes more
commodiously lodged; but when we had the chance to see it
within, we found it was enriched (beyond all island expectation) with coloured advertisements and cuts from illustrated
papers. Even before the gate some of the treasures of the
crown stand public: a bell of good magnitude, two pieces of
cannon, and a single shell. The bell cannot be rung nor the
guns fired; they are curiosities, proofs of wealth, a part of the
parade of the royalty, and stand to be admired like statues in
a square. A straight gut of water like a canal runs almost to
the palace door; the containing quay-walls excellently built
of coral; over against the mouth, by what seems an effect of
landscape art, the martello-like islet of the gaol breaks the
lagoon. Vassal chiefs with tribute, neighbour monarchs
come a-roving, might here sail in, view with surprise these
extensive public works, and be awed by these mouths of
silent cannon. It was impossible to see the place and not to
fancy it designed for pageantry. But the elaborate theatre
then stood empty; the royal house deserted, its doors and
windows gaping; the whole quarter of the town immersed in
silence. On the opposite bank of the canal, on a roofed stage,
an ancient gentleman slept publicly, sole visible inhabitant;
and beyond on the lagoon a canoe spread a striped lateen, the
sole thing moving.

The canal is formed on the south by a pier or causeway
with a parapet. As the far end the parapet stops, and the quay
expands into an oblong peninsula in the lagoon, the
breathing-place and summer parlour of the king. The midst
is occupied by an open house or permanent marquee—called
here a maniapa, or, as the word is now pronounced, a
maniap'—at the lowest estimation forty feet by sixty. The
iron roof, lofty but exceedingly low-browed, so that a woman
must stoop to enter, is supported externally on pillars of
coral, within by a frame of wood. The floor is of broken
coral, divided in aisles by the uprights of the frame; the
house far enough from shore to catch the breeze, which
enters freely and disperses the mosquitoes; and under the

low eaves the sun is seen to glitter and the waves to dance on the lagoon.

It was now some while since we had met any but slumberers; and when we had wandered down the pier and stumbled at last into this bright shed, we were surprised to find it occupied by a society of a wakeful people, some twenty souls in all, the court and guardsmen of Butaritari. The court ladies were busy making mats; the guardsmen yawned and sprawled. Half a dozen rifles lay on a rock and a cutlass was leaned against a pillar: the armoury of these drowsy musketeers. At the far end, a little closed house of wood displayed some tinsel curtains, and proved, upon examination, to be a privy of the European model. In front of this, upon some mats, lolled Tebureimoa, the king[1]; behind him, on the panels of the house, two crossed rifles represented fasces. He wore pyjamas which sorrowfully misbecame his bulk; his nose was hooked and cruel, his body overcome with sodden corpulence, his eye timorous and dull; he seemed at once oppressed with drowsiness and held awake by apprehension: a pepper rajah muddled with opium, and listening for the march of a Dutch army, looks perhaps not otherwise. We were to grow better acquainted, and first and last I had the same impression; he seemed always drowsy, yet always to hearken and start; and, whether from remorse or fear, there is no doubt he seeks a refuge in the abuse of drugs.

The rajah displayed no sign of interest in our coming. But the queen, who sat beside him in a purple sacque, was more accessible; and there was present an interpreter so willing that his volubility became at last the cause of our departure. He had greeted us upon our entrance:—'That is the honourable King, and I am his interpreter,' he had said, with more stateliness than truth. For he held no appointment in the

1. Tebureimoa, Nantemat' by name and a carpenter to trade was the last of four brothers who had been kings of Butaritari before him. He earned the nick-name 'Mr Corpse' because of his bloody service as hatchetman to his oldest brother, the tyrant Nakaeia. He proved to be a weak and guilt-ridden figure when finally installed as king in his own right.

court, seemed extremely ill-acquainted with the island language, and was present, like ourselves, upon a visit of civility. Mr Williams was his name: an American darkey, runaway ship's cook, and bar-keeper at *The Land we Live in* tavern, Butaritari. I never knew a man who had more words in his command or less truth to communicate; neither the gloom of the monarch, nor my own efforts to be distant, could in the least abash him; and when the scene closed, the darkey was left talking.

The town still slumbered, or had but just begun to turn and stretch itself; it was still plunged in heat and silence. So much the more vivid was the impression that we carried away of the house upon the islet, the Micronesian Saul wakeful amid his guards, and his unmelodious David, Mr Williams, chattering through the drowsy hours.

from The Gilberts

AROUND OUR HOUSE

When we left the palace we were still but seafarers ashore;
and within the hour we had installed our goods in one of the
six foreign houses of Butaritari, namely, that usually
occupied by Maka, the Hawaiian missionary. Two San
Francisco firms are here established, Messrs Crawford and
Messrs Wightman Brothers; the first hard by the palace of
the mid town, the second at the north entry; each with a
store and bar-room. Our house was in the Wightman
compound, betwixt the store and bar, within a fenced
enclosure. Across the road a few native houses nestled in the
margin of the bush, and the green wall of palms rose solid,
shutting out the breeze. A little sandy cove of the lagoon ran
in behind, sheltered by a verandah pier, the labour of
queens' hands. Here, when the tide was high, sailed boats
lay to be loaded; when the tide was low, the boats took
ground some half a mile away, and an endless series of
natives descended the pier stair, tailed across the sand in
strings and clusters, waded to the waist with the bags of
copra, and loitered backward to renew their charge. The
mystery of the copra trade tormented me, as I sat and
watched the profits drip on the stair and the sands.[1]

In front, from shortly after four in the morning until nine
at night, the folk of the town streamed by us intermittently
along the road: families going up the island to make copra
on their lands; women bound for the bush to gather flowers
against the evening toilet; and, twice a day, the toddy-

1. Copra is dried coconut kernel from which coconut-oil
   could be extracted for use in food fats, soap, detergents
   and candles. Sold by weight, it is heavier when moist.

78

cutters,[1] each with his knife and shell. In the first grey of
the morning, and again late in the afternoon, these would
straggle past about their tree-top business, strike off here
and there into the bush, and vanish from the face of earth.
At about the same hour, if the tide be low in the lagoon, you
are likely to be bound yourself across the island for a bath,
and may enter close at their heels alleys of the palm wood.
Right in front, although the sun is not yet risen, the east is
already lighted with preparatory fires, and the huge
accumulations of the trade-wind cloud glow with and
heliograph the coming day. The breeze is in your face;
overhead in the tops of the palms, its playthings, it maintains a lively bustle; look where you will, above or below,
there is no human presence, only the earth and shaken
forest. And right overhead the song of an invisible singer
breaks from the thick leaves; from farther on a second
tree-top answers; and beyond again, in the bosom of the
woods, a still more distant minstrel perches and sways and
sings. So, all round the isle, the toddy-cutters sit on high,
and are rocked by the trade, and have a view far to seaward,
where they keep watch for sails, and like huge birds utter
their songs in the morning. They sing with a certain
lustiness and Bacchic glee; the volume of sound and the
articulate melody fall unexpected from the tree-top, whence
we anticipate the chattering of fowls. And yet in a sense
these songs also are but chatter; the words are ancient,
obsolete, and sacred; few comprehend them, perhaps no
one perfectly; but it was understood the cutters 'prayed to
have good toddy, and sang of their old wars'. The prayer is
at least answered; and when the foaming shell is brought to
your door, you have a beverage well 'worthy of a grace'. All
forenoon you may return and taste; it only sparkles, and
sharpens, and grows to be a new drink, not less delicious;
but with the progress of the day the fermentation quickens
and grows acid; in twelve hours it will be yeast for bread, in
two days more a devilish intoxicant, the counsellor of crime.

The men are of a marked Arabian cast of features, often

1. A toddy-palm is a coconut or other palm, the juice of
   which can be fermented to make toddy.

bearded and moustached, often gaily dressed, some with bracelets and anklets, all stalking hidalgo-like, and accepting salutations with a haughty lip. The hair (with the dandies of either sex) is worn turban-wise in a frizzled bush; and like the daggers of the Japanese, a pointed stick (used for a comb) is thrust gallantly among the curls. The women from this bush of hair look forth enticingly: the race cannot be compared with the Tahitian for female beauty; I doubt even if the average be high; but some of the prettiest girls, and one of the handsomest women I ever saw, were Gilbertines. Butaritari, being the commercial centre of the group, is Europeanised; the coloured sacque or the white shift are common wear, the latter for the evening; the trade hat, loaded with flowers, fruit, and ribbons, is unfortunately not unknown; and the characteristic female dress of the Gilberts no longer universal. The *ridi* is its name: a cutty petticoat or fringe of the smoked fibre of cocoa-nut leaf, not unlike tarry string; the lower edge not reaching the mid-thigh, the upper adjusted so low upon the haunches that it seems to cling by accident. A sneeze, you think, and the lady must surely be left destitute. 'The perilous, hairbreadth ridi' was our word for it; and in the conflict that rages over women's dress it has the misfortune to please neither side, the prudish condemning it as insufficient, the more frivolous finding it unlovely in itself. Yet if a pretty Gilbertine would look her best, that must be her costume. In that, and naked otherwise, she moves with an incomparable liberty and grace and life, that marks the poetry of Micronesia. Bundle her in a gown, the charm is fled, and she wriggles like an Englishwoman.

Towards dusk the passers-by became more gorgeous. The men broke out in all the colours of the rainbow—or at least of the trade-room,—and both men and women began to be adorned and scented with new flowers. A small white blossom is the favourite, sometimes sown singly in a woman's hair like little stars, now composed in a thick wreath. With the night, the crowd sometimes thickened in the road, and the padding and brushing of bare feet became continuous; the promenades mostly grave, the silence only interrupted by some giggling and scampering of girls; even

the children quiet. At nine, bed-time struck on a bell from
the cathedral, and the life of the town ceased. At four the
next morning the signal is repeated in the darkness, and the
innocent prisoners set free; but for seven hours all must
lie—I was about to say within doors, of a place where doors,
and even walls, are an exception—housed, at least, under
their airy roofs and clustered in the tents of the mosquito-
nets. Suppose a necessary errand to occur, suppose it
imperative to send abroad, the messenger must then go
openly, advertising himself to the police with a huge brand
of cocoa-nut, which flares from house to house like a
moving bonfire. Only the police themselves go darkling,
and grope in the night of misdemeanants. I used to hate
their treacherous presence; their captain in particular, a
crafty old man in white, lurked nightly about my premises
till I could have found it in my heart to beat him. But the
rogue was privileged.

Not one of the eleven resident traders came to town, no
captain cast anchor in the lagoon, but we saw him ere the
hour was out. This was owing to our position between the
store and the bar—the *Sans Souci*, as the last was called. Mr
Rick was not only Messrs Wightman's manager, but con-
sular agent for the States; Mrs Rick was the only white
woman on the island, and one of the only two in the
archipelago; their house besides, with its cool verandahs, its
bookshelves, its comfortable furniture, could not be rivalled
nearer than Jaluit or Honolulu. Every one called in consequence, save such as might be prosecuting a South Sea
quarrel, hingeing on the price of copra and the odd cent, or
perhaps a difference about poultry. Even these, if they did
not appear upon the north, would be presently visible to the
southward, the *Sans Souci* drawing them as with cords. In
an island with a total population of twelve white persons,
one of the two drinking-shops might seem superfluous; but
every bullet has its billet, and the double accommodation of
Butaritari is found in practice highly convenient by the
captains and crews of ships: *The Land we Live in* being
tacitly resigned to the forecastle, the *Sans Souci* tacitly
reserved for the afterguard. So aristocratic were my habits,
so commanding was my fear of Mr Williams, that I have

never visited the first; but in the other, which was the club
or rather the casino of the island, I regularly passed my
evenings. It was small, but neatly fitted, and at night (when
the lamp was lit) sparkled with glass and glowed with
coloured pictures like a theatre at Christmas. The pictures
were advertisements, the glass coarse enough, the carpentry
amateur; but the effect, in that incongruous isle, was of
unbridled luxury and inestimable expense. Here songs were
sung, tales told, tricks performed, games played. The
Ricks, ourselves, Norwegian Tom the bar-keeper, a captain
or two from the ships, and perhaps three or four traders
come down the island in their boats or by the road on foot,
made up the usual company. The traders, all bred to the
sea, take a humorous pride in their new business; 'South
Sea Merchants' is the title they prefer. 'We are all sailors
here'—'Merchants, if you please'—'*South Sea* Merchants'—
was a piece of conversation endlessly repeated, that never
seemed to lose in savour. We found them at all times
simple, genial, gay, gallant, and obliging; and, across some
interval of time, recall with pleasure the traders of
Butaritari. There was one black sheep indeed. I tell of him
here where he lived, against my rule; for in this case I have
no measure to preserve, and the man is typical of a class of
ruffians that once disgraced the whole field of the South
Seas, and still linger in the rarely visited isles of Micronesia.
He had the name on the beach of 'a perfect gentleman when
sober', but I never saw him otherwise than drunk. The few
shocking and savage traits of the Micronesian he has singled
out with the skill of a collector, and planted in the soil of his
original baseness. He has been accused and acquitted of a
treacherous murder; and has since boastfully owned it,
which inclines me to suppose him innocent. His daughter is
defaced by his erroneous cruelty, for it was his wife he had
intended to disfigure, and, in the darkness of the night and
the frenzy of cocoa-brandy, fastened on the wrong victim.
The wife has since fled and harbours in the bush with
natives; and the husband still demands from deaf ears her
forcible restoration. The best of his business is to make
natives drink, and then advance the money for the fine upon
a lucrative mortgage. 'Respect for whites' is the man's

word: 'What is the matter with this island is the want of
respect for whites.' On his way to Butaritari, while I was
there, he spied his wife in the bush with certain natives and
made a dash to capture her; whereupon one of her
companions drew a knife, and the husband retreated: 'Do
you call that proper respect for whites?' he cried. At an
early stage of the acquaintance we proved our respect for his
kind of white by forbidding him our enclosure under pain of
death. Thenceforth he lingered often in the neighbourhood
with I knew not what sense of envy or design of mischief;
his white, handsome face (which I beheld with loathing)
looked in upon us at all hours across the fence; and once,
from a safe distance, he avenged himself by shouting a
recondite island insult, to us quite inoffensive, on his
English lips incredibly incongruous.

Our enclosure, round which this composite of degrad-
ations wandered, was of some extent. In one corner was a
trellis with a long table of rough boards. Here the Fourth of
July feast had been held not long before with memorable
consequences, yet to be set forth; here we took our meals;
here entertained to a dinner the king and notables of Makin.
In the midst was the house, with a verandah front and back,
and three rooms within. In the verandah we slung our
man-of-war hammocks, worked there by day, and slept at
night. Within were beds, chairs, a round table, a fine
hanging lamp, and portraits of the royal family of Hawaii.
Queen Victoria proves nothing; Kalakaua[1] and Mrs
Bishop[2] are diagnostic; and the truth is we were the
stealthy tenants of the parsonage. On the day of our arrival
Maka was away; faithless trustees unlocked his doors; and
the dear rigorous man, the sworn foe of liquor and tobacco,
returned to find his verandah littered with cigarettes and his
parlour horrible with bottles. He made but one condition—

1. King of Hawaii, whom Stevenson got to know well
   during the six month stay at Waikiki.
2. Probably a reference to Bernice Pauaohi Bishop, after
   whom Honolulu's Bishop Museum was founded in
   1889, the year Stevenson was in Hawaii. She was the
   wife of missionary Charles Reed Bishop and a member
   of the Hawaiian royal family.

on the round table, which he used in the celebration of the
sacraments, he begged us to refrain from setting liquor; in
all else he bowed to the accomplished fact, refused rent,
retired across the way into a native house, and, plying in his
boat, beat the remotest quarters of the isle for provender.
He found us pigs—I could not fancy where—no other pigs
were visible; he brought us fowls and taro; when we gave
our feast to the monarch and gentry, it was he who supplied
the wherewithal, he who superintended the cooking, he
who asked grace at table, and when the king's health was
proposed, he also started the cheering with an English
hip-hip-hip. There was never a more fortunate conception;
the heart of the fatted king exulted in his bosom at the
sound.

Take him for all in all, I have never known a more
engaging creature than this parson of Butaritari: his mirth,
his kindness, his noble, friendly feelings, brimmed from the
man in speech and gesture. He loved to exaggerate, to act
and overact the momentary part, to exercise his lungs and
muscles, and to speak and laugh with his whole body. He
had the morning cheerfulness of birds and healthy children;
and his humour was infectious. We were next neighbours
and met daily, yet our salutations lasted minutes at a
stretch—shaking hands, slapping shoulders, capering like a
pair of Merry-Andrews, laughing to split our sides upon
some pleasantry that would scarce raise a titter in an
infant-school. It might be five in the morning, the toddy-
cutters just gone by, the road empty, the shade of the island
lying far on the lagoon: and the ebullition cheered me for
the day.

Yet I always suspected Maka of a secret melancholy;
these jubilant extremes could scarce be constantly maintained. He was besides long, and lean, and lined, and
corded, and a trifle grizzled; and his Sabbath countenance
was even saturnine. On that day we made a procession to
the church, or (as I must always call it) the cathedral; Maka
(a blot on the hot landscape) in tall hat, black frockcoat,
black trousers; under his arm the hymn-book and the
Bible; in his face, a reverent gravity:—beside him Mary his
wife, a quiet, wise, and handsome elderly lady, seriously

attired:—myself following with singular and moving
thoughts. Long before, to the sound of bells and streams
and birds, through a green Lothian glen, I had accompanied
Sunday by Sunday a minister in whose house I lodged; and
the likeness, and the difference, and the series of years and
deaths, profoundly touched me. In the great, dusky, palm-
tree cathedral the congregation rarely numbered thirty: the
men on one side, the women on the other, myself posted
(for a privilege) amongst the women, and the small missionary contingent gathered close around the platform, we
were lost in that round vault. The lessons were read
antiphonally, the flock was catechised, a blind youth
repeated weekly a long string of psalms, hymns were
sung—I never heard worse singing,—and the sermon
followed. To say I understood nothing were untrue; there
were points that I learned to expect with certainty; the name
of Honolulu, that of Kalakaua, the word Cap'n-man-o'-wa',
the word ship, and a description of a storm at sea, infallibly
occurred; and I was not seldom rewarded with the name of
my own Sovereign in the bargain. The rest was but sound to
the ears, silence for the mind; a plain expanse of tedium,
rendered unbearable by heat, a hard chair, and the sight
through the wide doors of the more happy heathen on the
green. Sleep breathed on my joints and eyelids, sleep
hummed in my ears; it reigned in the dim cathedral. The
congregation stirred and stretched; they moaned, they
groaned aloud; they yawned upon a singing note, as you
may sometimes hear a dog when he has reached the tragic
bitterest of boredom. In vain the preacher thumped the
table; in vain he singled and addressed by name particular
hearers. I was myself perhaps a more effective excitant; and
at least to one old gentleman the spectacle of my successful
struggles against sleep—and I hope they were successful—
cheered the flight of time. He, when he was not catching
flies or playing tricks upon his neighbours, gloated with a
fixed, truculent eye upon the stages of my agony; and once,
when the service was drawing towards a close, he winked at
me across the church.

I write of the service with a smile; yet I was always
there—always with respect for Maka, always with admir-

ation for his deep seriousness, his burning energy, the fire of his roused eye, the sincere and various accents of his voice. To see him weekly flogging a dead horse and blowing a cold fire was a lesson in fortitude and constancy. It may be a question whether if the mission were fully supported, and he was set free from business avocations, more might not result; I think otherwise myself; I think not neglect but rigour had reduced his flock, that which has once provoked a revolution, and which today, in a man so lively and engaging, amazes the beholder. No song, no dance, no tobacco, no liquor, no alleviative of life—only toil and church-going; so says a voice from his face; and the face is the face of the Polynesian Esau, but the voice is the voice of a Jacob from a different world. And a Polynesian at the best makes a singular missionary in the Gilberts, coming from a country recklessly unchaste to one conspicuously strict; from a race hag-ridden with bogies to one comparatively bold against the terrors of the dark. The thought was stamped one morning in my mind, when I chanced to be abroad by moonlight, and saw all the town lightless, but the lamp faithfully burning by the missionary's bed. It requires no law, no fire, and no scouting police, to withhold Maka and his countrymen from wandering in the night unlighted.

from The Gilberts

A TALE OF A TAPU[1]
On the morrow of our arrival (Sunday, 14th July 1889) our
photographers were early stirring. Once more we traversed
a silent town; many were yet abed and asleep; some sat
drowsily in their open houses; there was no sound of
intercourse or business. In that hour before the shadows,
the quarter of the palace and canal seemed like a landing-
place in the *Arabian Nights* or from the classic poets; here
were the fit destination of some 'faery frigot', here some
adventurous prince might step ashore among new characters and incidents; and the island prison, where it floated
on the luminous face of the lagoon, might have passed for
the repository of the Grail. In such a scene, and at such an
hour, the impression received was not so much of foreign
travel—rather of past ages; it seemed not so much degrees
of latitude that we had crossed, as centuries of time that we
had re-ascended; leaving, by the same steps, home and
to-day. A few children followed us, mostly nude, all silent;
in the clear, weedy waters of the canal some silent damsels
waded, baring their brown thighs; and to one of the
maniap's before the palace gate we were attracted by a low
but stirring hum of speech.

The oval shed was full of men sitting cross-legged. The
king was there in striped pyjamas, his rear protected by four
guards with Winchesters, his air and bearing marked by
unwonted spirit and decision; tumblers and black bottles
went the round; and the talk, throughout loud, was general
and animated. I was inclined at first to view this scene with
suspicion. But the hour appeared unsuitable for a carouse;

1. A taboo, a proscription.

drink was besides forbidden equally by the law of the land and the canons of the church; and while I was yet hesitating, the king's rigorous attitude disposed of my last doubt. We had come, thinking to photograph him surrounded by his guards, and at the first word of the design his piety revolted. We were reminded of the day—the Sabbath, in which thou shalt take no photographs—and returned with a flea in our ear, bearing the rejected camera.

At church, a little later, I was struck to find the throne unoccupied. So nice a Sabbatarian might have found the means to be present; perhaps my doubts revived; and before I got home they were transformed to certainties. Tom, the bar-keeper of the *Sans Souci*, was in conversation with two emissaries from the court. The 'keen', they said, wanted 'din', failing which 'perandi'.* No din, was Tom's reply, and no perandi; but 'pira' if they pleased. It seems they had no use for beer, and departed sorrowing.

'Why, what is the meaning of all this?' I asked. 'Is the island on the spree?''

Such was the fact. On the 4th of July a feast had been made, and the king, at the suggestion of the whites, had raised the tapu against liquor. There is a proverb about horses; it scarce applies to the superior animal, of whom it may be rather said, that any one can start him drinking, not any twenty can prevail on him to stop. The tapu, raised ten days before, was not yet re-imposed; for ten days the town had been passing the bottle or lying (as we had seen it the afternoon before) in hoggish sleep; and the king, moved by the Old Men and his own appetites, continued to maintain the liberty, to squander his savings on liquor, and to join in and lead the debauch. The whites were the authors of this crisis; it was upon their own proposal that the freedom had been granted at the first; and for a while, in the interests of trade, they were doubtless pleased it should continue. That pleasure had now sometime ceased; the bout had been prolonged (it was conceded) unduly; and it now began to be a question how it might conclude. Hence Tom's refusal. Yet that refusal was avowedly only for the moment, and it was

* Gin and brandy. [R.L.S.]

avowedly unavailing; the king's foragers, denied by Tom at the *Sans Souci,* would be supplied at *The Land we Live in* by the gobbling Mr Williams.

The degree of the peril was not easy to measure at the time, and I am inclined to think now it was easy to exaggerate. Yet the conduct of drunkards even at home is always matter for anxiety; and at home our populations are not armed from the highest to the lowest with revolvers and repeating rifles, neither do we go on a debauch by the whole townful—and I might rather say, by the whole polity— king, magistrates, police, and army joining in one common scene of drunkenness. It must be thought besides that we were here in barbarous islands, rarely visited, lately and partly civilised. First and last, a really considerable number of whites have perished in the Gilberts, chiefly through their own misconduct; and the natives have displayed in at least one instance a disposition to conceal an accident under a butchery, and leave nothing but dumb bones. This last was the chief consideration against a sudden closing of the bars; the bar-keepers stood in the immediate breach and dealt direct with madmen; too surly a refusal might at any moment precipitate a blow, and the blow might prove the signal for a massacre.

Monday, 15th—At the same hour we returned to the same maniap'. Kümmel (of all drinks) was served in tumblers; in the midst sat the crown prince, a fatted youth, surrounded by fresh bottles and busily plying the corkscrew; and king, chief, and commons showed the loose mouth, the uncertain joints, and the blurred and animated eye of the early drinker. It was plain we were impatiently expected; the king retired with alacrity to dress, the guards were despatched after their uniforms; and we were left to await the issue of these preparations with a shedful of tipsy natives. The orgie had proceeded further than on Sunday. The day promised to be of great heat; it was already sultry, the courtiers were already fuddled; and still the kümmel continued to go round, and the crown prince to play butler. Flemish freedom followed upon Flemish excess; and a funny dog, a handsome fellow, gaily dressed, and with a full turban of frizzed hair, delighted the company with a humorous courtship of a lady in a manner not to be described. It was our diversion, in this time of waiting, to observe the gathering of the guards. They have European arms, European uniforms, and (to their sorrow) European shoes. We saw one warrior (like Mars) in the article of being armed; two men and a stalwart woman were scarce strong enough to boot him; and after a single appearance on parade the army is crippled for a week.

At last, the gates under the king's house opened; the army issued, one behind another, with guns and epaulettes; the colours stooped under the gateway; majesty followed in his uniform bedizened with gold lace; majesty's wife came next in a hat and feathers, and an ample trained silk gown; the royal imps succeeded; there stood the pageantry of Makin marshalled on its chosen theatre. Dickens might have told how serious they were; how tipsy; how the king melted and streamed under his cocked hat; how he took station by the larger of his two cannons—austere, majestic, but not truly vertical; how the troops huddled, and were staightened out, and clubbed again; how they and their firelocks raked at various inclinations like the masts of ships; and how an amateur photographer reviewed, arrayed, and adjusted them, to see his dispositions change before he reached the camera.

The business was funny to see; I do not know that it is graceful to laugh at; and our report of these transactions was received on our return with the shaking of grave heads.

The day had begun ill; eleven hours divided us from sunset; and at any moment, on the most trifling chance, the trouble might begin. The Wightman compound was in a military sense untenable, commanded on three sides by houses and thick bush; the town was computed to contain over a thousand stand of excellent new arms; and retreat to ships, in the case of an alert, was a recourse not to be thought of. Our talk that morning must have closely reproduced the talk in English garrisons before the Sepoy mutiny;[1] the sturdy doubt that any mischief was in

1. The Indian Mutiny of 1857, in which many of the
   Sepoy troops of the East India Company's Bengal army
   mutinied.

prospect, the sure belief that (should any come) there was nothing left but to go down fighting, the half amused, half anxious attitude of mind in which we were awaiting fresh developments.

The kümmel soon ran out; we were scarce returned before the king had followed us in quest of more. Mr Corpse was now divested of his more awful attitude, the lawless bulk of him again encased in striped pyjamas; a guardsman brought up the rear with his rifle at the trail; and his majesty was further accompanied by a Rarotongan[1] whalerman and the playful courtier with the turban of frizzed hair. There was never a more lively deputation. The whalerman was gapingly, tearfully tipsy; the courtier walked on air; the king himself was even sportive. Seated in a chair in the Ricks' sitting-room, he bore the brunt of our prayers and menaces unmoved. He was even rated, plied with historic instances, threatened with the men-of-war, ordered to restore the tapu on the spot—and nothing in the least affected him. It should be done tomorrow, he said; today it was beyond his power, today he durst not. 'Is that royal?' cried indignant Mr Rick. No, it was not royal; had the king been of a royal character we should ourselves have held a different language; and royal or not, he had the best of the dispute. The terms indeed were hardly equal; for the king was the only man who could restore the tapu, but the Ricks were not the only people who sold drink. He had but to hold his ground on the first question, and they were sure to weaken on the second. A little struggle they still made for the fashion's sake; and then one exceedingly tipsy deputation departed, greatly rejoicing, a case of brandy wheeling beside them in a barrow. The Rarotongan (whom I had never seen before) wrung me by the hand like a man bound on a far voyage. 'My dear frien'!' he cried, 'good-bye, my dear frien'!'—tears of kümmel standing in his eyes; the king lurched as he went, the courtier ambled—a strange party of intoxicated children to be intrusted with that barrowful of madness.

1. Rarotonga, the largest of the Cook Islands, a scattered Polynesian group in the Central Pacific.

You could never say the town was quiet; all morning there was a ferment in the air, an aimless movement and congregation of natives in the street. But it was not before half-past one that a sudden hubbub of voices called us from the house, to find the whole white colony already gathered on the spot as by concerted signal. The *Sans Souci* was overrun with rabble, the stair and verandah thronged. From all these throats an inarticulate babbling cry went up incessantly; it sounded like the bleating of young lambs, but angrier. In the road his royal highness (whom I had seen so lately in the part of butler) stood crying upon Tom; on the top step, tossed in the hurly-burly, Tom was shouting to the prince. Yet a while the pack swayed about the bar, vociferous. Then came a brutal impulse; the mob reeled, and returned and was rejected; the stair showed a stream of heads; and there shot into view, through the disbanding ranks, three men violently dragging in their midst a fourth. By his hair and his hands, his head forced as low as his knees, his face concealed, he was wrenched from the verandah and whisked along the road into the village, howling as he disappeared. Had his face been raised, we should have seen it bloodied, and the blood was not his own. The courtier with the turban of frizzed hair had paid the costs of this disturbance with the lower part of one ear.

So the brawl passed with no other casualty than might seem comic to the inhumane. Yet we looked round on serious faces and—a fact that spoke volumes—Tom was putting up the shutters on the bar. Custom might go elsewhither, Mr Williams might profit as he pleased, but Tom had had enough of bar-keeping for that day. Indeed the event had hung on a hair. A man had sought to draw a revolver—on what quarrel I could never learn, and perhaps he himself could not have told; one shot, when the room was so crowded, could scarce have failed to take effect; where many were armed and all tipsy, it could scarce have failed to draw others; and the woman who spied the weapon and the man who seized it may very well have saved the white community.

The mob insensibly melted from the scene; and for the rest of the day our neighbourhood was left in peace and a good deal in solitude. But the tranquility was only local; *din* and *perandi* still flowed in other quarters; and we had one more sight of Gilbert Island violence. In the church, where we had wandered photographing, we were startled by a sudden piercing outcry. The scene, looking forth from the doors of that great hall of shadow, was unforgettable. The palms, the quaint and scattered houses, the flag of the island streaming from its tall staff, glowed with intolerable sunshine. In the midst two women rolled fighting on the grass. The combatants were the more easy to be distinguished, because the one was stripped to the *ridi* and the other wore a holoku[1] (sacque) of some lively colour. The first was uppermost, her teeth locked in her adversary's face, shaking her like a dog; the other impotently fought and scratched. So for a moment we saw them wallow and grapple there like vermin; then the mob closed and shut them in.

It was a serious question that night if we should sleep ashore. But we were travellers, folk that had come far in quest of the adventurous; on the first sign of an adventure it would have been a singular inconsistency to have withdrawn; and we sent on board instead for our revolvers. Mindful of Taahauku, Mr Rick, Mr Osbourne, and Mrs Stevenson held an assault of arms on the public highway, and fired at bottles to the admiration of the natives. Captain Reid of the *Equator* stayed on shore with us to be at hand in case of trouble, and we retired to bed at the accustomed hour, agreeably excited by the day's events. The night was exquisite, the silence enchanting; yet as I lay in my hammock looking on the strong moonshine and the quiescent palms, one ugly picture haunted me of the two women, the naked and the clad, locked in that hostile embrace. The harm done was probably not much, yet I could have looked on death and massacre with less revolt. The return to these primeval weapons, the vision of man's beastliness, of his ferality, shocked in me a deeper sense than that with which we count the cost of

1. A dress rather like a nightgown introduced after
   European contact in an effort to make Polynesian
   women cover themselves modestly.

battles. There are elements in our state and history which it is a pleasure to forget, which it is perhaps the better wisdom not to dwell on. Crime, pestilence, and death are in the day's work; the imagination readily accepts them. It instinctively rejects, on the contrary, whatever shall call up the image of our race upon its lowest terms, as the partner of beasts, beastly itself, dwelling pell-mell and hugger-mugger, hairy man with hairy woman, in the caves of old. And yet to be just to barbarous islanders we must not forget the slums and dens of our cities: I must not forget that I have passed dinnerward through Soho, and seen that which cured me of my dinner.

A TALE OF A TAPU. PART TWO

Tuesday, July 16.—It rained in the night, sudden and loud, in Gilbert Island fashion. Before the day, the crowing of a cock aroused me and I wandered in the compound and along the street. The squall was blown by, the moon shone with incomparable lustre, the air lay dead as in a room, and yet all the isle sounded as under a strong shower, the eaves thickly pattering, the lofty palms dripping at larger intervals and with a louder note. In this bold nocturnal light the interior of the houses lay inscrutable, one lump of blackness, save when the moon glinted under the roof, and made a belt of silver, and drew the slanting shadows of the pillars on the floor. Nowhere in all the town was any lamp or ember; not a creature stirred; I thought I was alone to be awake; but the police were faithful to their duty; secretly vigilant, keeping account of time; and a little later, the watchman struck slowly and repeatedly on the cathedral bell; four o'clock, the warning signal. It seemed strange that, in a town resigned to drunkenness and tumult, curfew and réveillé should still be sounded and still obeyed.

The day came, and brought little change. The place still lay silent; the people slept, the town slept. Even the few who were awake, mostly women and children, held their peace and kept within under the strong shadow of the thatch, where you must stop and peer to see them. Through the deserted streets, and past the sleeping houses, a deputation took its way at an early hour to the palace; the king was suddenly awakened, and must listen (probably with a headache) to unpalatable truths. Mrs Rick, being a sufficient mistress of that difficult tongue, was spokeswoman; she explained to the sick monarch that I was an intimate personal friend of Queen Victoria's; that immediately on my return I should make her a report upon Butaritari; and that if my house should have been again invaded by natives, a man-of-war would be despatched to make reprisals. It was scarce the fact—rather a just and necessary parable of the fact, corrected for latitude; and it certainly told upon the king. He was much affected; he had conceived the notion (he said) that I was a man of some importance, but not dreamed it was as bad as this; and the missionary house was tapu'd under a fine of fifty dollars.

So much was announced on the return of the deputation; not any more; and I gathered subsequently that much more had passed. The protection gained was welcome. It had been the most annoying and not the least alarming feature of the day before, that our house was periodically filled with tipsy natives, twenty or thirty at a time, begging drink, fingering our goods, hard to be dislodged, awkward to quarrel with. Queen Victoria's friend (who was soon promoted to be her son) was free from these intrusions. Not only my house, but my neighbourhood as well, was left in peace; even on our walks abroad we were guarded and prepared for; and, like great persons visiting a hospital, saw only the fair side. For the matter of a week we were thus suffered to go out and in and live in a fool's paradise, supposing the king to have kept his word, the tapu to be revived and the island once more sober.

Tuesday, July 23.—We dined under a bare trellis erected for the Fourth of July; and here we used to linger by lamplight over coffee and tobacco. In that climate evening approaches without sensible chill; the wind dies out before sunset; heaven glows a while and fades, and darkens into the blueness of the tropical night; swiftly and insensibly the shadows thicken, the stars multiply their number; you look around you and the day is gone. It was then that we would see our Chinaman draw near across the compound in a lurching sphere of light, divided by his shadows; and with the coming of the lamp the night closed about the table. The faces of the company, the spars of the trellis, stood out suddenly bright on a ground of blue and silver, faintly designed with palm-tops and the peaked roofs of houses. Here and there the gloss upon a leaf, or the fracture of a stone, returned an isolated sparkle. All else had vanished. We hung there, illuminated like a galaxy of stars *in vacuo*; we sat, manifest and blind, amid the general ambush of the darkness; and the islanders, passing with light footfalls and low voices in the sand of the road, lingered to observe us, unseen.

On Tuesday the dusk had fallen, the lamp had just been brought, when a missile struck the table with a rattling smack and rebounded past my ear. Three inches to one side and this page had never been written; for the thing travelled like a cannon ball. It was supposed at the time to be a nut, though even at the time I thought it seemed a small one and fell strangely.

Wednesday, July 24.—The dusk had fallen once more, and the lamp been just brought out, when the same business was repeated. And again the missile whistled past my ear. One nut I had been willing to accept; a second, I rejected utterly. A cocoa-nut does not come slinging along on a windless evening, making an angle of about fifteen degrees with the horizon; cocoa-nuts do not fall on successive nights at the same hour and spot; in both cases, besides, a specific moment seemed to have been chosen, that when the lamp was just carried out, a specific person threatened, and that the head of the family. I may have been right or wrong, but I believed I was the mark of some intimidation; believed the missile was a stone, aimed not to hit, but to frighten.

No idea makes a man more angry. I ran into the road, where the natives were as usual promenading in the dark; Maka joined me with a lantern; and I ran from one to another, glared in quite innocent faces, put useless questions, and proffered idle threats. Thence I carried my wrath (which was worthy the son of any queen in history) to the Ricks. They heard me with depression, assured me this trick of throwing a stone into a family dinner was not new; that it meant mischief, and was of a piece with the alarming disposition of the natives. And then the truth, so long concealed from us, came out. The king had broken his promise, he had defied the deputation; the tapu was still dormant, *The Land we Live in* still selling drink, and that quarter of the town disturbed and menaced by perpetual broils. But there was worse ahead: a feast was now preparing for the birthday of the little princess; and the tributary chiefs of Kuma and Little Makin were expected daily. Strong in a following of numerous and somewhat savage clansmen, each of these was believed, like a Douglas of old, to be of doubtful loyalty. Kuma (a little pot-bellied fellow) never visited the place, never entered the town, but sat on the beach on a mat, his gun across his knees, parading his mistrust and scorn; Karaiti of Makin, although he was more bold, was not supposed to be more friendly; and not only were these vassals jealous of the throne, but the followers on either side shared in the animosity. Brawls had already taken place; blows had passed which might at any moment be repaid in blood. Some of the strangers were already here and already drinking; if the debauch continued after the bulk of them had come, a collision, perhaps a revolution, was to be expected.

The sale of drink is in this group a measure of the jealousy of traders; one begins, the others are constrained to follow; and to him who has the most gin, and sells it the most recklessly, the lion's share of copra is assured. It is felt by all to be an extreme expedient, neither safe, decent, nor dignified. A trader on Tarawa,[1] heated by an eager rivalry, brought many cases of gin. He told me he sat afterwards day and night in his house till it was finished, not daring to arrest the sale, not venturing to go forth, the bush all round him filled with howling drunkards. At night, above all, when he was afraid to sleep, and heard shots and voices about him in the darkness, his remorse was black.

'My God!' he reflected, 'if I was to lose my life on such a wretched business!' Often and often, in the story of the Gilberts, this scene has been repeated; and the remorseful trader sat beside his lamp, longing for the day, listening

1. Tarawa. Also known as the Knox Islands, part of the Gilbert group.

with agony for the sound of murder, registering resolutions for the future. For the business is easy to begin, but hazardous to stop. The natives are in their way a just and law-abiding people, mindful of their debts, docile to the voice of their own institutions; when the tapu is re-enforced they will cease drinking; but the white who seeks to antedate the movement by refusing liquor does so at his peril.

Hence, in some degree, the anxiety and helplessness of Mr Rick. He and Tom, alarmed by the rabblement of the *Sans Souci*, had stopped the sale; they had done so without danger, because *The Land we Live in* still continued selling; it was claimed, besides, that they had been the first to begin. What step could be taken? Could Mr Rick visit Mr Muller (with whom he was not on terms) and address him thus: 'I was getting ahead of you, now you are getting ahead of me, and I ask you to forgo your profits. I got my place closed in safety, thanks to your continuing; but now I think you have continued long enough. I begin to be alarmed; and because I am afraid I ask you to confront a certain danger'? It was not to be thought of. Something else had to be found; and there was one person at one end of the town who was at least not interested in copra. There was little else to be said in favour of myself as an ambassador. I had arrived in the Wightman schooner, I was living in the Wightman compound, I was the daily associate of the Wightman coterie. It was egregious enough that I should now intrude unasked in the private affairs of Crawford's agent, and press upon him the sacrifice of his interests and the venture of his life. But bad as I might be, there was none better; since the affair of the stone I was, besides, sharp-set to be doing, the idea of a delicate interview attracted me, and I thought it policy to show myself abroad.

The night was very dark. There was service in the church, and the building glimmered through all its crevices like a dim Kirk Allowa'.[1] I saw few other lights, but was

1. Alloway in Ayrshire is the birthplace of Robert Burns.
   In Burns's famous poem 'Tam o'Shanter' Tam encounters 'warlocks and witches' in Alloway kirkyard during
   a drunken ride home.

indistinctly aware of many people stirring in the darkness, and a hum and splutter of low talk that sounded stealthy. I believe (in the old phrase) my beard was sometimes on my shoulder as I went. Muller's was but partly lighted, and quite silent, and the gate was fastened. I could by no means manage to undo the latch. No wonder, since I found it afterwards to be four or five feet long—a fortification in itself. As I still fumbled, a dog came on the inside and snuffed suspiciously at my hands, so that I was reduced to calling 'House ahoy!' Mr Muller came down and put his chin across the paling in the dark. 'Who is that?' said he, like one who has no mind to welcome strangers.

'My name is Stevenson,' said I.

'O, Mr Stevens! I didn't know you. Come inside.'

We stepped into the dark store, when I leaned upon the counter and against the wall. All the light came from the sleeping-room, where I saw his family being put to bed; it struck full in my face, but Mr Muller stood in shadow. No doubt he expected what was coming, and sought the advantage of position; but for a man who wished to persuade and had nothing to conceal, mine was the preferable.

'Look here,' I began, 'I hear you are selling to the natives.'

'Others have done that before me,' he returned pointedly.

'No doubt,' said I, 'and I have nothing to do with the past, but the future. I want you to promise you will handle these spirits carefully.'

'Now what is your motive in this?' he asked, and then, with a sneer, 'Are you afraid of your life?'

'That is nothing to the purpose,' I replied. 'I know, and you know, these spirits ought not to be used at all.'

'Tom and Mr Rick have sold them before.'

'I have nothing to do with Tom and Mr Rick. All I know is I have heard them both refuse.'

'No, I suppose you have nothing to do with them. Then you are just afraid of your life.'

'Come now,' I cried, being perhaps a little stung, 'you know in your heart I am asking a reasonable thing. I don't ask you to lose your profit—though I would prefer to see no spirits brought here, as you would—'

'I don't say I wouldn't. I didn't begin this,' he inter-jected.

'No, I don't suppose you did,' said I. 'And I don't ask you to lose; I ask you to give me your word, man to man, that you will make no native drunk.'

Up to now Mr Muller had maintained an attitude very trying to my temper; but he had maintained it with difficulty, his sentiment being all upon my side; and here he changed ground for the worse. 'It isn't me that sells,' said he.

'No, it's that nigger,' I agreed. 'But he's yours to buy and sell; you have your hand on the nape of his neck; and I ask you—I have my wife here—to use the authority you have.'

He hastily returned to his old ward. 'I don't deny I could if I wanted,' said he. 'But there's no danger, the natives are all quiet. You're just afraid of your life.'

I do not like to be called a coward, even by implication; and here I lost my temper and propounded an untimely ultimatum. 'You had better put it plain,' I cried. 'Do you mean to refuse me what I ask?'

'I don't want either to refuse it or grant it,' he replied.

'You'll find you have to do the one thing or the other, and right now!' I cried, and then, striking into a happier vein, 'Come,' said I, 'you're a better sort than that. I see what's wrong with you—you think I came from the opposite camp. I see the sort of man you are, and you know that what I ask is right.'

Again he changed ground. 'If the natives get any drink, it isn't safe to stop them,' he objected.

'I'll be answerable for the bar,' I said. 'We are three men and four revolvers; we'll come at a word, and hold the place against the village.'

'You don't know what you're talking about; it's too dangerous!' he cried.

'Look here,' said I, 'I don't mind much about losing that life you talk so much of; but I mean to lose it the way I want to, and that is, putting a stop to all this beastliness.'

He talked a while about his duty to the firm; I minded not at all, I was secure of victory. He was but waiting to capitulate, and looked about for any potent to relieve the strain. In the gush of light from the bedroom door I spied a cigar-holder on the desk. 'That is well coloured,' said I.

'Will you take a cigar?' said he.

I took it and held it up unlighted. 'Now,' said I, 'you promise me.'

'I promise you you won't have any trouble from natives that have drunk at my place,' he replied.

'That is all I ask,' said I, and showed it was not by immediately offering to try his stock.

So far as it was anyway critical our interview here ended. Mr Muller had thenceforth ceased to regard me as an emissary from his rivals, dropped his defensive attitude, and spoke as he believed. I could make out that he would already, had he dared, have stopped the sale himself. Not quite daring, it may be imagined how he resented the idea of interference from those who had (by his own statement) first led him on, then deserted him in the breach, and now (sitting themselves in safety) egged him on to a new peril, which was all gain to them, all loss to him. I asked him what he thought of the danger from the feast.

'I think worse of it than any of you,' he answered. 'They were shooting around here last night, and I heard the balls too. I said to myself, "That's bad." What gets me is why you should be making this row up at your end. I should be the first to go.'

It was a thoughtless wonder. The consolation of being second is not great; the fact, not the order of going—there was our concern.

Scott talks moderately of looking forward to a time of fighting 'with a feeling that resembled pleasure'. The resemblance seems rather an identity. In modern life, contact is ended; man grows impatient of endless manoeuvres; and to approach the fact, to find ourselves where we can push our advantage home, and stand a fair risk, and see at last what we are made of, stirs the blood. It was so at least with all my family, who bubbled with delight at the approach of trouble; and we sat deep into the night like a pack of schoolboys, preparing the revolvers and arranging plans against the morrow. It promised certainly to be a busy and eventful day. The Old Men were to be summoned to confront me on the question of the tapu; Muller might call us at any moment to garrison his bar; and suppose Muller to fail, we decided in a family council to take that matter into our own hands, *The Land we Live in* at the pistol's mouth, and with the polysyllabic Williams, dance to a new tune. As I recall our humour, I think it would have gone hard with the mulatto.

Wednesday, July 24.—It was as well, and yet it was disappointing that these thunder-clouds rolled off in silence. Whether the Old Men recoiled from an interview with Queen Victoria's son, whether Muller had secretly intervened, or whether the step flowed naturally from the fears of the king and the nearness of the feast, the tapu was early that morning re-enforced; not a day too soon, from the manner the boats began to arrive thickly, and the town was filled with the big rowdy vassals of Karaiti.

The effect lingered for some time on the minds of the traders; it was with the approval of all present that I helped to draw up a petition to the United States, praying for a law against the liquor trade in the Gilberts; and it was at this request that I added, under my own name, a brief testimony of what had passed;—useless pains; since the whole reposes, probably unread and possibly unopened, in a pigeon-hole at Washington.

Sunday, July 28.—This day we had the afterpiece of the debauch. The king and queen, in European clothes, and followed by armed guards, attended church for the first time, and sat perched aloft in a precarious dignity under the barrel-hoops. Before sermon his majesty clambered from the dais, stood lopsidedly upon the gravel floor, and in a few words abjured drinking. The queen followed suit with a yet briefer allocution. All the men in church were next addressed in turn; each held up his right hand, and the affair was over—throne and church were reconciled.

from The Gilberts

HUSBAND AND WIFE

The trader accustomed to the manners of Eastern Polynesia has a lesson to learn among the Gilberts. The *ridi* is but a spare attire; as late as thirty years back the women went naked until marriage; within ten years the custom lingered; and these facts, above all when heard in description, conveyed a very false idea of the manners of the group. A very intelligent missionary described it (in its former state) as a 'Paradise of naked women' for the resident whites. It was at least a platonic Paradise, where Lothario ventured at his peril. Since 1860, fourteen whites have perished on a single island, all for the same cause, all found where they had no business, and speared by some indignant father of a family; the figure was given me by one of their contemporaries who had been more prudent and survived. The strange persistence of these fourteen martyrs might seem to point to monomania or a series of romantic passions; gin is the more likely key. The poor buzzards sat alone in their houses by an open case; they drank; their brain was fired; they stumbled towards the nearest houses on chance; and the dart went through their liver. In place of a Paradise the trader found an archipelago of fierce husbands and of virtuous women. 'Of course if you wish to make love to them, it's the same as anywhere else,' observed a trader innocently; but he and his companions rarely so choose.

The trader must be credited with a virtue; he often makes a kind and loyal husband. Some of the worst beachcombers in the Pacific, some of the last of the old school, have fallen in my path, and some of them were admirable to their native wives, and one made a despairing widower. The position of a trader's wife in the Gilberts is, besides, unusually enviable. She shares the immunities of her husband. Curfew in Butaritari sounds for her in vain. Long after the bell is rung and the great island ladies are confined for the night to their own roof, this chartered libertine may scamper and giggle through the deserted streets or go down to bathe in the dark. The resources of the store are at her hand; she goes arrayed like a queen, and feasts delicately every day upon tinned meats. And she who was perhaps of no regard or station among natives sits with captains, and is entertained on board of schooners. Five of these privileged dames were some time our neighbours. Four were handsome skittish lasses, gamesome like children, and like children liable to fits of pouting. They wore dresses by day, but there was a tendency after dark to strip these lendings and to career and squall about the compound in the aboriginal *ridi*. Games of cards were continually played, with shells for counters; their course was much marred by cheating; and the end of a round (above all if a man was of the party) resolved itself into a scrimmage for the counters. The fifth was a matron. It was a picture to see her sail to church on a Sunday, a parasol in hand, a nursemaid following, and the baby buried in a trade hat and armed with a patent feeding-bottle. The service was enlivened by her continual supervision and correction of the maid. It was impossible not to fancy the baby was a doll, and the church some European playroom. All these women were legitimately married. It is true that the certificate of one, when she proudly showed it, proved to run thus, that she was 'married for one night', and her gracious partner was at liberty to 'send her to hell' the next morning; but she was none the wiser or the worse for the dastardly trick. Another, I heard, was married on a work of mine in a pirated edition; it answered the purpose as well as a Hall Bible. Notwithstanding all these allurements of social distinction, rare food and raiment, a comparative vacation from toil, and legitimate marriage contracted on a pirated edition, the trader must sometimes seek long before he can be mated. While I was in the group one had been eight months on the quest, and he was still a bachelor.

Within strictly native society the old laws and practices were harsh, but not without a certain stamp of high-mindedness. Stealthy adultery was punished with death; open elopement was properly considered virtue in comparison, and compounded for a fine in land. The male adulterer alone seems to have been punished. It is correct manners for a jealous man to hang himself; a jealous woman had a different remedy—she bites her rival. Ten or twenty years ago it was a capital offence to raise a woman's *ridi*; to this day it is still punished with a heavy fine; and the garment itself is still symbolically sacred. Suppose a piece of land to be disputed in Butaritari, the claimant who shall first hang a *ridi* on the tapu-post has gained his cause, since no one can remove or touch it but himself.

The *ridi* was the badge not of the woman but the wife, the mark not of her sex but of her station. It was the collar on the slave's neck, the brand on merchandise. The adulterous woman seems to have been spared; were the husband offended, it would be a poor consolation to send his draught cattle to the shambles. Karaiti, to this day, calls his eight wives 'his horses', some trader having explained to him the employment of these animals on farms; and Nanteitei hired out his wives to do mason-work. Husbands, at least when of high rank, had the power of life and death; even whites seem to have possessed it; and their wives, when they had trangressed beyond forgiveness, made haste to pronounce the formula of deprecation—*I Kana Kim*. This form of words had so much virtue that a condemned criminal, repeating it on a particular day to the king who had condemned him, must be instantly released. It is an offer of abasement, and, strangely enough, the reverse—the imitation—is a common vulgar insult in Great Britain to this day. I give a scene between a trader and his Gilbert Island wife, as it was told me by the husband, now one of the oldest residents, but then a freshman in the group.

'Go and light a fire,' said the trader, 'and when I have brought this oil I will cook some fish.'

The woman grunted at him, island fashion.

'I am not a pig that you should grunt at me,' said he.

'I know you are not a pig,' said the woman, 'neither am I your slave.'

'To be sure you are not my slave, and if you do not care to

stop with me, you had better go home to your people,' said
he. 'But in the meantime go and light the fire; and when I
have brought this oil I will cook some fish.'

She went as if to obey; and presently when the trader
looked she had built a fire so big that the cook-house was
catching in flames.

'*I Kana Kim!*' she cried, as she saw him coming; but he
recked not, and hit her with a cooking-pot. The leg pierced
her skull, blood spouted, it was thought she was a dead
woman, and the natives surrounded the house in a
menacing expectation. Another white was present, a man of
older experience. 'You will have us both killed if you go on
like this,' he cried. 'She had said *I Kana Kim!*' If she had
not said *I Kana Kim* he might have struck her with a
caldron. It was not the blow that made the crime, but the
disregard of an accepted formula.

Polygamy, the particular sacredness of wives, their semi-
servile state, their seclusion in kings' harems, even their
privilege of biting, all would seem to indicate a Moham-
medan society and the opinion of the soullessness of
woman. And not so in the least. It is a mere appearance.
After you have studied these extremes in one house, you
may go to the next and find all reversed, the woman the
mistress, the man only the first of her thralls. The authority
is not with the husband as such, nor the wife as such. It
resides in the chief or the chief-woman; in him or her who
had inherited the lands of the clan, and stands to the
clansman in the place of parent, exacting their service,
answerable for their fines. There is but the one source of
power and the one ground of dignity—rank. The king
married a chief-woman; she became his menial, and must
work with her hands on Messrs Wightman's pier. The king
divorced her; she regained at once her former state and
power. She married the Hawaiian sailor, and behold the
man is her flunkey and can be shown the door at pleasure.
Nay, and such low-born lords are even corrected physically,
and, like grown but dutiful children, must endure the
discipline.

We were intimate in one such household, that of Nei
Takauti and Nan Tok'; I put the lady first of necessity.

During one week of fool's paradise, Mrs Stevenson had gone alone to the sea-side of the island after shells. I am very sure the proceeding was unsafe; and she soon perceived a man and woman watching her. Do what she would, her guardians held her steadily in view; and when the afternoon began to fall, and they thought she had stayed long enough, took her in charge, and by signs and broken English ordered her home. On the way the lady drew from her earring-hole a clay-pipe, the husband lighted it, and it was handed to my unfortunate wife, who knew not how to refuse the incommodious favour; and when they were all come to our house, the pair sat down beside her on the floor, and improved the occasion with prayer. From that day they were our family friends; bringing thrice a day the beautiful island garlands of white flowers, visiting us any evening, and frequently carrying us down to their own maniap' in return, the woman leading Mrs Stevenson by the hand like one child with another.

Nan Tok', the husband, was young, extremely hand-some, of the most approved good humour, and suffering in his precarious station from suppressed high spirits. Nei Takauti, the wife, was getting old; her grown son by a former marriage had just hanged himself before his mother's eyes in despair at a well-merited rebuke. Perhaps she had never been beautiful, but her face was full of character, her eye of sombre fire. She was a high chief-woman, but by a strange exception for a person of her rank, was small, spare, and sinewy, with lean small hands and corded neck. Her full dress of an evening was invariably a white chemise— and for adornment, green leaves (or sometimes white blossoms) stuck in her hair and thrust through her huge earring-holes. The husband on the contrary changed to view like a kaleidoscope. Whatever pretty thing my wife might have given to Nei Takauti—a string of beads, a ribbon, a piece of bright fabric—appeared the next evening on the person of Nan Tok'. It was plain he was a clothes-horse; that he wore livery; that, in a word, he was his wife's wife. They reversed the parts indeed, down to the least particular; it was the husband who showed himself the ministering angel in the hour of pain, while the wife displayed the apathy and heartlessness of the proverbial man.

When Nei Takauti had a headache Nan Tok' was full of attention and concern. When the husband had a cold and a racking toothache the wife heeded not, except to jeer. It is always the woman's part to fill and light the pipe; Nei Takauti handed hers in silence to the wedded page; but she carried it herself, as though the page were not entirely trusted. Thus she kept the money, but it was he who ran the errands, anxiously sedulous. A cloud on her face dimmed instantly his beaming looks; on an early visit to their maniap' my wife saw he had cause to be wary. Nan Tok' had a friend with him, a giddy young thing, of his own age and sex; and they had worked themselves into that stage of jocularity when consequences are too often disregarded. Nei Takauti mentioned her own name. Instantly Nan Tok' held up two fingers, his friend did likewise, both in an ecstasy of slyness. It was plain the lady had two names; and from the nature of their merriment, and the wrath that gathered on her brow, there must be something ticklish in the second. The husband pronounced it; a well-directed cocoa-nut from the hand of his wife caught him on the side of the head, and the voices and the mirth of these indiscreet young gentlemen ceased for the day.

The people of Eastern Polynesia are never at a loss; their etiquette is absolute and plenary; in every circumstance it tells them what to do and how to do it. The Gilbertines are seemingly more free, and pay for their freedom (like ourselves) in frequent perplexity. This was often the case with the topsy-turvy couple. We had once supplied them during a visit with a pipe and tobacco; and when they had smoked and were about to leave; they found themselves confronted with a problem; should they take or leave what remained of the tobacco. The piece of plug was taken up, it was laid down again, it was handed back and forth, and argued over, till the wife began to look haggard and the husband elderly. They ended by taking it, and I wager were not yet clear of the compound before they were sure they had decided wrong. Another time they had been given each a liberal cup of coffee, and Nan Tok' with difficulty and disaffection made an end of his. Nei Takauti had taken some, she had no mind for more, plainly conceived it would be a breach of manners to set down the cup unfinished, and ordered her wedded retainer to dispose of what was left. 'I have swallowed all I can, I cannot swallow more, it is a physical impossibility,' he seemed to say; and his stern officer reiterated her commands with secret imperative signals. Luckless dog! but in mere humanity we came to the rescue and removed the cup.

I cannot but smile over this funny household; yet I remember the good souls with affection and respect. Their attention to ourselves was surprising. The garlands are much esteemed, the blossooms must be sought far and wide; and though they had many retainers to call to their aid, we often saw themselves passing afield after the blossoms, and the wife engaged with her own hands in putting them together. It was no want of heart, only that disregard so incident to husbands, that made Nei Takauti despise the sufferings of Nan Tok'. When my wife was unwell she proved a diligent and kindly nurse; and the pair, to the extreme embarrassment of the sufferer, became fixtures in the sick-room. This rugged, capable, imperious old dame, with the wild eyes, had deep and tender qualities: her pride in her young husband it seemed that she dissembled, fearing possibly to spoil him; and when she spoke of her dead son there came something tragic in her face. But I seemed to trace in the Gilbertines a virility of sense and sentiment which distinguishes them (like their harsh and uncouth language) from their brother islanders in the east.

Fiction

Throughout his time in the Pacific Stevenson was writing fiction, both short stories and full-length novels. Of the three stories included here 'The Bottle Imp' was probably written first, during Stevenson's first stay in Samoa in December 1889 and January 1890. It was published in instalments in the New York *Herald* in February 1891, and in *Black and White* (London) in March and April. 'The Isle of Voices' was written in the autumn of 1892 and published in the *National Observer* in February 1893. *The Beach of Falesá* was begun in November 1890, but most of it was written during the following September. It was published in the *Illustrated London News* in six instalments in July and August 1892, but Stevenson was put under pressure to make a number of alterations. The editor felt changes were needed to render the story more palatable to his readers. Stevenson was extremely unhappy about this, and referred to the published version as 'slashed and gaping ruins'.[1]

Thanks to the researches of Professor Barry Menikoff the full extent of the changes forced on the manuscript are now known, and reproduced here is Stevenson's original text. All three stories appeared in *Island Nights' Entertainments* (1893) although Stevenson would have preferred to keep the two stories 'The Bottle Imp' and 'The Isle of Voices', written for a Polynesian audience, separate from *The Beach of Falesá*. I have brought them together here as they are equally the products of Stevenson's sympathetic interest in all aspects of the South Seas. The text of 'The Bottle Imp' and 'The Isle of Voices' is taken from the first collected edition of Stevenson's work, the Edinburgh Edition, which was in preparation at the time of his death.

1. Letter to J. M. Barrie, *Letters* ed. Sidney Colvin,
   vol iv, p.257

THE BOTTLE IMP

There was a man of the Island of Hawaii, whom I shall call
Keawe; for the truth is, he still lives, and his name must be
kept secret; but the place of his birth was not far from
Honaunau, where the bones of Keawe the Great lie hidden in
a cave. This man was poor, brave, and active; he could read
and write like a schoolmaster; he was a first-rate mariner
besides, sailed for some time in the island steamers, and
steered a whaleboat on the Hamakua coast. At length it came
in Keawe's mind to have a sight of the great world and
foreign cities, and he shipped on a vessel bound to San
Francisco.

This is a fine town, with a fine harbour, and rich people
uncountable; and, in particular, there is one hill which is
covered with palaces. Upon this hill Keawe was one day
taking a walk with his pocket full of money, viewing the
great houses upon either hand with pleasure. 'What fine
houses these are!' he was thinking, 'and how happy must
those people be who dwell in them, and take no care for the
morrow!' The thought was in his mind when he came
abreast of a house that was smaller than some others, but all
finished and beautified like a toy; the steps of that house
shone like silver, and the borders of the garden bloomed

NOTE: Any student of that very unliterary product, the
English drama of the early part of the century, will here
recognise the name and the root idea of a piece once
rendered popular by the redoubtable O. Smith. The
root idea is there, and identical, and yet I hope I have
made it a new thing. And the fact that the tale has been
designed and written for a Polynesian audience may
lend it some extraneous interest nearer home.   R.L.S.

like garlands, and the windows were bright like diamonds; and Keawe stopped and wondered at the excellence of all he saw. So stopping, he was aware of a man that looked forth upon him through a window so clear that Keawe could see him as you see a fish in a pool upon the reef. The man was elderly, with a bald head and a black beard; and his face was heavy with sorrow, and he bitterly sighed. And the truth of it is, that as Keawe looked in upon the man, and the man looked out upon Keawe, each envied the other.

All of a sudden the man smiled and nodded, and beckoned Keawe to enter, and met him at the door of the house.

'This is a fine house of mine,' said the man, and bitterly sighed. 'Would you not care to view the chambers?'

So he led Keawe all over it, from the cellar to the roof, and there was nothing there that was not perfect of its kind, and Keawe was astonished.

'Truly,' said Keawe, 'this is a beautiful house; if I lived in the like of it I should be laughing all day long. How comes it, then, that you should be sighing?'

'There is no reason,' said the man, 'why you should not have a house in all points similar to this, and finer, if you wish. You have some money, I suppose?'

'I have fifty dollars,' said Keawe; 'but a house like this will cost more than fifty dollars.'

The man made a computation. 'I am sorry you have no more,' said he, 'for it may raise you trouble in the future; but it shall be yours at fifty dollars.'

'The house?' asked Keawe.

'No, not the house,' replied the man; 'but the bottle. For I must tell you, although I appear to you so rich and fortunate, all my fortune, and this house itself and its garden, came out of a bottle not much bigger than a pint. This is it.'

And he opened a lockfast place, and took out a round-bellied bottle with a long neck; the glass of it was white like milk, with changing rainbow colours in the grain. Within-sides something obscurely moved, like a shadow and a fire.

'This is the bottle,' said the man; and, when Keawe laughed, 'You do not believe me?' he added. 'Try, then, for yourself. See if you can break it.'

So Keawe took the bottle up and dashed it on the floor till he was weary; but it jumped on the floor like a child's ball, and was not injured.

'This is a strange thing,' said Keawe. 'For by the touch of it, as well as by the look, the bottle should be of glass.'

'Of glass it is,' replied the man, sighing more heavily than ever; 'but the glass of it was tempered in the flames of hell. An imp lives in it, and that is the shadow we behold there moving; or so I suppose. If any man buy this bottle the imp is at his command; all that he desires—love, fame, money, houses like this house, ay, or a city like this city—all are his at the word uttered. Napoleon had this bottle, and by it he grew to be the king of the world; but he sold it at last, and fell. Captain Cook had this bottle, and by it he found his way to so many islands; but he, too, sold it, and was slain upon Hawaii. For, once it is sold, the power goes and the protection; and unless a man remain content with what he has, ill will befall him.'

'And yet you talk of selling it yourself?' Keawe said.

'I have all I wish, and I am growing elderly,' replied the man. 'There is one thing the imp cannot do—he cannot prolong life; and, it would not be fair to conceal from you, there is a drawback to the bottle; for if a man die before he sells it, he must burn in hell for ever.'

'To be sure, that is a drawback and no mistake,' cried Keawe. 'I would not meddle with the thing. I can do without a house, thank God; but there is one thing I could not be doing with one particle, and that is to be damned.'

'Dear me, you must not run away with things,' returned the man. 'All you have to do is to use the power of the imp in moderation, and then sell it to someone else, as I do to you, and finish your life in comfort.'

'Well, I observe two things,' said Keawe. 'All the time you keep sighing like a maid in love, that is one; and, for the other, you sell this bottle very cheap.'

'I have told you already why I sigh,' said the man. 'It is because I fear my health is breaking up; and, as you said yourself, to die and go to the devil is a pity for any one. As for why I sell so cheap, I must explain to you there is a peculiarity about the bottle. Long ago, when the devil brought it first upon earth, it was extremely expensive, and was sold first of all to Prester John[1] for many millions of dollars; but it cannot be sold at all, unless sold at a loss. If you sell it for as much as you paid for it, back it comes to you again like a homing pigeon. It follows that the price has kept falling in these centuries, and the bottle is now remarkably cheap. I bought it myself from one of my great neighbours on this hill, and the price I paid was only ninety dollars. I could sell it for as high as eighty-nine dollars and ninety-nine cents, but not a penny dearer, or back the thing must come to me. Now, about this there are two bothers. First, when you offer a bottle so singular for eighty odd dollars, people do not suppose you to be jesting. And second—but there is no hurry about that—and I need not go into it. Only remember it must be coined money that you sell it for.'

'How am I to know that this is all true?' asked Keawe.

'Some of it you can try at once,' replied the man. 'Give me your fifty dollars, take the bottle, and wish your fifty dollars back into your pocket. If that does not happen, I pledge you my honour I will cry off the bargain and restore your money.'

'You are not deceiving me?' said Keawe.

The man bound himself with a great oath.

'Well, I will risk that much,' said Keawe, 'for that can do no harm.' And he paid over his money to the man, and the man handed him the bottle.

'Imp of the bottle,' said Keawe, 'I want my fifty dollars back.' And sure enough he had scarce said the word before his pocket was as heavy as ever.

'To be sure this is a wonderful bottle,' said Keawe.

'And now good-morning to you, my fine fellow, and the devil go with you for me!' said the man.

'Hold on,' said Keawe, 'I don't want any more of this fun. Here, take your bottle back.'

'You have bought it for less than I paid for it,' replied the man, rubbing his hands. 'It is yours now; and, for my part, I am only concerned to see the back of you.' And with that he

1. Legendary Christian ruler in the East. The legend had its origins in the eleventh and twelfth centuries. Later, Prester John was associated with Ethiopia.

rang for his Chinese servant, and had Keawe shown out of the house.

Now, when Keawe was in the street, with the bottle under his arm, he began to think. 'If all is true about this bottle, I may have made a losing bargain,' thinks he. 'But perhaps the man was only fooling me.' The first thing he did was to count his money; the sum was exact—forty-nine dollars American money, and one Chili piece. 'That looks like the truth,' said Keawe. 'Now I will try another part.'

The streets in that part of the city were as clean as a ship's decks, and though it was noon, there were no passengers. Keawe set the bottle in the gutter and walked away. Twice he looked back, and there was the milky round-bellied bottle where he left it. A third time he looked back, and turned a corner; but he had scarce done so, when something knocked upon his elbow, and behold! it was the long neck sticking up; and as for the round belly, it was jammed into the pocket of his pilotcoat.

'And that looks like the truth', said Keawe.

The next thing he did was to buy a corkscrew in a shop, and go apart into a secret place in the fields. And there he tried to draw the cork, but as often as he put the screw in, out it came again, and the cork as whole as ever.

'This is some new sort of cork,' said Keawe, and all at once he began to shake and sweat, for he was afraid of that bottle.

On his way back to the port-side he saw a shop where a man sold shells and clubs from the wild islands, old heathen deities, old coined money, pictures from China and Japan, and all manner of things that sailors bring in their sea-chests. And here he had an idea. So he went in and offered the bottle for a hundred dollars. The man of the shop laughed at him at the first, and offered him five; but, indeed, it was a curious bottle—such glass was never blown in any human glassworks, so prettily the colours shone under the milky white, and so strangely the shadow hovered in the midst; so, after he had disputed a while after the manner of his kind, the shopman gave Keawe sixty silver dollars for the thing, and set it on a shelf in the midst of his window.'

'Now,' said Keawe, 'I have sold that for sixty which I bought for fifty—or, to say truth, a little less, because one of my dollars was from Chili. Now I shall know the truth upon another point.'

So he went back on board his ship, and, when he opened his chest, there was the bottle, and had come more quickly than himself. Now Keawe had a mate on board whose name was Lopaka.

'What ails you?' said Lopaka, 'that you stare in your chest?'

They were alone in the ship's forecastle, and Keawe bound him to secrecy, and told all.

'This is a very strange affair,' said Lopaka; 'and I fear you will be in trouble about this bottle. But there is one point very clear—that you are sure of the trouble, and you had better have the profit in the bargain. Make up your mind what you want with it; give the order, and if it is done as you desire, I will buy the bottle myself; for I have an idea of my own to get a schooner, and go trading through the islands.'

'That is not my idea,' said Keawe; 'but to have a beautiful house and garden on the Kona Coast, where I was born, the sun shining in at the door, flowers in the garden, glass in the windows, pictures on the walls, and toys and fine carpets on the tables, for all the world like the house I was in this day—only a story higher, and with balconies all about like the King's palace; and to live there without care and make merry with my friends and relatives.'

'Well,' said Lopaka, 'let us carry it back with us to Hawaii; and if all comes true, as you suppose, I will buy the bottle, as I said, and ask a schooner.'

Upon that they were agreed, and it was not long before the ship returned to Honolulu, carrying Keawe and Lopaka, and the bottle. They were scarce come ashore when they met a friend upon the beach, who began at once to condole with Keawe.

'I do not know what I am to be condoled about,' said Keawe.

'Is it possible you have not heard,' said the friend, 'your uncle—that good old man—is dead, and your cousin—that beautiful boy—was drowned at sea?'

Keawe was filled with sorrow, and, beginning to weep and to lament, he forgot about the bottle. But Lopaka was thinking to himself, and presently, when Keawa's grief was a little abated, 'I have been thinking,' said Lopaka. 'Had not your uncle lands in Hawaii, in the district of Kaü?'

'No,' said Keawe, 'not in Kaü; they are on the mountain side—a little way south of Hookena.'

'These lands will now be yours?' asked Lopaka.

'And so they will,' says Keawe, and began again to lament for his relatives.

'No,' said Lopaka, 'do not lament at present. I have a thought in my mind. How if this should be the doing of the bottle? For here is the place ready for your house.'

'If this be so,' cried Keawe, 'it is a very ill way to serve me by killing my relatives. But it may be indeed; for it was in just such a station that I saw the house with my mind's eye.'

'The house, however, is not yet built,' said Lopaka.

'No, nor like to be!' said Keawa; 'for though my uncle has some coffee and ava[1] and bananas, it will not be more than will keep me in comfort; and the rest of that land is the black lava.'

'Let us go to the lawyer,' said Lopaka; 'I have still this idea in my mind.'

Now, when they came to the lawyer's, it appeared Keawe's uncle had grown monstrous rich in the last days, and there was a fund of money.

'And here is the money for the house!' cried Lopaka.

'If you are thinking of a new house,' said the lawyer, 'here is the card of a new architect, of whom they tell me great things.'

'Better and better!' cried Lopaka. 'Here is all made plain for us. Let us continue to obey orders.'

So they went to the architect, and he had drawings of houses on his table.

'You want something out of the way,' said the architect. 'How do you like this?' and he handed a drawing to Keawe.

Now, when Keawe set eyes on the drawing, he cried out aloud, for it was the picture of his thought exactly drawn.

'I am in for this house,' thought he. 'Little as I like the way

1. The palm-lily tree, which yields an intoxicating liquor.

it comes to me, I am in for it now, and I may as well take the good along with the evil.'

So he told the architect all that he wished, and how he would have that house furnished, and about the pictures on the wall and the knickknacks on the tables; and he asked the man plainly for how much he would undertake the whole affair.

The architect put many questions, and took his pen and made a computation; and when he had done he named the very sum that Keawe had inherited.

Lopaka and Keawe looked at one another and nodded.

'It is quite clear,' thought Keawe, 'that I am to have this house, whether or no. It comes from the devil, and I fear I will get little good by that; and of one thing I am sure, I will make no more wishes as long as I have this bottle. But with the house I am saddled, and I may as well take the good along with the evil.'

So he made his terms with the architect, and they signed a paper; and Keawe and Lopaka took ship again and sailed to Australia; for it was concluded between them they should not interfere at all, but leave the architect and the bottle imp to build and adorn that house at their own pleasure.

The voyage was a good voyage, only all the time Keawe was holding in his breath, for he had sworn he would utter no more wishes, and take no more favours from the devil. The time was up when they got back. The architect told them that the house was ready, and Keawe and Lopaka took a passage in the *Hall*, and went down Kona way to view the house, and see if all had been done fitly according to the thought that was in Keawe's mind.

Now, the house stood on the mountain side, visible to ships. Above, the forest ran up into the clouds of rain; below, the black lava fell in cliffs, where the kings of old lay buried. A garden bloomed about that house with every hue of flowers; and there was an orchard of papaia on the one hand and an orchard of bread-fruit on the other, and right in front, toward the sea, a ship's mast had been rigged up and bore a flag. As for the house, it was three stories high, with great chambers and broad balconies on each. The windows were of glass, so excellent that it was as clear as water and as bright as day. All manner of furniture adorned the chambers. Pictures hung upon the wall in golden frames: pictures of ships, and men fighting, and of the most beautiful women, and of singular places; nowhere in the world are there pictures of so bright a colour as those Keawe found hanging in his house. As for the knickknacks, they were extraordinary fine; chiming clocks and musical boxes filled with pictures, weapons of price from all quarters of the world, and the most elegant puzzles to entertain the leisure of a solitary man. And as no one would care to live in such chambers, only walk through and view them, the balconies were made so broad that a whole town might have lived upon them in delight; and Keawe knew not which to prefer, whether the back porch, where you got the land-breeze, and looked upon the orchards and the flowers, or the front balcony, where you could drink the wind of the sea, and look down the steep wall of the mountain and see the *Hall* going by once a week or so between Hookena and the hills of Pele, or the schooners plying up the coast for wood and ava and bananas.

When they had viewed all, Keawe and Lopaka sat on the porch.

'Well,' asked Lopaka, 'is it all as you designed?'

'Words cannot utter it,' said Keawe. 'It is better than I dreamed, and I am sick with satisfaction.'

'There is but one thing to consider,' said Lopaka; 'all this may be quite natural, and the bottle imp have nothing whatever to say to it. If I were to buy the bottle, and got no schooner after all, I should have put my hand in the fire for nothing. I gave you my word, I know; but yet I think you would not grudge me one more proof.'

'I have sworn I would take no more favours,' said Keawe. 'I have gone already deep enough.'

'This is no favour I am thinking of,' replied Lopaka. 'It is only to see the imp himself. There is nothing to be gained by that, and so nothing to be ashamed of; and yet, if I once saw him, I should be sure of the whole matter. So indulge me so far, and let me see the imp; and, after that, here is the money in my hand, and I will buy it.'

'There is only one thing I am afraid of,' said Keawe. 'The

imp may be very ugly to view: and if you once set eyes upon him you might be very undesirous of the bottle.'

'I am a man of my word,' said Lopaka. 'And here is the money betwixt us.'

'Very well,' replied Keave. 'I have a curiosity myself.— So, come, let us have one look at you, Mr Imp.'

Now as soon as that was said the imp looked out of the bottle, and in again, swift as a lizard; and there sat Keawe and Lopaka turned to stone. The night had quite come, before either found a thought to say or voice to say it with; and then Lopaka pushed the money over and took the bottle.

'I am a man of my word,' said he, 'and had need to be so, or I would not touch this bottle with my foot. Well, I shall get my schooner, and a dollar or two for my pocket; and then I will be rid of this devil as fast as I can. For to tell you the plain truth, the look of him has cast me down.'

'Lopaka,' said Keawe, 'do not you think any worse of me than you can help; I know it is night, and the roads bad, and the pass by the tombs an ill place to go by so late, but I declare since I have seen that little face, I cannot eat or sleep or pray till it is gone from me. I will give you a lantern, and a basket to put the bottle in, and any picture or fine thing in all my house that takes your fancy;—and be gone at once, and go sleep at Hookena with Nahinu.'

'Keawe,' said Lopaka, 'many a man would take this ill; above all, when I am doing you a turn so friendly as to keep my word and buy the bottle; and for that matter, the night, and the dark, and the way by the tombs, must be all tenfold more dangerous to a man with such a sin upon his conscience, and such a bottle under his arm. But for my part, I am so extremely terrified myself, I have not the heart to blame you. Here I go then; and I pray God you may be happy in your house, and I fortunate with my schooner, and both get to heaven in the end in spite of the devil and his bottle.'

So Lopaka went down the mountain; and Keawe stood in his front balcony, and listened to the clink of the horse's shoes, and wached the lantern go shining down the path, and along the cliff of caves where the old dead are buried; and all the time he trembled and clasped his hands, and prayed for his friend, and gave glory to God that he himself was escaped out of that trouble.

But the next day came very brightly, and that new house of his was so delightful to behold that he forgot his terrors. One day followed another, and Keawe dwelt there in perpetual joy. He had his place on the back porch; it was there he ate and lived, and read the stories in the Honolulu newspapers; but when any one came by they would go in and view the chambers and the pictures. And the fame of the house went far and wide; it was called *Ka-Hale Nui*—the Great House—in all Kona; and sometimes the Bright House, for Keawe kept a Chinaman, who was all day dusting and furbishing; and the glass and the gilt, and the fine stuffs, and the pictures, shone as bright as the morning. As for Keawe himself, he could not walk in the chambers without singing, his heart was so enlarged; and when ships sailed by upon the sea, he would fly his colours on the mast.

So time went by, until one day Keawe went upon a visit as far as Kailua to certain of his friends. There he was well feasted; and left as soon as he could the next morning, and rode hard, for he was impatient to behold his beautiful house; and, besides, the night then coming on was the night in which the dead of old days go abroad in the sides of Kona; and having already meddled with the devil, he was the more chary of meeting with the dead. A little beyond Honaunau, looking far ahead, he was aware of a woman bathing in the edge of the sea; and she seemed a well-grown girl, but he thought no more of it. Then he saw her white shift flutter as she put it on, and then her red holoku; and by the time he came abreast of her she was done with her toilet, and had come up from the sea, and stood by the track side in her red holoku, and she was all freshened with the bath, and her eyes shone and were kind. Now Keawe no sooner beheld her than he drew rein.

'I thought I knew every one in this country,' said he. 'How comes it that I do not know you?'

'I am Kokua, daughter of Kiano,' said the girl, 'and I have just returned from Oahu. Who are you?'

'I will tell you who I am in a little,' said Keawe, dismounting from his horse, 'but not now. For I have a thought in my mind, and if you knew who I was, you might have heard of me, and would not give me a true answer. But tell me, first of all, one thing: Are you married?'

At this Kokua laughed out aloud. 'It is you who ask questions,' she said. 'Are you married yourself?'

'Indeed, Kokau, I am not,' replied Keawe, 'and never thought to be until this hour. But here is the plain truth. I have met you here at the roadside, and I saw your eyes, which are like the stars, and my heart went to you as swift as a bird. And so now, if you want none of me, say so, and I will go on to my own place; but if you think me no worse than any other young man, say so, too, and I will turn aside to your father's for the night, and tomorrow I will talk with the good man.'

Kokua said never a word, but she looked at the sea and laughed.

'Kokua,' said Keawe, 'if you say nothing, I will take that for the good answer; so let us be stepping to your father's door.'

She went ahead of him, still without speech; only sometimes she glanced back and glanced away again, and she kept the strings of her hat in her mouth.

Now, when they had come to the door, Kiano came out on his verandah, and cried out and welcomed Keawe by name. At that the girl looked over, for the fame of the great house had come to her ears; and, to be sure, it was a great temptation. All that evening they were very merry together; and the girl was as bold as brass under the eyes of her parents, and made a mock of Keawe, for she had a quick wit. The next day he had a word with Kiano, and found the girl alone.

'Kokua', said he, 'you made a mock of me all the evening; and it is still time to bid me go. I would not tell you who I was, because I have so fine a house, and I feared you would think too much of that house, and too little of the man that loves you. Now you know all, and if you wish to have seen the last of me, say so at once.'

'No,' said Kokua; but this time she did not laugh, nor did Keawe ask for more.

This was the wooing of Keawe; things had gone quickly; but so an arrow goes, and the ball of a rifle swifter still, and yet both may strike the target. Things had gone fast, but they had gone far also, and the thought of Keawe rang in the maiden's head; she heard his voice in the breach of the surf upon the lava, and for this young man that she had seen but twice she would have left father and mother in her native islands. As for Keawe himself, his horse flew up the path of the mountain under the cliff of tombs, and the sound of the hoofs, and the sound of Keawe singing to himself for pleasure, echoed in the caverns of the dead. He came to the Bright House, and still he was singing. He sat and ate in the broad balcony, and the Chinaman wondered at his master, to hear how he sang between the mouthfuls. The sun went down into the sea, and the night came; and Keawe walked the balconies by lamplight, high on the mountains, and the voice of his singing startled men on ships.

'Here am I now upon my high place,' he said to himself. 'Life may be no better; this is the mountain top; and all shelves about me toward the worse. For the first time I will light up the chambers, and bathe in my fine bath with the hot water and the cold, and sleep alone in the bed of my bridal chamber.'

So the Chinaman had word, and he must rise from sleep and light the furnaces; and as he wrought below, beside the boilers, he heard his master singing and rejoicing above him in the lighted chambers. When the water began to be hot the Chinaman cried to his master; and Keawe went into the bathroom; and the Chinaman heard him sing as he filled the marble basin; and heard him sing, and the singing broken, as he undressed; until of a sudden the song ceased. The Chinaman listened, and listened; he called up the house to Keawe to ask if all were well, and Keawe answered him 'Yes', and bade him go to bed; but there was no more singing in the Bright House; and all night long the Chinaman heard his master's feet go round and round the balconies without repose.

Now the truth of it was this; as Keawe undressed for his bath, he spied upon his flesh a patch like a patch of lichen on a rock, and it was then that he stopped singing. For he knew the likeness of that patch, and knew that he was fallen in the Chinese Evil.*

Now, it is a sad thing for any man to fall into this sickness. And it would be a sad thing for any one to leave a house so beautiful and so commodious, and depart from all his friends to the north coast of Molokai between the mighty cliff and the sea-breakers. But what was that to the case of the man Keawe, he who had met his love but yesterday, and won her but that morning, and now saw all his hopes break, in a moment, like a piece of glass?

A while he sat upon the edge of the bath; then sprang, with a cry, and ran outside; and to and fro, to and fro, along the balcony, like one despairing.

'Very willingly could I leave Hawaii, the home of my fathers,' Keawe was thinking. 'Very lightly could I leave my house, the high-placed, the many-windowed, here upon the mountains. Very bravely could I go to Molokai, to Kalaupapa by the cliffs, to live with the smitten and to sleep there, far from my fathers. But what wrong have I done, what sin lies upon my soul, that I should have encountered Kokua coming cool from the seawater in the evening? Kokua, the soul-ensnarer! Kokua, the light of my life! Her may I never wed, her may I look upon no longer, her may I no more handle with my loving hand; and it is for this, it is for you, O Kokua! that I pour my lamentations!'

Now you are to observe what sort of man Keawe was, for he might have dwelt there in the Bright House for years, and no one been the wiser of his sickness; but he reckoned nothing of that, if he must lose Kokua. And again, he might have wed Kokua even as he was; and so many would have done, because they have the souls of pigs; but Keawe loved the maid manfully, and he would do her no hurt and bring her in no danger.

A little beyond the midst of the night, there came in his mind the recollection of the bottle. He went round to the back porch, and called to memory the day when the devil had looked forth; and at the thought ice ran in his veins.

'A dreadful thing is the bottle,' thought Keawe, 'and

* Leprosy [R.L.S.]

dreadful is the imp, and it is a dreadful thing to risk the flames of hell. But what other hope have I to cure my sickness or to wed Kokua? What!' he thought, 'would I beard the devil once, only to get me a house, and not face him again to win Kokua?'

Thereupon he called to mind it was the next day the *Hall* went by on her return to Honolulu. 'There must I go first,' he thought, 'and see Lopaka. For the best hope that I have now is to find that same bottle I was so pleased to be rid of.'

Never a wink could he sleep; the food stuck in his throat; but he sent a letter to Kiano, and, about the time when the steamer would be coming, rode down beside the cliff of the tombs. It rained; his horse went heavily; he looked up at the black mouths of the caves, and he envied the dead that slept there and were done with trouble; and called to mind how he had galloped by the day before, and was astonished. So he came down to Hookena, and there was all the country gathered for the steamer as usual. In the shed before the store they sat and jested and passed the news; but there was no matter of speech in Keawe's bosom, and he sat in their midst and looked without on the rain falling on the houses, and the surf beating among the rocks, and the sighs arose in his throat.

'Keawe of the Bright House is out of spirits,' said one to another. Indeed, and so he was, and little wonder.

Then the *Hall* came, and the whaleboat carried him on board. The after-part of the ship was full of Haoles,* who had been to visit the volcano, as their custom is; and the midst was crowded with Kanakas, and the forepart with wild bulls from Hilo and horses from Kaü; but Keawe sat apart from all in his sorrow, and watched for the house of Kiano. There it sat, low upon the shore in the black rocks, and shaded by the cocoa palms, and there by the door was a red holoku, no greater than a fly. and going to and from with a fly's busyness. 'Ah, queen of my heart,' he cried, 'I'll venture my dear soul to win you!'

Soon after, darkness fell, and the cabins were lit up, and the Haoles sat and played at the cards and drank whisky as

---

* Whites [R.L.S.]

their custom is; but Keawe walked the deck all night; and all the next day, as they steamed under the lee of Maui or of Molokai, he was still pacing to and fro like a wild animal in a menagerie.

Towards evening they passed Diamond Head, and came to the pier of Honolulu. Keawe stepped out among the crowd and began to ask for Lopaka. It seemed he had become the owner of a schooner—none better in the islands—and was gone upon an adventure as far as Pola-Pola or Kahiki; so there was no help to be looked for from Lopaka. Keawe called to mind a friend of his, a lawyer in the town (I must not tell his name), and inquired of him. They said he was grown suddenly rich, and had a fine new house upon Waikiki shore; and this put a thought in Keawe's head, and he called a hack and drove to the lawyer's house.

The house was all brand new, and the trees in the garden no greater than walking-sticks, and the lawyer, when he came, had the air of a man well pleased.

'What can I do to serve you?' said the lawyer.

'You are a friend of Lopaka's,' replied Keawe, 'and Lopaka purchased from me a certain piece of goods that I thought you might enable me to trace.'

The lawyer's face became very dark. 'I do not profess to misunderstand you, Mr Keawe,' said he, 'though this is an ugly business to be stirring in. You may be sure I know nothing, but yet I have a guess, and if you would apply in a certain quarter I think you might have news.'

And he named the name of a man, which, again, I had better not repeat. So it was for days, and Keawe went from one to another, finding everywhere new clothes and carriages, and fine new houses, and men everywhere in great contentment, although, to be sure, when he hinted at his business their faces would cloud over.

'No doubt I am upon the track,' thought Keawe. 'These new clothes and carriages are all the gifts of the little imp, and these glad faces are the faces of men who have taken their profit and got rid of the accursed thing in safety. When I see pale cheeks and hear sighing, I shall know I am near the bottle.'

So it befell at last that he was recommended to a Haole in

Beritania Street. When he came to the door, about the hour
of the evening meal, there were the usual marks of the new
house, and the young garden, and the electric light shining in
the windows; but when the owner came, a shock of hope and
fear ran through Keawe; for here was a young man, white as
a corpse, and black about the eyes, the hair shedding from
his head, and such a look in his countenance as a man may
have when he is waiting for the gallows.

'Here it is, to be sure,' thought Keawe, and so with this
man he noways veiled his errand. 'I am come to buy the
bottle,' said he.

At the word the young Haole of Beritania Street reeled
against the wall.

'The bottle!' he gasped. 'To buy the bottle!' Then he
seemed to choke, and seizing Keawe by the arm carried him
into a room and poured out wine in two glasses.

'Here is my respects,' said Keawe, who had been much
about with Haoles in his time. 'Yes,' he added, 'I am come to
buy the bottle. What is the price by now?'

At that word the young man let his glass slip through his
fingers, and looked upon Keawe like a ghost.

'The price,' says he; 'the price! You do not know the
price?'

'It is for that I am asking you,' returned Keawe. 'But why
are you so much concerned? Is there anything wrong about
the price?'

'It has dropped a great deal in value since your time, Mr
Keawe,' said the young man, stammering.

'Well, well, I shall have the less to pay for it,' says Keawe.
'How much did it cost you?'

The young man was as white as a sheet. 'Two cents,' said
he.

'What!' cried Keawe, 'two cents? Why, then, you can
only sell it for one. And he who buys it——' The words died
upon Keawe's tongue; he who bought it could never sell it
again, the bottle and the bottle imp must abide with him
until he died, and when he died must carry him to the red
end of hell.

The young man of Beritania Street fell upon his knees.
'For God's sake, buy it!' he cried. 'You can have all my

fortune in the bargain. I was mad when I bought it at that price. I had embezzled money at my store; I was lost else; I must have gone to jail.'

'Poor creature,' said Keawe, 'you would risk your soul upon so desperate an adventure, and to avoid the proper punishment of your own disgrace; and you think I could hesitate with love in front of me. Give me the bottle, and the change, which I make sure you have all ready. Here is a five-cent piece.'

It was as Keawe supposed; the young man had the change ready in a drawer; the bottle changed hands, and Keawe's fingers were no sooner clasped upon the stalk than he had breathed his wish to be a clean man. And, sure enough, when he got home to his room, and stripped himself before a glass, his flesh was whole like an infant's. And here was the strange thing: he had no sooner seen this miracle than his mind changed within him, and he cared naught for the Chinese Evil, and little enough for Kokua; and had but the one thought, that here he was bound to the bottle imp for time and for eternity, and had no better hope but to be a cinder for ever in the flames of hell. Away ahead of him he saw them blaze with his mind's eye, and his soul shrank, and darkness fell upon the light.

When Keawe came to himself a little, he was aware it was the night when the band played at the hotel. Thither he went, because he feared to be alone; and there, among happy faces, walked to and fro, and heard the tunes go up and down, and saw Berger beat the measure, and all the while he heard the flames crackle, and saw the red fire burning in the bottomless pit. Of a sudden the band played *Hiki-ao-ao*; that was a song that he had sung with Kokua, and at the strain courage returned to him.

'It is done now,' he thought, 'and once more let me take the good along with the evil.'

So it befell that he returned to Hawaii by the first steamer, and as soon as it could be managed he was wedded to Kokua, and carried her up the mountain side to the Bright House.

Now it was with these two, that when they were together, Keawe's heart was stilled; but so soon as he was alone he fell into a brooding horror, and heard the flames crackle, and saw the red fire burn in the bottomless pit. The girl, indeed, had come to him wholly; her heart leapt in her side at the sight of him, her hand clung to his; and she was so fashioned from the hair upon her head to the nails upon her toes that none could see her without joy. She was pleasant in her nature. She had the good word always. Full of song she was, and went to and fro in the Bright House, the brightest thing in its three stories, carolling like the birds. And Keawe beheld and heard her with delight, and then must shrink upon the side, and weep and groan to think upon the price that he had paid for her; and then he must dry his eyes, and wash his face, and go and sit with her on the broad balconies, joining in her songs, with a sick spirit, answering her smiles.

There came a day when her feet began to be heavy and her songs more rare; and now it was not Keawe only that would weep apart, but each would sunder from the other and sit in opposite balconies with the whole width of the Bright House betwixt. Keawe was so sunk in his despair he scarce observed the change, and was only glad he had more hours to sit alone and brood upon his destiny, and was not so frequently condemned to pull a smiling face on a sick heart. But one day, coming softly through the house, he heard the sound of a child sobbing, and there was Kokua rolling her face upon the balcony floor, and weeping like the lost.

'You do well to weep in this house, Kokua,' he said. 'And yet I would give the head off my body that you (at least) might have been happy.'

'Happy!' she cried. 'Keawe, when you lived alone in your Bright House you were the word of the island for a happy man; laughter and song were in your mouth, and your face was as bright as the sunrise. Then you wedded poor Kokua; and the good God knows what is amiss in her—but from that day you have not smiled. O!' she cried, 'what ails me? I thought I was pretty, and I knew I loved him. What ails me that I throw this cloud upon my husband?'

'Poor Kokua,' said Keawe. He sat down by her side, and sought to take her hand; but that she plucked away. 'Poor Kokua!' he said again. 'My poor child—my pretty. And I had thought all this while to spare you! Well, you shall know

all. Then, at least, you will pity poor Keawe; then you will
understand how much he loved you in the past—that he
dared hell for your possession—and how much he loves you
still (the poor condemned one), that he can yet call up a
smile when he beholds you.'

With that he told her all, even from the beginning.

'You have done this for me?' she cried. 'Ah, well, then
what do I care!'—and she clasped and wept upon him.

'Ah, child!' said Keawe, 'and yet, when I consider of the
fire of hell, I care a good deal!'

'Never tell me,' said she; 'no man can be lost because he
loved Kokua, and no other fault. I tell you, Keawe, I shall
save you with these hands, or perish in your company.
What! you loved me, and gave your soul, and you think I will
not die to save you in return?'

'Ah, my dear! you might die a hundred times, and what
difference would that make?' he cried, 'except to leave me
lonely till the time comes of my damnation?'

'You know nothing,' said she. 'I was educated in a school
in Honolulu; I am no common girl. And I tell you, I shall
save my lover. What is this you say about a cent? But all the
world is not American. In England they have a piece they call
a farthing, which is about half a cent. Ah! sorrow!' she cried,
'that makes it scarcely better, or the buyer must be lost, and
we shall find none so brave as my Keawe! But then, there is
France: they have a small coin there which they call a
centime, and these go five to the cent, or thereabout. We
could not do better. Come, Keawe, let us go to the French
islands; let us go to Tahiti as fast as ships can bear us. There
we have four centimes, three centimes, two centimes, one
centime; four possible sales to come and go on; and two of us
to push the bargain. Come, my Keawe! kiss me, and banish
care. Kokua will defend you.'

'Gift of God!' he cried. 'I cannot think that God will
punish me for desiring aught so good! Be it as you will, then;
take me where you please: I put my life and my salvation in
your hands.'

Early the next day Kokua was about her preparations. She
took Keawe's chest that he went with sailoring; and first she
put the bottle in a corner; and then packed it with the richest

of their clothes and the bravest of the knickknacks in the house. 'For,' said she, 'we must seem to be rich folks, or who will believe in the bottle?' All the time of her preparation she was as gay as a bird; only when she looked upon Keawe the tears would spring in her eye, and she must run and kiss him. As for Keawe, a weight was off his soul; now that he had his secret shared, and some hope in front of him, he seemed like a new man, his feet went lightly on the earth, and his breath was good to him again. Yet was terror still at his elbow; and ever and again, as the wind blows out a taper, hope died in him, and he saw the flames toss and the red fire burn in hell.

It was given out in the country they were gone pleasuring to the States, which was thought a strange thing, and yet not so strange as the truth, if any could have guessed it. So they went to Honolulu in the *Hall*, and thence in the *Umatilla* to San Francisco with a crowd of Haoles, and at San Francisco took their passage by the mail brigantine, the *Tropic Bird*, for Papeete, the chief place of the French in the south islands. Thither they came, after a pleasant voyage, on a fair day of the Trade Wind, and saw the reef with the surf breaking, and Motuiti with its palms, and the schooner riding within-side, and the white houses of the town low down along the shore among green trees, and overhead the mountains and the clouds of Tahiti, the wise island.

It was judged the most wise to hire a house, which they did accordingly, opposite the British Consul's, to make a great parade of money, and themselves conspicuous with carriages and horses. This it was easy to do, so long as they had the bottle in their possession; for Kokua was more bold than Keawe, and, whenever she had a mind, called on the imp for twenty or a hundred dollars. At this rate they soon grew to be remarked in the town; and the strangers from Hawaii, their riding and their driving, the fine holokus and the rich lace of Kokua, became the matter of much talk.

They got on well after the first with the Tahitian language, which is indeed like to the Hawaiian, with a change of certain letters; and as soon as they had any freedom of speech, began to push the bottle. You are to consider it was not an easy subject to introduce; it was not easy to persuade people you

were in earnest, when you offered to sell them for four
centimes the spring of health and riches inexhaustible. It was
necessary besides to explain the dangers of the bottle; and
either people disbelieved the whole thing and laughed, or
they thought the more of the darker part, became overcast
with gravity, and drew away from Keawe and Kokua, as
from persons who had dealings with the devil. So far from
gaining ground, these two began to find they were avoided in
the town; the children ran away from them screaming, a
thing intolerable to Kokua; Catholics crossed themselves as
they went by; and all persons began with one accord to
disengage themselves from their advances.

Depression fell upon their spirits. They would sit at night
in their new house, after a day's weariness, and not exchange
one word, or the silence would be broken by Kokua bursting
suddenly into sobs. Sometimes they would pray together;
sometimes they would have the bottle out upon the floor, and
sit all evening watching how the shadow hovered in the
midst. At such times they would be afraid to go to rest. It was
long ere slumber came to them, and, if either dozed off, it
would be to wake and find the other silently weeping in the
dark, or, perhaps, to wake alone, the other having fled from
the house and the neighbourhood of that bottle, and to pace
under the bananas in the little garden, or to wander on the
beach by moonlight.

One night it was so when Kokua awoke. Keawe was gone.
She felt in the bed, and his place was cold. Then fear fell
upon her, and she sat up in bed. A little moonshine filtered
throught the shutters. The room was bright, and she could
spy the bottle on the floor. Outside it blew high, the great
trees of the avenue cried aloud, and the fallen leaves rattled
in the verandah. In the midst of this Kokua, was aware of
another sound; whether of a beast or of a man she could
scarce tell, but it was as sad as death, and cut her to the soul.
Softly she arose, set the door ajar, and looked forth into the
moonlit yard. There, under the bananas, lay Keawe, his
mouth in the dust, and as he lay he moaned.

It was Kokua'a first thought to run forward and console
him; her second potently withheld her. Keawe had borne
himself before his wife like a brave man; it became her little

in the hour of weakness to intrude upon his shame. With the thought she drew back into the house.

'Heaven!' she thought, 'how careless have I been—how weak! It is he, not I, that stands in this eternal peril; it was he, not I, that took the curse upon his soul. It is for my sake, and for the love of a creature of so little worth and such poor help, that he now beholds so close to him the flames of hell—ay, and smells the smoke of it, lying without there in the wind and moonlight. Am I so dull of spirit that never till now I have surmised my duty, or have I seen it before and turned aside? But now, at least, I take up my soul in both the hands of my affection; now I say farewell to the white steps of heaven and the waiting faces of my friends. A love for a love, and let mine be equalled with Keawe's! A soul for a soul, and be it mine to perish!'

She was a deft woman with her hands, and was soon apparelled. She took in her hands the change—the precious centimes they kept ever at their side; for this coin is little used, and they had made provision at a Government office. When she was forth in the avenue clouds came on the wind, and the moon was blackened. The town slept, and she knew not whither to turn till she heard one coughing in the shadow of the trees.

'Old man,' said Kokua, 'what do you here abroad in the cold night?'

The old man could scarce express himself for coughing, but she made out that he was old and poor, and a stranger in the island.

'Will you do me a service?' said Kokua. 'As one stranger to another, and as an old man to a young woman, will you help a daughter of Hawaii?'

'Ah,' said the old man. 'So you are the witch from the Eight Islands, and even my old soul you seek to entangle. But I have heard of you, and defy your wickedness.'

'Sit down here,' said Kokua, 'and let me tell you a tale.' And she told him the story of Keawe from the beginning to the end.

'And now,' said she, 'I am his wife, whom he bought with his soul's welfare. And what should I do? If I went to him myself and offered to buy it, he would refuse. But if you go, he will sell it eagerly; I will await you here; you will buy it for four centimes, and I will buy it again for three. And the Lord strengthen a poor girl!'

'If you meant falsely,' said the old man, 'I think God would strike you dead.'

'He would!' cried Kokua. 'Be sure he would. I could not be so treacherous—God would not suffer it.'

'Give me the four centimes and await me here,' said the old man.

Now, when Kokua stood alone in the street, her spirit died. The wind roared in the trees, and it seemed to her the rushing of flames of hell; the shadows tossed in the light of the street lamp, and they seemed to her the snatching hands of evil ones. If she had had the strength, she must have run away, and if she had had the breath she must have screamed aloud; but in truth she could do neither, and stood and trembled in the avenue, like an affrighted child.

Then she saw the old man returning, and he had the bottle in his hand.

'I have done your bidding,' said he. 'I left your husband weeping like a child; tonight he will sleep easy.' And he held the bottle forth.

'Before you give it me,' Kokua panted, 'take the good with the evil—ask to be delivered from your cough.'

'I am an old man,' replied the other, 'and too near the gate of the grave to take a favour from the devil.—But what is this? Why do you not take the bottle? Do you hesitate?'

'Not hesitate!' cried Kokua. 'I am only weak. Give me a moment. It is my hand resists, my flesh shrinks back from the accursed thing. One moment only!'

The old man looked upon Kokua kindly. 'Poor child!' said he, 'you fear; your soul misgives you. Well, let me keep it. I am old, and can never more be happy in this world, and as for the next——'

'Give it me!' gasped Kokua. 'There is your money. Do you think I am so base as that? Give me the bottle.'

'God bless you, child,' said the old man.

Kokua concealed the bottle under her holoku, said farewell to the old man, and walked off along the avenue, she cared not whither. For all roads were now the same to her, and led equally to hell. Sometimes she walked, and sometimes ran; sometimes she screamed out loud in the night, and sometimes lay by the wayside in the dust and wept. All that she had heard of hell came back to her; she saw the flames blaze, and she smelt the smoke, and her flesh withered on the coals.

Near day she came to her mind again, and returned to the house. It was even as the old man said—Keawe slumbered like a child. Kokua stood and gazed upon his face.

'Now, my husband,' said she, 'it is your turn to sleep. When you wake it will be your turn to sing and laugh. But for poor Kokua, alas! that meant no evil—for poor Kokua, no more sleep, no more singing, no more delight, whether in earth or heaven.'

With that she lay down in the bed by his side, and her misery was so extreme that she fell in a deep slumber instantly.

Late in the morning her husband woke her and gave her the good news. It seemed he was silly with delight, for he paid no heed to her distress, ill though she dissembled it. The words stuck in her mouth, it mattered not; Keawe did the speaking. She ate not a bite, but who was to observe it? for Keawe cleared the dish. Kokua saw and heard him, like some strange thing in a dream; there were times when she forgot or doubted, and put her hands to her brow; to know herself doomed and hear her husband babble seemed so monstrous.

All the while Keawe was eating and talking, and planning the time of their return, and thanking her for saving him, and fondling her, and calling her the true helper after all. He laughed at the old man that was fool enough to buy that bottle.

'A worthy old man he seemed,' Keawe said. 'But no one can judge by appearances. For why did the old reprobate require the bottle?'

'My husband,' said Kokua humbly, 'his purpose may have been good.'

Keawe laughed like an angry man.

'Fiddle-de-dee!' cried Keawe. 'An old rogue, I tell you, and an old ass to boot. For the bottle was hard enough to sell at four centimes; and at three it will be quite impossible. The margin is not broad enough, the thing begins to smell of scorching——brrr!' said he, and shuddered. 'It is true I bought it myself at a cent, when I knew not there were smaller coins. I was a fool for my pains; there will never be found another: and whoever has that bottle now will carry it to the pit.'

'O my husband!' cried Kokua. 'Is it not a terrible thing to save oneself by the eternal ruin of another? It seems to me I could not laugh. I would be humbled. I would be filled with melancholy. I would pray for the poor holder.'

Then Keawe, because he felt the truth of what she said, grew the more angry. 'Heighty-teighty!' cried he. 'You may be filled with melancholy if you please. It is not the mind of a good wife. If you thought at all of me you would sit shamed.'

Thereupon he went out, and Kokua was alone.

What chance had she to sell that bottle at two centimes? None, she perceived. And if she had any, here was her husband hurrying her away to a country where there was nothing lower than a cent. And here—on the morrow of her sacrifice—was her husband leaving her and blaming her.

She would not even try to profit by what time she had, but sat in the house, and now had the bottle out and viewed it with unutterable fear, and now, with loathing, hid it out of sight.

By and by Keawe came back, and would have her take a drive.

'My husband, I am ill,' she said. 'I am out of heart. Excuse me, I can take no pleasure.'

Then was Keawe more wroth than ever. With her, because he thought she was brooding over the case of the old man; and with himself, because he thought she was right, and was ashamed to be so happy.

'This is your truth,' cried he, 'and this your affection! Your husband is just saved from eternal ruin, which he encountered for the love of you—and you can take no pleasure! Kokua, you have a disloyal heart.'

He went forth again furious, and wandered in the town all day. He met friends, and drank with them; they hired a carriage and drove into the country, and there drank again. All the time Keawe was ill at ease, because he was taking this pastime while his wife was sad, and because he knew in his heart that she was more right than he; and the knowledge made him drink the deeper.

Now there was an old brutal Haole drinking with him, one that had been a boatswain of a whaler, a runaway, a digger in gold mines, a convict in prisons. He had a low mind and a foul mouth; he loved to drink and to see others drunken; and he pressed the glass upon Keawe. Soon there was no more money in the company.

'Here, you!' says the boatswain, 'you are rich, you have been always saying. You have a bottle or some foolishness.'

'Yes,' says Keawe, 'I am rich; I will go back and get some money from my wife, who keeps it.'

'That's a bad idea, mate,' said the boatswain. 'Never you trust a petticoat with dollars. They're all false as water; you keep an eye on her.'

Now this word stuck in Keawe's mind; for he was muddled with what he had been drinking.

'I should not wonder but she was false, indeed,' thought he. 'Why else should she be so cast down at my release? But I will show her I am not the man to be fooled. I will catch her in the act.'

Accordingly, when they were back in town, Keawe bade the boatswain wait for him at the corner, by the old calaboose, and went forward up the avenue alone to the door of his house. The night had come again; there was a light within, but never a sound; and Keawe crept about the corner, opened the back-door softly, and looked in.

There was Kokua on the floor, the lamp at her side; before her was a milk-white bottle, with a round belly and a long neck; and as she viewed it, Kokua wrung her hands.

A long time Keawe stood and looked in the doorway. At first he was struck stupid; and then fear fell upon him that the bargain had been made amiss, and the bottle had come back to him as it came at San Francisco; and at that his knees were loosened, and the fumes of the wine departed from his head like mists off a river in the morning. And then he had another thought; and it was a strange one, that made his cheeks to burn.

'I must make sure of this,' thought he.

So he closed the door, and went softly round the corner again, and then came noisily in, as though he were but now returned. And, lo! by the time he opened the front door no bottle was to be seen; and Kokua sat in a chair and started up like one awakened out of sleep.

'I have been drinking all day and making merry,' said Keawe. 'I have been with good companions, and now I only come back for money, and return to drink and carouse with them again.'

Both his face and voice were as stern as judgment, but Kokua was too troubled to observe.

'You do well to use your own, my husband,' said she, and her words trembled.

'O, I do well in all things,' said Keawe, and he went straight to the chest and took out money. But he looked besides in the corner where they kept the bottle, and there was no bottle there.

At that the chest heaved upon the floor like a sea-billow, and the house span about him like a wreath of smoke, for he saw he was lost now, and there was no escape. 'It is what I feared,' he thought. 'It is she who has bought it.'

And then he came to himself a little and rose up; but the sweat streamed on his face as thick as the rain and as cold as the well-water.

'Kokua,' said he, 'I said to you today what ill became me. Now I return to carouse with my jolly companions,' and at that he laughed a little quietly. 'I will take more pleasure in the cup if you forgive me.'

She clasped his knees in a moment; she kissed his knees with flowing tears.

'O,' she cried, 'I asked but a kind word!'

'Let us never one think hardly of the other,' said Keawe, and was gone out of the house.

Now, the money that Keawe had taken was only some of that store of centime pieces they had laid in at their arrival. It was very sure he had no mind to be drinking. His wife had given her soul for him, now he must give his for hers; no other thought was in the world with him.

At the corner, by the old calaboose, there was the boatswain waiting.

'My wife has the bottle,' said Keawe, 'and, unless you help me to recover it, there can be no more money and no more liquor tonight.'

'You do not mean to say you are serious about that bottle?' cried the boatswain.

'There is the lamp,' said Keawe. 'Do I look as if I was jesting?'

'That is so,' said the boatswain. 'You look as serious as a ghost.'

'Well, then,' said Keawe, 'here are two centimes; you must go to my wife in the house, and offer her these for the bottle, which (if I am not much mistaken) she will give you instantly. Bring it to me here, and I will buy it back from you for one; for that is the law with this bottle, that it still must be sold for a less sum. But whatever you do, never breathe a word to her that you come from me.'

'Mate, I wonder are you making a fool of me?' asked the boatswain.

'It will do you no harm if I am,' returned Keawe.

'That is so, mate,' said the boatswain.

'And if you doubt me,' added Keawe, 'you can try. As soon as you are clear of the house, wish to have your pocket full of money, or a bottle of the best rum, or what you please, and you will see the virtue of the thing.'

'Very well, Kanaka,' says the boatswain. 'I will try; but if you are having your fun out of me, I will take my fun out of you with a belaying-pin.'

So the whaler-man went off up the avenue; and Keawe stood and waited. It was near the same spot where Kokua had waited the night before; but Keawe was more resolved, and never faltered in his purpose; only his soul was bitter with despair.

It seemed a long time he had to wait before he heard a voice singing in the darkness of the avenue. He knew the voice to be the boatswain's; but it was strange how drunken it appeared upon a sudden.

Next, the man himself came stumbling into the light of the lamp. He had the devil's bottle buttoned in his coat; another bottle was in his hand; and even as he came in view he raised it to his mouth and drank.

'You have it,' said Keawe. 'I see that.'

'Hands off!' cried the boatswain, jumping back. 'Take a step near me and I'll smash your mouth. You thought you could make a cat's-paw of me, did you?'

'What do you mean?' cried Keawe.

'Mean?' cried the boatswain, 'This is a pretty good bottle, this is; that's what I mean. How I got it for two centimes I can't make out; but I'm sure you shan't have it for one.'

'You mean you won't sell it?' gasped Keawe.

'No, *sir*!' cried the boatswain. 'But I'll give you a drink of the rum, if you like.'

'I tell you,' said Keawe, 'the man who has that bottle goes to hell.'

'I reckon I'm going anyway,' returned the sailor; 'and this bottle's the best thing to go with I've struck yet. No, sir!' he cried again, 'this is my bottle now, and you can go and fish for another.'

'Can this be true?' Keawe cried. 'For your own sake, I beseech you, sell it me!'

'I don't value any of your talk,' replied the boatswain. 'You thought I was a flat; now you see I'm not; and there's an end. If you won't have a swallow of the rum I'll have one myself. Here's your health, and good-night to you!'

So off he went down the avenue towards town, and there goes the bottle out of the story.

But Keawe ran to Kokua light as the wind; and great was their joy that night; and great, since then, has been the peace of all their days in the Bright House.

Keola was married with Lehua, daughter of Kalamake, the wise man of Molokai, and he kept his dwelling with the father of his wife. There was no man more cunning than that prophet; he read the stars, he could divine by the bodies of the dead, and by the means of evil creatures: he could go alone into the highest parts of the mountain, into the region of the hobgoblins, and there he would lay snares to entrap the spirits of ancient.

For this reason no man was more consulted in all the Kingdom of Hawaii. Prudent people bought, and sold, and married, and laid out their lives by his counsels; and the King had him twice to Kona to seek the treasures of Kamehameha.[1] Neither was any man more feared: of his enemies, some had dwindled in sickness by the virtue of his incantations, and some had been spirited away, the life and the clay both, so that folk looked in vain for so much as a bone of their bodies. It was rumoured that he had the art or the gift of the old heroes. Men had seen him at night upon the mountains, stepping from one cliff to the next; they had seen him walking in the high forest, and his head and shoulders were above the trees.

This Kalamake was a strange man to see. He was come of the best blood in Molokai and Maui, of a pure descent; and yet he was more white to look upon than any foreigner: his hair the colour of dry grass, and his eyes red and very blind, so that 'Blind as Kalamake, that can see across tomorrow' was a byword in the islands.

1. Dynastic name of the late eighteenth- and nineteenth-century kings of Hawaii. Kamehameha I united the Hawaiian Islands.

Of all these doings of his father-in-law, Keola knew a little by the common repute, a little more he suspected, and the rest he ignored. But there was one thing troubled him. Kalamake was a man that spared for nothing, whether to eat or to drink or to wear; and for all he paid in bright new dollars. 'Bright as Kalamake's dollars' was another saying in the Eight Isles. Yet he neither sold, nor planted, nor took hire—only now and then for his sorceries—and there was no source conceivable for so much silver coin.

It chanced one day Keola's wife was gone upon a visit to Kaunakakai, on the lee side of the island, and the men were forth at the sea-fishing. But Keola was an idle dog, and he lay in the verandah and watched the surf beat on the shore and the birds fly about the cliff. It was a chief thought with him always—the thought of the bright dollars. When he lay down to bed he would be wondering why they were so many, and when he woke at morn he would be wondering why they were all new; and the thing was never absent from his mind. But this day of all days he made sure in his heart of some discovery. For it seems he had observed the place where Kalamake kept his treasure, which was a lockfast desk against the parlour wall, under the print of Kamehameha the Fifth, and a photograph of Queen Victoria with her crown; and it seems again that, no later than the night before, he found occasion to look in, and behold! the bag lay there empty. And this was the day of the steamer; he could see her smoke off Kalaupapa; and she must soon arrive with a month's goods, tinned salmon and gin, and all manner of rare luxuries for Kalamake.

'Now if he can pay for his goods today,' Keola thought, 'I shall know for certain that the man is a warlock, and the dollars come out of the Devil's pocket.'

While he was thinking, there was his father-in-law behind him, looking vexed.

'Is that the steamer?' he asked.

'Yes,' said Keola. 'She has but to call at Pelekunu, and then she will be here.'

'There is no help for it then,' returned Kalamake, 'and I must take you in my confidence, Keola, for the lack of any one better. Come here within the house.'

So they stepped together into the parlour, which was a very fine room, papered and hung with prints, and furnished with a rocking-chair, and a table and a sofa in the European style. There was a shelf of books besides, and a family Bible in the midst of the table, and the lockfast writing-desk against the wall; so that any one could see it was the house of a man of substance.

Kalamake made Keola close the shutters of the windows, while he himself locked all the doors and set open the lid of the desk. From this he brought forth a pair of necklaces hung with charms and shells, a bundle of dried herbs, and the dried leaves of trees, and a green branch of palm.

'What I am about,' said he, 'is a thing beyond wonder. The men of old were wise; they wrought marvels, and this among the rest; but that was at night, in the dark, under the fit stars and in the desert. The same will I do here in my own house and under the plain eye of day.'

So saying, he put the Bible under the cushion of the sofa so that it was all covered, brought out from the same place a mat of a wonderfully fine texture, and heaped the herbs and leaves on sand in a tin pan. And then he and Keola put on the necklaces and took their stand upon the opposite corners of the mat.

'The time comes,' said the warlock; 'be not afraid.'

With that he set flame to the herbs, and began to mutter and wave the branch of palm. At first the light was dim because of the closed shutters; but the herbs caught strongly afire, and the flames beat upon Keola, and the room glowed with the burning: and next the smoke rose and made his head swim and his eyes darken, and the sound of Kalamake muttering ran in his ears. And suddenly, to the mat on which they were standing came a snatch or twitch, that seemed to be more swift than lightning. In the same wink the room was gone and the house, the breath all beaten from Keola's body. Volumes of light rolled upon his eyes and head, and he found himself transported to a beach of the sea, under a strong sun, with a great surf roaring: he and the warlock standing there on the same mat, speechless, gasping and grasping at one another, and passing their hands before their eyes.

'What was this?' cried Keola, who came to himself the

first, because he was the younger. 'The pang of it was like death.'

'It matters not,' panted Kalamake. 'It is now done.'

'And in the name of God where are we?' cried Keola.

'That is not the question,' replied the sorcerer. 'Being here, we have matter in our hands, and that we must attend to. Go, while I recover my breath, into the borders of the wood, and bring me the leaves of such and such a herb, and such and such a tree, which you will find to grow there plentifully—three handfuls of each. And be speedy. We must be home again before the steamer comes; it would seem strange if we had disappeared.' And he sat on the sand and panted.

Keola went up the beach, which was of shining sand and coral, strewn with singular shells; and he thought in his heart—

'How do I not know this beach? I will come here again and gather shells.'

In front of him was a line of palms against the sky; not like the palms of the Eight Islands, but tall and fresh and beautiful, and hanging out withered fans like gold among the green, and he thought in his heart—

'It is strange I should not have found this grove. I will come here again, when it is warm, to sleep.' And he thought, 'How warm it has grown suddenly!' For it was winter in Hawaii, and the day had been chill. And he thought also, 'Where are the grey mountains? And where is the high cliff with the hanging forest and the wheeling birds?' And the more he considered, the less he might conceive in what quarter of the islands he was fallen.

In the border of the grove, where it met the beach, the herb was growing, but the tree farther back. Now, as Keola went toward the tree, he was aware of a young woman who had nothing on her body, but a belt of leaves.

'Well!' thought Keola, 'they are not very particular about their dress in this part of the country.' And he paused, supposing she would observe him and escape; and, seeing that she still looked before her, stood and hummed aloud. Up she leaped at the sound. Her face was ashen; she looked this way and that, and her mouth gaped with the terror of her soul. But it was a strange thing that her eyes did not rest upon Keola.

'Good-day,' said he. 'You need not be so frightened; I will not eat you.' And he had scarce opened his mouth before the young woman fled into the bush.

'These are strange manners,' thought Keola. And, not thinking what he did, ran after her.

As she ran, the girl kept crying in some speech that was not practised in Hawaii, yet some of the words were the same, and he knew she kept calling and warning others. And presently he saw more people running—men, women and children, one with another, all running and crying like people at a fire. And with that he began to grow afraid himself, and returned to Kalamake, bringing the leaves. Him he told what he had seen.

'You must pay no heed,' said Kalamake. 'All this is like a dream and shadows. All will disappear and be forgotten.'

'It seemed none saw me,' said Keola.

'And none did,' replied the sorcerer. 'We walk here in the broad sun invisible by reason of these charms. Yet they hear us; and therefore it is well to speak softly, as I do.'

With that he made a circle round the mat with stones, and in the midst he set the leaves.

'It will be your part,' said he, 'to keep the leaves alight, and feed the fire slowly. While they blaze (which is but for a little moment) I must do my errand; and before the ashes blacken, the same power that brought us carries us away. Be ready now with the match; and do you call me in good time, lest the flames burn out and I be left.'

As soon as the leaves caught, the sorcerer leaped like a deer out of the circle, and began to race along the beach like a hound that has been bathing. As he ran he kept stooping to snatch shells; and it seemed to Keola that they glittered as he took them. The leaves blazed with a clear flame that consumed them swiftly; and presently Keola had but a handful left, and the sorcerer was far off, running and stopping.

'Back!' cried Keola. 'Back! The leaves are near done.'

At that Kalamake turned, and if he had run before, now he flew. But fast as he ran, the leaves burned faster. The flame was ready to expire when, with a great leap, he bounded on the mat. The wind of his leaping blew it out; and with that the beach was gone, and the sun and the sea, and they stood once more in the dimness of the shuttered parlour, and were once more shaken and blinded; and on the mat betwixt them lay a pile of shining dollars. Keola ran to the shutters; and there was the steamer tossing in the swell close in.

The same night Kalamake took his son-in-law apart, and gave him five dollars in his hand.

'Keola,' said he, 'if you are a wise man (which I am doubtful of) you will think you slept this afternoon on the verandah, and dreamed as you were sleeping. I am a man of few words, and I have for my helpers people of short memories.'

Never a word more said Kalamake, nor referred again to that affair. But it ran all the while in Keola's head—if he were lazy before he would now do nothing.

'Why should I work,' thought he, 'when I have a father-in-law who makes dollars of sea-shells?'

Presently his share was spent. He spent it all upon fine clothes. And then he was sorry:

'For,' thought he, 'I had done better to have bought a concertina, with which I might have entertained myself all day long.' And then he began to grow vexed with Kalamake.

'This man has the soul of a dog,' thought he. 'He can gather dollars when he pleases on the beach, and he leaves me to pine for a concertina! Let him beware: I am no child, I am as cunning as he, and hold his secret.' With that he spoke to his wife Lehua, and complained of her father's manners.

'I would let my father be,' said Lehua. 'He is a dangerous man to cross.'

'I care that for him!' cried Keola; and snapped his fingers. 'I have him by the nose. I can make him do what I please.' And he told Lehua the story.

But she shook her head.

'You may do what you like,' said she; 'but as sure as you thwart my father, you will be no more heard of. Think of this person, and that person; think of Hua, who was a noble of the House of Representatives, and went to Honolulu every year; and not a bone or a hair of him was found. Remember Kamau, and how he wasted to a thread, so that his wife lifted him with one hand. Keola, you are a baby in my father's hands; he will take you with his thumb and finger and eat you like a shrimp.'

Now Keola was truly afraid of Kalamake, but he was vain too; and these words of his wife incensed him.

'Very well,' said he, 'if that is what you think of me, I will show how much you are deceived.' And he went straight to where his father-in-law was sitting in the parlour.

'Kalamake,' said he, 'I want a concertina.'

'Do you indeed?' said Kalamake.

'Yes,' said he, 'and I may as well tell you plainly, I mean to have it. A man who picks up dollars on the beach can certainly afford a concertina.'

'I had no idea you had so much spirit,' replied the sorcerer. 'I though you were a timid, useless lad, and I cannot describe how much pleased I am to find I was mistaken. Now I begin to think I may have found an assistant and successor in my difficult business. A concertina? You shall have the best in Honolulu. And tonight, as soon as it is dark, you and I will go and find the money.'

'Shall we return to the beach?' asked Keola.

'No, no!' replied Kalamake; 'you must begin to learn more of my secrets. Last time I taught you to pick shells; this time I shall teach you to catch fish. Are you strong enough to launch Pili's boat?'

'I think I am,' returned Keola. 'But why should we not take your own, which is afloat already?'

'I have a reason which you will understand thoroughly before tomorrow,' said Kalamake. 'Pili's boat is the better suited for my purpose. So, if you please, let us meet there as soon as it is dark; and in the meanwhile let us keep our own counsel, for there is no cause to let the family into our business.'

Honey is not more sweet than was the voice of Kalamake, and Keola could scarce contain his satisfaction.

'I might have had my concertina weeks ago,' thought he, 'and there is nothing needed in this world but a little courage.'

Presently after he spied Lehua weeping, and was half in a mind to tell her all was well.

'But no,' thinks he; 'I shall wait till I can show her the concertina; we shall see what the chit will do then. Perhaps she will understand in the future that her husband is a man of some intelligence.'

As soon as it was dark father and son-in-law launched Pili's boat and set the sail. There was a great sea, and it blew strong from the leeward; but the boat was swift and light and dry, and skimmed the waves. The wizard had a lantern, which he lit and held with his finger through the ring; and the two sat in the stern and smoked cigars, of which Kalamake had always a provision, and spoke like friends of magic and the great sums of money which they could make by its exercise, and what they should buy first, and what second; and Kalamake talked like a father.

Presently he looked all about, and above him at the stars, and back at the island, which was already three parts sunk under the sea, and he seemed to consider ripely his position.

'Look!' says he, 'there is Molokai already behind us, and Maui like a cloud; and by the bearing of these three stars I know I am come where I desire. This part of the sea is called the Sea of the Dead. It is in this place extraordinarily deep, and the floor is all covered with the bones of men, and in the holes of this part gods and goblins keep their habitation. The flow of the sea is to the north, stronger than a shark can swim, and any man who shall here be thrown out of a ship it bears away like a wild horse into the uttermost ocean. Presently he is spent and goes down, and his bones are scattered with the rest, and the gods devour his spirit.'

Fear came on Keola at the words, and he looked, and by the light of the stars and the lantern the warlock seemed to change.

'What ails you?' cried Keola, quick and sharp.

'It is not I who am ailing,' said the wizard; 'but there is one here very sick.'

With that he changed his grasp upon the lantern, and, behold! as he drew his finger from the ring, the finger stuck and the ring was burst, and his hand was grown to be of the bigness of three.

At that sight Keola screamed and covered his face.

But Kalamake held up the lantern. 'Look rather at my face!' said he—and his head was huge as a barrel; and still he grew and grew as a cloud grows on a mountain, and Keola sat before him screaming, and the boat raced on the great seas.

'And now,' said the wizard, 'what do you think about that concertina? and are you sure you would not rather have a flute? No?' says he; 'that is well, for I do not like my family to be changeable of purpose. But I begin to think I had better get out of this paltry boat, for my bulk swells to a very unusual degree, and if we are not the more careful, she will presently be swamped.'

With that he threw his legs over the side. Even as he did so, the greatness of the man grew thirty-fold and forty-fold as swift as sight or thinking, so that he stood in the deep seas to the armpits, and his head and shoulders rose like a high isle, and the swell beat and burst upon his bosom, as it beats and breaks against a cliff. The boat ran still to the north, but he reached out his hand, and took the gunwhale by the finger and thumb, and broke the side like a biscuit, and Keola was spilled into the sea. And the pieces of the boat the sorcerer crushed into the hollow of his hand and flung miles away into the night.

'Excuse me taking the lantern,' said he; 'for I have a long wade before me, and the land is far, and the bottom of the sea uneven, and I feel the bones under my toes.'

And he turned and went off walking with great strides; and as often as Keola sank in the trough he could see him no longer; but as often as he was heaved upon the crest, there he was striding and dwindling, and he held the lamp high over his head, and the waves broke white about him as he went.

Since first the islands were fished out of the sea there was never a man so terrified as this Keola. He swam indeed, but he swam as puppies swim when they are cast in to drown, and knew not wherefore. He could but think of the hugeness of the swelling of the warlock, of that face which was great as a mountain, of those shoulders that were broad as an isle, and of the seas that beat on them in vain. He thought, too, of the concertina, and shame took hold upon him; and of the dead men's bones, and fear shook him.

Of a sudden he was aware of something dark against the stars that tossed, and a light below, and a brightness of the cloven sea; and he heard speech of men. He cried out aloud and a voice answered; and in a twinkling the bows of a ship hung above him on a wave like a thing balanced, and swooped down. He caught with his two hands in the chains of her, and the next moment was buried in the rushing seas, and the next hauled on board by seamen.

They gave him gin and biscuit and dry clothes, and asked him how he came where they found him, and whether the light which they had seen was the lighthouse Lae o Ka Laau. But Keola knew white men are like children and only believe their own stories; so about himself he told them what he pleased, and as for the light (which was Kalamake's lantern) he vowed he had seen none.

This ship was a schooner bound for Honolulu, and then to trade in the low islands; and by a very good chance for Keola she had lost a man off the bowsprit in a squall. It was no use talking. Keola durst not stay in the Eight Islands. Word goes so quickly, and all men are so fond to talk and carry news, that if he hid in the north end of Kauai or in the south end of Kaü, the wizard would have wind of it before a month, and he must perish. So he did what seemed the most prudent, and shipped sailor in the place of the man who had been drowned.

In some ways the ship was a good place. The food was extraordinarily rich and plenty, with biscuits and salt beef every day, and pea-soup and puddings made of flour and suet twice a week, so that Keola grew fat. The captain also was a good man, and the crew no worse than other whites. The trouble was the mate, who was the most difficult man to please Keola had ever met with, and beat and cursed him daily, both for what he did and what he did not. The blows that he dealt were very sore, for he was strong; and the words he used were very unpalatable, for Keola was come of a good family and accustomed to respect. And what was the worst of all, whenever Keola found a chance to sleep, there was the mate awake and stirring him up with a rope's end. Keola saw it would never do; and he made up his mind to run away.

They were about a month out from Honolulu when they

made the land. It was a fine starry night, the sea was smooth as well as the sky fair; it blew a steady trade; and there was the island on their weather bow, a ribbon of palm-trees lying flat along the sea. The captain and the mate looked at it with the night-glass, and named the name of it, and talked of it, beside the wheel where Keola was steering. It seemed it was an isle where no traders came. By the captain's way, it was an isle besides where no man dwelt; but the mate thought otherwise.

'I don't give a cent for the directory,' said he. 'I've been past here one night in the schooner *Eugenie*; it was just such a night as this; they were fishing with torches, and the beach was thick with lights like a town.'

'Well, well,' says the captain, 'its steep-to, that's the great point; and there ain't any outlying dangers by the chart, so we'll just hug the lee side of it. —Keep her romping full, don't I tell you!' he cried to Keola, who was listening so hard that he forgot to steer.

And the mate cursed him, and swore that Kanaka was for no use in the world, and if he got started after him with a belaying-pin, it would be a cold day for Keola.

And so the captain and mate lay down on the house together, and Keola was left to himself.

'This island will do very well for me,' he thought; 'if no traders deal there, the mate will never come. And as for Kalamake, it is not possible he can ever get as far as this.'

With that he kept edging the schooner nearer in. He had to do this quietly, for it was the trouble with these white men, and above all with the mate, that you could never be sure of them; they would all be sleeping sound, or else pretending, and if a sail shook they would jump to their feet and fall on you with a rope's end. So Keola edged her up little by little, and kept all drawing. And presently the land was close on board, and the sound of the sea on the sides of it grew loud.

With that the mate sat up suddenly upon the house.

'What are you doing?' he roars. 'You'll have the ship ashore!'

And he made one bound for Keola, and Keola made another clean over the rail and plump into the starry sea.

When he came up again, the schooner had payed off on her true course, and the mate stood by the wheel himself, and Keola heard him cursing. The sea was smooth under the lee of the island; it was warm besides, and Keola had his sailor's knife, so he had no fear of sharks. A little way before him the trees stopped; there was a break in the line of the land like the mouth of a harbour; and the tide, which was then flowing, took him up and carried him through. One minute he was without, and the next within; had floated there in a wide shallow water, bright with ten thousand stars, and all about him was the ring of the land, with its string of palm-trees. And he was amazed, because this was a kind of island he had never heard of.

The time of Keola in that place was in two periods—the period when he was alone, and the period when he was there with the tribe. At first he sought everywhere and found no man; only some houses standing in a hamlet, and the marks of fires. But the ashes of the fires were cold and the rains had washed them away; and the winds had blown, and some of the huts were overthrown. It was here he took his dwelling; and he made a fire drill, and a shell hook, and fished and cooked his fish, and climbed after green cocoa-nuts, the juice of which he drank, for in all the isle there was no water. The days were long to him, and the nights terrifying. He made a lamp of cocoa-shell, and drew the oil of the ripe nuts, and made a wick of fibre; and when evening came he closed up his hut, and lit his lamp, and lay and trembled till morning. Many a time he thought in his heart he would have been better in the bottom of the sea, his bones rolling there with the others.

All this while he kept by the inside of the island, for the huts were on the shore of the lagoon, and it was there the palms grew best, and the lagoon itself abounded with good fish. And to the outer side he went once only, and he looked but the once at the beach of the ocean, and came away shaking. For the look of it, with its bright sand, and strewn shells, and strong sun and surf, went sore against his inclination.

'It cannot be,' he thought, 'and yet it is very like. And how do I know? These white men, although they pretend to know where they are sailing, must take their chance like other people. So that after all we may have sailed in a circle, and I may be quite near to Molokai, and this may be the very beach where my father-in-law gathers his dollars.'

So after that he was prudent, and kept to the land side.

It was perhaps a month later, when the people of the place arrived—the fill of six great boats. They were a fine race of men, and spoke a tongue that sounded different from the tongue of Hawaii, but so many of the words were the same that it was not difficult to understand. The men besides were very courteous, and the women very towardly; and they made Keola welcome, and built him a house, and gave him a wife; and, what surprised him the most, he was never sent to work with the young men.

And now Keola had three periods. First he had a period of being very sad, and then he had a period when he was pretty merry. Last of all came the third, when he was the most terrified man in the four oceans.

The cause of the first period was the girl he had to wife. He was in doubt about the island, and he might have been in doubt about the speech, of which he had heard so little when he came there with the wizard on the mat. But about his wife there was no mistake conceivable, for she was the same girl that ran from him crying in the wood. So he had sailed all this way, and might as well have stayed in Molokai; and had left home and wife and all his friends for no other cause but to escape his enemy, and the place he had come to was that wizard's hunting-ground, and the shore where he walked invisible. It was at this period when he kept the most close to the lagoon side, and, as far as he dared, abode in the cover of his hut.

The cause of the second period was talk he heard from his wife and the chief islanders. Keola himself said little. He was never so sure of his new friends, for he judged they were too civil to be wholesome, and since he had grown better acquainted with his father-in-law the man had grown more cautious. So he told them nothing of himself, but only his name and descent, and that he came from the Eight Islands, and what fine islands they were; and about the king's palace in Honolulu, and how he was a chief friend of the king and

the missionaries. But he put many questions and learned
much. The island where he was was called the Isle of Voices;
it belonged to the tribe, but they made their home upon
another, three hours' sail to the southward. There they lived
and had their permanent houses, and it was a rich island,
where were eggs and chickens and pigs, and ships came
trading with rum and tobacco. It was there the schooner had
gone after Keola deserted; there, too, the mate had died, like
the fool of a white man as he was. It seems, when the ship
came, it was the beginning of the sickly season in that isle;
when the fish of the lagoon are poisonous, and all who eat of
them swell up and die. The mate was told of it; he saw the
boats preparing, because in that season the people leave that
island and sail to the Isle of Voices; but he was a fool of a
white man, who would believe no stories but his own, and he
caught one of these fish, cooked it and ate it, and swelled up
and died, which was good news to Keola. As for the Isle of
Voices, it lay solitary the most part of the year; only now and
then a boat's crew came for copra, and in the bad season,
when the fish at the main isle were poisonous, the tribe dwelt
there in a body. It had its name from a marvel, for it seemed
the seaside of it was all beset with invisible devils; day and
night you heard them talking one with another in strange
tongues; day and night little fires blazed up and were ext-
inguished on the beach; and what was the cause of these
doings no man might conceive. Keola asked them if it were
the same in their island where they stayed, and they told him
no, not there; nor yet in any other of some hundred isles that
lay all about them in that sea; but it was a thing peculiar to
the Isle of Voices. They told him also that these fires and
voices were ever on the seaside and in the seaward fringes of
the wood, and a man might dwell by the lagoon two
thousand years (if he could live so long) and never be any
way troubled; and even on the seaside the devils did no harm
if let alone. Only once a chief had cast a spear at one of the
voices, and the same night he fell out of a cocoa-nut palm and
was killed.

Keola thought a good bit with himself. He saw he would
be all right when the tribe returned to the main island, and
right enough where he was, if he kept by the lagoon, yet he

had a mind to make things righter if he could. So he told the
high chief he had once been in an isle that was pestered the
same way, and the folk had found a means to cure that
trouble.

'There was a tree growing in the bush there,' says he, 'and
it seems these devils came to get the leaves of it. So the people
of the isle cut down the tree wherever it was found, and the
devils came no more.'

They asked what kind of tree this was, and he showed
them the tree of which Kalamake burned the leaves. They
found it hard to believe, yet the idea tickled them. Night
after night the old men debated it in their councils, but the
high chief (though he was a brave man) was afraid of the
matter, and reminded them daily of the chief who cast a
spear against the voices and was killed, and the thought of
that brought all to a stand again.

Though he could not yet bring about the destruction of the
trees, Keola was well enough pleased, and began to look
about him and take pleasure in his days; and, among other
things, he was the kinder to his wife, so that the girl began to
love him greatly. One day he came to the hut, and she lay on
the ground lamenting.

'Why,' said Keola, 'what is wrong with you now?'

She declared it was nothing.

The same night she woke him. The lamp burned very low,
but he saw by her face she was in sorrow.

'Keola', she said, 'put your ear to my mouth that I may
whisper, for no one must hear us. Two days before the boats
begin to be got ready, go you to the seaside of the isle and lie
in a thicket. We shall choose that place beforehand, you and
I; and hide food; and every night I shall come near by there
singing. So when a night comes and you do not hear me, you
shall know we are clean gone out of the island, and you may
come forth again in safety.

The soul of Keola died within him.

'What is this?' he cried, 'I cannot live among devils. I will
not be left behind upon this isle. I am dying to leave it.'

'You will never leave it alive, my poor Keola,' said the
girl; 'for to tell you the truth, my people are eaters of men;
but this they keep secret. And the reason they will kill you

before we leave is because in our island ships come, and Donat-Kimaran comes and talks for the French, and there is a white trader there in a house with a verandah, and a catechist. O, that is a fine place indeed! The trader has barrels filled with flour; and a French warship once came in the lagoon and gave everybody wine and biscuit. Ah, my poor Keola, I wish I could take you there, for great is my love to you, and it is the finest place in the seas except Papeete.'

So now Keola was the most terrified man in the four oceans. He had heard tell of eaters of men in the south islands, and the thing had always been a fear to him; and here it was knocking at his door. He had heard besides, by travellers, of their practices, and how when they are in a mind to eat a man they cherish and fondle him like a mother with a favourite baby. And he saw this must be his own case; and that was why he had been housed, and fed, and wived, and liberated from all work; and why the old men and the chiefs discoursed with him like a person of weight. So he lay on his bed and railed upon his destiny; and the flesh curdled on his bones.

The next day the people of the tribe were very civil, as their way was. They were elegant speakers, and they made beautiful poetry, and jested at meals, so that a missionary must have died laughing. It was little enough Keola cared for their fine ways; all he saw was the white teeth shining in their mouths, and his gorge rose at the sight; and when they were done eating, he went and lay in the bush like a dead man.

The next day it was the same, and then his wife followed him.

'Keola,' she said, 'if you do not eat, I tell you plainly you will be killed and cooked tomorrow. Some of the old chiefs are murmuring already. They think you are fallen sick and must lose flesh.'

With that Keola got to his feet, and anger burned in him.

'It is little I care one way or the other,' said he. 'I am between the devil and the deep sea. Since die I must, let me die the quickest way; and since I must be eaten at the best of it, let me rather be eaten by hobgoblins than by men. Farewell,' said he, and he left her standing, and walked to the seaside of the island.

It was all bare in the strong sun; there was no sign of man, only the beach was trodden, and all about him as he went the voices talked and whispered, and the little fires sprang up and burned down. All tongues of the earth were spoken there; the French, the Dutch, the Russian, the Tamil, the Chinese. Whatever land knew sorcery, there were some of its people whispering in Keola's ear. That beach was thick as a cried fair, yet no man seen; and as he walked he saw the shells vanish before him, and no man to pick them up. I think the devil would have been afraid to be alone in such a company: but Keola was past fear and courted death. When the fires sprang up, he charged for them like a bull. Bodiless voices called to and fro; unseen hands poured sand upon the flames; and they were gone from the beach before he reached them.

'It is plain Kalamake is not here,' he thought, 'or I must have been killed long since.'

With that he sat him down in the margin of the wood, for he was tired, and put his chin upon his hands. The business before his eyes continued: the beach babbled with voices, and the fires sprang up and sank, and the shells vanished and were renewed again even while he looked.

'It was a by-day when I was here before,' he thought, 'for it was nothing to this.'

And his head was dizzy with the thought of these millions and millions of dollars, and all these hundreds and hundreds of persons culling them upon the beach and flying in the air higher and swifter than eagles.

'And to think how they have fooled me with their talk of mints,' says he, 'and that money was made there, when it is clear that all the new coin in all the world is gathered on these sands! But I will know better the next time!' said he.

And at last, he knew not very well how or when, sleep fell on Keola, and he forgot the island and all his sorrows.

Early the next day, before the sun was yet up, a bustle woke him. He awoke in fear, for he though the tribe had caught him napping; but it was no such matter. Only, on the beach in front of him, the bodiless voices called and shouted one upon another, and it seemed they all passed and swept beside him up the coast of the island.

'What is afoot now?' thinks Keola. And it was plain to him it was something beyond ordinary, for the fires were not lighted nor the shells taken, but the bodiless voices kept posting up the beach, and hailing and dying away; and others following, and by the sound of them these wizards should be angry.

'It is not me they are angry at,' thought Keola, 'for they pass me close.'

As when hounds go by, or horses in a race, or city folk coursing to a fire, and all men join and follow after, so it was now with Keola; and he knew not what he did, nor why he did it, but there, lo and behold! he was running with the voices.

So he turned one point of the island, and this brought him in view of a second; and there he remembered the wizard trees to have been growing by the score together in a wood. From this point there went up a hubbub of men crying not to be described; and by the sound of them, those that he ran with shaped their course of the same quarter. A little nearer, and there began to mingle with the outcry the crash of many axes. And at this a thought came at last into his mind that the high chief had consented; that the men of the tribe had set-to cutting down these trees; that word had gone about the isle from sorcerer to sorcerer, and these were all now assembling to defend their trees. Desire of strange things swept him on. He posted with the voices, crossed the beach, and came into the borders of the wood, and stood astonished. One tree had fallen, others were part hewed away. There was the tribe clustered. They were back to back, and bodies lay, and blood flowed among their feet. The hue of fear was on all their faces: their voices went up to heaven shrill as a weasel's cry.

Have you seen a child when he is all alone and has a wooden sword, and fights, leaping and hewing with the empty air? Even so the man-eaters huddled back to back, and heaved up their axes, and laid on, and screamed as they laid on, and behold! no man to contend with them! only here and there Keola saw an axe swinging over against them without hands; and time and again a man of the tribe would fall before it, clove in twain or burst assunder, and his soul sped howling.

For a while Keola looked upon this prodigy like one that dreams, and then fear took him by the midst as sharp as death, that he should behold such doings. Even in that same flash the high chief of the clan espied him standing, and pointed and called out his name. Thereat the whole tribe saw him also, and their eyes flashed, and their teeth clashed.

'I am too long here,' thought Keola, and ran further out of the wood and down the beach, not caring whither.

'Keola!' said a voice close by upon empty sand.

'Lehua! is that you?' he cried, and gasped, and looked in vain for her; but by the eyesight he was stark alone.

'I saw you pass before,' the voice answered; 'but you would not hear me.—Quick! get the leaves and herbs, and let us free.'

'You are there with the mat?' he asked.

'Here, at your side,' said she. And he felt her arms about him.—Quick! the leaves and the herbs, before my father can get back!'

So Keola ran for his life, and fetched the wizard fuel: and Lehua guided him back, and set his feet upon the mat, and made the fire. All the time of its burning the sound of battle towered out of the wood; the wizards and the man-eaters hard at fight; the wizards, the viewless ones, roaring out aloud like bulls upon a mountain, and the men of the tribe replying shrill and savage out of the terror of their souls. And all the time of the burning, Keola stood there and listened, and shook, and watched how the unseen hands of Lehua poured the leaves. She poured them fast, and the flame burned high, and scorched Keola's hands; and she speeded and blew the burning with her breath. The last leaf was eaten, the flame fell, and the shock followed, and there were Keola and Lehua in the room at home.

Now, when Keola could see his wife at last he was mightily pleased, and he was mighty pleased to be home again in Molokai and sit down beside a bowl of poi[1]—for they make no poi on board ships, and there was none in the Isle of Voices—and he was out of the body with pleasure to be clean escaped out of the hands of the eaters of men. But there was

1. A fermented porridge made from the ground-up roots of the taro plant.

another matter not so clear, and Lehua and Keola talked of it all night and were troubled. There was Kalamake left upon the isle. If, by the blessing of God, he could but stick there, all were well; but should he escape and return to Molokai, it would be an ill day for his daughter and her husband. They spoke of his gift of swelling, and whether he could wade that distance in the seas. But Keola knew by this time where that island was—and that is to say, in the Low or Dangerous Archipelago. So they fetched the atlas and looked upon the distance in the map, and by what they could make of it, it seemed a far way for an old gentleman to walk. Still, it would not do to make too sure of a warlock like Kalamake, and they determined at last to take counsel of a white missionary.

So the first one that came by, Keola told him everything. And the missionary was very sharp on him for taking the second wife in the low island; but for all the rest, he vowed he could make neither head nor tail of it.

'However,' says he, 'if you think this money of your father's ill gotten, my advice to you would be, give some of it to the lepers and some to the missionary fund. And as for this extraordinary rigmarole, you cannot do better than keep it to yourselves.'

But he warned the police at Honolulu that, by all he could make out, Kalamake and Keola had been coining false money, and it would not be amiss to watch them.

Keola and Lehua took his advice, and gave many dollars to the lepers and the fund. And no doubt the advice must have been good, for from that day to this Kalamake has never more been heard of. But whether he was slain in the battle by the trees, or whether he is still kicking his heels upon the Isle of Voices, who shall say?

ONE. A SOUTH SEA BRIDAL

I saw that island first when it was neither night nor morning.
The moon was to the west, setting but still broad and bright.
To the east, and right amidships of the dawn, which was all
pink, the daystar sparkled like a diamond. The land breeze
blew in our faces and smelt strong of wild lime and vanilla:
other things besides, but these were the most plain; and the
chill of it set me sneezing. I should say I had been for years
on a low island near the line, living for the most part solitary
among natives. Here was a fresh experience; even the tongue
would be quite strange to me; and the look of these woods
and mountains, and the rare smell of them, renewed my
blood.

The captain blew out the binnacle lamp.

'There,' said he, 'there goes a bit of smoke, Mr Wiltshire,
behind the break of the reef. That's Falesá[1] where your
station is, the last village to the east; nobody lives to
windward, I don't know why. Take my glass, and you can
make the houses out.'

I took the glass; and the shores leaped nearer, and I saw
the tangle of woods and the breach of the surf, and the brown
roofs and the black insides of houses peeped among the trees.

'Do you catch a bit of white there to the east'ard?' the
captain continued. 'That's your house. Coral built, stands
high, verandah you could walk on three abreast: best station
in the South Pacific. When old Adams saw it, he took and
shook me by the hand.—"I've dropped into a soft thing
here," says he.—"So you have," says I, "and time too!"

1. A fictional place. The word means 'sacred house'.
   Stevenson knew the meaning of the word, and
   presumably chose it deliberately.

Poor Johnny! I never saw him again but the once, and then he had changed his tune—couldn't get on with the natives, or the whites, or something; and the next time we came round, there he was dead and buried. I took and put up a bit of a stick to him: "John Adams, *obit* eighteen and sixty eight. Go thou and do likewise." I missed that man; I never could see much harm in Johnny.'

'What did he die of?' I inquired.

'Some kind of a sickness,' says the captain. 'It appears it took him sudden. Seems he got up in the night, and filled up on Pain-Killer and Kennedy's Discovery: no go—he was booked beyond Kennedy. Then he had tried to open a case of gin; no go again—not strong enough. Then he must have turned to and run out on the verandah, and capsized over the rail. When they found him the next day, he was clean crazy—carried on all the time about somebody watering his copra. Poor John!'

'Was it thought to be the island?' I asked.

'Well, it was thought to be the island, or the trouble, or something,' he replied. 'I never could hear but what it was a healthy place. Our last man, Vigours, never turned a hair. He left because of the beach; said he was afraid of Black Jack and Case and Whistling Jimmie, who was still alive at the time but got drowned soon afterward when drunk. As for old Captain Randall, he's been here any time since eighteen forty, forty five. I never could see much harm in Billy, nor much change. Seems as if he might live to be old Kafoozleum. No, I guess its healthy.'

'There's a boat coming now,' said I. 'She's right in the pass; looks to be a sixteen foot whale; two white men in the stern sheets.'

'That's the boat that drowned Whistling Jimmie!' cried the captain. 'Let's see the glass. Yes: that's Case, sure enough, and the darkie. They've got a gallows bad reputation, but you know what a place the beach is for talking. My belief, that Whistling Jimmie was the worst of the trouble; and he's gone to glory, you see. What'll you bet they ain't after gin? Lay you five to two they take six cases.'

When these two traders came aboard I was pleased with the looks of them at once, or rather, with the looks of both, and the speech of one. I was sick for white neighbours after my four years at the line, which I always counted years of prison; getting tabooed, and going down to the Speak House to see and get it taken off; buying gin, and going on a break, and then repenting; sitting in my house at night with the lamp for company; or walking on the beach and wondering what kind of a fool to call myself for being where I was. There were no other whites upon my island; and when I sailed to the next, rough customers made the most of the society. Now to see these two when they came aboard, was a pleasure. One was a negro to be sure; but they were both rigged out smart in striped pyjamas and straw hats, and Case would have passed muster in a city. He was yellow and smallish; had a hawk's nose to his face, pale eyes, and his beard trimmed with scissors. No man knew his country, beyond he was of English speech; and it was clear he came of a good family and was splendidly educated. He was accomplished too; played the accordion first rate; and give him a piece of string or a cork or a pack of cards, and he could show you tricks equal to any professional. He could speak when he chose fit for a drawing room; and when he chose he could blaspheme worse than a Yankee boatswain and talk smut to sicken a kanaka. The way he thought would pay best at the moment, that was Case's way; and it always seemed to come natural and like as if he was born to it. He had the courage of a lion and the cunning of a rat; and if he's not in Hell today, there's no such place. I know but one good point to the man; that he was fond of his wife and kind to her. She was a Sāmoa woman, and dyed her hair red, Sāmoa style; and when he came to die (as I have to tell of) they found one strange thing, that he had made a will like a christian and the widow got the lot. All his, they said, and all Black Jack's, and the most of Billy Randall's in the bargain; for it was Case that kept the books. So she went off home in the schooner *Manu'a*, and does the lady to this day in her own place.

But of all this, on that first morning, I knew no more than a fly. Case used me like a gentleman and like a friend, made me welcome to Falesá, and put his services at my disposal, which was the more helpful from my ignorance of the native. All the early part of the day, we sat drinking better acquaintance in the cabin, and I never heard a man talk more to the point. There was no smarter trader, and none dodgier, in the islands. I remember one bit of advice he gave that morning, and one yarn he told. The bit of advice was this. 'Whenever you get hold of any money,' says he—'any christian money, I mean—the first thing to do is to fire it up to Sydney to the bank. It's only a temptation to a copra merchant; some day, he'll be in a row with the other traders, and he'll get his shirt out and buy copra with it. And the name of the man that buys copra with gold is Damfool,' says he. That was the advice; and this was the yarn, which might have opened my eyes to the danger of that man for a neighbour, if I had been anyway suspicious. It seems Case was trading somewhere in the Ellices. There was a man Miller a Dutchman there, who had a strong hold with the natives and handled the bulk of what there was. Well one fine day a schooner got wrecked in the lagoon, and Miller bought her (the way these things are usually managed) for an old song, which was the ruin of him. For having a lot of trade on hand that had cost him practically nothing, what does he do but begin cutting rates? Case went round to the other traders. 'Wants to lower prices?' says Case. 'All right, then. He has five times the turn-over of any of us; if buying at a loss is the game, he stands to lose five times more. Let's give him the bed rock; let's bilge the————!' And so they did, and five months after, Miller had to sell out his boat and station, and begin again somewhere in the Carolines.

All this talk suited me, and my new companion suited me, and I thought Falesá seemed to be the right kind of a place; and the more I drank, the lighter my heart. Our last trader had fled the place at half an hour's notice, taking a chance passage in a labour ship from up west; the captain, when he came, had found the station closed, the keys left with the native pastor, and a letter from the runaway confessing he was fairly frightened of his life. Since then the firm had not been represented and of course there was no cargo; the wind besides was fair, the captain hoped he could make his next island by dawn, with a good tide; and the business of landing my trade was gone about lively. There was no call for me to fool with it, Case said; nobody would touch my things, everyone was honest in Falesá, only about chickens or an odd knife or an odd stick of tobacco; and the best I could do was to sit quiet till the vessel left, then come straight to his house, see old Captain Randall, the father of the Beach, take pot luck, and go home to sleep when it got dark. So it was high noon, and the schooner was under way, before I set my foot on shore at Falesá.

I had a glass or two on board, I was just off a long cruise and the ground heaved under me like a ship's deck. The world was like all new painted; my foot went along to music; Falesá might have been Fiddler's Green, if there is such a place, and more's the pity if there isn't! It was good to foot the grass, to look aloft at the green mountains, to see the men with their green wreaths and the women in their bright dresses, red and blue. On we went, in the strong sun and the cool shadow, liking both; and all the children in the town came trotting after with their shaven heads and their brown bodies, and raising a thin kind of a cheer in our wake, like crowing poultry.

'By the by,' says Case, 'we must get you a wife.'

'That's so,' said I, 'I had forgotten.'

There was a crowd of girls about us, and I pulled myself up and looked among them like a Bashaw. They were all dressed out for the sake of the ship being in; and the women of Falesá are a handsome lot to see. If they have a fault, they are a trifle broad in the beam; and I was just thinking so when Case touched me.

'That's pretty,' says he.

I saw one coming on the other side alone. She had been fishing; all she wore was a chemise, and it was wetted through, and a cutty sark at that. She was young and very slender for an island maid, with a long face, a high forehead, and a sly, strange, blindish look between a cat's and a baby's.

'Who's she?' said I. 'She'll do.'

'That's Uma,' said Case, and he called her up and spoke to her in the native. I didn't know what he said; but when he was in the midst, she looked up at me quick and timid like a child dodging a blow; then down again; and presently smiled. She had a wide mouth, the lips and the chin cut like any statue's; and the smile came out for a moment and was gone. There she stood with her head bent and heard Case to an end; spoke back in the pretty Polynesian voice, looking him full in the face; heard him again in answer; and then with an obeisance started off. I had just a share of the bow, but never another shot of her eye; and there was no more word of smiling.

'I guess it's all right,' said Case. 'I guess you can have her. I'll make it square with the old lady. You can have your pick of the lot for a plug of tobacco,' he added, sneering.

I suppose it was the smile stuck in my memory, for I spoke back sharp. 'She doesn't look that sort,' I cried.

'I don't know that she is,' said Case. 'I believe she's as right as the mail. Keeps to herself, don't go round with the gang, and that. O, no, don't you misunderstand me—Uma's on the square.' He spoke eager I thought, and that surprised and pleased me. 'Indeed,' he went on, 'I shouldn't make so sure of getting her, only she cottoned to the cut of your jib. All you have to do is to keep dark and let me work the mother my own way; and I'll bring the girl round to the captain's for the marriage.'

I didn't care for the word marriage, and I said so.

'O, there's nothing to hurt in the marriage,' says he. 'Black Jack's the chaplain.'

By this time we had come in view of the house of these three white men; for a negro is counted a white man—and so is a Chinese! a strange idea, but common in the islands. It was a board house with a strip of ricketty verandah. The store was to the front, with a counter, scales and the poorest possible display of trades: a case or two of tinned meats; a barrel of hard bread; a few bolts of cotton stuff, not to be compared with mine; the only thing well represented being the contraband—fire arms and liquor. 'If these are my only rivals,' thinks I, 'I should do well in Falesá.' Indeed there was only the one way they could touch me, and that was with the guns and drink.

In the back room was old Captain Randall, squatting on the floor native fashion, fat and pale, naked to the waist, gray as a badger and his eyes set with drink. His body was covered with gray hair and crawled over by flies; one was in the corner of his eye—he never heeded; and the mosquitoes hummed about the man like bees. Any clean-minded man would have had the creature out at once and buried him; and to see him, and think he was seventy, and remember he had once commanded a ship, and come ashore in his smart togs, and talked big in bars and consulates, and sat in club verandahs, turned me sick and sober.

He tried to get up when I came in, but that was hopeless, so he reached me a hand instead and stumbled out some salutation.

'Papa's pretty full this morning,' observed Case. 'We've had an epidemic here; and Captain Randall takes gin for a prophylactic—don't you, papa?'

'Never took such thing my life!' cried the captain, indignantly. 'Take gin for my health's sake, Mr Wha's-ever-your-name. 'S a preacaution'ry measure.'

'That's all right, papa,' said Case. 'But you'll have to brace up. There's going to be a marriage, Mr Wiltshire here is going to get spliced.'

The old man asked to whom.

'To Uma,' said Case.

'Uma?' cried the captain. 'Wha's he want Uma for? 'S he come here for his health, anyway? Wha' 'n hell's he want Uma for?'

'Dry up papa,' said Case. ''Tain't you that's to marry her. I guess you're not her godfather and godmother, I guess Mr Wiltshire's going to please himself.'

With that he made an excuse to me that he must move about the marriage, and left me alone with the poor wretch that was his partner and (to speak truth) his gull. Trade and station belonged both to Randall; Case and the negro were parasites; they crawled and fed upon him like the flies, he none the wiser. Indeed I have no harm to say of Billy Randall, beyond the fact that my gorge rose at him, and the time I now passed in his company was like a nightmare.

The room was stifling hot and full of flies; for the house was dirty and low and small, and stood in a bad place, behind the village, in the borders of the bush, and sheltered from the trade. The three men's beds were on the floor, and a litter of pans and dishes. There was no standing furniture, Randall, when he was violent, tearing it to laths. There I sat, and had a meal which was served us by Case's wife; and there I was entertained all day by that remains of man, his tongue stumbling among low old jokes and long old stories, and his own wheezy laughter always ready, so that he had no sense of depression. He was nipping gin all the while; sometimes he fell asleep and awoke again whimpering and shivering, and every now and again he would ask me why in Hell I wanted to marry Uma. 'My friend,' I was telling myself all day, 'you must not be an old gentleman like this.'

It might be four in the afternoon perhaps, when the backdoor was thrust slowly open, and a strange old native woman crawled into the house almost on her belly. She was swathed in black stuff to her heels; her hair was gray in swatches; her face was tattooed, which was not the practise in that island; her eyes big and bright and crazy. These she fixed upon me with a wrapt expression that I saw to be part acting; she said no plain word, but smacked and mumbled with her lips, and hummed aloud, like a child over its Christmas pudding. She came straight across the house heading for me, and as soon as she was alongside, caught up my hand and purred and crooned over it like a great cat. From this she slipped into a kind of song.

'Who in the devil's this?' cried I, for the thing startled me.

'It's Faavao,' says Randall, and I saw he had hitched along the floor into the farthest corner.

'You ain't afraid of her?' I cried.

'Me 'fraid!' cried the captain. 'My dear friend, I defy her! I don't let her put her foot in here. Only I suppose 's diff'ent today for the marriage. 'S Uma's mother.'

'Well, suppose it is, what's she carrying on about?' I asked, more irritated, perhaps more frightened than I cared to show; and the captain told me she was making up a quantity of poetry in my praise because I was to marry Uma. 'All right, old lady,' says I, with rather a failure of a laugh. 'Anything to oblige. But when you're done with my hand, you might let me know.'

She did as though she understood; the song rose into a cry and stopped; the woman crouched out of the house the same way that she came in, and must have plunged straight into the bush, for when I followed her to the door she had already vanished.

'These are rum manners,' said I.

''S a rum crowd,' said the captain, and to my surprise he made the sign of the cross on his bare bosom.

'Hillo!' says I, 'are you a papist?'

He repudiated the idea with contempt. 'Hard-shell Baptis',' said he. 'But, my dear friend, the papists got some good ideas too; and tha' 's one of 'em. You take my advice, and whenever you come across Uma or Faavao or Vigours or any of that crowd, you take a leaf out o' the priests, and do what I do: savvy?' says he, repeated the sign, and winked his dim eye at me. 'No, *sir!*' he broke out again, 'no papists here!' and for a long time entertained me with his religious opinions.

I must have been taken with Uma from the first, or I should certainly have fled from that house and got into the clean air, and the clean sea or some convenient river. Though it's true I was committed to Case; and besides I could never have held my head up in that island, if I had run from a girl upon my wedding night.

The sun was down, the sky all on fire and the lamp had been sometime lighted, when Case came back with Uma and the negro. She was dressed and scented; her kilt was of fine tapa,[1] looking richer in the folds than any silk; and behind which was of the colour of dark honey, she wore bare only for some half a dozen necklaces of seeds and flowers; and behind her ears and in her hair, she had the scarlet flowers of the hybiscus. She showed the best bearing for a bride conceivable, serious and still; and I thought shame to stand up with her in that mean house and before that grinning negro. I thought shame I say; for the mountebank was dressed with a big paper collar, the book he made believe to read from was an odd volume of a novel, and the words of his service not fit to be set down. My conscience smote me when we joined hands; and when she got her certificate, I was tempted to throw up in bargain and confess. Here is the document: it

1. Bark cloth, a material made in many parts of the Pacific.

was Case that wrote it, signatures and all, in a leaf out of the ledger.

This is to certify that *Uma* daughter of *Faavao* of Falesá island of ——, is illegally married to *Mr John Wiltshire* for one night, and Mr John Wiltshire is at liberty to send her to hell next morning.

John Blackamoor
Chaplain to the Hulks

Extracted from the register
by William T. Randall
Master Mariner.

That was a nice paper to put in a girl's hand and see her hide away like gold. A man might easily feel cheap for less. But it was the practise in these parts, and (as I told myself) not the least the fault of us White Men but of the missionaries. If they had let the natives be, I had never needed this deception, but taken all the wives I wished, and left them when I pleased, with a clear conscience.

The more ashamed I was, the more hurry I was in to be gone; and our desires thus jumping together, I made the less remark of a change in the traders. Case had been all eagerness to keep me; now, as though he had attained a purpose, he seemed all eagerness to have me go. Uma, he said, could show me to my house, and the three bade us farewell indoors.

The night was nearly come; the village smelt of trees, and flowers and the sea, and breadfruit cooking; there came a fine roll of sea from the reef, and from a distance, among the woods and houses, many pretty sounds of men and children. It did me good to breathe free air; it did me good to be done with the captain and see, instead, the creature at my side. I felt for all the world as though she were some girl at home in the old country, and forgetting myself for a minute, took her hand to walk with. Her fingers nestled into mine; I heard her breathe deep and quick; and all at once she caught my hand to her face and pressed it there. 'You good!' she cried, and ran ahead of me, and stopped and looked back and smiled, and ran ahead of me again; thus guiding me through the edge of the bush and by a quiet way to my own house.

The truth is Case had done the courting for me in style;

told her I was mad to have her and cared nothing for the consequence; and the poor soul, knowing that which I was still ignorant of, believed it every word, and had her head nigh turned with vanity and gratitude. Now of all this I had no guess; I was one of those most opposed to any nonsense about native women, having seen so many whites eaten up by their wives' relatives and made fools of in the bargain; and I told myself I must make a stand at once and bring her to her bearings. But she looked so quaint and pretty as she ran away and then awaited me, and the thing was done so like a child or a kind of dog, that the best I could do was just to follow her whenever she went on, to listen for the fall of her bare feet, and to watch in the dusk for the shining of her body. And there was another thought came in my head. She played kitten with me now when we were alone; but in the house she had carried it the way a countess might, so proud and humble. And what with her dress—for all there was so little of it, and that native enough—what with her fine tapa and fine scents, and her red flowers and seeds that were quite as bright as jewels, only larger—it came over me she was a kind of a countess really, dressed to hear great singers at a concert, and no even mate for a poor trader like myself.

She was the first in the house; and while I was still without, I saw a match flash and the lamplight kindle in the windows. The station was a wonderful fine place, coral built, with quite a wide verandah, and the main room high and wide. My chest and cases had been piled in, and made rather of a mess; and there, in the thick of the confusion, stood Uma by the table, awaiting me. Her shadow went all the way up behind her into the hollow of the iron roof; she stood against it bright, the lamplight shining on her skin. I stopped in the door, and she looked at me, not speaking, with eyes that were eager and yet daunted. Then she touched herself on the bosom. 'Me—your wifie,' she said. It had never taken me like that before; but the want of her took and shook all through me, like the wind in the luff of a sail.

I could not speak, if I had wanted; and if I could, I would not. I was ashamed to be so much moved about a native, ashamed of the marriage too, and the certificate she had treasured in her kilt; and I turned aside and made believe to

rummage among my cases. The first thing I lighted on was a
case of gin, the only one that I had brought; and partly for
the girl's sake, and partly for the horror of the recollection of
old Randall, took a sudden resolve. I prized the lid off; one
by one, I drew the bottles with a pocket corkscrew, and sent
Uma out to pour the stuff from the verandah.

She came back after the last, and looked at me puzzled
like.

'Why you do that?' she asked.

'No good,' said I, for I was now a little better master of my
tongue. 'Man he drink, he no good.'

She agreed with this but kept considering. 'Why you bring
him?' she asked presently. 'Suppose you no want drink, you
no bring him, I think.'

'That's all right,' said I. 'One time I want drink too much;
now no want. You see I no savvy I get one little wifie.
Suppose I drink gin, my little wifie he 'fraid.'

To speak to her kindly was about more than I was fit for; I
had made my vow I would never let on to weakness with a
native; and I had nothing for it but to stop.

She stood looking gravely down at me where I sat by the
open case. 'I think you good man,' she said. And suddenly
she had fallen before me on the floor. 'I belong you all-e-
same pig!' she cried.

TWO. THE BAN

I came on the verandah just before the sun rose on the morrow. My house was the last on the east; there was a cape of woods and cliffs behind that hid the sunrise. To the west, a swift cold river ran down, and beyond was the green of the village, dotted with cocoapalms and breadfruits and houses. The shutters were some of them down and some open; I saw the mosquito bars still stretched, with shadows of people new wakened sitting up inside; and all over the green others were stalking silent, wrapped in their many-coloured sleeping clothes like Bedouins in bible pictures. It was mortal still and solemn and chilly; and the light of the dawn on the lagoon was like the shining of a fire.

But the thing that troubled me was nearer hand. Some dozen young men and children made a piece of a half circle, flanking my house; the river divided them, some were on the near side, some on the far, and one on a boulder in the midst; and they all sat silent, wrapped in their sheets, and stared at me and my house as straight as pointer dogs. I thought it strange as I went out. When I had bathed and come back again, and found them all there, and two or three more along with them, I thought it stranger still. What could they see to gaze at in my house? I wondered, and went in.

But the thought of these starers stuck in my mind, and presently I came out again. The sun was now up, but it was still behind the cape of woods: say quarter of an hour had come and gone. The crowd was greatly increased, the far bank of the river was lined for quite a way; perhaps thirty grown folk, and of children twice as many, some standing, some squatted on the ground, and all staring at my house. I have seen a house in a South Sea village thus surrounded, but then a trader was thrashing his wife inside, and she singing out. Here was nothing: the stove was alight, the smoke going up in a Christian manner; all was shipshape and Bristol fashion. To be sure, there was a stranger come; but they had a chance to see that stranger yesterday and took it quiet enough. What ailed them now? I leaned my arms on the rail and stared back. Devil a wink they had in them. Now and then I could see the children chatter, but they spoke so low not even the hum of their speaking came my length. The rest were like graven images; they stared at me, dumb and sorrowful, with their bright eyes; and it came upon me things would look not much different, if I were on the platform of the gallows, and these good folk had come to see me hanged.

I felt I was getting daunted, and began to be afraid I looked it, which would never do. Up I stood, made believe to stretch myself, came down the verandah stair, and strolled towards the river. There went a short buzz from one to the other, like what you hear in theatres when the curtain goes up; and some of the nearest gave back the matter of a pace. I saw a girl lay one hand on a young man and make a gesture upward with the other; at the same time she said something in the native with a gasping voice. Three little boys sat beside my path, where I must pass within three feet of them. Wrapped in their sheets, with their shaved heads and bits of topknots, and queer faces, they looked like figures on a chimney piece. Awhile they sat their ground, solemn as judges; I came up hand over fist, doing my five knots, like a man that meant business; and I thought I saw a sort of a wink and gulp in the three faces. The one jumped up (he was the farthest off) and ran for his mammy. The other two, trying to follow suit, got foul, came to ground together bawling, wriggled right out of their sheets—and in a moment there were all three of them, two mother naked, scampering for their lives and singing out like pigs. The natives, who would never let a joke slip even at a burial, laughed and let up, as short as a dog's bark.

They say it scares a man to be alone. No such thing. What scares him in the dark or the high bush, is that he can't make sure, and there might be an army at his elbow. What scares him worst is to be right in the midst of a crowd, and have no guess of what they're driving at. When that laugh stopped, I stopped too. The boys had not yet made their offing, they were still on the full stretch going the one way, when I had already gone about ship and was sheering off the other. Like a fool I had come out, doing my five knots, like a fool I went back again. It must have been the funniest thing to see, and what knocked me silly, this time no one laughed; only one old woman gave a kind of pious moan, the way you have heard dissenters in their chapels at the sermon.

'I never saw such damfool kanakas as your people here,' I said once to Uma, glancing out of the window at the starers.

'Savvy nothing,' says Uma, with a kind of a disgusted air that she was good at.

And that was all the talk we had upon the matter, for I was put out, and Uma took the thing so much as a matter of course, that I was fairly ashamed.

All day, off and on, now fewer and now more, the fools sat about the west end of my house and across the river, waiting for the show, whatever that was—fire to come down from heaven, I suppose, and consume me bones and baggage. But by evening, like real islanders, they had wearied of the business; and got away and had a dance instead in the big house of the village, where I heard them singing and clapping hands till maybe ten at night; and the next day, it seemed they had forgotten I existed. If fire had come down from heaven or the earth opened and swallowed me, there would have been nobody to see the sport or take the lesson, or whatever you like to call it. But I was to find they hadn't forgot either, and kept an eye lifting for phenomena over my way.

I was hard at it both these days getting my trade in order, and taking stock of what Vigours had left. This was a job that made me pretty sick, and kept me from thinking on much else. Ben had taken stock the trip before, I knew I could trust Ben; but it was plain somebody had been making free in the meantime. I found I was out by what might easy cover six months salary and profit; and I could have kicked myself all round the village to have been such a blamed ass, sitting boozing with that Case, instead of attending to my own affairs and taking stock.

However, there's no use crying over spilt milk. It was done now and couldn't be undone. All I could do was to get what was left of it, and my new stuff (my own choice) in order, to go round and get after the rats and cockroaches, and to fix up that store regular Sydney style. A fine show I made of it; and the third morning, when I had lit my pipe and stood in the doorway and looked in—and turned and looked far up the mountain, and saw the cocoanuts waving, and saw the island dandies, and reckoned up the yards of print they wanted for their kilts and dresses—I felt as if I was in the right place to make a fortune, and go home again, and start a public house. There was I sitting in that verandah, in as handsome a piece of scenery as you could find, a splendid sun, and a fine, fresh healthy trade that stirred up a man's blood like seabathing; and the whole thing was clean gone from me, and I was dreaming England, which is after all a nasty, cold, muddy hole, with not enough light to see to read by—and dreaming the looks of my public, by a kant of a broad highroad like an avenue and with the sign on a green tree.

So much for the morning, but the day passed and the devil any one looked near me, and from all I knew of natives in other islands, I thought this strange. People laughed a little at our firm, and their fine stations, and at this station of Falesá in particular: all the copra in the district wouldn't pay for it (I had heard them say) in fifty years; which I supposed was an exaggeration. But when the day went and no business came at all, I began to get down-hearted, and about three in the afternoon, I went out for a stroll to cheer me up. On the green I saw a white man coming with a cassock on, by which and by the face of him, I knew he was a priest. He was a good natured old soul to look at, gone a little grizzled, and so dirty you could have written with him on a piece of paper.

'Good day, sir,' says I.

He answered me eagerly in native.

'Don't you speak any English?' said I.

'Franch,' says he.

'Well,' said I, 'I'm sorry, but I can't do anything there.'

He tried me awhile in the French, and then again in

native, which he seemed to think was the best chance. I made out he was after more than passing the time of day with me, but had something to communicate, and I listened the harder. I heard the names of Adams and Case and of Randall—Randall the oftenest; and the word 'poison' or something like it; and a native word that he said very often. I went home repeating it to myself.

'What does *fussy-ocky* mean?' I asked of Uma, for that was as near as I could come to it.

'Make dead,' said she.

'The devil does it!' says I. 'Did ever you hear that Case had poisoned Johnny Adams?'

'Every man he savvy that,' says Uma, scornful like. 'Give him white sand—bad sand. He got the bottle still. Suppose he give you gin, you no take him.'

Now I had heard much the same sort of story in other islands, and the same white powder always to the front, which made me think the less of it. For all that I went over to Randall's place, to see what I could pick up, and found Case on the door step cleaning a gun.

'Good shooting here?' says I.

'A one,' says he. 'The bush is full of all kinds of birds. I wish copra was as plenty,' says he, I thought slyly, 'but there don't seem anything doing.'

I could see Black Jack in the store serving a customer.

'That looks like business, though,' said I.

'That's the first sale we've made in three weeks,' said he.

'You don't tell me?' says I. 'Three weeks? Well, well.'

'If you don't believe me,' he cries, a little hot, 'you can go and look at the copra house. It's half empty to this blessèd hour.'

'I shouldn't be much the better for that, you see,' says I. 'For all I can tell, it might have been whole empty yesterday.'

'That's so,' says he, with a bit of a laugh.

'By the by,' I said, 'what sort of a party is that priest? Seems rather a friendly sort.'

At this Case laughed right out loud. 'Ah,' says he, 'I see what ails you now! Galuchet's been at you.' *Father Galoshes* was the name he went by mostly, but Case always gave it the

French quirk, which was another reason we had for thinking him above the common.

'Yes, I have seen him,' says I. 'I made out he didn't think much of you or Captain Randall.'

'That he don't!' says Case. 'It was the trouble about poor Adams. The last day, when he lay dying, there was young Buncombe round. Ever met Buncombe?'

I told him no.

'He's a cure, is Buncombe!' laughs Case. 'Well, Buncombe took it in his head that as there was no other clergyman about, bar kanaka pastors, we ought to call in Father Galuchet, and have the old man administered and take the sacrament. It was all the same to me, you may suppose; but I said I thought Adams was the fellow to consult. He was jawing away about watered copra and a sight of foolery. "Look here," I said. "You're pretty sick. Would you like to see Galoshes?" He sat right up on his elbow. "Get the priest," says he, "get the priest, don't let me die here like a dog." He spoke kind of fierce and eager, but sensible enough; there was nothing to say against that; so we went and asked Galuchet if he would come. You bet he would! He jumped in his dirty linen at the thought of it. But we had reckoned without Papa. He's a hard-shell Baptist, is Papa; no papists need apply; and he took and locked the door. Buncombe told him he was bigoted, and I thought he would have had a fit. "Bigoted!" he says. "Me bigoted? Have I lived to hear it from a jackanapes like you?" And he made for Buncombe, and I had to hold them apart—and there was Adams in the middle, gone luny again and carrying on about copra like a born fool. It was good as the play, and I was about knocked out of time with laughing, when all of a sudden Adams sat up, clapped his hands to his chest, and went into the horrors.[1] He died hard, did John Adams,' says Case with a kind of a sudden sternness.

'And what became of the priest?' I asked.

'The priest?' says Case. 'O, he was hammering on the door

---

1. Delirium tremens. It is tempting to think that when in
   Heart of Darkness Conrad invokes 'the horror' it might
   be an echo of Stevenson.

outside, and crying on the natives to come and beat it in, and singing out it was a soul he wished to save, and that. He was in a hell of a taking was the priest. But what would you have? Johnny had slipped his cable; no more Johnny in the market! and the administration racket clean played out. Next thing, word came to Randall the priest was praying upon Johnny's grave. Papa was pretty full, and got a club, and lit out straight for the place; and there was Galoshes on his knees, and a lot of natives looking on. You wouldn't think papa cared that much about anything, unless it was liquor; but he and the priest stuck to it two hours, slanging each other in native; and every time Galoshes tried to kneel down, papa went for him with the club. There never were such larks in Falesá. The end of it was that Captain Randall knocked over with some kind of a fit or stroke, and the priest got in his goods after all. But he was the angriest priest you ever heard of; and complained to the chiefs about the outrage, as he called it. That was no account, for our chiefs are protestant here; and anyway he had been making trouble about the drum for morning school, and they were glad to give him a wipe. Now he swears old Randall gave Adams poison or something, and when the two meet they grin at each other like baboons.'

He told this story as natural as could be, and like a man that enjoyed the fun; though now I come to think of it after so long, it seems rather a sickening yarn. However Case never set up to be soft, only to be square and hearty and a man all round; and to tell the truth, he puzzled me entirely.

I went home, and asked Uma if she were a *Popey*, which I had made out to be the native word for catholics.

'*E le ai*!' says she—she always used the native when she meant 'no' more than usually strong, and indeed there's more of it. 'No good, popey,' she added.

Then I asked her about Adams and the priest, and she told me much the same yarn in her own way. So that I was left not much farther on; but inclined upon the whole, to think the bottom of the matter was the row about the sacrament, and the poisoning only talk.

The next day was a Sunday, when there was no business to be looked for. Uma asked me in the morning if I was going to

'pray'; I told her she bet not; and she stopped home herself
with no more words. I thought this seemed unlike a native,
and a native woman, and a woman that had new clothes to
show off; however, it suited me to the ground and I made the
less of it. The queer thing was that I came next door to going
to church after all, a thing I'm little likely to forget. I had
turned out for a stroll, and heard the hymn tune up. You
know how it is; if you hear folk singing, it seems to draw
you; and pretty soon I found myself alongside the church. It
was a little long low place, coral built, rounded off at both
ends like a whale boat, a big native roof on the top of it,
windows without sashes and doorways without doors. I
stuck my head into one of the windows, and the sight was so
new to me—for things went quite different in the islands I
was acquainted with—that I stayed and looked on. The
congregation sat on the floor on mats, the women on one
side, the men on the other; all rigged out to kill, the women
with dresses and trade hats, the men in white jackets and
shirts. The hymn was over; the pastor, a big, buck kanaka,
was in the pulpit preaching for his life; and by the way he
wagged his hand, and worked his voice, and made his points,
and seemed to argue with the folk, I made out he was a gun at
the business. Well, he looked up suddenly and caught my
eye; and I give you my word he staggered in the pulpit. His
eyes bulged out of his head, his hand rose and pointed at me
like as if against his will, and the sermon stopped right there.

It isn't a fine thing to say for yourself, but I ran away; and
if the same kind of a shock was given me, I should run away
again tomorrow. To see that palavering kanaka struck all of a
heap at the mere sight of me, gave me a feeling as if the
bottom had dropped out of the world. I went right home,
and stayed there, and said nothing. You might think I would
tell Uma, but that was against my system. You might have
thought I would have gone over and consulted Case; but the
truth was I was ashamed to speak of such a thing, I thought
everyone would blurt out laughing in my face. So I held my
tongue, and thought all the more, and the more I thought,
the less I liked the business.

By Monday night, I got it clearly in my head I must be
tabooed. A new store to stand open two days in a village, and

not a man or woman come to see the trade, was past
believing.

'Uma,' said I, 'I think I'm tabooed.'

'I think so,' said she.

I thought awhile whether I should ask her more, but it's a
bad idea to set natives up with any notion of consulting
them, so I went to Case. It was dark, and he was sitting
alone, as he did mostly, smoking on the stairs.

'Case,' said I, 'here's a queer thing. I'm tabooed.'

'O, fudge!' says he. 'Tain't the practise in these islands.'

'That may be, or it mayn't,' said I. 'It's the practise where
I was before; you can bet I know what it's like; and I tell it
you for a fact: I'm tabooed.'

'Well,' said he; 'it ain't possible. However I'll tell you
what I'll do; just to put your mind at rest, I'll go round and
find out for sure. Just you waltz in and talk to papa.'

'Thank you,' I said, 'I'd rather stay right out here on the
verandah: your house is so close.'

'I'll call papa out here, then,' says he.

'My dear fellow,' I says, 'I wish you wouldn't. The fact is I
don't take to Mr Randall.'

Case laughed, took a lantern from the store, and set out
into the village. He was gone perhaps quarter of an hour, and
he looked mighty serious when he came back.

'Well,' said he, clapping down the lantern on the verandah
steps, 'I would never have believed it. I don't know where
the impudence of these kanakas 'll go next, they seem to have
lost all idea of respect for whites. What we want is a man of
war: a German, if we could—they know how to manage
kanakas.'

'I *am* tabooed then?' I cried.

'Something of the sort,' said he. 'It's the worst thing of the
kind I've heard yet. But I'll stand by you, Wiltshire, man to
man. You come round here tomorrow about nine and we'll
have it out with the chiefs. They're afraid of me; or they used
to be, but their heads are so big now I don't know what to
think. Understand me, Wiltshire, I don't count this your
quarrel,' he went on with a great deal of resolution; 'I count it
all of our quarrel, I count it the White Man's Quarrel, and I'll
stand to it through thick and thin, and there's my hand on it.'

'Have you found out what's the reason?' I asked.

'Not yet,' said Case. 'But we'll fix them down tomorrow.'

Altogether I was pretty well pleased with his attitude, and almost more the next day when we met to go before the chiefs, to see him so stern and resolved. The chiefs awaited us in one of their big oval houses, which was marked out to us from a long way off by the crowd about the eaves, a hundred strong if there was one, men, women and children. Many of the men were on their way to work and wore green wreaths; and it put me in thoughts of the first of May at home. This crowd opened and buzzed about the pair of us as we went in, with a sudden angry animation. Five chiefs were there, four mighty stately men, the fifth old and puckered. They sat on mats in their white kilts and jackets; they had fans in their hands like fine ladies; and two of the younger ones wore catholic medals, which gave me matter of reflection. Our place was set and the mats laid for us over against these grandees on the near side of the house; the midst was empty; the crowd, close at our backs, murmured and craned and jostled to look on, and the shadows of them tossed in front of us on the clean pebbles of the floor. I was just a hair put out by the excitement of the commons, but the quiet, civil appearance of the chiefs reassured me: all the more when their spokesman began and made a long speech in a low tone of voice, sometimes waving his hand toward Case, sometimes toward me, and sometimes knocking with his knuckles on the mat. One thing was clear: there was no sign of anger in the chiefs.

'What's he been saying?' I asked, when he had done.

'O, just that they're glad to see you, and they understand by me you wish to make some kind of a complaint, and you're to fire away, and they'll do the square thing.'

'It took a precious long time to say that,' said I.

'O, the rest was sawder and *bonjour* and that,' says Case—'you know what kanakas are!'

'Well, they don't get much *bonjour* out of me,' said I. 'You tell who I am. I'm a white man, and a British Subject, and no end of a big chief at home; and I've come here to do them good and bring them civilisation; and no sooner have I got my trade sorted out, than they go and taboo me and no one dare come near my place! Tell them I don't mean to fly in the face of anything legal; and if what they want's a present, I'll do what's fair. I don't blame any man looking out for himself, tell them, for that's human nature; but if they think they're going to come any of their native ideas over me, they'll find themselves mistaken. And tell them plain, that I demand the reason of this treatment as a White Man and a British Subject.'

That was my speech. I know how to deal with kanakas; give them plain sense and fair dealing, and I'll do them that much justice, they knuckle under every time. They haven't any real government or any real law, that's what you've got to knock into their heads; and even if they had, it would be a good joke if it was to apply to a white man. It would be a strange thing if we came all this way and couldn't do what we pleased. The mere idea has always put my monkey up, and I rapped my speech out pretty big. Then Case translated it, or made believe to, rather; and the first chief replied, and then a second and a third, all in the same style, easy and genteel but solemn underneath. Once a question was put to Case, and he answered it, and all hands (both chiefs and commons) laughed out loud and looked at me. Last of all, the puckered old fellow and the big young chief that spoke first, started in to put Case through a kind of catechism. Sometimes I made out that Case was trying to fence, and they stuck to him like hounds, and the sweat ran down his face, which was no very pleasant sight to me; and at some of his answers, the crowd moaned and murmured, which was a worse hearing. It's a cruel shame I knew no native; for (as I now believe) they were asking Case about my marriage, and he must have had a tough job of it to clear his feet. But leave Case alone: he had the brains to run a parliament.

'Well, is that all?' I asked, when a pause came.

'Come along,' says he, mopping his face. 'I'll tell you outside.'

'Do you mean they won't take the taboo off?' I cried.

'It's something queer,' said he. 'I'll tell you outside. Better come away.'

'I won't take it at their hands,' cried I. 'I ain't that kind of a man. You don't find me turn my back on a parcel of kanakas.'

'You'd better,' said Case.

He looked at me with a signal in his eye; and the five chiefs looked at me civilly enough but kind of pointed; and the people looked at me and craned and jostled. I remembered the folks that watched my house, and how the pastor had jumped in his pulpit at the bare sight of me; and the whole business seemed so out of the way that I rose and followed Case. The crowd opened again to let us through, but wider than before, the children on the skirts running and singing out; and as we two white men walked away, they all stood and watched us.

'And now,' said I, 'what is all this about?'

'The truth is I can't rightly make it out myself. They have a down on you,' says Case.

'Taboo a man because they have a down on him!' I cried. 'I never heard the like.'

'It's worse than that, you see,' said Case. 'You ain't tabooed, I told you that couldn't be. The people won't go near you, Wiltshire; and there's where it is.'

'They won't go near me? What do you mean by that? Why won't they go near me?' I cried.

Case hesitated. 'Seems they're frightened,' says he, in a low voice.

I stopped dead short. 'Frightened?' I repeated. 'Are you gone crazy, Case? What are they frightened of?'

'I wish I could make out,' Case answered, shaking his head. 'Appears like one of their tomfool superstitions. That's what I don't cotton to,' he said; 'it's like the business about Vigours.'

'I'd like to know what you mean by that, and I'll trouble you to tell me,' says I.

'Well, you know, Vigours lit out and left all standing,' said he. 'It was some superstition business—I never got the hang of it—but it began to look bad before the end.'

'I've heard a different story about that,' said I, 'and I had better tell you so. I heard he ran away because of you.'

'O, well, I suppose he was ashamed to tell the truth,' says Case, 'I guess he thought it silly. And it's a fact that I packed

him off. "What would you do, old man?" says he—"Get,"
says I, "and not think twice about it." I was the gladdest
kind of man to see him clear away. It ain't my notion to turn
back on a mate when he's in a tight place; but there was that
much trouble in the village that I couldn't see where it might
likely end. I was a fool to be so much about with Vigours.
They cast it up to me today; didn't you hear Maea—that's
the young chief, the big one—ripping out about "Vika"?
That was him they were after; they don't seem to forget it,
somehow."

'This is all very well,' said I, 'but it don't tell me what's
wrong; it don't tell me what they're afraid of—what their
idea is.'

'Well, I wish I knew,' said Case. 'I can't say fairer than
that.'

'You might have asked, I think,' says I.

'And so I did,' says he; 'but you must have seen for
yourself, unless you're blind, that the asking got the other
way. I'll go far as I dare for another white man; but when I
find I'm in the scrape myself, I think first of my own bacon.
The loss of me is I'm too good natured. And I'll take the
freedom of telling you, you show a queer kind of gratitude to
a man who's got into all this mess along of your affairs.'

'There's a thing I'm thinking of,' said I. 'You were a fool
to be so much about with Vigours. One comfort, you haven't
been much about with me. I notice you've never been inside
my house. Own up, now: you had word of this before?'

'It's a fact I haven't been,' said he. 'It was an oversight,
and I'm sorry for it, Wiltshire. But about coming now, I'll be
quite plain.'

'You mean you won't?' I asked.

'Awfully sorry, old man, but that's the size of it,' says
Case.

'In short, you're afraid?' says I.

'In short, I'm afraid,' says he.

'And I'm still to be tabooed for nothing?' I asked.

'I tell you you're not tabooed,' said he. 'The kanakas won't
go near you, that's all. And who's to make 'em? We traders
have a lot of gall, I must say; we make these poor kanakas
take back their laws, and take up their taboos, and that,

whenever it happpens to suit us. But you don't mean to say you expect a law obliging people to deal in your store whether they want to or not? You don't mean to tell me you've got the gall for that! And if you had, it would be a queer thing to propose to me. I would just like to point out to you, Wiltshire, that I'm a trader myself.'

'I don't think I would talk of gall if I was you,' said I. 'Here's about what it comes to, as well as I can make out. None of the people are to trade with me, as they're all to trade with you. You're to have the copra, and I'm to go to the devil and shake myself. And I don't know any native, and you're the only man here worth mention that speaks English, and you have the gall to up and hint to me my life's in danger, and all you've got to tell me is, you don't know why?'

'Well, it is all I have to tell you,' said he. 'I don't know, I wish I did.'

'And so you turn your back and leave me to myself: is that the position?' says I.

'If you like to put it nasty,' says he. 'I don't put it so. I say merely I'm going to keep clear of you, or if I don't I'll get in danger for myself.'

'Well,' said I, 'you're a nice kind of a white man!'

'O, I understand you're riled,' said he. 'I would be myself. I can make excuses.'

'All right,' I said, 'go and make excuses somewhere else. Here's my way, there's yours.'

With that we parted, and I went straight home, in a holy temper, and found Uma trying on a lot of trade goods like a baby.

'Here,' I said, 'you quit that foolery. Here's a pretty mess to have made—as if I wasn't bothered enough anyway! And I thought I told you to get dinner?'

And then I believe I gave her a bit of the rough side of my tongue, as she deserved. She stood up at once, like a sentry to his officer; for I must say she was always well brought up and had a great respect for whites.

'And now,' says I, 'you belong round here, you're bound to understand this. What am I tabooed for anyway? or if I ain't tabooed, what makes the folks afraid of me?'

She stood and looked at me with eyes like saucers.

'You no savvy?' she gasps at last.

'No,' said I. 'How would you expect me to? We don't have any such craziness where I come from.'

'Ese no tell you?' she asked again.

(*Ese* was the name the natives had for Case; it may mean foreign, or extraordinary; or it might mean a mummy apple; but most like it was only his own name misheard and put in the kanaka spelling.)

'Not much!' said I.

'Damn Ese,' she cried.

You might think it was funny to hear this kanaka girl come out with a big swear. No such thing. There was no swearing in her; no, nor anger; she was beyond anger, and meant the word simple and serious. She stood there straight as she said it; I cannot justly say that ever I saw a woman look like that before or after, and it struck me mum. Then she made a kind of an obeisance, but it was the proudest kind, and threw her hands out open.

'I 'shamed,' she said. 'I think you savvy. Ese he tell me you savvy, he tell me you no mind—tell me you love me too much. Taboo belong me,' she said, touching herself on the bosom, as she had done upon our wedding night. 'Now I go 'way, taboo he go 'way too. Then you get too much copra. You like more better, I think. Tofá, alii,' says she in the native—'Farewell, chief!'

'Hold on,' I cried. 'Don't be in such a blamed hurry.'

She looked at me sidelong with a smile. 'You see, you get copra,' says she, the same as you might offer candies to a child.

'Uma,' said I, 'hear reason. I didn't know, and that's a fact; and Case seems to have played it pretty mean upon the pair of us. But I do know now, and I don't mind: I love you too much. You no go 'way, you no leave me, I too much sorry.'

'You no love me!' she cried, 'you talk me bad words!' And she threw herself in a corner on the floor, and began to cry.

Well, I'm no scholar, but I wasn't born yesterday, and I thought the worst of that trouble was over. However, there she lay—her back turned, her face to the wall—and shook with sobbing like a little child, so that her feet jumped with it. It's strange how it hits a man when he's in love; for there's no use mincing things; kanaka and all, I was in love with her, or just as good. I tried to take her hand, but she would none of that. 'Uma,' I said, 'there's no sense in carrying on like this. I want you stop here, I want my little wifie, I tell you true.'

'No tell me true!' she sobbed.

'All right,' says I, 'I'll wait till you're through with this.' And I sat right down beside her on the floor, and set to smoothe her hair with my hand. At first she wriggled away when I touched her; then she seemed to notice me no more; then her sobs grew gradually less and presently stopped; and the next thing I knew, she raised her face to mine.

'You tell me true? You like me stop?' she asked.

'Uma,' I said, 'I would rather have you than all the copra in the South Seas,' which was a very big expression, and the strangest thing was that I meant it.

She threw her arms about me, sprang close up, and pressed her face to mine in the island way of kissing, so that I was all wetted with her tears and my heart went out to her wholly. I never had anything so near me as this little brown bit of a girl. Many things went together and all helped to turn my head. She was pretty enough to eat; it seemed she was my only friend in that queer place; I was ashamed that I had spoken rough to her; and she was a woman, and my wife, and a kind of a baby besides that I was sorry for; and the salt of her tears was in my mouth. And I forgot Case and the natives; and I forgot that I knew nothing of the story, or only remembered it to banish the remembrance; and I forgot that I was to get no copra and so could make no livelihood; and I forgot my employers, and the strange kind of service I was doing them, when I preferred my fancy to their business; and I forgot even that Uma was no true wife of mine, but just a maid beguiled, and that in a pretty shabby style. But that is to look too far on. I will come to that part of it next.

It was late before we thought of getting dinner. The stove was out, and gone stone-cold; but we fired up after awhile, and cooked each a dish, helping and hindering each other, and making a play of it like children. I was so greedy of her nearness that I sat down to dinner with my lass upon my knee, made sure of her with one hand, and ate with the other. Ay, and more than that. She was the worst cook I suppose God made; the things she set her hand to, it would have sickened an entire horse to eat of; yet I made my meal that day on Uma's cookery, and can never call to mind to have been better pleased.

I didn't pretend to myself, and I didn't pretend to her. I saw I was clean gone; and if she was to make a fool of me, she must. And I suppose it was this that set her talking, for now she made sure that we were friends. A lot she told me, sitting in my lap and eating my dish, as I ate hers, from foolery: a lot about herself and her mother and Case, all which would be very tedious and fill sheets if I set it down in Beach de Mar, but which I must give a hint of in plain English—and one thing about myself, which had a very big effect on my concerns, as you are soon to hear.

It seems she was born in one of the Line islands; had been only two or three years in these parts, where she had come with a white man who was married to her mother and then died; and only the one year in Falesá. Before that, they had been a good deal on the move, trekking about after the white man, who was one of these rolling stones that keep going round after a soft job. They talk about looking for gold at the end of the rainbow; but if a man wants an employment that'll last him till he dies, let him start out on the soft-job hunt. There's meat and drink in it too, and beer and skittles; for you never hear of them starving and rarely see them sober; and as for steady sport, cockfighting isn't in the same county with it. Anyway, this beachcomber carried the woman and her daughter all over the shop, but mostly to out of the way islands, where there were no police and he thought perhaps the soft-job hung out. I've my own view of this old party; but I was just as glad he had kept Uma clear of Apia and Papeete and these flash towns. At last he struck Fale-alii on this island, got some trade the Lord knows how! muddled it all away in the usual style, and died worth next to nothing, bar a bit of land at Falesá that he had got for a

bad debt, which was what put it in the minds of the mother
and daughter to come there and live. It seems Case encouraged them all he could, and helped to get their house built.
He was very kind those days, and gave Uma trade, and
there is no doubt he had his eye on her from the beginning.
However, they had scarce settled, when up turned a young
man, a native, and wanted to marry her. He was a small
chief, and had some fine mats and old songs in his family,
and was 'very pretty', Uma said; and altogether it was an
extraordinary match for a penniless girl and an out-
islander.

At the first word of this, I got downright sick with
jealousy.

'And you mean to say you would have married him!' I
cried.

'*Ioe*,' says she. 'I like too much!'

'Well!' I said. 'And suppose I had come round after?'

'I like you more better now,' said she. 'But suppose I
marry Ioane, I one good wife. I no common kanaka: good
girl!' says she.

Well, I had to be pleased with that; but I promise you I
didn't care about the business one little bit, and liked the
end of that yarn better than the beginning. For it seems this
proposal of marriage was the start of all the trouble. It
seems, before that, Uma and her mother had been looked
down upon of course for kinless folk and out-islanders, but
nothing to hurt; and even when Ioane came forward there
was less trouble at first than might have been looked for.
And then all of a sudden, about six months before my
coming, Ioane backed out and left that part of the island,
and from that day to this, Uma and her mother had found
themselves alone. None called at their house, none spoke to
them on the roads. If they went to church, the other women
drew their mats away and left them in a clear space by
themselves. It was a regular excommunication, like what
you read of in the middle ages; and the cause or sense of it
beyond guessing. It was some *tala pepelo*, Uma said, some
lie, some calumny; and all she knew of it was that the girls
who had been jealous of her luck with Ioane used to twit her
with his desertion, and cry out, when they met her alone in

the woods, that she would never be married. 'They tell me no man he marry me. He too much 'fraid,' she said.

The only soul that came about them after this desertion was Master Case; even he was chary of showing himself, and turned up mostly by night; and pretty soon he began to table his cards and make up to Uma. I was still sore about Ioane, and when Case turned up in the same line of business, I cut up downright rough.

'Well,' I said sneering, 'and I suppose you thought Case "very pretty" and "liked too much".'

'Now you talk silly,' said she. 'White man he come here, I marry him all-e-same kanaka; very well then, he marry me all-e-same white woman. Suppose he no marry, he go 'way, woman he stop. All-e-same thief; empty hand, Tonga-heart—no can love! Now you come marry me; you big heart—you no 'shamed island girl. That thing I love you for too much. I proud.'

I don't know that ever I felt sicker all the days of my life. I laid down my fork and I put away 'the island girl'; I didn't seem somehow to have any use for either; and I went and walked up and down in the house, and Uma followed me with her eyes, for she was troubled, and small wonder! But troubled was no word for it with me; I so wanted, and so feared, to make a clean breast of the sweep that I had been.

And just then there came a sound of singing out of the sea; it sprang up suddenly clear and near, as the boat turned the headland; and Uma, running to the window, cried out it was 'Misi' come upon his rounds.

I thought it was a strange thing I should be glad to have a missionary; but if it was strange, it was still true.

'Uma,' said I, 'you stop here in this room, and don't budge a foot out of it till I come back.'

THREE. THE MISSIONARY

As I came out on the verandah, the mission boat was shooting for the mouth of the river. She was a long whale boat painted white; a bit of an awning astern; a native pastor crouched on the wedge of the poop, steering; some four and twenty paddles flashing and dipping, true to the boat-song; and the missionary under the awning, in his white clothes, reading in a book, and set him up! It was pretty to see and hear; there's no smarter sight in the islands than a missionary boat with a good crew and a good pipe to them; and I considered it for half a minute with a bit of envy perhaps, and then strolled towards the river.

From the opposite side there was another man aiming for the same place, but he ran and got there first. It was Case; doubtless his idea was to keep me apart from the missionary who might serve me as interpreter; but my mind was upon other things, I was thinking how he had jockeyed us about the marriage, and tried his hand on Uma before; and at the sight of him, rage flew in my nostrils.

'Get out of that, you low, swindling thief!' I cried.

'What's that you say?' says he.

I gave him the word again, and rammed it down with a good oath. 'And if ever I catch you within six fathoms of my house,' I cried, 'I'll clap a bullet in your measly carcase.'

'You must do as you like about your house,' said he, 'where I told you I have no thought of going. But this is a public place.'

'It's a place where I have private business,' said I. 'I have no idea of a hound like you eavesdropping, and I give you notice to clear out.'

'I don't take it though,' says Case.

'I'll show you, then,' said I.

'We'll have to see about that,' said he.

He was quick with his hands, but he had neither the height nor the weight, being a flimsy creature alongside a man like me; and besides I was blazing to that height of wrath that I could have bit into a chisel. I gave him first the one and then the other, so that I could hear his head rattle and crack, and he went down straight.

'Have you had enough?' cries I. But he only looked up white and blank, and the blood spread upon his face like wine upon a napkin. 'Have you had enough?' I cried again. 'Speak up, and don't lie malingering there, or I'll take my feet to you!'

He sat up at that, and held his head—by the look of him you could see it was spinning—and the blood poured on his pyjamas.

'I've had enough for this time,' says he, and he got up staggering and went off by the way that he had come.

The boat was close in; I saw the missionary had laid his book to one side, and I smiled to myself. 'He'll know I'm a man, anyway,' thinks I.

This was the first time, in all my years in the Pacific, I had ever exchanged two words with any missionary; let alone asked one for a favour. I didn't like the lot, no trader does; they look down upon us and make no concealment; and besides they're partly kanakaised, and suck up with natives instead of with other white men like themselves. I had on a rig of clean, striped pyjamas, for of course I had dressed decent to go before the chiefs; but when I saw the missionary step out of his boat in the regular uniform, white duck clothes, pith helmet, white shirt and tie, and yellow boots to his feet, I could have bunged stones at him. As he came nearer, queering me pretty curious (because of the fight I suppose) I saw he looked mortal sick, for the truth was he had a fever on and had just had a chill in the boat.

'Mr Tarleton, I believe?' says I, for I had got his name.

'And you, I suppose, are the new trader?' says he.

'I want to tell you first that I don't hold with missions,' I went on, 'and that I think you and the likes of you do a sight of harm, filling up the natives with old wives' tales and bumptiousness.'

'You are perfectly entitled to your opinions,' says he, looking a bit ugly, 'but I have no call to hear them.'

'It so happens that you've got to hear them,' I said. 'I'm no missionary nor missionary lover; I'm no kanaka nor favourer of kanakas: I'm just a trader, I'm just a common, low, god-damned white man and British subject, the sort you would like to wipe your boots on. I hope that's plain.'

'Yes, my man,' said he. 'It's more plain than creditable. When you are sober, you'll be sorry for this.'

He tried to pass on, but I stopped him with my hand. The kanakas were beginning to growl; guess they didn't like my tone, for I spoke to that man as free as I would to you.

'Now you can't say I've deceived you,' said I, 'and I can go on. I want a service, I want two services in fact; and if you care to give me them, I'll perhaps take more stock in what you call your christianity.'

He was silent for a moment. Then he smiled. 'You are rather a strange sort of man,' says he.

'I'm the sort of a man God made me,' says I. 'I don't set up to be a gentleman,' I said.

'I am not quite so sure,' said he. 'And what can I do for you, Mr ——?'

'Wiltshire,' I says, 'though I'm mostly called Welsher; but Wiltshire is the way it's spellt, if the people on the beach could only get their tongues about it. And what do I want? Well, I'll tell you the first thing. I'm what you call a sinner—what I call a sweep—and I want you to help me make it up to a person I've deceived.'

He turned and spoke to his crew in the native. 'And now I am at your service,' said he, 'but only for the time my crew are dining. I must be much farther down the coast before night. I was delayed at Papa-mālūlū till this morning, and I have an engagement in Fale-alii tomorrow night.'

I led the way to my house in silence and rather pleased with myself for the way I had managed the talk, for I like a man to keep his self-respect.

'I was sorry to see you fighting,' says he.

'O, that's part of a yarn I want to tell you,' I said. 'That's service number two. After you've heard it, you'll let me know whether you're sorry or not.'

We walked right in through the store, and I was surprised to find Uma had cleared away the dinner things. This was so unlike her ways, that I saw she had done it out of gratitude, and liked her the better. She and Mr Tarleton called each other by name, and he was very civil to her seemingly. But I thought little of that; they can always find civility for a kanaka; it's us white men they lord it over. Besides I didn't want much Tarleton just then: I was going to do my pitch.

'Uma,' said I, 'give us your marriage certificate.' She looked put out. 'Come,' said I. 'You can trust me. Hand it up.'

She had it about her person as usual; I believe she thought it was a pass to heaven, and if she died without having it handy she would go to hell. I couldn't see where she put it the first time, I couldn't see now where she took it from; it seemed to jump in her hand like that Blavatsky[1] business in the papers. But it's the same way with all island women, and I guess they're taught it when young.

'Now,' said I, with the certificate in my hand, 'I was married to this girl by Black Jack the negro. The certificate was wrote by Case, and it's a dandy piece of literature, I promise you. Since then I've found that there's a kind of cry in the place against this wife of mine, and so long as I keep her, I cannot trade. Now what would any man do in my place, if he was a man?' I said. 'The first thing he would do is this, I guess.' And I took and tore up the certificate and bunged the pieces on the floor.

'*Aué*!' cried Uma, and began to clap her hands, but I caught one of them in mine.

'And the second thing that he would do,' said I, 'if he was what I would call a man, and you would call a man, Mr Tarleton, is to bring the girl right before you or any other missionary, and to up and say: "I was wrong married to this wife of mine, but I think a heap of her, and now I want to be married to her right." Fire away, Mr Tarleton. And I guess

1. Madame Blavatsky, the spiritualist, who was active at the time Stevenson was writing.

you'd better do it in native, it'll please the old lady,' I said, giving her the proper name of a man's wife upon the spot.

So we had in two of the crew to witness, and were spliced in our own house; and the parson prayed a good bit, I must say, but not so long as some, and shook hands with the pair of us.

'Mr Wiltshire,' he says, when he had made out the lines and packed off the witnesses, 'I have to thank you for a very lively pleasure. I have rarely performed the marriage ceremony with more grateful emotions.'

That was what you would call talking. He was going on besides with more of it, and I was ready for as much taffy as he had in stock, for I felt good. But Uma had been taken up with something half through the marriage, and cut straight in.

'How your hand he get hurt?' she asked.

'You ask Case's head, old lady,' says I.

She jumped with joy, and sang out.

'You haven't made much of a christian of this one,' says I to Mr Tarleton.

'We didn't think her one of our worst,' says he, 'when she was at Fale-alii; and if Uma bears malice, I shall be tempted to fancy she has good cause.'

'Well, there we are at service number two,' said I. 'I want to tell you our yarn, and see if you can let a little daylight in.'

'Is it long?' he asked.

'Yes,' I said, 'it's a goodish bit of a yarn.'

'Well, I'll give you all the time I can spare,' says he, looking at his watch. 'But I must tell you fairly I haven't eaten since five this morning; and unless you can let me have something, I am not likely to eat again before seven or eight tonight.'

'By God, we'll give you dinner!' I cried.

I was a little caught up at my swearing, just when all was going straight; and so was the missionary I suppose, but he made believe to look out of the window and thanked us.

So we ran him up a bit of a meal. I was bound to let the old lady have a hand in it, to show off; so I deputised her to brew the tea. I don't think I ever met such tea as she turned out. But that was not the worst, for she got round with the salt-box, which she considered an extra European touch, and turned my stew into sea water. Altogether, Mr Tarleton had a devil of a dinner of it; but he had plenty entertainment by the way, for all the while that we were cooking, and afterwards when he was making believe to eat, I kept posting him up on Master Case and the beach of Falesá, and he putting questions that showed he was following close.

'Well,' said he at last, 'I am afraid you have a dangerous enemy. This man Case is very clever and seems really wicked. I must tell you I have had my eye on him for nearly a year, and have rather had the worst of our encounters. About the time when the last representative of your firm ran so suddenly away, I had a letter from Namu, the native pastor, begging me to come to Falesá at my earliest convenience, as his flock were all "adopting catholic practices." I had great confidence in Namu; I fear it only shows how easily we are deceived. No one could hear him preach and not be persuaded he was a man of extraordinary parts. All our islanders easily acquire a kind of eloquence, and can roll out and illustrate with a great deal of vigour and fancy secondhand sermons; but Namu's sermons are his own, and I cannot deny that I have found them means of grace. Moreover he has a keen curiosity in secular things, does not fear work, is clever at carpentering, and has made himself so much respected among the neighbouring pastors that we call him, in a jest which is half serious, the Bishop of the East. In short I was proud of the man; all the more puzzled by his letter; and took occasion to come this way. The morning before my arrival, Vigours had been set on board the *Lion*, and Namu was perfectly at ease, apparently ashamed of his letter, and quite unwilling to explain it. This of course I could not allow; and he ended by confessing that he had been much concerned to find his people using the sign of the cross, but since he had learned the explanation his mind was satisfied. For Vigours had the Evil Eye, a common thing in a country of Europe called Italy, where men were often struck dead by that kind of devil; and it appeared the sign of the cross was a charm against its power.

'"And I explain it, Misi," said Namu in this way. "The country in Europe is a Popey country, and the devil of the Evil Eye may be a catholic devil, or at least used to catholic ways. So then I reasoned thus; if this sign of the cross were used in a Popey manner, it would be sinful; but when it is used only to protect men from a devil, which is a thing harmless in itself, the sign too must be harmless. For the sign is neither good nor bad, even as a bottle is neither good nor bad. But if the bottle be full of gin, the gin is bad; and if the sign be made in idolatry, so is the idolatry bad." And very like a native pastor, he had a text apposite about the casting out of devils.

'"And who has been telling you about the Evil Eye?" I asked.

'He admitted it was Case. Now I am afraid you will think me very narrow, Mr Wiltshire, but I must tell you I was displeased, and cannot think a trader at all a good man to advise or have an influence upon my pastors. And besides there had been some flying talk in the country of old Adams and his being poisoned, to which I had paid no great heed; but it came back to me at the moment.

'"And is this Case a man of sanctified life?" I asked.

'He admitted he was not; for though he did not drink, he was profligate with women and had no religion.

'"Then," said I, "I think the less you have to do with him the better."

'But it is not easy to have the last word with a man like Namu; he was ready in a moment with an illustration. "Misi," said he, "you have told me there were wise men, not pastors, not even holy, who knew many things useful to be taught, about trees for instance, and beasts, and to print books, and about the stones that are burned to make knives of. Such men teach you in your college, and you learn from them, but take care not to learn to be unholy. Misi, Case is my college."

'I knew not what to say. Mr Vigours had evidently been driven out of Falesá by the machinations of Case and with something not very unlike the collusion of my pastor. I called to mind it was Namu who had reassured me about Adams and traced the rumour to the ill will of the priest.

And I saw I must inform myself more thoroughly from an impartial source. There is an old rascal of a chief here, Faiaso, whom I daresay you saw today at the council; he has been all his life turbulent and sly, a great fomenter of rebellions, and a thorn in the side of the mission and the island. For all that he is very shrewd, and except in politics or about his own misdemeanours, a teller of the truth. I went to his house, told him what I had heard, and besought him to be frank. I do not think I had ever a more painful interview. Perhaps you will understand me, Mr Wiltshire, if I tell you that I am perfectly serious in these old wives' tales with which you reproached me, and as anxious to do well for these islands as you can be to please and to protect your pretty wife. And you are to remember that I thought Namu a paragon, and was proud of the man as one of the first ripe fruits of the mission. And now I was informed that he had fallen in a sort of dependence upon Case. The beginning of it was not corrupt; it began doubtless in fear and respect produced by trickery and pretence; but I was shocked to find that another element had been lately added, that Namu helped himself in the store, and was believed to be deep in Case's debt. Whatever the trader said, that Namu believed with trembling. He was not alone in this; many in the village lived in similar subjection; but Namu's case was the most influential, it was through Namu Case had wrought most evil; and with a certain following among the chiefs, and the pastor in his pocket, the man was as good as master of the village. You know something of Vigours and Adams; but perhaps you have never heard of old Underhill, Adam's predecessor. He was a quiet, mild old fellow, I remember, and we were told he had died suddenly: white men die very suddenly in Falesá. The truth, as I now heard it, made my blood run cold. It seems he was struck with a general palsy, all of him dead but one eye, which he continually winked. Word was started that the helpless old man was now a devil; and this vile fellow Case worked upon the natives' fears, which he professed to share, and pretended he durst not go into the house alone. At last a grave was dug, and the living body buried at the far end of the village. Namu, my pastor, whom I had helped to educate, offered up prayer at the hateful scene.

'I felt myself in a very difficult position. Perhaps too it was my duty to have denounced Namu and had him deposed; perhaps I think so now; but at the time, it seemed less clear. He had a great influence, it might prove greater than mine. The natives are prone to superstition; perhaps by stirring them up. I might but ingrain and spread these dangerous fancies. And Namu besides, apart from this novel and accursed influence, was a good pastor, an able man and spiritually minded. Where should I look for a better? how was I to find as good? At that moment with Namu's failure fresh in my view, the work of my life appeared a mockery; hope was dead in me; I would rather repair such tools as I had, than go abroad in quest of others that must certainly prove worse; and a scandal is, at the best, a thing to be avoided when humanly possible. Right or wrong then, I determined on a quiet course. All that night I denounced and reasoned with the erring pastor; twitted him with his ignorance and want of faith; twitted him with his wretched attitude, making clean the outside of the cup and platter, callously helping at a murder, childishly flying in excitement about a few childish, unnecessary and inconvenient gestures; and long before day, I had him on his knees and bathed in tears of what seemed a genuine repentance. On Sunday I took the pulpit in the morning and preached from First Kings, nineteenth, on the fire, the earthquake and the voice: distinguishing the true spiritual power, and referring with such plainness as I dared to recent events in Falesá. The effect produced was great; and it was much increased, when Namu rose in his turn, and confessed that he had been wanting in faith and conduct, and was convinced of sin. So far, then all was well; but there was one unfortunate circumstance. It was nearing the time of our 'May' in the island, when the native contributions to the mission are received; it fell in my duty to make a notification on the subject; and this gave my enemy his chance, by which he was not slow to profit.

'News of the whole proceedings must have been carried to Case as soon as church was over; and the same afternoon he made an occasion to meet me in the midst of the village.

He came up with so much intentness and animosity that I felt it would be damaging to avoid him.

"'So," he says in native, "here is the holy man. He has been preaching against me, but that was not in his heart. He has been preaching the love of God, but that was not in his heart—it was between his teeth. Will you know what was in his heart?" cried he. "I will show it you." And making a snatch at my head, he made believe to pluck out a dollar, and held it in the air.

'There went that rumour through the crowd with which Polynesians receive a prodigy. As for myself, I stood amazed. The thing was a common, conjuring trick, which I have seen performed at home a score of times; but how was I to convince the villagers of that? I wished I had learned legerdemain instead of Hebrew, that I might have paid the fellow out with his own coin. But there I was, I could not stand there silent, and the best that I could find to say was weak.

"'I will trouble you not to lay hands on me again," said I.

"'I have no such thought," said he, "nor will I deprive you of your dollar. Here it is," he said, and flung it at my feet. I am told it lay where it fell three days.'

'I must say it was well played,' said I.

'O, he is clever,' said Mr Tarleton, 'and you can now see for yourself how dangerous. ᴴe was a party to the horrid death of the paralytic; he is accused of poisoning Adams; he drove Vigours out of the place by lies that might have led to murder; and there is no question but he has now made up his mind to rid himself of you. How he means to try, we have no guess; only be sure it's something new. There is no end to his readiness and invention.'

'He gives himself a sight of trouble,' says I. 'And after all, what for?'

'Why, how many tons of copra may they make in this district?' asked the missionary.

'I daresay as much as sixty tons,' says I.

'And what is the profit to the local trader?' he asked.

'You may call it three pounds,' said I.

'Then you can reckon for yourself how much he does it for,' said Mr Taleton. 'But the more important thing is to defeat him. It is clear he spread some report against Uma, in order to isolate and have his wicked will of her; failing of that, and seeing a new rival come upon the scene, he used her in a different way. Now the first point to find out is about Namu. Uma, when people began to leave you and your mother alone, what did Namu do?'

'Stop away all-e-same,' says Uma.

'I fear the dog has returned to his vomit,' said Mr Tarleton. 'And now what am I to do for you? I will speak to Namu, I will warn him he is observed; it will be strange if he allow anything to go on amiss, when he is put upon his guard. At the same time, this precaution may fail, and then you must turn elsewhere. You have two people at hand to whom you might apply. There is first of all the priest, who might protect you by the catholic interest; they are a wretchedly small body, but they count two chiefs. And then there is old Faiaso. Ah, if it had been some years ago, you would have needed no one else; but his influence is much reduced, it has gone into Maea's hands, and Maea, I fear, is one of Case's jackalls. In fine, if the worst comes to the worst, you must send up or come yourself to Fale-alii, and though I am not due at this end of the island for a month, I will see what can be done.'

So Mr Tarleton said farewell; and half an hour later, the crew were singing and the paddles flashing in the missionary boat.

FOUR. DEVIL-WORK

Near a month went by without much doing. The same night of our marriage, Galoshes called round, made himself mighty civil, and got into a habit of dropping in about dark and smoking his pipe with the family. He could talk to Uma of course, and started to teach me native and French at the same time. He was a kind old buffer, though the dirtiest you would wish to see, and he muddled me up with foreign languages worse than the tower of Babel.

That was one employment we had, and it made me feel less lonesome; but there was no profit in the thing; for though the priest came and sat and yarned, none of his folks could be enticed into my store; and if it hadn't been for the other occupation I struck out, there wouldn't have been a pound of copra in the house. This was the idea: Fa'avao (Uma's mother) had a score of bearing trees. Of course, we could get no labour, being all as good as tabooed. And the two women and I turned to make copra with our own hands. It was copra to make your mouth water, when it was done—I never understood how much the natives cheated me till I had made that four hundred pounds of my own hand—and it weighed so light, I felt inclined to take and water it myself.

When we were at the job, a good many kanakas used to put in the best of the day looking on, and once that nigger turned up. He stood back with the natives, and laughed, and did the big don and the funny dog, till I began to get riled.

'Here, you, nigger!' says I.

'I don't address myself to you, sah,' says the nigger. 'Only speak to gen'le'um.'

204

'I know,' says I, 'but it happens I was addressing myself to you, Mr Black Jack. And all I want to know is just this: did you see Case's figurehead about a week ago?'

'No, sah,' says he.

'That's all right, then, says I; 'for I'll show you the own brother to it, only black, in the inside of about two minutes.'

And I began to walk towards him, quite slow and my hands down; only there was trouble in my eye, if anybody took the pains to look.

'You're a low, obstropulous fellow, sah,' says he.

'You bet!' says I.

By that time he thought I was about as near as was convenient, and lit out so it would have done your heart good to see him travel. And that was all I saw of that precious gang, until what I am about to tell you.

It was one of my chief employments these days to go pot-hunting in the woods, which I found (as Case had told me) very rich in game. I have spoken of the cape, which shut up the village and my station from the east. A path went about the end of it, and led into the next bay. A strong wind blew here daily, and as the line of the barrier reef stopped at the end of the cape, a heavy surf ran on the shores of the bay. A little cliffy hill cut the valley in two parts, and stood close on the beach; and at high water the sea broke right on the face of it, so that all passage was stopped. Woody mountains hemmed the place all round; the barrier to the east was particularly steep and leafy; the lower parts of it, along the sea, falling in sheer black cliffs streaked with cinnabar; the upper part lumpy with the tops of the great trees. Some of the trees as black as your shoes. Many birds hovered round the bay, some of them snow white; and the flying-fox (or vampire) flew there in broad daylight, gnashing its teeth.

For a long while I came as far as this shooting and went no farther. There was no sign of any path beyond; and the cocoapalms in the front of the foot of the valley were the last this way. For the whole 'eye' of the island, as natives call the windward end, lay desert. From Falesá round about to Papa-mālūlū, there was neither house, nor man, nor planted fruit tree; and the reef being mostly absent and the shores bluff, the sea beat direct among crags, and there was scarce a landing place.

I should tell you that after I began to go in the woods, although no one offered to come near my store, I found people willing enough to pass the time of day with me where nobody could see them. And as I had begun to pick up native, and most of them had a word or two of English, I began to hold little odds and ends of conversation, not to much purpose, to be sure, but they took off the worst of the feeling. For it's a miserable thing to be made a leper of.

It chanced one day, towards the end of the month, that I was sitting in this bay in the edge of the bush, looking east, with a kanaka. I had given him a fill of tobacco, and we were making out to talk as best we could; indeed he had more English than most.

I asked him if there was no road going eastward.

'One time one road,' said he. 'Now he dead.'

'Nobody he go there?' I asked.

'No good,' said he. 'Too much devil he stop there.'

'Oho!' says I, 'got-um plenty devil, that bush?'

'Man devil, woman devil: too much devil,' said my friend. 'Stop there all-e-time. Man he go there, no come back.'

I thought, if this fellow was so well posted on devils and spoke of them so free, which is not common, I had better fish for a little information about myself and Uma.

'You think me one devil?' I asked.

'No think devil,' said he soothingly. 'Think all-e-same fool.'

'Uma, she devil?' I asked again.

'No, no: no devil; devil stop bush,' said the young man.

I was looking in front of me across the bay, and I saw the hanging front of the woods pushed suddenly open, and Case with a gun in his hand step forth into the sunshine on the black beach. He was got up in light pyjamas, near white, his gun sparkled, he looked mighty conspicuous; and the land crabs scuttled from all round him to their holes.

'Hullo, my friend,' says I, 'you no talk all-e-same true. Ese he go, he come back.'

'Ese no all-e-same. Ese *Tiapolo*,' says my friend; and with a good bye, slunk off among the trees.

I watched Case all round the beach, where the tide was low; and let him pass me on the homeward way to Falesá. He was in deep thought; and the birds seemed to know it, trotting quite near him on the sand and wheeling and calling in his ears. Where he passed nearest me, I could see by the working of his lips that he was talking in to himself, and what pleased me mightily, he had still my trademark on his brow. I tell you the plain truth, I had a mind to give him a gunfull in his ugly mug, but I thought better of it.

All this time, and all the time I was following home, I kept repeating that native word, which I remembered by 'Polly, put the kettle on and make us all some tea': tea-a-pollo.

'Uma,' says I, when I got back, 'what does Tiapolo mean?'

'Devil,' says she.

'I thought *aitu* was the word for that?' I said.

'*Aitu* 'nother kind of devil,' said she; 'stop bush, eat kanaka. Tiapolo big-chief devil, stop home; all-e-same Christian devil.'

'Well then,' said I. 'I'm no further forward. How can Case be Tiapolo?'

'No all-e-same,' said she. 'Ese belong Tiapolo; Tiapolo too much like; Ese all-e-same his son. Suppose Ese he wish something, Tiapolo he make him.'

'That's mighty convenient for Ese,' says I. 'And what kind of things does he make for him?'

Well, out came a rigmarole of all sorts of stories, many of which (like the blue dollar he took from Mr Tarleton's head) were plain enough to me, but others I could make nothing of; and the thing that most surprised the kanakas was what surprised me least; namely, that he could go in the desert among all the *aitus*. Some of the boldest, however, had accompanied him, and had heard him speak with the dead and give them orders, and safe in his protection, had returned unscathed. Some said he had a church there where he worshippped Tiapolo, and Tiapolo appeared to him;

others swore there was no sorcery at all, that he performed
his miracles by the power of prayer, and the church was no
church but a prison in which he had confined a dangerous
aitu. Namu had been in the bush with him once, and
returned glorifying God for these wonders. Altogether I
began to have a glimmer of the man's position, and the
means by which he had acquired it, and though I saw he was
a tough nut to crack, I was noways cast down.

'Very well,' said I, 'I'll have a look at Master Case's place
of worship myself, and we'll see about the glorifyng.'

At this time Uma fell in a terrible taking; if I went in the
high bush, I should never return; none could go there but
by the protection of Tiapolo.

'I'll chance it on God's,' said I. 'I'm a good sort of a
fellow, Uma, as fellows go; and I guess God'll con me
through.'

She was silent for awhile. 'I think,' said she, mighty
solemn; and then presently: 'Victoreea he big chief?'

'You bet,' said I.

'He like you too much?' she asked again.

I told her with a grin I believed the old lady was rather
partial to me.

'All right,' said she. 'Victoreea he big chief, like you too
much; no can help you here in Falesá; no can do, too far
off. Maea he small chief; stop here; suppose he like you,
make you all right. All-e-same God and Tiapolo. God he big
chief, got too much work. Tiapolo he small chief, he like too
much make-see, work very hard.'

'I'll have to hand you over to Mr Tarleton,' said I. 'Your
theology's out of its bearings, Uma.'

However we stuck at this business all the evening, and
with the stories she told me of the desert and its dangers,
she came near frightening herself into a fit. I don't remember half a quarter of them of course, for I paid little heed;
but two come back to me kind of clear.

About six miles up the coast there is a sheltered cove,
they call *Fanga-anaana*, 'the haven full of caves'. I've seen it
from the sea myself, as near as I could get my boys to
venture in, and it's a little strip of yellow sand. Black cliffs
overhang it full of the black mouths of caves, great trees

overhang the cliffs and dangle down lianas, and in one place, about the middle, a big brook pours over in a cascade. Well, there was a boat going by here with six young men of Falesá, 'all very pretty,' Uma said, which was the loss of them. It blew strong, there was a heavy head sea; and by the time they opened Fanga-anaana, and saw the white cascade and the shady beach, they were all tired and thirsty, and their water had run out. One proposed to land and get a drink; and being reckless fellows, they were all of the same mind except the youngest. Lotu was his name; he was a very good young gentleman and very wise; and he held out they were crazy, telling them the place was given over to spirits and devils and the dead, and there were no living folk nearer than six miles the one way and maybe twelve the other. But they laughed at his words; and being five to one, pulled in, beached the boat, and landed. It was a wonderful pleasant place, Lotu said, and the water excellent. They walked round the beach, but could see nowhere any way to mount the cliffs, which made them easier in their mind; and at last they sat down to make a meal on the food they had brought with them. They were scarce set, when there came out of the mouth of one of the black caves six of the most beautiful ladies ever seen; they had flowers in their hair, and the most beautiful breasts, and necklaces of scarlet seeds; and began to jest with these young gentlemen, and the young gentlemen to jest back with them, all but Lotu. As for Lotu, he saw there could be no living women in such a place, and ran, and flung himself in the bottom of the boat, and covered his face, and prayed. All the time the business lasted, Lotu made one clean break of prayer; and that was all he knew of it, until his friends came back, and made him sit up, and they put to sea again out of the bay, which was now quite desert, and no word of the six ladies. But what frightened Lotu worst, not one of the five remembered anything of what had passed, but they were all like drunken men, and sang and laughed in the boat, and skylarked. The wind freshened and came squally, the sea rose extraordinary high; it was such weather as any man in the islands would have turned back to and fled home to Falesá; but these five were like crazy folk, and cracked on all sail, and drove their boat into the seas. Lotu went to the bailing; none of the others thought to help him, but sang and skylarked and carried on, and spoke singular things beyond a man's comprehension, and laughed out loud when they said them. So the rest of that day, Lotu bailed for his life in the bottom of the boat, and was all drenched with sweat and cold sea water; and none heeded him. Against all expectation, they came safe in a dreadful tempest to Papa-mālūlū, where the palms were singing out and the cocoanuts flying like cannon balls about the village green; and the same night the five young gentlemen sickened and spoke never a reasonable word until they died.

'And do you mean to tell me you can swallow a yarn like that?' I asked.

She told me the thing was well known, and with handsome young men alone, it was even common. But this was the only case where five had been slain the same day and in a company by the love of the women devils; and it had made a great stir in the island; and she would be crazy if she doubted.

'Well anyway,' says I, 'you needn't be frightened about me. I've got no use for the women devils; you're all the women I want, and all the devil too, old lady.'

To that she answered there were other sorts, and she had seen one with her own eyes. She had gone one day alone to the next bay, and perhaps got too near the margin of the bad place. The boughs of the high bush overshadowed her from the kant of the hill; but she herself was outside in a flat place, very stony and growing full of young mummy-apples, four and five feet high. It was a dark day in the rainy season; and now there came squalls that tore off the leaves and sent them flying, and now it was all still as in a house. It was in one of these still times, that a whole gang of birds and flying-foxes came pegging out of the bush like creatures frightened. Presently after she heard a rustle nearer hand, and saw coming out of the margin of the trees among the mummy-apples, the appearance of a lean, gray, old boar. It seemed to think as it came, like a person, and all of a sudden, as she looked at it coming, she was aware it was no boar but a thing that was a man with a man's thoughts. At that she ran, and the pig after her, and as the pig ran it hollered aloud, so that the place rang with it.

'I wish I had been there with my gun,' said I. 'I guess the pig would have hollered so as to surprise himself.'

But she told me a gun was of no use with the like of these, which were the spirits of the dead.

Well, this kind of talk put in the evening, which was the best of it; but of course it didn't change my notion; and the next day, with my gun and a good knife, I set off upon a voyage of discovery. I made as near as I could for the place where I had seen Case come out; for if it was true he had some kind of establishment in the bush, I reckoned I should find a path. The beginning of the desert was marked off by a wall—to call it so, for it was more of a long mound of stones; they say it reached right across the island, but how they know it is another question, for I doubt if anyone has made the journey in a hundred years; the natives sticking chiefly to the sea and their little colonies along the coast, and that part being mortal high and steep and full of cliffs. Up to the west side of the wall, the ground has been cleared, and there are cocoapalms, and mummy-apples, and guavas, and lots of sensitive.[1] Just across, the bush begins outright; high bush at that: trees going up like the masts of ships, and ropes of liana hanging down like a ship's rigging, and nasty orchids growing in the forks like funguses. The ground, where there was no underwood, looked to be a heap of boulders. I saw many green pigeons which I might have shot, only I was there with a different idea; a number of butterflies flopped up and down along the ground like dead leaves; sometimes I would hear a bird calling, sometimes the wind overhead, and always the sea along the coast.

But the queerness of the place, it's more difficult to tell of; unless to one who has been alone in the high bush himself. The brightest kind of a day, it is always dim down there. A man can see to the end of nothing; whichever way he looks, the wood shuts up, one bough folding with

1. Sensitive plant. Stevenson had a close acquaintance
   with sensitive plant as it grew profusely at Vailima and
   was very hard to eradicate.

another, like the fingers of your hand; and whenever he listens, he hears always something new—men talking, children laughing, the strokes of an axe a far way ahead of him, and sometimes a sort of quick, stealthy scurry near at hand that makes him jump and look to his weapons. It's all very well for him to tell himself that he's alone, bar trees and birds; he can't make out to believe it: whichever way he turns, the whole place seems to be alive and looking on. Don't think it was Uma's yarns that put me out; I don't value native talk a fourpenny piece: it's a thing that's natural in the bush, and that's the end of it.

As I got near the top of the hill, for the ground of the wood goes up in this place steep as a ladder, the wind began to sound straight on, and the leaves to toss and switch open and let in the sun. This suited me better; it was the same noise all the time and nothing to startle. Well, I had got to a place where there was an underwood of what they call wild cocoanut—mighty pretty with its scarlet fruits—when there came a sound of singing in the wind that I thought I had never heard the like of. It was all very fine to tell myself it was the branches; I knew better. It was all very fine to tell myself it was a bird; I knew never a bird that sang like that. It rose, and swelled, and died away, and swelled again; and now I thought it was like some one weeping, only prettier; and now I thought it was like harps; and there was one thing I made sure of, it was a sight too sweet to be wholesome in a place like that. You may laugh if you like; but I declare I called to mind the six young ladies that came, with their scarlet necklaces, out of the cave at Fanga-anaana, and wondered if they sang like that. We laugh at the natives and their superstitions; but see how many traders take them up, splendidly educated white men, that have been bookkeepers (some of them) and clerks in the old country! It's my belief a superstition grows up in a place like the different kinds of weeds; and as I stood there, and listened to that wailing, I twittered in my shoes.

You may call me a coward to be frightened; I thought myself brave enough to go on ahead. But I went mighty carefully, with my gun cocked, spying all about me like a hunter, fully expecting to see a handsome young woman

sitting somewhere in the bush, and fully determined (if I
did) to try her with a charge of duckshot. And sure enough I
had not gone far, when I met with a queer thing. The wind
came on the top of the wood in a strong puff, the leaves in
front of me burst open, and I saw for a second something
hanging in a tree. It was gone in a wink, the puff blowing by
and the leaves closing. I tell you the truth; I had made up
my mind to see an *aitu*; and if the think had looked like a
pig or a woman, it wouldn't have given me the same turn.
The trouble was that it seemed kind of square; and the idea
of a square thing that was alive and sang, knocked me sick
and silly. I must have stood quite a while; and I made pretty
certain it was right out of the same tree that the singing
came. Then I began to come to myself a bit.

'Well,' says I, 'if this is really so, if this is a place where
there are square things that sing, I'm gone up anyway. Let's
have my fun for my money.'

But I thought I might as well take the off-chance of a
prayer being any good; so I plumped on my knees and
prayed out loud; and all the time I was praying, the strange
sounds came out of the tree, and went up and down, and
changed, for all the world like music; only you could see it
wasn't human—there was nothing there that you could
whistle.

As soon as I had made an end in proper style, I laid down
my gun, stuck my knife between my teeth, walked right up
to that tree, and began to climb. I tell you my heart was like
ice. But presently, as I went up, I caught another glimpse of
the thing, and that relieved me, for I thought it seemed
woundy like a box; and when I had got right up to it, I near
fell out of the tree with laughter. A box it was, sure enough,
and a candle box at that, with the brand upon the side of it;
and it had banjo strings stretched so as to sound when the
wind blew. I believe they call the thing a Tyrolean harp,
whatever that may mean.

'Well, Mr Case,' said I, 'you've frightened me once. But I
defy you to frighten me again,' I says, and slipped down the
tree, and set out again to find my enemy's head office, which
I guessed would not be far away.

The undergrowth was thick in this part. I couldn't see

before my nose, and must burst my way through by main force and ply the knife as I went, slicing the cords of the lianas and slashing down whole trees at a blow. I call them trees for the bigness, but in truth they were just big weeds and sappy to cut through like a carrot. From all this crowd and kind of vegetation, I was just thinking to myself the place might have once been cleared, when I came on my nose over a pile of stones, and saw in a moment it was some kind of a work of man. The Lord knows when it was made or when deserted; for this part of the island has lain undisturbed since long before the whites came. A few steps beyond, I hit into a path I had been always looking for. It was narrow but well beaten, and I saw that Case had plenty of disciples. It seems indeed it was a piece of fashionable boldness to venture up here with the trader; and a young man scarce reckoned himself grown, till he had got his breech tattooed for one thing, and seen Case's devils for another. This is mighty like kanakas; but if you look at it another way, it's mighty like white folks too.

A bit along the path, I was brought to a clean stand and had to rub my eyes. There was a wall in front of me, the path passing it by a gap; it was tumble down and plainly very old, but built of big stones very well laid; and there is no native alive today upon that island that could dream of such a piece of building. Along all the top of it was a line of queer figures, idols, or scare-crows, or what not. They had carved and painted faces, ugly to view their eyes and teeth were of shell; their hair and their bright clothes blew in the wind, and some of them worked with the tugging. There are islands up west, where they make these kinds of figures till today; but if ever they were made in this island, the practise and the very recollection of it are now long forgotten. And the singular thing was that all these bogies were as fresh as toys out of a shop.

Then it came in my mind what Case had let out to me the first day, that he was a good forger of island curiosities: a thing by which so many traders turn an honest penny. And with that I saw the whole business, and how this display served the man a double purpose: first of all to season his curiosities, and then to frighten those that came to visit him.

But I should tell you (what made the thing more curious) that all the time the Tyrolean harps were harping round me in the trees, and even while I looked a green and yellow bird (that I suppose was building) began to tear the hair off the head of one of the figures.

A little farther on, I found the last curiosity of the museum. The first I saw of it was a longish mound of earth with a twist to it. Digging off the earth with my hands, I found underneath tarpaulin stretched on boards, so that this was plainly the roof of a cellar. It stood right on the top of the hill, and the entrance was on the far side, between two rocks, like the entrance to a cave. I went in as far as the bend, and looking round the corner, saw a shining face. It was big and ugly like a pantomime mask, and the brightness of it waxed and dwindled, and at times it smoked.

'Oho,' says I, 'luminous paint!'

And I must say I rather admired the man's ingenuity. With a box of tools and a few mighty simple contrivances, he had made out to have a devil of a temple. Any poor kanaka brought up here in the dark, with the harps whining all round him, and shown that smoking face in the bottom of a hole, would make no kind of doubt but he had seen and heard enough devils for a lifetime. It's easy to find out what kanakas think. Just go back to yourself anyway round from ten to fifteen years old, and there's an average kanaka. There are some pious, just as there are pious boys; and the most of them, like the boys again, are middling honest and yet think it rather larks to steal, and are easy scared and rather like to be so. I remembered a boy I was at school with at home, who played the Case business. He didn't know anything, that boy; he couldn't do anything; he had no luminous paint and no Tyrolean harps; he just boldly said he was a sorcerer, and frightened us out of our boots, and we loved it. And then it came in my mind how the master had once flogged that boy, and the surprise we were all in to see the sorcerer catch it and bum like anybody else. Thinks I to myself: 'I must find some way of fixing it so for Master Case.' And the next moment I had my idea.

I went back by the path which, when once you had found it, was quite plain and easy walking; and when I stepped out on the black sands, who should I see but Master Case himself?' I cocked my gun and held it handy; and we marched up and passed without a word, each keeping the tail of his eye on the other; and no sooner had we passed, than we each wheeled round like fellows drilling and stood face to face. We had each taken the same notion in his head, you see, that the other fellow might give him the load of a gun in the stern.

'You've shot nothing,' says Case.

'I'm not on the shoot today,' says I.

'Well, the devil go with you for me,' says he.

'The same to you,' says I.

But we stuck just the way we were; no fear of either of us moving.

Case laughed. 'We can't stop here all day, though,' said he.

'Don't let me detain you,' says I.

He laughed again. 'Look here, Wiltshire, do you think me a fool?' he asked.

'More of a knave if you want to know,' says I.

'Well, do you think it would better me to shoot you here on this open beach?' said he, 'because I don't. Folks come fishing every day. There may be a score of them up the valley now, making copra; there may be half a dozen on the hill behind you after pigeons; they might be watching us this minute, and I shouldn't wonder. I give you my word I don't want to shoot you. Why should I? You don't hinder me any; you haven't got one pound of copra but what you made with your own hands like a negro slave. You're vegetating, that's what I call it; and I don't care where you vegetate, nor yet how long. Give me your word you don't mean to shoot me, and I'll give you a lead and walk away.'

'Well,' said I, 'you're frank and pleasant, ain't you? and I'll be the same. I don't mean to shoot you today. Why should I? This business is beginning; it ain't done yet, Mr Case. I've given you one turn already, I can see the marks of my knuckles on your head to this blooming hour; and I've more cooking for you. I'm not a paralee like Underhill; my name ain't Adams and it ain't Vigours; and I mean to show you that you've met your match.'

'This is a silly way to talk,' said he. 'This is not the talk to make me move on with.'

'All right,' said I. 'Stay where you are. I ain't in any hurry, and you know it. I can put in the day on this beach, and never mind. I ain't got any copra to bother with. I ain't got any luminous paint to see to.'

I was sorry I said that last, but it whipped out before I knew. I could see it took the wind out of his sails, and he stood and stared at me with his brow drawn up. Then I suppose he made up his mind he must get to the bottom of this.

'I take you at your word,' says he, and turned his back, and walked right into the devil's bush.

I let him go of course, for I had passed my word. But I watched him as long as he was in sight, and after he was gone, lit out for cover as lively as you would want to see, and went the rest of the way home under the bush. For I didn't trust him sixpenceworth. One thing I saw: I had been ass enough to give him warning; and that which I meant to do, I must do at once.

You would think I had had about enough excitement for one morning; but there was another turn waiting me. As soon as I got far enough round the cape to see my house, I made out there were strangers there; a little farther, and no doubt about it, there were a couple of armed sentries squatting at my door. I could only suppose the trouble about Uma must have come to a head, and the station been seized. For aught I could think Uma was taken up already, and these armed men were waiting to do the like by me.

However, as I came nearer, which I did at top speed, I saw there was a third native sitting on the verandah like a guest, and Uma was talking with him like a hostess. Nearer still I made out it was the big young chief Maea, and that he was smiling away and smoking; and what was he smoking? —none of your European cigarettes fit for a cat; not even the genuine, big, knock-me-down native article, that a fellow can really put in the time with, if his pipe is broke; but a cigar, and one of my Mexicans at that, that I could swear to. At sight of this, my heart started beating; and I took a wild hope in my head that the trouble was over, and Maea had come round.

Uma pointed me out to him, as I came up, and he met me at the head of my own stairs like a thorough gentleman.

'Vilivili,' said he, which was the best they could make of my name, 'I pleased.'

There is no doubt when an island chief wants to be civil he can do it. I saw the way things were from the word go. There was no call for Uma to say to me: 'He no 'fraid Ese now; come bring copra.' I tell you I shook hands with that kanaka like as if he was the best white man in Europe.

The fact was Case and he had got after the same girl, or Maea suspected it and concluded to make hay of the trader on the chance. He had dressed himself up, got a couple of retainers cleaned and armed to kind of make the thing more public, and just waiting till Case was clear of the village, came round to put the whole of his business my way. He was rich as well as powerful, I suppose that man was worth fifty thousand nuts per annum. I gave him the price of the beach and a quarter cent better, and as for credit, I would have advanced him the inside of the store and the fittings besides, I was so pleased to see him. I must say he bought like a gentleman: rice and tins and biscuit enough for a week's feast, and stuffs by the bolt. He was agreeable besides; he had plenty fun to him; and we cracked jests together, mostly through Uma for interpreter, because he had mighty little English, and my native was still off colour. One thing I made out: he could never really have thought much harm of Uma; he could never have been really frightened, and must just have made believe from dodginess and because he thought Case had a strong pull in the village and could help him on.

This set me thinking that both he and I were in a tightish place. What he had done was to fly in the face of the whole village, and the thing might cost him his authority. More than that, after my talk with Case on the beach, I thought it might very well cost me my life. Case had as good as said he would pot me if ever I got copra; he would come home to find the best business in the village had changed hands, and

the best thing I thought I could do was to get in first with
the potting.

'See here, Uma,' says I, 'tell him I'm sorry I made him
wait, but I was looking for Case's Tiapolo store in the bush.'

'He want savvy if you no 'fraid?' translated Uma.

I laughed out. 'Not much!' says I. 'Tell him the place is a
blooming toyshop! Tell him in England we give these things
to the kids to play with.'

'He want savvy if you hear devil sing?' she asked next.

'Look here,' I said, 'I can't do it now because I've got no
banjo strings in stock; but the next time the ship comes
round, I'll have one of these same contraptions right here in
my verandah, and he can see for himself how much devil
there is to it. Tell him, as soon as I can get the strings, I'll
make one for his picaninnies. The name of the concern is a
Tyrolean harp; and you can tell him the name means in
English, that nobody but damfools give a cent for it.'

This time he was so pleased he had to try his English
again. 'You talk true?' says he.

'Rather!' said I. 'Talk all-e-same bible. Bring out a bible
here, Uma, if you've got such a thing, and I'll kiss it. Or I'll
tell you what's better still,' says I, taking a header. 'Ask him
if he's afraid to go up there himself by day.'

It appeared he wasn't; he could venture as far as that by
day in company.

'That's the ticket, then!' said I. 'Tell him the man's a
fraud and the place foolishness, and if he'll go up there
tomorrow, he'll see all that's left of it. But tell him this,
Uma, and mind he understands it; if he gets talking, it's
bound to come to Case and I'm a dead man. I'm playing his
game, tell him, and if he says one word, my blood will be at
his door and be the damnation of him here and after.'

She told him, and he shook hands with me up to the hilts,
and says he: 'No talk. Go up tomollow. You my friend?'

'No, sir!' says I. 'No such foolishness. I've come here to
trade, tell him, and not to make friends. But as to Case, I'll
send that man to glory.'

So off Maea went, pretty well pleased, as I could see.

FIVE. NIGHT IN THE BUSH

Well, I was committed now; Tiapolo had to be smashed up before next day; and my hands were pretty full, not only with preparations, but with argument. My house was like a mechanics' debating society; Uma was so made up that I shouldn't go into the bush by night, or that if I did I was never to come back again. You know her style of arguing, you've had a specimen about Queen Victoria and the devil; and I leave you to fancy if I was tired of it before dark.

At last, I had a good idea; what was the use of casting my pearls before her? I thought: some of her own chopped hay would be likelier to do the business.

'I'll tell you what, then,' said I. 'You fish out your bible, and I'll take that up along with me. That'll make me right.'

She swore a bible was no use.

'That's just your blamed kanaka ignorance,' said I. 'Bring the bible out.'

She brought it, and I turned to the title page where I thought there would likely be some English, and so there was. 'There!' said I. 'Look at that! *"London: printed for the British and Foreign Bible Society, Blackfriars"*; and the date, which I can't read, owing to its being in these X's. There's no devil in hell can look near the Bible Society, Blackfriars. Why, you silly!' I said, 'how do you suppose we get along with our own *aitus* at home? All Bible Society!'

'I think you no got any,' said she. 'White man he tell me you no got.'

'Sounds likely, don't it?' I asked. 'Why would these islands all be chock full of them, and none in Europe?'

'Well, you no got breadfruit,' said she.

I could have tore my hair. 'Now, look here, old lady,' said

220

I, 'you dry up, for I'm tired of you. I'll take the bible, which'll put me as straight as the mail; and that's the last word I've got to say.'

The night fell extraordinary dark, clouds coming up with sundown and overspreading all; not a star showed; there was only an end of a moon, and that not due before the small hours. Round the village, what with the lights and the fires in the open houses and the torches of many fishers moving on the reef, it kept as gay as an illumination; but the sea and the mountains and woods were all clean gone. I suppose it might be eight o'clock when I took the road, loaden like a donkey. First there was that bible, a book as big as your head, which I had let myself in for by my own tomfoolery. Then there was my gun and knife and lantern and patent matches, all necessary. And then there was the real plant of the affair in hand, a mortal weight of gunpowder, a pair of dynamite fishing-bombs, and two or three pieces of slow match that I had hauled out of the tin cases and spliced together the best way I could; for the match was only trade stuff, and a man would be crazy that trusted it. Altogether, you see, I had the materials of a pretty good blow up. Expense was nothing to me; I wanted that thing done right.

As long as I was in the open, and had the lamp in my house to steer by, I did well. But when I got to the path, it fell so dark I could make no headway, walking into trees and swearing there, like a man looking for the matches in his bedroom. I knew it was risky to light up; for my lantern would be visible all the way to the point of the cape; and as no one went there after dark, it would be talked about and come to Case's ears. But what was I to do? I had either to give the business over and lose caste with Maea, or light up, take my chance, and get through the thing the smartest I was able.

As long as I was on the path, I walked hard; but when I came to the black beach, I had to run. For the tide was now nearly flowed; and to get through with my powder dry between the surf and the steep hill, took all the quickness I possessed. As it was even, the wash caught me to the knees and I came near falling on a stone. All this time, the hurry I

was in, and the free air and the smell of the sea, kept my
spirits lively; but when I was once in the bush and began to
climb the path, I took it easier. The fearsomeness of the
wood had been a good bit rubbed off for me by Master
Case's banjo strings and graven images; yet I thought it was
a dreary walk, and guessed, when the disciples went up
there, they must be badly scared. The light of the lantern,
striking among all these trunks, and forked branches, and
twisted rope's-ends of lianas, made the whole place, or all
that you could see it, a kind of a puzzle of turning shadows.
They came to meet you, solid and quick like giants, and
then span off and vanished; they hove up over your head
like clubs, and flew away into the night like birds. The floor
of the bush glimmered with dead wood, the way the
matchbox used to shine after you had struck a lúcifer. Big
cold drops fell on me from the branches overhead like
sweat. There was no wind to mention, only a little icy
breath of a land breeze that stirred nothing; and the harps
were silent.

The first landfall I made was when I got through the bush
of wild cocoanuts, and came in view of the bogies on the
wall. Mighty queer they looked by the shining of the
lantern, with ther painted faces, and shell eyes, and their
clothes and their hair hanging. One after another I pulled
them all up and piled them in a bundle on the cellar roof, so
as they might go to glory with the rest. Then I chose a place
behind one of the big stones at the entrance, buried my
powder and the two shells, and arranged my match along
the passage. And then I had a look at the smoking head, just
for good-bye. It was doing fine.

'Cheer up,' says I. 'You're booked.'

It was my first idea to light up and be getting homeward;
for the darkness, and the glimmer of the dead wood, and the
shadows of the lantern made me lonely. But I knew where
one of the harps hung; it seemed a pity it shouldn't go with
the rest; and at the same time I couldn't help letting on to
myself that I was mortal tired of my employment and would
like best to be at home and have the door shut. I stepped out
of the cellar, and argued it fore and back. There was a sound
of the sea far down below me on the coast; nearer hand, not

a leaf stirred; I might have been the only living creature this side Cape Horn. Well, as I stood there thinking, it seemed the bush woke and became full of little noises. Little noises they were, and nothing to hurt—a bit of a crackle, a bit of a brush—but the breath jumped right out of me and my throat went as dry as a biscuit. It wasn't Case I was afraid of, which would have been common sense; I never thought of Case; what took me, as sharp as the cholic, was the old wives' tales, the devil-women and the man-pigs. It was the toss of a penny whether I should run; but I got a purchase on myself, and stepped out, and held up the lantern (like a fool) and looked all round.

In the direction of the village and the path, there was nothing to be seen; but when I turned inland, it's a wonder to me I didn't drop. There—coming right up out of the desert and the bad bush—there, sure enough, was a devil-woman, just the way I had figured she would look. I saw the light shine on her bare arms and her bright eyes. And there went out of me a yell so big that I thought it was my death.

'Ah! No sing out!' says the devil-woman, in a kind of a high whisper. 'Why you talk big voice? Put out light! Ese he come.'

'My God Almighty, Uma, is that you?' says I.

'*Ioe*,' says she. 'I come quick. Ese here soon.'

'You come alone?' I asked. 'You no 'fraid?'

'Ah, too much 'fraid!' she whispered, clutching me. 'I think die.'

'Well,' says I, with a kind of a weak grin. 'I'm not the one to laugh at you, Mrs Wiltshire, for I'm about the worst scared man in the South Pacific myself.'

She told me in two words what brought her. I was scarce gone, it seems, when Faavao came in; and the old woman had met Black Jack running as hard as he was fit from our house to Case's. Uma neither spoke nor stopped, but lit right out to come and warn me. She was so close at my heels that the lantern was her guide across the beach, and afterwards, by the glimmer of it in the trees, she got her line up hill. It was only when I had got to the top or was in the cellar, that she wandered—Lord knows where!—and lost a sight of precious time, afraid to call out lest Case was at the

heels of her, and falling in the bush so that she was all
knocked and bruised. That must have been when she got
too far to the southward, and how she came to take me in
the flank at last, and frighten me beyond what I've got the
words to tell of.

Well, anything was better than a devil-woman; but I
thought her yarn serious enough. Black Jack had no call to
be about my house, unless he was set there to watch; and it
looked to me as if my tomfool word about the paint and
perhaps some chatter of Maea's had got us all in a clove
hitch. One thing was clear: Uma and I were here for the
night; we daren't try to go home before day, and even then
it would be safer to strike round up the mountain and come
in by the back of the village, or we might walk into an
ambuscade. It was plain too that the mine should be sprung
immediately, or Case might be in time to stop it.

I marched into the tunnel, Uma keeping tight hold of me,
opened my lantern and lit the match. The first length of it
burned like a spill of paper; and I stood stupid, watching it
burn, and thinking we were going aloft with Tiapolo, which
was none of my views. The second took to a better rate,
though faster than I cared about; and at that I got my wits
again, hauled Uma clear of the passage, blew out and
dropped the lantern; and the pair of us groped our way into
the bush until I thought it might be safe, and lay down
together by a tree.

'Old lady,' I said, 'I won't forget this night. You're a
trump, and that's what's wrong with you.'

She humped herself close up to me. She had run out the
way she was with nothing on but her kilt; and she was all
wet with the dews and the sea on the black beach, and shook
straight on with cold and the terror of the dark and the
devils.

'Too much 'fraid,' was all she said.

The far side of Case's hill goes down near as steep as a
precipice into the next valley. We were on the very edge of
it, and I could see the dead wood shine and hear the sea
sound far below. I didn't care about the position, which left
me no retreat, but I was afraid to change. Then I saw I had
made a worse mistake about the lantern, which I should

have left lighted, so that I could have had a crack at Case when he stepped into the shine of it. And even if I hadn't the wit to do that, it seemed a senseless thing to leave the good lantern to blow up with the graven images; the thing belonged to me, after all, and was worth money, and might come in handy. If I could have trusted the match, I might have run in still and rescued it. But who was going to trust the match? You know what trade is; the stuff was good enough for kanakas to go fishing with, where they've got to look lively anyway, and the most they risk is only to have their hand blown off; but for any one that wanted to fool around a blow-up like mine, that match was rubbish.

Altogether, the best I could do was to lie still, see my shot gun handy, and wait for the explosion. But it was a solemn kind of a business; the blackness of the night was like solid; the only thing you could see was the nasty, bogy glimmer of the dead wood, and that showed you nothing but itself; and as for sounds, I stretched my ears till I thought I could have heard the match burn in the tunnel, and that bush was as silent as a coffin. Now and then there was a bit of a crack, but whether it was near or far, whether it was Case stubbing his toes within a few yards of me or a tree breaking miles away, I knew no more than the babe unborn.

And then all of a sudden Vesuvius went off. It was a long time coming; but when it came (though I say it that shouldn't) no man could ask to see a better. At first it was just a son of a gun of a row, and a spout of fire, and the wood lighted up so that you could see to read. And then the trouble began. Uma and I were half buried under a waggonful of earth, and glad it was no worse; for one of the rocks at the entrance of the tunnel was fired clean into the air, fell within a couple of fathom of where we lay, and bounded over the edge of the hill, and went pounding down into the next valley. I saw I had rather under-calculated our distance, or overdone the dynamite and powder, which you please.

And presently I saw I had made another slip. The noise of the thing began to die off, shaking the island; the dazzle was over; and yet the night didn't come back the way that I expected. For the whole wood was scattered with red coals and brands from the explosion; they were all round me on the flat, some had fallen below in the valley, and some stuck and flared in the treetops. I had no fear of fire, for these forests are too wet to kindle. But the trouble was that the place was all lit up, not very bright but good enough to get a shot by; and the way the coals were scattered, it was just as likely Case might have the advantage of myself. I looked all round for his white face, you may be sure; but there was not a sign of him. As for Uma, the life seemed to have been knocked right out of her by the bang and blaze of it.

There was one bad point in my game. One of the blessed graven images had come down all afire, hair and clothes and body, not four yards away from me. I cast a mighty noticing glance all round; there was still no Case; and I made up my mind I must get rid of that burning stick before he came, or I should be shot there like a dog.

It was my first idea to have crawled; and then I thought speed was the main thing, and stood half up to make a rush. The same moment, from somewhere between me and the sea, there came a flash and a report, and a rifle bullet screeched in my ear. I swung straight round, and up with my gun. But the brute had a Winchester; and before I could as much as see him, his second shot knocked me over like a ninepin. I seemed to fly in the air, then came down by the run and lay half a minute silly; and then I found my hands empty and my gun had flown over my head as I fell. It makes a man mighty wide awake to be in the kind of box that I was in. I scarce knew where I was hurt, or whether I was hurt or not, but turned right over on my face to crawl after my weapon. Unless you have tried to get about with a smashed leg, you don't know what pain is, and I let a howl out like a bullock's.

This was the unluckiest noise that I ever made in my life. Up to then, Uma had stuck to her tree like a sensible woman, knowing she would be only in the way. But as soon as she heard me sing out, she ran forward—the Winchester cracked again—and down she went.

I had sat up, leg and all, to stop her; but when I saw her tumble, I clapped down again where I was, lay still, and felt the handle of my knife. I had been scurried and put out before. No more of that for me; he had knocked over my girl, I had got to fix him for it; and I lay there and gritted my teeth, and footed up the chances. My leg was broke, my gun was gone, Case had still ten shots in his Winchester, it looked a kind of hopeless business. But I never despaired nor thought upon despairing: that man had got to go.

For a goodish bit, not one of us let on. Then I heard Case begin to move nearer in the bush, but mighty careful. The image had burned out; there were only a few coals left here and there; and the wood was main dark, but had a kind of a low glow in it like a fire on its last legs. It was by this that I made out Case's head looking at me over a big tuft of ferns; and at the same time the brute saw me and shouldered his Winchester. I lay quite still and as good as looked into the barrel; it was my last chance; but I thought my heart would have come right out of its bearings. Then he fired. Lucky for me it was no shot gun, for the bullet struck within an inch of me and knocked the dirt in my eyes.

Just you try and see if you can lie quiet, and let a man take a sitting shot at you, and miss you by a hair! But I did, and lucky too. Awhile Case stood with the Winchester at the port-arms; then he gave a little laugh to himself, and stepped round the ferns.

'Laugh!' thought I. 'If you had the wit of a louse, you would be praying!'

I was all as taut as a ship's hauser or the spring of a watch; and as soon as he came within reach of me, I had him by the ankle, plucked the feet right from under him, laid him out, and was upon the top of him, broken leg and all, before he breathed. His Winchester had gone the same road as my shot gun; it was nothing to me; I defied him now. I'm a pretty strong man anyway, but I never knew what strength was till I got hold of Case. He was knocked out of time by the rattle he came down with, and threw up his hands together, more like a frightened woman, so that I caught both of them with my left. This wakened him up, and he fixed his teeth in my forearm like a weasel. Much I cared! My leg gave me all the pain I had any use for; and I drew my knife, and got it in the place.

'Now,' said I, 'I've got you; and you're gone up, and a

good job too. Do you feel the point of that? That's for Underhill. And there's for Adams. And now here's for Uma, and that's going to knock your blooming soul right out of you.'

With that, I gave him the cold steel for all I was worth. His body kicked under me like a spring sofa; he gave a dreadful kind of a long moan, and lay still.

'I wonder if you're dead. I hope so,' I thought, for my head was swimming. But I wasn't going to take chances; I had his own example too close before me for that; and I tried to draw the knife out to give it him again. The blood came over my hands, I remember, hot as tea; and with that I fainted clean away and fell with my head on the man's mouth.

When I came to myself, it was pitch dark; the cinders had burned out, there was nothing to be seen but the shine of the dead wood; and I couldn't remember where I was, nor why I was in such pain, nor what I was all wetted with. Then it came back; and the first thing I attended to was to give him the knife again a half a dozen times up to the handle. I believe he was dead already; but it did him no harm and did me good.

'I bet you're dead now,' I said, and then I called to Uma.

Nothing answered; and I made a move to go and grope for her, fouled my broken leg, and fainted again.

When I came to myself the second time, the clouds had all cleared away except a few that sailed there, white as cotton. The moon was up, a tropic moon. The moon at home turns a wood black; but even this old but-end of a one showed up that forest as green as by day. The night birds—or rather they're a kind of early morning bird—sang out with their long, falling notes like nightingales. And I could see the dead man that I was still half resting on, looking right up into the sky with his open eyes, no paler than when he was alive; and a little way off, Uma tumbled on her side. I got over to her the best way I was able; and when I got there, she was broad awake and crying and sobbing to herself with no more noise than an insect. It appears she was afraid to cry out loud, because of the *aitus*. Altogether she was not much hurt, but scared beyond belief; she had come to her senses a long while ago, cried out to me, heard nothing in reply, made out we were both dead, and had lain there ever since, afraid to budge a finger. The ball had ploughed up her shoulder; and she had lost a main quantity of blood; but I soon had that tied up the way it ought to be with the tail of my shirt and a scarf I had on, got her head on my sound knee and my back against a trunk, and settled down to wait for morning. Uma was for neither use nor ornament; and could only clutch hold of me, and shake, and cry; I don't suppose there was ever anybody worse scared, and to do her justice, she had had a lively night of it. As for me, I was in a good bit of pain and fever, but not so bad when I sat still; and every time I looked over to Case, I could have sung and whistled. Talk about meat and drink! to see that man lying there dead as a herring filled me full.

The night birds stopped after a while; and then the light began to change, the east came orange, the whole wood began to whirr with singing like a musical box, and there was the broad day.

I didn't expect Maea for a long while yet; and indeed I thought there was an off chance he might go back on the whole idea and not come at all. I was the better pleased when, about an hour after daylight, I heard sticks smashing and a lot of kanakas laughing and singing out to keep their courage up. Uma sat up quite brisk at the first word of it; and presently we saw a party come stringing out of the path, Maea in front and behind him a white man in a pith helmet. It was Mr Tarleton who had turned up late last night in Falesá, having left his boat and walked the last stage with a lantern.

They buried Case upon the field of glory, right in the hole where he had kept the smoking head. I waited till the thing was done; and Mr Tarleton prayed, which I thought tomfoolery, but I'm bound to say he gave a pretty sick view of the dear departed's prospects, and seemed to have his own ideas of hell. I had it out with him afterwards, told him he had scamped his duty, and what he had ought to have done was to up like a man and tell the kanakas plainly Case was damned, and a good riddance; but I never could get

him to see it my way. Then they made me a litter of poles
and carried me down to the station. Mr Tarleton set my leg,
and made a regular missionary splice of it, so that I limp to
this day. That done, he took down my evidence, and Uma's
and Maea's, wrote it all out fair, and had us sign it; and then
he got the chiefs and marched over to Papa Randall's to
seize Case's papers.

All they found was a bit of a diary, kept for a good many
years, and all about the price of copra and chickens being
stolen and that; and the books of the business, and the will I
told you of in the beginning, by both of which the whole
thing (stock lock and barrel) appeared to belong to the
Sāmoa woman. It was I that bought her out, at a mighty
reasonable figure, for she was in a hurry to get home. As for
Randall and the black, they had to tramp; got into some
kind of a station on the Papa-mālūlū side; did very bad
business, for the truth is neither of the pair was fit for it;
and lived mostly on fish, which was the means of Randall's
death. It seems there was a nice shoal in one day, and papa
went after them with dynamite; either the match burned too
fast or papa was full, or both, but the shell went off (in the
usual way) before he threw it; and where was papa's hand?
Well, there's nothing to hurt in that; the islands up north
are all full of one-handed men, like the parties in the
Arabian Nights; but either Randall was too old, or he drank
too much, and the short and the long of it was that he died.
Pretty soon after, the nigger was turned out of the islands
for stealing from white men, and went off to the west,
where he found men of his own colour, in case he liked
that, and the men of his own colour took and ate him at
some kind of a corroborree and I'm sure I hope he was to
their fancy!

So there was I left alone in my glory at Falesá; and when
the schooner came round I filled her up and gave her a deck
cargo half as high as the house. I must say Mr Tarleton did
the right thing by us; but he took a meanish kind of a
revenge.

'Now, Mr Wiltshire,' said he, 'I've put you all square
with everybody here. It wasn't difficult to do, Case being
gone; but I have done it, and given my pledge besides that

you will deal fairly with the natives. I must ask you to keep my word.'

Well, so I did. I used to be bothered about my balances, but I reasoned it out this way. We all have queerish balances, and the natives all know it and water their copra in a proportion; so that it's fair all round. But the truth is, it did use to bother me; and though I did well in Falesá, I was half-glad when the firm moved me on to another station, where I was under no kind of pledge, and could look my balances in the face.

As for the old lady, you know her as well as I do. She's only the one fault; if you don't keep your eye lifting, she would give away the roof off the station. Well, it seems it's natural in kanaka. She's turned a powerful big woman now, and could throw a London bobby over her shoulder. But that's natural in kanakas too; and there's no manner of doubt that she's an A one wife.

Mr Tarleton's gone home, his trick being over; he was the best missionary I ever struck, and now it seems he's parsonizing down Somerset ways. Well, that's best for him; he'll have no kanakas there to get luny over.

My public house? Not a bit of it, nor ever likely; I'm stuck here, I fancy; I don't like to leave the kids, you see; and there's no use talking—they're better here than what they would be in a white man's country. Though Ben took the eldest up to Auckland, where he's being schooled with the best. But what bothers me is the girls. They're only half castes of course; I know that as well as you do, and there's nobody thinks less of half castes than I do; but they're mine, and about all I've got; I can't reconcile my mind to their taking up with kanakas, and I'd like to know where I'm to find them whites?